The Big Rip Off

(of Significant Proportions)

Steven Polederos

Copyright © 2009 by Steven Polederos

ISBN 0-7414-5148-4

Published by:

INFINITY
PUBLISHING.COM

1094 New DeHaven Street, Suite 100
West Conshohocken, PA 19428-2713
Info@buybooksontheweb.com
www.buybooksontheweb.com
Toll-free (877) BUY BOOK
Local Phone (610) 941-9999
Fax (610) 941-9959

Printed in the United States of America

Printed on Recycled Paper

Published February 2009

This book is dedicated to my mother and father

I extend my sincerest thanks to all my loved ones who supported me during this project and for all the feedback and inventiveness as this became somewhat of a collaborative effort through collective ideas.

A special thanks to Michael McIrvin and Caine for their amazing contributions to this project.

And lastly, thank you Winchester Buckley Johnson, wherever you are hiding now.

"The worst is not, So long as we can say,
'This is the worst.' "

- William Shakespeare, *King Lear*

How dreadful knowledge of the truth can be
When there's no help in truth!

Sophocles, *Oedipus Rex*

Prologue

A Determinable Clause for Patenting the Human Condition

By the year 2008, humankind had achieved an indescribable complexity in its brief but apparently critical history. This complexity was not guided by any one individual, nor was it the product of a single voice looming dreamily over the crowd, candidly mesmerizing mankind about the nature of man and his role on earth, about what constitutes appropriate ideas and feelings, though there have been those from our illustrious past who have certainly provided this service. No, humankind's complex situation in 2008 was a product of concurrent adjoining spirits—battle cries and weapons and fevers and fires lighting the skies as a rabid energy charged the particles like ominous clouds about to spill an ominous rain on the earth below. And like their predecessors who witnessed the last synergetic symphonies, the wonder and awesome nature of the circumstances contain enough lasting energy to make it a complete and whole reality.

A single thread-like band of energy sweeps through the earth's core as if matter does not exist. The earth is not merely penetrable but dominated for moments die in its arms, and the tremors and shock waves created by this band of energy leave behind a state of determinable chaos. The shallow sheath of film that had covered the eyes of humanity for so long—humanity who had searched through those filtered, foggy spectacles for so long—is now lifted.

Some choose not to discard their lenses, however, for their world, although at times brutal and unforgiving, was comfortable and so the aggregate mind of humanity defines itself by its ability to ornamentalize its outer being at any moment's notice, and at any moment this ornament can be misconstrued as soul. The inner-self was discarded, however. Submission to a greater mind has always guided the hands that rule us, and we are effectively ruled by those who wield said hands.

So our story goes. So our story shapes itself in the guise of this understandable but nevertheless misunderstood existence. Not that chaos is unavoidable. Human existence could have been different. At least the possibilities did exist, but everyone knows this drill: without conflict, parallel lines can lead to blindness, but somehow they intersect and the infinite once again becomes rational and we lend it a name, or a face, or a state of characterization in a film plot. A sphere of pure energy binds the great wind that sweeps across the land, whips through our skin and reaches our chilled bones. On distant shores, the seas open up. On the streets by our homes, the dogs sniff the neatly paved roads hoping to find some sense that coordinates their instincts with their logical thoughts. In cities teeming with life, Mother Nature rips through on occasion, showing us who is boss—and we thought there were going to be *no complications* resulting from the rape of our own planet? This is not a query about what economic policy is best, or which solution provides the most jobs, or what platform one stands on relating to drilling in the few remaining unexcavated plots of earth. The operative question is in regard to the recognition of consequences. There are *always* consequences to *every* action.

On divergent paths, we seek retribution. We seek the hollow feelings that are restless within us, for they provide something to measure all of our feelings by, and we then seek to fill that hollowness with feelings that are whole and complicated. We seek to release the pressure that assaults us with the knowledge that perhaps the deepest void does exist—the blackest holes sucking up the matter of energy spinning through the universe. We walk different roads, and on these roads we meet, and on occasion, if we are fortunate, we can share a moment with someone special who can see the same point on the road we see. We wear shoes on our feet that are conducive to life in the fields and in the streets. We cultivate our land. We build our towers and monuments to show our currencies' worth. We bustle about with little on our minds except love and darkness and evolving creation, and our understanding of life spans the generations. We trace our lineage and demand more wine. We drink until our bellies are full. We search for the way to keep the viruses still. And at the end of every day, when we lie down for rest, we put ourselves through an unconscious test. And our dreams reflect that which we know not to be whole and return it to us, and we know beyond doubt that our minds are beyond our understanding, no matter how hard we study and learn and grow.

So we wait for the day that all minds are joined as one, a single, adjoining thought guiding the movements of all. We wait and wait and hope it does not arrive, for we also seek independence of spirit, solitary lives. Can the two truly be combined? Or perhaps the better question is: should they be combined?

Deeply embedded within the cavities of our souls, there is something we seek to expose, something we seek to show. And as it closes in on our sun, our hearts feel the sensations of a once begotten son, one kept behind closed doors, one that is hidden in books and dreams. The streets of the cities of the world are filled with alchemical mixes of desire and sin, profit and loss, happiness, failure to move swiftly from within and a fatally cynical grin.

Martial law in the 5th dimension: time is its own slave controlled by its further kin. Distance appears to mean very little as we shake our thoughts clear. We see moons like we see our hands. Technology has advanced our movement outward. Love makes our movement stir from within. We shake them together and feast on the delight of humanity coming closer to ending that long and seemingly endless night.

One man travels in this time, one man who is the paradigmatic man of his time. There are many who cannot fathom events even as they witness them, but, somehow, unbeknownst to us, there is always one who, from the moment he is born to the moment he dies exists at the center of all the changes occurring. Is he pushed and pulled by circumstance? Or does he just know? Is he guided by voices, by stars, by instincts? Does he make decisions based on visions in solitude? Based on love? Based merely on fate? As distractions for himself? Does he move about without a clue in mind, constructing ideas based on what the moment, for him, defines? The man in question in 2008 was not a hero, not a man with some great plan, but a man disguised by his fortitude. His opinions are set apart from the rest, his momentous discussions with no one in mind but himself, and whether those opinions are right or wrong does not matter, for he exists to have *his* opinions and no others.

He exists in our thoughts, our fights, our dreams, and our desires. All of our mistakes are his fault and all our victories are his doing. We scoff at madness in the streets and high atop the penthouse office spaces, for he exists in both places. He avoids war but charges directly into it. He sees famine and interprets it as anorexia. He cannot read or spell anything including the word read. He exists perfectly in our times, the ones that define now. But, someday, time will end and all will be different. Waiting in the wings, patiently, is a womb that will give birth to something so extraordinary that no words exist in any language to define it.

Again, so the story goes, and with it, the antecedents that will cross your mind at every minute as you read this piece, for hidden within the main character is something very special indeed. It is as though he *is* the dream of humanity, the often funny, sad, twisted, horrifying dream of humankind: the love and hatred, the ideologies, the healthy and the pestilent, the joy and sadness, the aggressiveness and pacifism, the dancing puppet in us all that embodies an everlasting state of confusion and balance at once, of certainty and regret simultaneously.

And in dreams we find our expressive qualities. Some of the oldest are the transcriptions of dreams into functional interpretations of one's individual reality. Whether it be the gentle weaving of occurrences in life regarding associations one has with other persons, or environmental influences, or the sudden awakening from centuries of sleep, the impact varies by strength of will and depth of perception. What follows is the story of a real adventure: part logical, part mystical, part religious, part macroeconomic, part phantasmagorical, part magical, part satire, but all adventure through time and space.

Our main character set his compass to wherever it would lead him, and it led him right to the heartland of modern civilization. The lead character, "Little Diarrhea" Winchester Buckley Johnson, is by no means representative of any *one* person (damned close though), and indeed he is obviously an amalgam of precious minerals and metals extracted from planet earth and possibly beyond. His dedication to blindness is favorable amongst cult groups and other locales of social bonding, like corporations, especially among Wall Street giants, daytime talk shows, and in countries with dictatorships. This is not to say that all persons involved with these groups are blind or espouse blindness as a preferable way of being, but a person who is physically deprived of sight has a far stronger eye than a 'Little Diarrhea' Winchester Buckley Johnson and that self-inflicted blindness allows him to be who he is, the one who is the paradigm of his time. However, blindness, or lack of a deeper vision as this would insinuate, can be cured. Since being blind is a central element to our misgivings, this type of blindness needs a sense of humor to be able to cope with it and requires a character to show us what self-deprived sight looks like from a larger perspective.

Sexuality is addressed as a mere contextual epigram. Its humorous usage serves as a contorted mirror as humankind places an enormous emphasis on it, and at times, rightly so. Sexuality has two, sometimes separate, functions: One of reproduction and one that is very abstract—expressionistic, metaphysically gratifying, euphorically experimental and psychologically controlling or demanding. In short, the emphasis on sexuality is part satire and part seriousness. It is the author's belief that we have more things to worry about—like chemical warfare and the loss of oxygen on our planet—than who is the year's sexiest soap star or teen idol (although there is merit to most soap operas and to idolizing teens). It is also the author's belief that racism is fundamentally stupid and that human beings are not born to be racist but learn this affliction, and if afflicted, a racist person makes deplorable decisions as well as comments, substituting understanding with irrational modes of psychological transportation. The use of racist commentary is an obvious extension of the lead character's self-inflicted blindness—and consequently this is at times funny and at times horrifying.

If time can be understood the way it truly exists, as it truly surrounds us, then the leaps in and out of memory and space may not be so farfetched from a scientifically, albeit lyrically scientific, standpoint. Obviously, to the reader of typical materials, typical in the sense that what most people read daily make it something typical, like poorly conceived articles, gossip magazines and trash novels, the strangeness of the work may override the underlying movements. In light of this, the author hopes (and sometimes prays) that consciousness is not an absolute for it grows daily as every individual mind helps it along—and on some days it certainly retracts. And who knows, by the time this work is read by more than two or three people, leaps in time may be the norm.

Look out—here comes the human race! Oh yes, and don't forget to vote while you still can, and indeed, if you are in a place where voting is actually legal.

Filed US Patent and Trademark Office March 15, 2008

Act 1.

Sleeping Benjamin

As a blade sharp as the morning sun cuts his throat and his blood streams down his arm to the floor, his thoughts become crippled by the notion that it ended just as soon as it began. The hand holding the crow feather quill, the same quill that he had used to write everything for what seems an eternity, loses its motor function and the quill falls toward the small pool of blood now accumulating beneath him. A rapid flow of ancient memories careens into his conscious thoughts, and he thinks, *"Darkness is not something I would have chosen for an end result if I could do it all over again, if I could change what has already occurred, the letters, the symbols, the thoughts, the arrangements of ideas, the juxtaposition of dissecting energies that created all of this turmoil, this avoidable descent. There could have been unity, which exists so completely already. Time plays a higher role, or so I thought at least, the idea that time is finite, which is definingly problematic."*

As his thoughts become more focused on the problem of time as a finite composition, his sensation of time begins to slow, and with it a feeling arises that strengthens in scope, like an eternal memory becoming an ethereal awareness that dangles in a directionless breeze, with no other discernible senses available to distract the overwhelming sensation that is.

*

When the playwright's central character reached the age of 62, a thought smacked him right in the mouth. He bit down on his old fragile lips with an ever-so-slight twitch. "Do I even like this piece I have written?" The very idea gave him shivers up and down his spine, for how could this be? He was never uncertain about anything, and this new sensation, this uncertainty, really shook him up. Perhaps the mistakes were his, and he could take responsibility for his mistakes—he had no problem with that. He went backward into his mind, deeper and deeper into the very construct of his play, looking for the reasons that gave birth to this new feeling, this disquiet.

His protagonist was such an unlearned man, and perhaps that was it, for how could an unlearned man be relevant? Yes, his subject was born into wealth and his family was worldly and considered elite in many ways, and these factors alone would give anyone a head start on the human race; but this character possessed no discernable skills related to human communication or relationships. This character was not intelligent, nor could he be thought of as especially likable, not in any way. The character did have a certain way of dealing with people that made him interesting, or so the playwright believed, but this lone fact should not make one important. This protagonist was not the cruelest or most sinister man alive, nor did he contribute his time or effort consciously to destroying anyone or anything for the sake of destruction, and hence, the character was not evil by definition. This is not to say that people who fit that treacherous mold did not surround him, as very often, such company did surround him, and for all practical purposes, this placed him in the circle of fire.

Nonetheless, the times rolled on like a galactic freight train, and this man, this character in a play, was neither the conductor nor a paid passenger, but a stowaway. This stowaway remained in plain sight, however, not hidden behind some old wooden crates with giant ink stamps on the sides.

"The story arrives from deep within the wells of the soul, from the outer reaches of imaginable spaces where all things come to a point. All recognizable things, the ones we usually take for granted, come to a focused point for all of humankind to see at the same time. The story is not filled with tireless profundity, nor does it provide a modicum of romance by way of making one feel better about their existence. The story is not morose, nor is it joyous. It is not filled with senseless chatter or omnipresent maliciousness. There is uncertainty about the ending, but the story does have a point." The playwright reiterates his next sentence aloud many, many times: "It must have a point."

Seated comfortably before a gathering of his ghostwriters and his editing staff, the playwright twirls a crow feather quill dripping chocolate colored ink between his rather worn fingers. He reminds them, "The story must be told, and it must be told in the way that makes the most sense. Sometimes sense is elusive, of course, and indeed, sometimes making sense means *not* making sense at all. Remember," he instructs his staff. "What is stated now will carry you through times of doubt, which you will surely have: everything is relevant in this story. Everything is relevant because it is a specific point of view, and this relevance cannot be overlooked."

This would be the last time anyone would lay eyes upon the playwright. He would be missed, for his presence was always well received by those who spent much thinking about him. He often disappeared from the visual plane of existence to lurk behind the shadows of his ghostwriters' transcriptions, interpretations, and modifications; but he did not disappear altogether until now. His image could be loosely translated as the collective ego, or at least, that is what the place where his words came from might be called. Even with the intervention of those ghostwriters and the others, words were often meaningless, like each small step during a million year journey; but every once in a while, if he were sufficiently aroused, he would run a little faster and stub his toe and it would bleed, and the words would stand so completely relevant that it is hard to believe that anything could exist without them.

"The blood makes you think," he once told his chief editor, and he now relates the same notion to his ghosts and so on. "It makes you squirm a little, and by making you squirm, you discover what your walls and boundaries are, and thereby you have no choice but to make the decision to obey them or transcend them. I love war. Why, one might ask, with so much destruction and devastation, would anyone love war? How could anyone enjoy a good bloodbath? Life would be so meaningless otherwise. Think about it. Feeling alive is often related to escaping boredom, the monotony of the daily flow of gravity, sleep, and lack of penetrable wisdom. The human brain activates a higher function when faced with the very idea of war on a massive scale, as it does with love in any context. I certainly do not subscribe to the constant manipulation of order, but within order there is always disorder looking to be exorcised, and within disorder, there is always an order to things." With that, he places the quill down on a small desk made of black marble and picks up a tiny book. He scribbles some notes in it, as if his clarity were growing with each passing moment, as if his complete fundamental comprehension were passing to another level not understood by anyone, anywhere, except himself and his mentor.

"And sometimes, you are just so bored because you just can't see the art in anything. If it doesn't blow up your eyelids and cover your stinking skin with shrapnel, you just can't feel a damn thing. I am especially fond of the impassioned nature of art when lying is involved and combined with worldly relevance. Lying in any form is absolutely wrong, but when measured against other human psychological ailments, it is worthless, unless it changes something important, and this importance can be of great value. When lying is of a diminutive denomination, lying is sinful, but on that grandest of scales, lying is the most complex form of truth possible. I like hearing lies told for it makes me feel better than those who are telling them. You just need to work out the details, stretch them out as wide as possible with broad strokes of the quill. Eventually, life becomes much simpler when the lie is exposed, confessed or leaked."

On the back porch facing the sea of a white splashed tidewater style house, a wayward and worn man sits quite comfortably in an old maple rocking chair gently moving the weight of his body back and forth. The creaking of the boards under the rudders of the chair makes a muted trumpet-like sound. Young Benjamin sleeps soundly on his grandfather's lap while the old man stares keenly into a jar that sits on the edge of the porch, which perfectly faces the sea.

"I have been one of the most fortunate human beings to ever have lived on this fine earth, my young grandson. I thought I had life figured out, and I will tell you, I have seen some really strange things in strange places with strange people who had strange sounding names." He laughs a little to himself as his mind searches the depths of his memories. A single teardrop rolls swiftly down his face onto his grandson's curly auburn locks.

That one droplet forces a gentle awakening. It was as though the young boy was born at that moment. His small eyes squint to allow the light to pass through slowly. For any young child to awaken is like witnessing a gift from creation, but when caused by a tear, it is especially sentimental. The young man's eyes widen to greet his grandfather's weathered smile.

Suddenly, as if something catches up with him, something inside of the old man turns on and his mindset changes as if controlled by a metaphorically schizophrenic remote control. He begins babbling to himself in fragmented sentences, seemingly unrelated words connecting his thoughts together.

But just as he begins to illustrate his memories, a thunderous sound rolls at them from the distance. The resonance reaches the old man and his grandson like a blaring crescendo climbing to the heavens to finalize a dramatic symphony that had never been heard before this moment, the kind of sound that defines a precise moment in life. The whole earth begins to rumble, and the grandfather looks to the plasma television that is mounted on the living room wall and observable from the porch. All he sees is static interference.

Act 2.

A Broad Stroke of Fear: Life in the Day of Winchester Buckley Johnson

As though an internal clock ticked to remind the human species that it is imperative to race against time to locate that one point of transfer where fears are reassigned and legends and wars converge as if on a giant map in the sky, the point that is referred to in science fiction movies and that may be a seed of utopian thinking, human hands are joined together. Some hands are covered with calluses, some with dirty long fingernails. Some fingers are tiny and undeveloped and some have brass knuckles snug tightly between the fingers; some are covered with hair and others with warts, and some have soft, never-worn skin. Some hands are covered in poisonous manmade fluids or bacterial infections from overused storyboards and dramatic links to nowhere. It is as though, as each person holds hands with the next, we look to our neighbor with contempt, for everyone is a criminal. At least, everyone *believes* that everyone else is a criminal, but they do not simply think it. They try to avoid the consideration because it is not reasonable for everyone to be engaged in criminal activity, is it?

"What kind of crime are we talking about? I want to verify my understanding of the plot so I can make necessary corrections," one of the many illustrious ghostwriters once asked him. Of course, there was no need to answer. The playwright never answered questions. Is there any other crime to talk about besides the abandonment of the sanctity of trust?

"Isn't trust a myth, a venerable hope never to be reached by human hands?" one of the younger, fresher, more idealistic staff members asked. "It is as though we never understood love, nor have we understood the meaning of friendship and brotherhood and sisterhood. It is as though, we remain with our hands clenched and our eyes closed as life spins to a point not anywhere near the place we want it to be spinning."

Life is ceremoniously falling from the limbs of the trees. There is a methodic humming to the wind. Around the edges of our vision, the darkness is slowly closing in on the center. On both sides of the Polar Regions, spatial directors are busy setting up tracking stations for the predicted demise of the top layer of our physical landscape. The magnetic winds force the streams to flow in consistently changing directions. There is a basic saneness to this flow. A stubborn asthenosphere boils deeply embedded rock and gas, furiously sending waves of its production careening through tectonic plates toward the surface. It curves up and around well-worn jagged rocks and exposed walls of ancient mantles, between the crevices and canyons formed from two billion years of water flow into a larger, wider space. As it touches our oxygen supply, the flow is cooled and balanced and this geologic maintenance allows us to coexist with nature.

The earth is a garden of elements containing such timeless beauty, but sadly, so much of this beauty is transforming into merely ephemeral visualizations. That is, we see the changes and yet we permit them. The transformation in nature and among man is something that can be charted like the stars were first charted by ancient astronomers. But are the charts accurate? Have the charts taken *all* things into account? Time is our only witness, and as we all learn, time itself does not forge a forgivable face. Time is sometimes a trickster, existing on its own. Time likes to play practical jokes no matter how we might protest.

From the bend, one can see the recently patented trademark of time, a small and very thin roadway dumping into a vast and implicitly infinite space of thick openness and unimaginable patterns of energy. This is where the transmission usually stops: at a feathered landing by a morphing Quetzalcoatl on Aztec temple steps, which are the iron gates to the underworld populated by the gun carrying heroes and villains of Western civilization, which are the streets of São Paulo at dusk, which are the decrepit but still operating Gulags of the vast Soviet Empire, which are the rampaging oil fires in the Persian Gulf. The landing must be subtle, unharmed by physical contact. It was ordinarily safer to have lived inside one's imagination prior to the woes of modern times: by definition, change, physiological demand, the evolution that began with discovering freedom and ends with learning how to conceal it so it does not become a serious problem just before annihilating it altogether. Previously, there were Gods in the skies and in the mountains and in the deserts and in the forests and in the caves and in the seas and in the churches and in the temples and in the mosques and on the battlefields and in the classrooms; but now, the Gods are a more discriminating bunch. There are bigger, tougher Gods in the conference rooms. A typical conversation:

Winchester Buckley Johnson (WBJ): "Look boss, the proverbial well has run dry. Where do we go from here?"

Chairman: "Well, let's get some of the programmers on it. Isn't that what we hire them for?"

WBJ: "I'll get it done."

Chairman: "Do it, or I *will* have your head on a platter!"

WBJ (kneeling, bowing his head): "Yes sir. Right away sir."

As if it were his perverse birthright, Winchester Buckley Johnson was nicknamed Little Diarrhea. Even as a very young boy he possessed the cruelest of ailments, a spastic colon coupled with incontinence, which baffled his doctors. This is not the rarest of problems for a person of this age, but there is usually some kind of recognizable physical cause that made a diagnosis reasonably material and possible treatments viable. It was as though he were born with the predisposition but without the physical signs. Little Diarrhea would eventually learn to live with his ailments when he grew up, but at times, in his younger years, this condition would be something of a nuisance for him, but more so, the consistent clarification to strangers that he was not physically sound. The need to be within the relative proximity of a bathroom was most apparent. He was humiliated at home, in school, on playgrounds. In fact, being in public in general was a terrible psychological mess he would eventually learn to endure. Needless to say, but for purposes of dramatic posturing, it will be stated, his life was in many ways a living hell. Alas, he learned to live with his condition day to day, and although he never really took the time to mend his diet despite the daily graveling by his innards, he became quite agile in his approach to living as his condition forced him to be alert regarding his surroundings at all times. And despite the forces within him, the forces that surrounded him, and the forces of nature at large, he became a man of relevance. His relevance would not be questioned, but his true identity would remain elusive, at least at the level of the identity that exposes the soul, that defines who one really is. His very nature was deemed slippery, and his very essence seemed to cast shadows over all who attempted to see through it. Oddly perhaps, his mysterious identity would define our moment in time like a ticking bomb in a dark tunnel beneath a large city.

In his more formative years, his great nickname was shed many times. However, beneath the surface, in his subconscious, his nickname remained as near as it ever was as though buried in a shallow grave beneath a ritualistic mask. He would later be known as Deej, which was a very clever nickname shrunk down from the original nickname, Diarrhea Johnson, which was given to him by his workmates and subordinates. His other nickname, Big Poopy Pants, was given to him by some children who knew him, a name that will forever be enshrined in the nickname hall of fame. Nicknames and physiological ailments aside, his significant rise into the public limelight commenced. Critically speaking, it was as if time itself carved a path for him, and considering all things from as far back as one can imagine, and perhaps further than anyone can possibly fathom, a thin wire lay perfectly situated through the center of existence for the ongoing stagecraft to be presented.

An unknown number of acts in a grand play are still waiting to be enacted in time's illustrious center. All the actors and actresses are busy rehearsing backstage, and the director is screaming for some focus while the producers are screaming at their publicists, who are screaming at their husbands and wives as the assisting ghostwriters are making changes as needed. Few argue about who is in the lead role. For most, there is only one main character. Like any time, there is someone we focus our criticisms upon, our fears, our anger, our joy and love, and our dedication. The focus exists without predetermination of thought or desire, as opposed to being some conscious decision we make. And in answer to the question "To be or not to be," Deej simply is.

Winchester Buckley Johnson resides in the Northeastern corridor of the United States of America. More specifically, he lives on the outskirts of Boston, Massachusetts, and more specifically still, in Marblehead, a fine seaside community, mostly of wealth and pomp.

His subordinates at his company's headquarters in Kendall Square in Cambridge, just across the Charles River from Boston, consider Deej to be a somewhat popular man. In many ways, this has everything to do with fear, and the psychological implications of fear are great. One of the many relevant implications is to idolize people who are stupid and have no meaning just because the bearer of stupidity and meaninglessness is powerful, and thus, most of Deej's staff idolizes him. Mr. Johnson can paint his existence and its worth with one explosion of gas from either his mouth or his ass, each the same, the only varying attribute being the width of the crack from which the sound escapes. To better understand the nature of the man, simply imagine a stench, an aroma that so bends the chords in the brain as it penetrates the nose. Sadly, the list of expletive adjectives that could be rattled off here is so long that it would be a travesty to even begin. Let's just say that the guy has really nothing good to say, nothing important to say, and nothing to say that either sounds or smells good.

Deej's appearance is somewhat deceptive. On some days, this pale man appears to be 40, but on other days, he appears a riper age of 60, mostly depending on his habits that day and how his habits affect his body. He stands approximately six feet tall. His approximate body weight fluctuates between 175 and 190 pounds. Of course, he drives a very expensive automobile, and actually, he has several of these, each with a purpose designated for it. Oh yes, he also drives an old pickup truck when he heads down to the local watering holes so he can fit in. He has an overpowering aroma of irrationally placed self-righteousness on his breath. He reeks of foulness explicable only in terms of overt vulgarity. Attempts to define his physicality have been made in his presence, but his presence overwhelms one so much so that basic instincts take over and the ability to rationalize clearly is quickly replaced with a sense of abhorrence. The end result is that no progress can be made in determining the nature of his foulness. It is only later, after the body's gages have been reset, that contemplation leads to the road of discovery. Ultimately, that may be his greatest defense mechanism, which grows like a weed in a garden that can never be eradicated. This strange quality masks its true nature unto appearing as something nutritious for the body and mind, something that belongs amongst the organic fruits and vegetables.

Deej has been known to offend a few people. As a matter of fact, all who meet him either love him for his blatantly crude behavior or hate him for precisely the same reason. There is no gray area, no debate over the kind of person he is or the attitude he portrays. He is one person that sickens even the most open-minded and tolerant of individuals. He epitomizes the unoriginal trash that invades our living space with too many shopping malls, gimmicky credit card outfits, and poorly managed energy companies.

This man has really nothing to offer humanity, which in and of itself does not separate him from most because, in actuality, few people are actually contributing something critical to the intellectual or metaphysical growth of civilization. Of course, one might contend that we all contribute something in our own small way, for isn't collective human consciousness a living, breathing organism? However, Deej is not a well-intentioned citizen in the kingdom of irresponsible addicts of vulgar racism, excruciatingly depleted self-control, and thoughtless enterprise. His days are filled with insulting his co-workers and making their daily lives miserable while his perfect nights are filled with love and affection, the kind of love that is displayed by all good, honest folk.

Deej vacates his office in the early moments of evening, taking one look back at his office building before stepping into his automobile. He glances toward a melon glazed autumn sky and breathes out one long sigh as though he had been holding his breath for 30 minutes. As he enters traffic, he glances over at three young men, probably 16-17 years of age, driving a beat up beige Volvo sedan. They wear baseball caps on their fragile heads and boast new Fruggedwear rugby shirts and Prangler jeans purchased on a United States Express Plutonium charge card in the Copley Square Mall's finest fashion boutique. They have the look of hyenas chasing a young zebra through the Serengeti night in their eyes. They have conscious hallucinations of women's breasts as they pass a billboard of a half-naked woman wearing a pair of half-buttoned designer jeans as the song *Hungry Like The Wolf* blares on the car radio's cassette deck. One of the young men makes a comment about rape, about permitting it in certain circumstances, an idea he said he heard on one of the daytime talk shows but couldn't remember which one—the other two simply shrug their shoulders. Sexual expressionism was once considered rebellious. What now? It just might be that conformity is the conscious wave of the future. It is a necessary bolt in the ruby, diamond, and blue sapphire-laced golden machine. A common American saying goes, "If you can't beat them, join them." It is probably more accurately understood as, "If you can't beat them, don't bother fighting at all, just lie down and take it. Take it hard and continuously until you die of starvation from lack of some real connection to this planet, or to anyone for that matter." Or, juxtaposed, read: "Don't try to beat them, just annihilate them."

Deej winks at one of the young men, hoping for some kind of response. Whether Deej's intention was to show camaraderie with the younger generation in terms of their sexual prowess or they turned him on is open to argument. The young man twists his mouth in an appalled manner and violently thrusts his middle finger, upward and erect, out the window as he glares ferociously at Deej, who envisions that finger doing what his proctologist recently did. Deej closes his eyes and almost causes several deaths to pedestrians waiting to cross the road. A hollow bubble of liquid comes rolling to the surface of his eye from his tear duct as he continues homeward. Alas, the dusk has turned to night. He pulls into his driveway; the lights emitted from the home are gripping, engulfing, like a knife in the belly of a very poor, uneducated young man running drugs on the streets of Mexico City. Deej shuts off the engine and listens for the noises from within his humble seaside mansion. With a faint shuffling sound, he raises the black curtain in his mind where the image of his counterpart, Johnnie, bears her place inside him. He sees her scurrying around their home like a demented mouse. His forethought of her represents a dab of model glue holding the hull to a damaged ship, and at any moment that glue might dry up. He enters gently through the front door. As Johnnie prances down the hallway toward the carpeted stairway, she hears his movement. A door slams open, smashing another dent into the wall.

"GET BACK HERE! Where do you think you're going?"

He murmurs his best reply. "Um, nowhere?"

Johnnie pulls the briefcase from his arm, throws it to the floor and exclaims bluntly, "We're going to blah, blah tonight. And we're having blah, blah, blah for dinner." There are actual words spoken, but because Deej has such an enormously high degree of fear built up inside of him, he never hears anything she is saying.

"Ah, all right..." He returns the message swiftly, and comparatively speaking, quite powerfully.

As the night continues onward, several ounces of good Midwestern-raised, top-quality, milk-fed baby cow meat and organically grown Idaho potato flakes have been consumed and several malt beverages have been inhaled whilst the pseudo-queen prepares her armor for the evening's battles. Deej and Johnnie have two children, fraternal twins who actually share the same identity. Therefore, only one of the two will be mentioned in this entire story. The reason the second child is identity-less will remain a mystery for some time, and this may or may not be discovered later. Deej and Johnnie's chauffeur drops off their "only" child. Jennifer Johnson is returning from her most recent pre-grade school psychotherapy group sessions. Her fascination with all things related to World War I, especially the Ottoman Theater, is quite remarkable. At the precious age of six, she is in fact consumed with war history. Her mother does not know why, and her father does not care why. She amplifies a popular music radio station and pretends to fire a sniper rifle into the mirror, as if she is firing at herself.

As they approach the seaside mansion, the lavish abode hosting the event they are to attend, Johnnie makes it very clear to Deej that he will, at all times, remain within 15 feet of the bathroom. "You will *not* drink. You will *not* soil yourself tonight! There are very special people here I am trying to impress. If you ruin tonight for me, I will call your mother!"

"No! Honey, I will not ruin it for you."

This night is a special night and wealthy sheep dot the landscape of an elaborately designed seaside fortress at this fully secured event with all the trimmings. Fourteen security guards stand around the perimeter armed with 9mm Glocks, and a police boat circles the waters outside the rear entrance of the home, which is nestled gently against the rocky cliff separating the ocean's waves from the housing structure, looking to ward off or shoot any unwanted guests. There is an entrance fee of $2500 per guest to hobnob with a campaigning U.S. Senator, and there will be drawing for a weekend excursion to a "surprise" Caribbean island location. All the Champagne and Beluga caviar one could ever imagine is also available for the price of admission. All faces are fully masked with smeared on smiles. The night to follow will indeed be filled with sincere cavorting and planned humor. The lines are drawn upon entrance, usually in terms of bank statements or political affiliations, which often go together. There is a tremendous fervor generated by this kind of social gathering, and excitement that generates altered states of random misdirection and cyclical change to atmospheric pressures resulting from an intense shift of dynamics in the gravitational field within a thinning dimension creating rings of fire and swirling tornados destroying the... Sorry, wrong part of the story. The fervor is precisely enacted as carefully timed insults are tossed inconspicuously behind each and every participant's back. Cultured compliments fill the claustrophobic spaces with almost futuristic patterns of breathing from the slimmest of air passages, like being in an apartment building in downtown Tokyo trying to talk to your neighbor in the next cubicle. This is a very well attended event. All of the self-proclaimed important people are there. The background music is quintessential, improvisational jazz accompanying lyrics of heartbreak and romance. There is complete order as the night ends. It is too late to share recently heard rumors of infidelity or voracious sexual appetite to be true. Everyone simply goes home. The gossip will begin at precisely 9:30 a.m. the next morning after the stock markets open and the beauty salons and yoga studios are filled to capacity.

Later that night, after all the filth has been gathered within the body, Deej leans forward, head between his knees. This time the movement is clean, fresh, almost inspired by the night. It meets its holder with a feverish splash. Some remnants ricochet off the surface of the water and strike the flesh. He moans in terrible discomfort while he hears the clicking of stations on the television and a voice behind it. "Are you coming to bed or what?" He quietly cleans himself up and meanders slowly but surely to the bedroom. The light is dimmed, and some Las Vegas country-type show tune music echoes in the background. "Songs of whiskey and heartbreak fill the progressively emptying spaces in their lives," thinks Deej, as he fearfully removes his clothing. He swallows some pills to get aroused and she stares at the clock until his penis becomes erect. The room turns red as man and woman engage in sexual intercourse, moan, grunt, and achieve mutual relief. Johnnie laughs at his shrinking phallus. They fall asleep.

At daybreak, Deej awakens to a morning filled with song and tenderness. The orioles are singing outside his seaside home as the waves gently tumble into the rocks. Slightly bent, he gathers himself in the bathroom in his familiar position. He releases the stream. A brownish-yellow film lines the toilet. He turns around to look at the inside of the toilet bowl, to admire his work. He showers and repeats process. He proceeds down the spiraling marble staircase and eats a neatly prepared meal, factory-fresh microwaved breakfast sausage, farm-fresh free-range organic brown eggs fried in vegetable oil, and burnt white toast await him at his place on the formal dining room table. He thanks Johnnie graciously for her servitude, and she gladly accepts his thanks. He eats, then once again he approaches the bathroom quietly so as not to awaken their sleeping daughter, who is passed out on the sofa in the nearby family room. He delivers himself from the depths of his innards, then emerges feeling relatively well. Winchester and Johnnie kiss good-bye, well they do not quite touch lips, or any flesh for that matter, but it remains the thought behind such an act of love that truly matters, or so Deej tells himself. Then, "Thus ends the self-inflicted torture; begin the assault."

Back on the morning roads, the corporate commuters are jammed like atoms in a vacuum-sealed jar. Deej leans to his right and pulls a flask out of the paper compartment. He takes one deep breath and slugs a generous portion of single malt scotch down his throat. He carefully screws the cap back on the flask so none of it spills. At his reserved parking space, he emerges from the car, punches in his password to the modestly secured building, and enters *his* domain. Two guards stand at the front

entrance with police issued batons in hand and a loaded
.44 Magnum dangling by their right hips. A lanky
unassuming man, G. Sport Magupati, awaits Deej's
arrival for the day, for today is not like any other day for
him. The unassuming man has a large idea that he has
planned to carry out for a very long time, that he plans to
carry out today.

This is Deej's playground, his territory. Despite all of his
weaknesses, within these walls, he has power, and
damned are those who would deny him the right to flaunt
it daily. Deej makes his entrance, grand as usual,
insulting one of the workers below him in corporate
status. He refers to this man with an olive skin tone as
dune-coon or sand-nigger. The man accepts the attack
and continues his solemn morning. A woman, *who* is not
important in this case—it is her *gender* that matters—
approaches and Deej makes a detour for the men's room.
His movement can be heard like a spring lamb screaming
in violent death across an acoustically beautiful hillside.
The waves of exposure continue to a deeper level as the
aroma fills the 20,000 square feet of floor space at an
unbelievable rate. One-half the speed of sound was the
later calculated travel time of this special odor, a fact
donated by the Institute of Special Odors, a branch of the
Yellow University School of Science, with a grant ordered
by the Executive Branch of the federal government to its
Dean, former Central Intelligence Bureau (CIB) deputy
chairman and four-star Army General, Richard E.
McKnuckles, to study the relevance of smell on the ability
to control.

Prior to the start of the workday, which begins like a gun
popping its cork at the local dog track, the participants
gather next to a canteen truck parked outside. They smile
at each other, taking mental notes of who is wearing
what that day, half-listening to each other's stories about
the night before and other inane things. They glance at
their watches, and almost in unison, they bend downward

to firmly secure their shoes to their feet. Then, tying the laces, adjusting the heel straps, and pulling up the socks or stockings with authority, they march to the door. Interestingly, the rituals conducted prior to a workday are fundamentally comparable to rituals conducted before a professional athletic match, or to a rite in which wild animals or virgins are sacrificed to satisfy some deranged idea of God or Devil. A bell rings in someone's head, like it does in the movies or at the opening of the stock markets. Messages flash across the mind-influencing board in the center of the room, the subliminal message clear to all, whether they know it or not: make money for the boys upstairs or you will be relieved of your duties. The day has begun. G. Sport Magupati awaits his cue for mask removal.

Lunchtime cannot come soon enough across the suburban corporate landscape as most employees stare at clocks or at their watches, waiting patiently for noontime to arrive so they can gather together elsewhere and share gossip after the morning caffeine has kicked in so that memories can be recovered more quickly and their lips and tongues are looser. The streets are repacked with cars. The parking lots of fast food solidified fat chain establishments are crammed by shiny cars that carry gray suits. Back at the office, G. Sport Magupati decides a bit of fun is well overdue. He shorts a few circuits in the central artery of the computer network, causing complete system failure. He learned this from reading *How to Make an A-Bomb in the Comfort of Your Own Home or Any Relevant Sabotage* (Homeland Terrorist Press, 1973). The Chairman of the Board, Henry VIII, returns from a short thirty-five-day weekend in St. Barths to find destruction. He swears revenge on the saboteur. "GET THE COMPUTER GUYS ON THIS NOW!!!"

G. Sport Magupati, who sits in the far corner where there are no windows, faceless and usually unrecognized because of his "B" personality type as determined on the

Neo-Freudian substratum survey given prior to employment for new hires, is immediately considered. His employment is highly important to the organization. His position, one of power and great responsibility, cannot be left unseated. However so, and after all, according to their phone records and the content of his interoffice electronic memos, he is somewhat risky and a bit out of line. They have also decided his sexuality for him. Through a detailed study, they have determined that he is gay, and since gays have been determined to be one of the hindrances to directing a mid-size to enormous company into one of the great financial leaders—this news is contained within their operative guide—his presence is now considered very dangerous. It is decided that he should be "handled accordingly." This information regarding gays was detailed in paragraph G of chapter 23A, entitled "Sexual Divergence May Slow Your Company Down": "Those who practice what we decide is not right in a highly polished organization such as this must either be reeducated or terminated." Incidentally, twenty-three months after publication, the author, Ka Zin Flow, was arrested in Geneva for numerous pedophilic crimes.

In truth, G. Sport Magupati is not homosexual, but because he is not a predator, he is deemed as one. Of course, this is not to say that homosexual men and women can't be predators. In fact, many are; however, the facts are the facts and G. Sport Magupati asked the truth to be conveyed shortly before his 'permanent' disappearance.

The machine loses a bolt. A team of modern Atomic Bomb scientists, corporate computer programmers, works incessantly on fixing the problem, as follows.

Genius #1: "There must be a way to reroute the whole system around the malfunctioning channel."

Genius #2: "I agree. The path can easily be redirected by some tricky maneuvering... Here it is. Okay, mission accomplished. The network is now rerouted."

Genius # 1: "Boss, our duty is done. May we go back to having sex with our terminals?"

Deej: "Good work, men. There may be a bonus in it for you."

"It was a work of genius, wasn't it? I disabled the system—promise you won't tell?" stated Mr. Magupati in a confession that will turn out to be an ever-so-minor miscalculation of reason.

"Of course I won't tell," exclaims his closest friend, a man named Weasel.

Suddenly, dramatically, the lights are dimmed on the main sales floor. Everyone stops his or her daily chores to focus on the balcony above. The first few stanzas of "You Are The Wind Beneath My Diamond-Encrusted 24 karat Golden Wings," the company song, can be heard playing. The crowd of young animals cheers in exuberance as their fearless leader, Henry VIII, who is actually the eighth Henry in his family and the name his employees have given him is mere coincidence, enters for an announcement. The lights dim and several strategically placed spotlights shine downward upon the top of his head, which glows brightly from a mixture of olive oil and silver glitter that he smeared through it.

"There will be a Holiday bonus, which will be announced at a particular time of the day, today. And when this bonus is announced, the first five winners will be in a drawing for a very special mouthwatering delight."

The last part of the announcement made half the company rush to the vending machines for some candy or other type of tasty snack while the other half of company personnel quickly scanned their manuals to find the section entitled "How to Win Bonuses." Later that afternoon, the actual bonus is announced over the intercom in a computerized pre-programmed voice: "Any information leading to the discovery and apprehension of the destructor of our system will result in a week's paid vacation and an internship with the company elite, including Saturday night Champagne and caviar at the Yacht Club."

Weasel sneaks around to the back of building, gaining speed as he heads toward the staircase that leads to the upper echelon of this organization. Winchester Buckley Johnson intercepts him.

"You must tell me everything you know first, for I must relay the message to Henry the VIII myself—he likes no visitors and I've seen good men like yourself fired for less," Deej calmly explains to his overexcited, free-vacation time moronic opportunist. The "friend" gives the needed information and Deej asks with a peculiar sense of admiration, "That faggot? I thought the only thing he was good for was cock sucking." Weasel shakes his head at the statement. He asks about his reward as Deej orders the security guards to escort him from the building after gathering up his belongings in a plain brown box labeled "FIRED."

"And don't let him talk to anyone!" he bellows, his arms crossed across his torso as he taps his right foot rapidly. Deej then patiently waits for the man's forced removal and then darts into Henry the VIII's office. He is asked to wait by one of Henry's many bodyguards because the Chairman of the Board is busy signing his autograph for a local Little League Baseball team. Upon the exit of the baseball squad, Deej slides into the office and proceeds to give a detailed story of how he apprehended the offender in mid-act, and of course, how he also caught his co-conspirator. He explains candidly to Henry the VIII that he needed to wait until he also apprehended the co-

conspirator before informing on the offender, in case the co-conspirator had more plans of destruction. Immediately, he is given the Golden Heart award, the company's equivalent of the Man of The Year award. And for all who care, this begins the end of the day.

This very day, Henry the VIII receives a huge honor from a well-regarded business magazine as the greatest philanthropist and progressive businessman in recent times, and later that evening, the Director of the CIB visits him to discuss some unmentionable business. Henry is showered with press coverage, fan mail, and some research grants from federal institutions, and oh yes, some Thai prostitutes thrown in for good measure. Meanwhile, Mr. Magupati finds himself in the hospital with the HIV-1 strain group X, the most secretive strain, which is largely unreported and supposedly originated in Grozny. He got it from a contaminated blood transfusion after a car "accident" the very next morning after the debacle for which he was sent packing. There is no cure in sight.

Meanwhile, Deej's wife is becoming exponentially aggravated with her life and the hypocrisy she has forced herself to live within, and Deej's "only" child had taken to dressing like the British Expeditionary Forces and half wants to die any way possible and half wants to, specifically, explode. Deej receives a charming vacation to Grand Turk Island and a down payment toward his fourth very expensive automobile. Deej's body is, this very moment, slightly bent over a toilet, uncontrollably ejecting the waste from his pressurized, highly sensitive colon. This has been just another wonderful day in the life of Winchester Buckley Johnson, AKA Little Diarrhea.

Act 3.

Kra Fere Infinite: A Prelude to Destiny, Or Just Another Day Hanging Around The Entrance To The Cave Smoking a Cigar?

In arguing his point about the cave analogy, which he illustrated some 2400 years ago, Plato contended that mankind would prefer to remain blind in order to justify its own existence with more ease. He gave this simplified explanation to Rudyard Kipling, who was smoking a pipe with an eagerly comical grin on his face while John Lennon sat nearby fading in and out of his morphing dream state composing a song about real love and partnerships on his 12 string—more on Wall's trailer park shortly.

Plato elaborates: "An ancient man emerged from a cave to find the truth of life was quite different than he imagined in his clouded, narrow brain. While he was chained to the cave, he faced only the cave's wall, and while the rumblings of life lie behind him and he could hear the world as it existed from time to time, the only truth he had ever seen was merely a shadow of the truth cast before his eyes. Soon after the man broke free from his cave and a greater truth was revealed to him, he excitedly returned to the cave to express this newfound truth to the other men still chained to the cave. Angered, they rejected it bitterly as though they were being fed poison.

"What form does truth need in order to break free from its darker emblematic precipice to become something acceptable? The answer may be more fundamental than we might suppose. Why does humankind seek out the truth, really? For purposes of following this current story properly, let us assume that humankind seeks truth in order to bear the feelings or notions of loneliness contained in certain moments, especially those related to loss of faith, fearing the end of all things, or fearing the infinite nature of the universe."

Plato goes on like this at length, but let us continue with the present tale by narrowing the notion to the more specific issue we are facing, the notion of what can possibly happen next.

Many have written about pathways in our human past. Some speak about it in their daily conversation, while others read the signs while hiking some semi-untamed mountainside, rocky desert-like plateau, or a bustling city sidewalk. They seek a place to tread, so to speak, a place hidden in the spaces between our words in some conversation, some logic, some bending of one's will perhaps. Or was the pathway they seek, mostly in simplicity, much more complex? Is our social structure, by definition, too complicated to truly understand? Could it be possible that mankind, even in the person of someone as complexly glib as Plato, did not find the pathway that may eventually lead to truth, nor did he discover forms or order to things, nor did he find higher ideals like democracy, but these formulations found him? Zapped into his unified brain directly from an unknown source? And if that is so, which is not likely except for the purposes of a singular, almost-linear plot in a story line, what pathway lies next?

A formulation is on the verge of raising its weary eyelids, blinking desperately to shield a bright sun, to walk this earth, to ride its transit systems, to sail high above the planet in its vessels. What lurks slightly apart from all interconnected living things? Is it a new science? Is it a methodology? Is it a new religion? Is it a new electoral system? Is it all of these things stuffed with slightly overripe camembert wrapped in a tortilla shell and fried on a medium heat in extra virgin olive oil to be eaten with gratification (and if so desired, add a pinch of salt just before removing it from the pan)? Despite the answers, which could be deliriously many, the fact is that no one human being has that solitary answer that we all seek, and just maybe, none should. For our fate is determined by our decisions, is it not? And the consequences of our decisions are quite usually far beyond our understanding in that moment. At least the minions of the CIB want us to believe this hogwash is the truth.

Kra Fere Infinite was founded and subsequently molded in such a world of shadows and false realities, excited engineers of a dying system desperately modifying ivy-covered walls and dirty emptiness to suit their automated responses. Wings burned by the sun, splintered feet bleeding and broken from running and running and running and running to the setting sun in the west, men and women share the burden of proof of their own existence. Such is the nature of our ways. And the keeper of broken feet lies here, solid as he or she ever was. Always complicating our lives, for as some things become easier to maintain, more automatic, others that were within our reach at one time are now far beyond it as shadows still cover our brightened eyes like foggy lenses in a darkened-sky-rainstorm inaccurately reflected on a cave wall.

High above the central plains, Deej peers out from the left side of an airplane window at the eastern border of the Rocky Mountains just ahead. Although he is visiting a potential customer in Colorado Springs, he will land in Denver because it is the only flight he could get on such short notice. He is decidedly very unhappy and thinks aloud, "Why did Henry VIII send me? The asshole knows that I hate the chinks and this is a goddamn chink company. He also knows that I want to win the next company bonus and," he laughs, "although not impossible, it is tough to win that bonus when you're not there to rig the competition." A Korean businessman sitting next to him shakes his head in disbelief, biting his lower lip as to not say anything.

Deej's anger finally turns to something altogether different as he enters a local microbrewery in the 16th Street Mall in Denver's downtown district. It is worth noting that destiny will not happen here and he will not meet his companion for the next twenty-three hours. He walks in and notices the newest American superheroes. He is surrounded by them actually, the desirable, fashionably exploitative men and women lost in a mirrored crowd of weary young, yet able cannibals upon obvious paths. Deej squats by a replicated Tivoli in the center of the Mall, hearing laughter and insults around him as he desperately holds in his waste. He thinks, "There are thousands of persons in this one area who are trying to take my right to release my waste away from me!" People stand around him while his pants hang loosely around his ankles. They conveniently form a large circle and prostrate themselves in spherical formations until they converge into one large Coliseum-like structure with another group forming an arrow pointing to the West.

"Wow! They are quite a troop of artists. Anyone who can pull that off deserves a television show," thinks Deej as he feels the waste caressing his colon. "I wonder if they play golf," Deej states as he pulls up his pants upon release and the center of Denver smells of a cesspool reminiscent of ancient Rome.

The signs are posted everywhere on the streets all the way to lower downtown, LoDo to the locals. Deej decides that he has enough time before his meeting the following morning so he can wait before driving down to Colorado Springs because he really wants to see what is going on. The signs read:

Today's Featured Event: Execute the Guilty— American Style

*Bring the Whole Family

**Children under 10 are admitted for free, and at the gate each will receive a free *Do the Bitch In* button and an oversized Styrofoam Amendment 26pi pointy finger hand

He walks to a large columned structure that is an enormous abandoned warehouse remodeled to represent the Roman Coliseum by edict of the Governor. He pays a nominal entrance fee and finds his seat in the vast audience of laborers, artists, professionals of every kind, housewives and househusbands, students, servicemen and servicewomen, and recently released criminals. They have all come to witness justice.

"Can you believe that this woman actually had an abortion? She deserves to be butchered in public," stated one onlooker to another just before snorting a line of cocaine from a hand-mirror while seated on the sidewalk waiting to get in to the event.

"Uh, well, I think she was the doctor who gave the abortion to an eleven year-old rape victim."

"Fuck it. They're both guilty."

According to moral law and the subsequent amendments now called guidelines, any woman who has an abortion or any doctor who provides the service of an abortion, for any reason, must be killed. A prior United States Supreme Court had ruled that the Courts have no right to legally stand against one's decision to have an abortion as a basic matter of privacy. However, times have changed and so did the law. The federal law permitted abortions for many years, and then state judges took it upon themselves to change their interpretation of the federal law and limited abortions to special circumstances. While the Supreme Court could have repealed these changes under federal law, they did not. Outlawing them was the next logical step, and of course, the current Supreme Court of the United States is always logical and reasonable. They are, in fact, the highest ruling judges in the world. Therefore, what they say goes, period. Or at least, whatever they are told to vote for or vote against, or to abstain from voting upon at all, stands.

Since that decision, the secret Constitutional amendment 26pi (ratified by President Rabbit on July 4th, 1984) was passed and enacted. It is a measure to provide tax funding for capital punishment, and under this measure, each Supreme Court Judge has the authority to mandate an execution based on his or her discretion or mood. Each Judge has a "creative execution team," the existence of which was also enacted into law by Congress, helping to stage these exciting executions for a worldwide television audience. Most team members are notable Hollywood directors, Pulitzer Prize winning writers, and nature film documentary producers who take on the work Pro Bono. However, kickbacks are likely as the Judges' budgets are rather sizable. Time is a funny thing, and so is competition, as each new execution—each Judge is limited by law to twenty-three per year—becomes more exciting, more dramatic and ultimately very entertaining for larger audiences. Even the Pseudalopex News Network established a groundbreaking 24-hour news station covering the executions shot in a new higher-grade digital format and distributed in real time by satellite directly to every household in the United States. How, one might ask, did a private media organization retrieve first-run military technology? The answer is in the question.

A 230-piece orchestra with both electric and acoustic instruments plays an overture that fuses romantic fugue with a death metal's electric thrashing, Bach meets Slayer. Interestingly, the whole string section methodically and violently rolls their heads in circles so that their hair appears as propellers in the air. The stubbornly valiant victim, Dr. Jane Doe, enters the arena with her head held high, showing great poise and complete confidence that her crime was justifiable even in the eyes of God. However, she is very guilty of the highest sins on earth, and she finds herself staged against this crowd of fanatical death lovers. Deej settles in to one of the obstructed view seats where he strikes up a tête-à-tête with a fellow observer.

"Who is the bitch that we're doing in today?" asks Deej of his newly found friend after they introduce themselves and as he leans far to his right, really far to his right, to get a better view of the execution ceremony.

"I am not sure who she is, but she undoubtedly is guilty of something!" Kra Fere Infinite answers with some hesitation and some exuberance rolled together into his voice, reflecting the complexity of this one moment of beauty and clarity.

"I love this country! You know, watching citizens get what they deserve. Hey, would you like to join me in anything that I decide to do later on?" asks Deej of his new friend.

"Well, let me give it some thought—okay, I'll do it!" Answers Kra excitedly.

"Great, but I have to warn you that I have a bit of a stomach problem. You see anytime anyone or any animal or artificial stimulant sexually arouses me, I am forced to relieve myself. So, if we decide to have sex, I would need, for comfort's sake, a toilet—or at least a small secluded area where I can release in relative peace."

"Oh, that is no problem. Shall we go back to my home now. I live just outside the city."

"Well, okay, but can't we watch the good Doctor get the axe? I love seeing a good pubic execution, I mean, public offering. Actually, excuse me while I call my stockbroker because the stock in Rapes Anonymous Technology should go up as a result of this." Deej dials. "Pops? It's me, Deej. Yes, I know I spoke to you an hour ago. Have you sold... Oh well, yes, I am *sorry* to wake you again. Please forgive me... Okay, thank you, and I will give your regards to Kra. Can you please give me 2000 more shares of RAT. Yeah, Dr. Jane Doe is getting what the bitch deserves today, and even the President of the World Federation of anti-anti-control is present at the festivities. You heard what? HOLY COW! You are kidding, right? HOLY COW, give me as much as you can and I WILL talk to you tomorrow. Arrivederci!"

In his excited state, Deej fails to realize that his stockbroker knew that he was with Kra. However, even if he did realize it, that may not have mattered much to Deej for the moment had a different level of awareness for him, a moment involving the notion of profit.

"What was that at the end?" Kra's mind begins to adjust to the situation. "If it's good, how can I get in on it?"

"Well, Mr. Infinite, I have some inside information that can make us rich! Do you have fifty grand US dollars? This is a onetime offer. Just write me a check and I'll call my agent back and up the ante!"

"Well, okay, but what is it? What am I investing in?"

"Let me just say that the futures in U.S. Government's stock is going to rise at least ten points at tomorrow's starting bell!"

"I'M IN!"

Kra and Deej then flee the scene just as Dr. Jane Doe's brains spill from her head. An anonymous figure in the crowd blew a massive hole in the back of her head from the stadium seating high above with a Yugoslav M76 gas operated semi-automatic sniper rifle with Kalashnikov iron sights, a fact in permanent concealment in CIB file server 46, just before the axe man could swing his axe. The mob cheered in wild acceptance and everyone exchanged money from their bets, mostly relating to the time taken for the blood to stop pouring from her face like one of earth's great natural fountains drying up. A few brawls broke out in the Gold Circle Seats, but for the most part, everyone acted non-violently despite how much this event excited them. Everyone is aware how violent abortion hooligans can get, but this particular crowd was tame, and the reasons for this could be many. Perhaps she was relatively unknown to them, or maybe the weather was not befitting a riot, or perhaps there were other inexplicable motives for keeping the balance of energy slightly off in order to not connect people with each other's rage.

Upon exiting the Coliseum, Kra and Deej are beckoned by a dwarf woman wearing a jester's outfit. They are not aware of any traveling circuses in town or any local bands with small people playing drums, or anything else of that nature, and so her appearance seems out of place. They follow her anyway, and as they approach a doorway, she points in and then runs away, actually almost skips away as her awkward little legs stumble a bit while running. Kra and Deej wander together into a dark, deep steel corridor-like tunnel that, from high above, would almost resemble a giant steel dildo. They find themselves submerged in a cesspool of frothing uncontrollable angst. They are really lost. Yet along the way, they seem to have discovered interesting bits of information about life in the Mobile Biblicized Nuclear Age of Preservation. And somehow, someway, inexplicably to either of them, they find themselves deep beneath the facade wondering where to emerge and how they will know when they should. They find a decaying staircase ascending toward a very dim light. They ascend and find a door that opens directly into a restaurant's bathroom. Deej is so very, very happy. This could not have come at a better time. Kra tells him that he will wait outside and Deej gets down to business.

After Deej is finished, he enters the dining area leading a peaceful trail of geometrically rotating octagonal shaped red neon moist floating particles. Later, it would be determined that it was a combination of the cherry Italian ice he ate at the Coliseum and the breakfast sausage he ate back home in Marblehead that caused this scientific phenomena. A half roll of toilet paper flows behind his penny loafers like a bride's train. Deej sits with Kra in the Superbowl booth in Denver's 23-hour MacDiddy's, a replicated Wall Street Dim Sum gourmet fast-food bistro. Deej's thoughts are just returning from a lapse into the unknown, his memory.

"My newly found bestest friend, Deej, you looked lost in your thoughts just now. Is everything okay?" Kra asks with such sincere clarity that his face literally molds into a three-foot replica of the Raising the Flag on Iwo Jima. "Looks like you've seen a ghost, or perhaps think at some point you may see ghosts unexpectedly."

"Nah! I was just thinking of how tough it must have been to lose a great leader like Hitler. I mean, I know how it felt when John Lennon died. I was torn between buying the Beatles 8-track collection and starting a band of my own." Deej smiles at Kra, who is staring firmly back.

Kra leans forward, his eyes empty with darkness except for a small spot of flaming orange emanating from his pupils. "Deej, I have a little mission for you. It may involve some danger—are you interested? Before you answer, let me also warn you that may see great respectable heroes of the people like Kublai Khan, J.

Edgar Hoover—even L. Ron Hubbard and Jener Shoke might be there."

"Did you say Jener Shoke. I know a Jener Shoke." He dismisses the idea immediately that this could be the same person from his university days, the very same man he dreamt about the night before. That is, the following future recollection occurred, and unlike in most foreshadowing devices used, he actually remembered something that was going to happen in the future. And in this recollection, he witnessed a fake priest performing magic with many onlookers about. The memories, the dreamscape, were so real in that moment that he devised his own connection with divinity. For how else could this be happening? And, without allowing a second-thought to wander into the terrain of sexual innuendos, because more often than not this is what happens with Deej's brain, his right hand was positioned perfectly down the rear of Kra's pants. As he stroked his backside, he noticed that Kra's skin was quite worn and definitely felt wrinkled, which did not quite match his 30-something appearance, and yet Deej continued with vigorous fortitude and remarkable rhythm, a sure sign of a natural tendency to excel at something meaningful.

He pronounced, "I have always wanted to do something like this, something wild and uncontrollable like having sex with my boss or his wife or a terribly abnormal fellow, one clearly of my dreams, in the President's booth at MacDiddy's. Tell me, my friend, Mr. Infinite, is the adventure going to be that stimulating? I need to know for I will not accept any arrangement without prior agreement of some guidelines suggesting enforceable laws against my freewill. It would be unthinkable to venture into something irrational and insensible without a pocket stuffed with German bonds or stock in a start-up alternative energy company headed by former CEOs of Saudi Natural Gas firms. I would need to call my broker

to clear it with him first. Can you wait a few moments?"
Deej is so excited now he begins to levitate from his chair.

"Forget about Pops. I am concerned with your dedication
to the matter. Do you consider yourself a dedicated
person?" Kra bears down on Deej's will.

"Dedicated? You should have seen me during the oil
shortage." He dreamily looks up in remembrance. "Oh,
how I profited from that scene. My company flopped, but I
made a killing!"

"I'm not concerned with your profiteering abilities. I am
speaking adamantly about a spiritual journey, of
traveling miles upon miles, set free from the crowd,
reality and dreamscapes becoming one as you rub elbows
with important persons, both dead and alive, and
seemingly, with no end sight, seeing a sudden reflection
like an opium hallucination bending wildly into itself
defining who you are and showing where in time you
exist." Kra awaits Deej's response.

"Now, hold on there, Kra. I was just curious if you wanted
to have sex with me. My wife is waiting for me in the
kitchen and she takes care of me on my (gulp) command.
Nevertheless, I still want to take advantage of this
situation here and now. After all, you like me and I like
you, and well, let's get it on! I can even share some trade
secrets with you about the future of mobile telephone
company stocks if you want."

"Okay, Deej—I'M IN!"

After an intense night of sharing sensitive moments, the
divulging of some very relevant marketing secrets, and
watching G-rated videos with microwaved popcorn, Deej
awakens to sparrows twittering in the trees just outside
Kra's home, which looks to be decorated as though it was
furnished just the day before. Most pieces of furniture
still have tags attached, and he begins to weep

ferociously. Kra awakens because of the infantile slobbering next to him and reaches out to rub Deej's back. "Are you okay, Little Diarrhea?" he states in a very caring, nurturing voice.

"What? How did you know that name?"

"Name? Your name is Deej right?"

"Yes, yes forget it. I'm fine, but for a moment, as I heard the birds chirping, I thought I was at home in Marblehead with my wife."

"Marblehead?" The word itself gives Kra a stinging pulse of pleasure.

"Damn, I'm going to be late. How far to Colorado Springs?"

"Oh, about an hour and a half, give or take some and depending on traffic. Hey, Deej, I'll drive you. I have nothing to do, and so, if you don't mind, I'll join you."

"Are you sure? I have to meet up with some chinks, little yellow mother fuckers. We should have bombed them too."

"Don't worry, we will."

"What?"

"I mean...umm... YES! I'M IN!"

Kra and Deej make the trek to Colorado Springs, stopping along the way to get a couple of Mountain Dews and some Twinkies. They eventually arrive at this enormous building, very secure. As they come to the gate, Deej looks directly into a video camera connected to a transmitter. "May we help you?" the other end speaks first.

"I am here to see Jonathan Lo. I have an appointment."

"Who is the man with the stain on the rear of his jeans?" asks the voice.

"How the hell did they see that?" asks Deej.

"We see everything! Just come in," answers the mysterious voice.

Kra and Deej enter the fortress as an enormous and dismal storm cloud rolls inward from the southeastern ridge of the Rockies. The cloud is brooding and resembles the opening to a very dark cave. Cut angle to mountainside view at 45 degrees to the northeast by the Seven Falls tourist trap, humans, deer and bears fighting over the same shelter: Wide angle lens, pan out to a larger scale perspective higher from the sky. All of Colorado is bright and sunny and clear, except a small patch of smog over downtown Denver. Colorado Springs, however, is completely immersed in darkness and all living things with legs or body parts of some kind to create motion move for cover. The streets empty. the steakhouses close, and the skiers hurry in off the slopes on the nearby peaks. Deej and Kra sign in. "Where do we meet Mr. Lo?" asks Deej of the guard.

"Ha, ha, ha, ha, ha-ha-ha-ha!" He responds courteously.

"What does that mean? Was I being funny, you chink-fuck-motherfucker?"

The man stops laughing and grabs for his gun, but he decides not to shoot and instead rips Deej apart with an evil stare. Blood begins to stream out from Deej's ears.

"Holy Cow! How'd he do that! Find me a medic, now!" Deej whines in disbelief.

The guard puts his gun away and gives Deej a don't-mess-with-me look. Deej is still whining and mumbling to himself as the guard leads the two of them down a long corridor into a chamber with hundreds of small tubes sprouting out of the walls. The chamber begins buzzing and the tubes spew out an electrical charge that links them all together. The chamber then evaporates and reconstructs simultaneously in a different place.

"Do you feel that? I feel like I just went through a fucking time machine," Deej blares at Kra.

"Yeah I felt it alright. I am assuredly tired of answering your dumb questions!" Kra loses his cool with Deej.

The guard informs Kra in Mandarin that he should have a breath mint. And, in Mandarin, Kra responds affirmatively and asks the man how his family is and tells him that the ridiculous man next to him needs one too. Deej is immediately consumed by the fact that Kra just spoke in Mandarin, and naturally, he feels very cornered.

"Ah...I...I was just kidding about that chink fuck call. I really love you little yellow mother fuckers, really."

"We do not care if you are an idiotic racist. We only want the plans," Kra says to Deej sincerely and confidently.

"Oh shoot, you're a spy. What the hell do you want with me? I'm just a low level manager at a stumbling energy firm and I'm losing my status pretty quick now that the housing market is coming back and interest rates are falling." Kra quickly repeats what Deej stated into a micro digital recording device. "I don't have any plans, really. Just let me go and we'll forget about the entire episode," Deej pleads.

"Boss, shall we kill him now or kill him later?" the guard asks Kra.

"We will wait—we need information from him."

Kra and the guard lead Deej down a slim hallway. They arrive at a room marked "men." Kra bellows, "Go now, we will not stand for you soiling our floors."

Deej enters the bathroom. Its layout is definitely Southwestern American and looks like it could be in a public office building in Santa Fe. Deej knows bathroom layouts. This is of no significant importance, however, because Deej still cannot get out. He enters a stall and lets it rip. The small stalls in this particular bathroom cannot handle the pressure, and the door blows off and hits the floor followed by a loud clanging sound. The bathroom immediately fills with armed Chinese guards. Deej sits there with his pants and rubber ducky boxers hanging down by his bare feet, smoking a Cuban cigar and looking at the pictures in the Dr. Seuss classic *Green Eggs and Ham*, which had been on the floor next to the toilet when he entered. "Do you mind? I'd like a little privacy." The guards disperse into the hallway coughing from the hideous odor.

A large bald man with sun blisters on his neck and wearing an orange robe designed with small green and black dragons enters the bathroom. He raises his robe and removes a silver belt that has markings and characters inscribed all over it. He lifts the belt from his waist and cracks it in the air. Deej hears a thunderous clap from outside, then hears what sound like balls of steamed rice pummeling the roof of the bathroom. Deej arises hurriedly and pulls up his pants and the walls disintegrate around him. He finds himself in the center of a modern orgy. Warm tropical weather, white sand beaches, coral reefs visible beneath an azure sea, macaws dressed in tiny black leather jackets, naked men running around playing flutes, nude women holding stone masks to their faces slithering over the ground in and out of each other, ensembles of musicians layering melodies and rhythms like he's never heard. The sun splits the darkness and aluminates Deej. A chorus from the sky chants some stanzas from "Mars, the Bringer of War" by Holst. Deej suddenly understands his reason for being and the scene begins folding back up into itself. The walls build furiously around him and he finds himself back in the stall. He hears the mountains moving outside and hears doors slamming and feet running. He leaves the stall quickly and finds Kra waiting outside of the bathroom entrance.

"So, are you done?" Kra asks quietly.

"Yeah, I'm done. Just take me where you have to and get this over with. I'm sick of this playing around."

"Take you? You brought me here," Kra whimpers softly.

"Hold on, comrade! A few minutes ago you wanted to steal some secrets from me."

"Comrade? Steal secrets? The only secret I have is my step-parents think I'm in Real Estate."

"You mean that you're not going to kill me?"

"Kill you? I love you."

"Love me? Just ten minutes ago, you wanted to have me killed. Okay fine, but what about that chink language you were speaking. That was not faked."

"Chink language? I love the Chinese culture, especially the opera, but I do not know any Chinese at all."

"None?"

"None."

"This is really messed up, dude. Oh darn, I've got to go again." Deej runs toward the bathroom but it is not there anymore. There is only a huge group of Chinese people jammed together in a tiny room and no one is moving. Most of them wear business suits and some of them are smoking unfiltered cigarettes. Deej awakens smack in the middle. Everyone is pushing and shoving but no one is moving. He thinks, "I can move this." Deej lets one really rip, and everyone starts farting and laughing, laughing and farting, on and on. The smell is like half-digested barbecued chicken feet and begins peeling the top layer of skin off Deej. Skin begins melting and burning and coiling. The stink wraps around his face like a plastic sheath. Bloody puddles of ripped, burned skin lie at everyone's feet, and then bodies wrapped in petrified flesh fall on top of one another forming a giant pyramid of mummified people. Instantly, they are all in an Egyptian burial chamber deep within the ground. Deej's body is the final step upward, the one at the pinnacle.

Winchester Buckley Johnson awakens on a plane back to Boston. He does not remember anything that happened in Colorado. He only knows for certain that his forearms are bandaged and his memories are clouded. He goes back to sleep.

Act 4.

Jener Shoke: Symphonies of Electrical Discharge and Magic in the Bedroom

Speaking candidly about cracks and spaces, there are spaces between the cracks where few people live their lives, but the road may be found if one travels near and far and above and beneath, a road consisting of all of a man's understanding and care and guidance.

Jener Shoke, now regarded as the herder of animals, once found such a road. The road was high upon a hill near where everyone that is everyone has lived at some point in their lives, at least this is believed to be true. He was walking by the ancient ruins, and his memories rushed to meet his every step with a physical connection to all that surrounded him in a way that is indefinable. He walked slowly past all the defunct technology company buildings and old industrial company buildings and decaying statues of past leaders and victorious men and women of battle, herding his small tribe of animals, genetically forged creatures made up of the DNA of a female giant tortoise, a male wolf, and mixed sex-DNA cocktail crocodile. Certain of these creatures' characteristics have been proven, through years of field and laboratory study, to be the most dedicated to survival. Of course, these are land animals. Otherwise, he would have been herding a school of sharks, whose capacity for survival is legendary.

Jener Shoke is one of those persons who is not fearful of his past, who is completely aware of his future, and who knows the present is a phantasmagorical marvel of time and space. Complex patterns of order dominate his clearer existential thoughts, and every notion that is given birth and lingers is filed away in his brain's memory banks as though it were only the subcontext of a far larger plot. He seems to have made the right decisions his entire life, despite the circumstances he was in and whatever corner he found himself backed into. The solvency of his issues was in real time, as he did no wrong, and at times, while even he was not completely aware that the decisions he made in those moments were ultimately the right ones, he trusted himself so completely that this quibble became unimportant.

On a certain road, Jener Shoke found Winchester Buckley Johnson. They were two old friends of an impenetrable fortress, the Delta Kappa Epsilon fraternity, often pronounced as Deek, at Yellow University. And although brotherhood held them together under one roof, there could be no greater opposites than Jener Shoke and Winchester Buckley Johnson. Winchester's proverbial school is of foolishness, while Jener's is of complete stability and balance both within and surrounding him. Winchester learned to care only about money, power, and influencing the weak with intimidation and withheld information; while to Jener, to take part in this type of thinking is not only madness but completely disquieting to his inner being.

Jener had just returned from an adventure to a place not far from Zaire, a place still not defined as a nation. The European colonialists were unable to conquer the state of Cloudernia, a small mountain society located within a very strategic place, East Central Africa's wildest, most untamed valley, which contains a very important meteorological condition of a completely stable nature. Since atmospheric change has seldom found its way to Cloudernia, the natives had dedicated their lives to creating sufficient disorder to balance the obviousness of their surroundings. Hence, life in this valley was quite unusual. Jener needed to learn more about chaos, and in this place, the fundamental reasons for it were carefully planned. And as much of a romantic idea as planned chaos might be, the likelihood of it seemed so outrageous to him that he had to observe it firsthand to believe it. Taking things on faith had never before been an issue to Jener, and so this seemed relevant to him.

Ceremonial events were planned and sabotaged on all social levels. Food was gathered, and then lost purposefully or guarded powerfully by leaders and followers alike. Men and women exchanged societal roles often, sometimes several times daily, and sometimes all at once as if on cue, as though there was a central command dictating what to do. For these reasons, the Central Intelligence Bureau, whose great clandestine operations are highly concealed from the general voting public under code name CIB, set up their newest state of the art technology laboratories.

Gene splicing and cloning has been successful for years, ever since certain characteristics of human personality have been mapped onto a supercomputer hidden in the underground tunnels of the US government's new headquarters, the Octagon, beneath Puget Sound, Washington. In this supercomputer, principles of magnetism, basic force, and subatomic propulsion are quantified. By alternating the probabilities of the levels of kinetic energy measured inside and outside controlled terminals of hydrogen and helium when certain critical factors are introduced, such as the gaseous results of burning human flesh or a child's exploding candy, are transmitted through laser light tubing and sent directly into the mainframe's brain. The prospects of serious discovery are quite unique in that tremendous promiscuity amongst the usual stagnant crew of researchers is so great that a movie will be made of it before this information is leaked.

As the experimentation is conducted, energy levels are consistently fluctuating at incalculable rates, and when this flux is captured on wave tables, the levels appear as symphonies of electrical discharge. The principles of movement are given symbols, and the probability of similar wave patterns of the same types of impulses occurring is calculated and then defined in ascending order of frequency. The patterns are then mapped into a replica of the human brain's mapping system and subjects are hooked up to a thought decoder, where an intricate web of circuitry joins humans and other organisms, from baboons and gorillas to centipedes and crawfish. The orders from the brains are then transmitted into the decoder to separate levels of activity based on factors of reason denoted by a system of logic as antiquated as three dimensional space. The decoder then transforms the signals into digitally modified holographic fractal images, projecting the accompanying images onto large, slightly convex white screens, images ranging from beads of water to images of Christ to detailed maps of our solar system.

The inherent danger involved in this type of experimentation is that one cannot know fully which images came from what subjects. This was a problem actually led to a couple of murders amongst scientists within a twelve-month time span. Notably, there were also cases, due almost exclusively to an overwhelming amount of information fed into the system, when the decoder accidentally sent the orders back to the sender, which caused severely violent spasms and wild uninhibited recklessness followed by cases of spontaneous combustion amongst creatures of a normally slower thought patterns. Of course, all testing is done in padded rooms to ensure the patient's health.

In Cloudernia, the process is currently being tested on certain natives, with their consent of course, to find more advanced levels of chaos and learn how to control it.

Descending from a dream, Jener was shown how to help read the problem many years ago. Perhaps days had passed before the realization became fantasy, perhaps it was months or years. He had really no way to tell, nor is that relevant, but it was to affect his state of mind for years to come. He had settled into a hole far beneath the surface, not so much to hide there but in order to dive more deeply into his self. Perhaps the fear was self-learned, or perhaps the fear became a regenerative sense of masking reassurance to keep him searching for truth. Eventually, though, the pressure from existing inside a vacuum was deafening. He began flinching from intimidators, for Jener knew, from all the years of experimentation and all his pilgrimages, there always exists one who is much stronger than you and at any time. The tornado whipped across the open fields, tore through the forests, ripped the roofs from their cemented foundations and tossed them up and around, whirling them quickly yet gently around the corners of this squared off sphere we call home. We are taught to hate those who are different from ourselves. Where did that come from? The CIB doesn't know either, but they *are* working on it.

Deej had just returned from Denver and was driving north on Route 1A toward Marblehead from Boston's Logan International Airport when he noticed a man with a small group of strange looking animals by the roadside. It was as though lightning flashed before his eyes and everything slowed down to a virtual halt as his tire blew flat, the man and his animals staring at him as he drove slowly by. His brain fired bullets into his mouth to scream aloud, "JENER?"

Jener Shoke and Winchester Buckley Johnson found themselves sharing a common uneasiness. The distance between them was too great. Winchester had too many skeletons to hide, or at least he wasn't certain if he could reveal them to his old pal for Jener's overstated sense of judgment was not conscientious. It simply existed in his completeness. They looked at each other hoping for some kind of breakdown. Winchester Buckley Johnson was educated, modified, and then reeducated in *his* domain. You mustn't speak first for the opponent will have an advantage. What he did not know is that Jener had worked so closely with military intelligence that he picked up some of the trade secrets along the way. He helped to train *the* masters of deception while they thought they were training him with their skills in combat and torture. Opposites sometimes attract, and opposites actually can work together, as counterintuitive as this may seem. Those who publicly claim that their ways are the only way, and get away with it without any questions, suddenly find their own brains questioning everything about what it is that they are doing. This is the power that Jener held in his singular body. We are speaking on behalf of the militant personnel of any fanatical cause, whether violent or peaceful in nature. The dedication, ah, the dedication. What more is there to say besides this simple phrase: dedication to a cause? Jener understands dedication to a cause just as he understands the value of breathing, just as he understands life and death and all that it means, and just as he unquestionably understands Winchester Buckley Johnson, his DKE brother.

By Jener's presence alone, Winchester is forced to remember the river of truth, the place that we are forced to swim in sometimes. The balance of things can often turn in one direction or another, and it appears, at least in this time, that Winchester's way of life has been externalized beyond the confines of his own cave, his own bathroom. He bleeds lines of waste into the streets. The stench can now be heard. It is in the breathing apparatus that regulates the body's heart rate and oxygen flow to the brain, and the ears always get a little taste. Moment of conception: Little Diarrhea beckons to the call: a loud rumble from the inner belly, pressure gathered from the center and equally thrusted to all sides and erupted through long nutrient rich tubes from a horribly mutated organ. This organ, you see, was formed when the stomach grew too large for the space it was given. High fats clotted the passages and the fats dug themselves into the walls. An emerald colored fluid flows through this organ into the colon, carrying with it universes of unimaginable and unspeakable horrors. There it meets Winchester Buckley Johnson's essence. It simulates a cross walk to the other side where large groups of pedestrians wait at the traffic light, wait for the signal to begin. The mouth located directly opposite the hole from the largest tube speaks. Jener's eyes blaze with a disgusted, bizarre terror as Winchester politely pulls off his pants and proceeds to remove a handkerchief from his pocket and swipe his bare ass, a moist, rather thick glob held in his hand. The whiteness of the cloth glistens the naked truth of Winchester's presence to his old pal Jener. The stained cloth is tossed into the nearby bushes where it strikes a gasping individual spying on them. Jener understands how some humans go astray, toward violent uptake, or more probably, a generally putrid disposition, which is the case of the man standing before him, which gives Jener a revelation of sorts, as though this moment were critical in his present and future states of mind. Notwithstanding Jener's lifespan and massive degree of understanding of all things seen and unseen, this moment makes an impact.

"Mr. Johnson," he says, extending his hand to be shaken, and then he retracts it quickly. "It has been many years since we last touched eyes. How have you been and how is your life?" Jener wastes no time asking important questions.

"Touched eyes? What are you, a faggot? Only faggots talk that way. I'm fine, and my life is fine. I drive three expensive automobiles and have a fourth coming, and I live in a mansion by the sea. Whatdya got here, a bunch of faggot animals?" Winchester so cordially asks in return.

"I see that you haven't changed a damn bit." Jener chuckles as Winchester wanders quickly away into the nearby bushes to perform sexual acts on several of the animals. He finishes in about three minutes, brushes himself off, and then the two of them load Jener's animals into one of Winchester's expensive automobiles. Jener had stood by during the deviant act, unimpressed, for he knows Winchester Buckley Johnson, but moreover, it is not Jener's way to try to stop him from doing anything. But he will later, rest assured, let Winchester know that he should take more care of his actions for some day they will come back to haunt him.

"So I've been told that you are working for the government. Is that true?" asks Winchester warily.

"The government? Hell no. They just showed up one day in the place where I was visiting, set up an entire high tech laboratory within weeks, and after observing me with the locals, the director of the lab decided to offer me a grant to raise a group of these delightful little beasts. They wanted to observe me at every stage of my animal care. Besides, this isn't like the days at college. Oh remember those DKE parties with all the naked bodies running around and all the animals you used to violate in the petting zoo. I never thought I would relive these memories so clearly again." Jener breaks into a stream of dedicated tears.

"I've forgotten about most of it. My wife and daughter don't know about the good ol' days, and I certainly don't need them to find out. Got it?!" Winchester Buckley Johnson stares a rich colorless fury into Jener's eyes.

"Hey Winchester, don't you worry about a thing," says Jener, assured now that Winchester doesn't have a clue why he had found him. And now is not the time to inform him because Jener's plan must be adhered to by the strictest terms he has given to himself. "I won't reveal your secrets, don't worry. By the way, I have to meet an old friend out in Seattle on Friday night. Join me for some cards and scotch? I don't drink, but my pal does, and I would guess that a good 12 or 18 year-old single malt is just your poison."

"I'll have to ask. It should be okay. An old friend?" He pauses. "Another from school?" Winchester Buckley Johnson's memory doesn't serve him here.

"Well he did attend Yellow, but only very briefly, and I did not know him when he was there. This gentleman and I met at the Hilton in Bali. I was there to sit in on a lecture about quantum physics, and he was there to meet with some members of a Balinese militia organizing against the government. I met him in the lounge while listening to really good British synthesizer pop music, new wave stuff, very cool actually. He's an interesting guy, and we became friendly very quickly. He's a very strong religious type, like you and me, and actually has a little power in the federal government."

The very words shone like rose-colored sapphires reflecting light in Winchester's eyes. He pictures lavish parties in the Gold House rubbing his moist brown nose on Congressmen's fat asses, the same fat asses that Winchester has often dined with in the company of his father, and in the past, his grandfather, but now, he imagines himself actually playing a part in the nature of the ass nuzzling, not just observing it. It is a picture of wonderment and beauty. Winchester slips into a state of euphoria. Jener glances over at the bumbling fool, lets loose a hearty chuckle, and assures Winchester that his friend will like him.

"So where are you staying?"

"Haven't decided yet. Was going to get a room at a nearby travel lodge somewhere on Route 1. Any suggestions?"

"No way. You're staying with us. I live only about five miles from here." Winchester is gleefully excited to have someone interfere with his home life.

Winchester Buckley Johnson and Jener Shoke arrive at the seaside mansion. Winchester's son, sorry, his daughter meets them. He bends downward and she gives him a nice big kiss on his forehead. He blushes and states, as she wanders into the house, "That's my BOY!" Jener is puzzled but dares not ask.

"Hey, those little freaky beasts can't come in the house. They'll meet death if they mess up the carpet." Fearful of the impact that dirty genetically engineered animals in his home will have on his wife's mood, Winchester screams these words at Jener.

"Fine, fine, no problem regarding that. They are used to adverse conditions. WB, can you help me load all of this equipment into the house?"

Winchester pauses for he has not heard anyone call him WB since the Fraternity days. "Uh, yeah sure!!!" He converts his deeper thoughts to an expressionistic externalization of his excitement. His eyes widen with feverish joy. He'll do anything to distract his wife from himself.

Once in the home, Jener is led to a bedroom adorned in dark rich mahogany with original impressionistic art by local artists on the walls. Johnnic supports the local artists because it gives her a decent social standing. He notices that the paintings on the wall are slightly crooked and the blinds haven't been cleaned in a while, as they are dusty and slightly discolored. The bathroom door adjacent to the bedroom is closed, and he feels as if someone is lurking behind the door listening to him unpack.

Jener begins to set up his equipment to ensure nothing has been broken in his long travels as Johnnie enters from the bathroom to greet him. He is shocked to see her unclothed. She immediately signals him not to peep a word by placing her erect index finger in front of her closed lips. In the back of his mind, he might have figured something to be slightly odd about this family, but his thoughts begin meandering.

"Let's see now," he begins to make assimilations. "He calls his daughter his son. His wife is approaching me nude. He claims to be disgusted by homosexuals, and yet he has sex with small genetically-mutated animals, and at least from our university days, he has had sex with other men." Jener was always good at reasoning things out. This is clearly one of his strengths. "Must be the new thing, deception as the moral majority! I can see that working in all facets of life. I love this country, but this is just not right," he thinks to himself.

Johnnie tries to climb on top of him. She has an organism growing out of her vagina that looks something like a plant but with teeth. Jener might normally allow something like this to be, because that is his style. This is not one of those times to indulge, but the oddity of the whole scene has opened up his more curious side, if only for a moment, and as he stands motionless, he is caught completely off-guard.

"Ah, that must be a Venus fly trap. Maybe they have too many flies in the house in the summer?" he thinks as he feels a pinch on his crotch. The teeth dig right into his genitalia and cause a stream of bleed to flow downward to the floor as he screams. Winchester and Jennifer give a hearty chuckle downstairs.

They both chime in unison, "She got him!"

Jener awakens from what seems to be two thousand years of sleep to find he has been hooked up to his own equipment, the same equipment that he has used so many times on his animals to test brain function. He notices that his small pack of animals and some Marblehead townspeople are gathered around the bed, more specifically, a couple of shop owners, a tavern wench, a couple of fake priests, the local butcher and a couple of scented-candle makers. There are several lighted two-meter high ruby red candles set in cast iron candelabrums with Egyptian Hieroglyphs and Amerindian Petroglyphs etched into them lining the perimeter of the room. The driving percussion of "The Rite of Spring" by Stravinsky is blaring on the Harmony Kardony music system in the background while Arabic belly dancers move as they purify themselves by conducting death rituals with venomous snakes. One of the fake priests standing over him in a black robe waves his arms downward, calming the crowd.

"I've been waiting a long time for this. Thank you for notifying me of his arrival," states one of the fake priests.

"Oh, no problem, Father. You once told me, if anyone significant from my past ever showed up, it would be a good idea to let you know about it."

"Yes, thank you my obedient son."

The fake priest whips his hands around in a circular fashion, and they glow a translucent yellow and Jener can see his bones through the glowing skin. Jener is suddenly presented with his past, present, and future all at once, causing a slight system overload in his already very expanded brain. He knows how to beat magicians though. He's been doing it for a long time. He levitates and notices a black hole forming inside the pearl-white wall, growing wider and deeper; and the more the hole opens up, the more he wants to leap in, but gravity begins to pull him in anyway. All stand in awe and gasp.

Outside in the driveway, by the front of the home, a group of Assemblies of God missionaries chant and simultaneously sacrifice themselves with double-edged hunting knives. A full rainbow is seen over the horizon. As Jener leaps from the scene, he grabs Johnnie on the way out and escapes through the hole. They split like an atom and a flash of light nearly blinds some of the onlookers. Jennifer cries to her father, who responds amiably. Even the animals are shocked. The butcher eyes some of the fatter animals, a trickle of drool rolling down his chin.

Act 5.

The Legend of Broken Stream: Birth of a True Leader or Puppet Master to the Inane?

With very limited perceptions, human understandings of God have by now been more widely accepted as the doorknob to the next dimension. Strike that comment. This is mostly untrue, as human perceptions vary by person, so such a generalization, albeit somewhat accurate, is not a good idea here. Perhaps the proposed gateway of divine significance can be discovered in the back brain, waiting to hop the train to the outside world for its momentary glory, or at least acceptance in the minds of its counterparts, which is vital for progress. Oh, has not the enlightened spirit actively sought out a larger field to travel within? Is it not nobler to find the far reaches of our physical existence than to make a little cash?

Which brings the movement to Seattle, where several conflicting forces have congregated to battle for power. Their presence can be felt at every turn, in every underground passage and every open space. Seattle is not only one of the most pertinent gateways in the Pacific between the United States and its Asian allies of commerce. It is a cultural megalith transforming each passing day like a never-ending dream, and most importantly, it is the center of the universe, at least for planet earth, and at least relating to fundamental principles of economic and political power. Not only is the central operation of the most promising company in the world in Seattle, the entire U.S. government picked up and moved from Washington, D.C., Pentagon City and Langley, Virginia in order to stay closer to the source of certain economic success and broadening superiority in all bureaucratic regards, that of Macrohard.

At cocktail parties and other forums of social interaction, like café hanging, church going, fish tossing and music producing, the elements of control are hard at work preserving their point of view as they lean complete control and carefully planned destruction. The situation is becoming the most significant of all social problems. Please do not confuse this with balancing the power between men and women, which will remain a constant struggle for all humankind's existence. This could be thought of as a balance of power that lies within and between the cracks of our thoughts and actions. The tribal security forces that have enveloped men and women for centuries, dating back to around 46023 BC, still exist today, despite technology's advancements as a method to destroy this arrangement.

"Damn trees always lose their leaves when the damn air gets cold," exclaims Crode Mag, the district manager for the lower south side street crew of the Dead Animal Removal Task Force. "Pick up these rotting carcasses, boys. They're wreckin' my view of that beautiful pavement."

Most of the time, his "boys" listen carefully to his every word, for Crode is the product of some interesting, relatively new breed of science. His face and nervous system are those of a man, his digestive system that of a gorilla, his muscular system that of a cheetah, and his genitalia and lower body those of a snake with large webbed vulture-like feet. His long, thin, spotted lower body slithers behind him, leaving small pebbles of waste strewn along the ground. His brain gives orders to the body, but since the genetic structure has been altered so dramatically, and no one really understood what they were doing when they accomplished this marvelous feat of science, the transmission is usually incomplete or far too intensely energized, causing convulsions of a horribly violent nature, including spitting acid and toxic fumes from his steaming breath. And on days when Crode's processes are smooth, his massively varied instincts cause severe disturbances in his memory coping mechanism, which needs to be changed quite often due to recent surges of simultaneously conflicting ideas and behavioral swings. Since his memory coping mechanism is only updated to version 12a.7, and the most current mechanism out on the military grade market is about 33 generations newer than this, well, let us say that sometimes it just is not pretty.

Crode Mag's workers scurry around piling up the raccoon, ferret, and cougar carcasses. "New orders from command central: Stop carcass gathering and help the street merchants close up their shops, and get there in ten minutes or you're all losing a day's wages." The workers, with no time to process what is really happening to them, sprint for the city center. Upon arrival, the policemen greet them on the street, the good ones who do their absolute best to keep order, or disorder, whichever they prefer at that time, in an increasingly depopulating center of the city. They are instructed to help the officers of the law quell a small gathering of objectors to the government recently taking over an island off the coast of Venezuela. In light of the arsenal of weapons shining brilliantly in the sunlight before them, the gathering breaks up peacefully.

The ionized channels are fed signals of distress. Chaos is slightly increased and then decreased, and random misfortune befalls those whose guard is down, engaged in activities like walking the dog too close to the curb and other basic actions of pedestrianism, or simply not keeping their fourth and fifth eyes open at all times. Three of those gathered are shot in the back after they were ordered to file away by a rambunctious street worker who is half human and half polar bear.

And nearby, at the social gatherings in the old rundown churches of the extreme right, elderly fundamentalists and those most easily manipulated by mass media are chanting verses pertaining to the recent rise in violence on the streets and the hunger and poverty of those not affiliated with the central core. A falsely ordained priest enters the scene clad in a maroon cloak and wearing a cross upside down and slung over his back. He summons his followers to beckon to those who are destroying "life," all those associated with choices. "We must destroy all opposition of this sect in our denomination in another crusade." Although most who listen are horrified, immediately a church leader takes charge of the unsure, hoping that his ass-kissing techniques will be duly noted by the priest and his current allowance will be more generous next payoff. Upon entrance, a physical search is completed of all attendees, the searcher stealing money from each unsuspecting fool. He then uses the money to coerce them into following the lead of the leader as he gives it back to them in a secretive manner. He conveys to them that they are part of a secret organization and if they remain silent about it, they will be paid handsomely. This is a very clever maneuver indeed by a well-informed member of secret-intelligence-type thinking. He steps up to the podium.

"The priest is correct. This pro-choice is nothing more than a mass slaying of unborn fetuses and a social gathering of our direct opposition. We must act as the responsible party and annihilate those conducting such acts against the Holy Bible and the word of our God." He is well aware that much of the meek opposition is trampled by fears of gossip and becoming outcaste by the central power element in the group, as well as overwhelming feelings of guilt, every time the Holy Bible is mentioned in a context of control.

"And if word gets back to the public at large about what we are doing here, you will be dealt with accordingly. Our enemies are always conspiring against us, waiting for any opportunity to take us down, to break up our coalition. The strictest confidence must be kept by all in attendance, and any leak in that confidence will insinuate to us that you are not a believer." The man makes his stately exit to a round of uplifting applause and a generous nod from the fake priest. A fleeting idea of questioning this operation or even open opposition crosses the minds of a few, but most simply agree in fear. Actually, several of the elders of this federally subsidized clan get a surge of excitement, indeed a molecular charge from new acts of citizenry bestowed upon them by their church. The crowd disperses into the street and Crode Mag meets Peter, one of the church attendees.

"So, Peter, how was your gathering this evening?" asks Crode Mag.

"It was quite delightful. We even had a visit from an important priest!"

"An important priest? Aren't all priests important? What in heaven warranted his presence? It must have been a very delightful ceremony."

"Actually... He just stopped by to offer his thanks for our support of the church. He also talked of the preservation of life, well in a much more Godlike context. He was admonishing the absolute rule of a well-defined omnipresence in common existence. Oh the harshness of this idea must drive the *liberal* minority absolutely crazy. This is what we want, a well laid plan, and anyone straying from the absolute must be tortured, in a divine sense anyway."

"Sounds like the Lord's work is well at hand," calmly announces Crode Mag as he turns to face his crew of helpers. He bends over to remove the rubber condom-like cap from the end of his tail. With a slow manipulative gesture of his head toward the sky, Crode Mag stretches the rubber cap out to use as a belt, places it around his arm, and ties it tightly, forcing a blockage in the blood flow and causing his veins to swell. He then removes an overused needle from his coat pocket, and with his condom-cap-strap between his straightened arm and the side of his torso, he forces the needle into a vein slightly below a crack in the elbow. As he pushes the needle in, he squeezes the rubber with his hairy arm, which stabilizes the pinch to lessen the strain on his nervous system. His claws dig into the cement below him. The flow was unique—it went straight for the brain and didn't pass any muscle blockage or blood clotting. He falls with a smack against the pavement while Peter stands by and yawns, mildly disapproving, but of course, he told himself, pity was in order.

On the far side of the street corner, Peter observes a woman jamming a needle into her vagina and throwing herself helplessly on the cement, wriggling around as if she'd been shot. Blood spilled out of her onto the littered ground, and she cried desperately for assistance but the people who stood by just shook their heads in shame and filed back into church for an offering of sympathy to their embarrassed Lord.

Peter, a sensitive type, helped the woman to her feet as he screamed some control rhetoric at her and spit on her forehead, telling her that she belonged where her discharged fetus lie—on the street corner. He then sent a Teflon bullet through the left side of her face. Crode Mag stood upright, seemingly awakened by the uproar. Momentary heroism took over his drug infested genetic structure and he rushed after Peter screaming words like sharpened knives, tying his words to bullets puncturing Peter's shallow skin and deep within Peter's instantaneously dying brain. The insanity from the situation caused an overload on Crode Mag's balancing memory chip enhancer, which led to a short in the central nervous core, spasms and convulsions, and stars twirling around his vision. Life flashed by, then all of existence, the universe unfolding, then the subsequent birth and void of consciousness for a seemingly infinite span of time. Because Crode is crippled by the overload of the linearly taught existence flowing into his main circuitry, because of the resulting spastic outburst of irrationality, the military engineers realized the need to revitalize the brain map with less reactionary genes and make his flaws less human, less instinctual. They realized the opportunity was at hand to move this project more toward tomorrow than toward today or yesterday.

A giant projection screen goes blank and a large oval table around which sit 16 angry, reasonably astute, old Caucasian men comes into focus, more or less. None other than former CIA director, and father of Winchester, Gerald Johnson, occupies the head of the table.

"We must advise our scientists to forge a more forgivable creature, less apt to destroy himself from alternating currents. I suggest a complete rewrite of the code," Gerald barks at the group.

"If we bestow pity on this form, shall we believe the creature will refrain from physical disorientation?" asks a member of this powerful elite.

"If you read the sacred texts like you are supposed to, you would understand more about life. Since Congress passed the Right to Life Bill for all to obey, any of those who lack the faith to preserve such an act should be disintegrated at once. This is not the 1960s! This is now, the present. Unbelievers must be destroyed. There is not enough room in our prisons, so the criminals, the drug addicts and the non-believers must be eliminated. We must systematically destroy the opposition," bellows the leader of the group. "If we allow the opposition any kind of escape to liberation, we may be weakened. Freethinking clearly went out of style after the War of 1812. We simply don't need it creeping back into style. We simply don't need to go 'retro.'" He uses his index and middle fingers on both hands to signify quotation marks.

"Have we not learned through history that we are a killing breed? We have a destructive core, worse than any other animals, brooding on the tyranny of our desires and need for control and power. Any meek amongst us shall not be destroyed for they will not matter. They will probably, eventually, just kill themselves. We must focus our energy on the leaders of the opposition, who will further their cause and destroy the ways that we believe should be. We must use the media outlets wisely to publicly defecate on the faces of their beloved leaders, for their say is dangerous to human well-being and to us. If there are any dissenters within this room, know that your position with this organization will be terminated and you will be trapped within a cavern far beneath the Nevadan wasteland where your bones and flesh will rot as God smiles and Jesus cries for you." Somewhere, Machiavelli scratches his head as his ideas seem to be categorically misunderstood.

A thundering applause captures all in attendance. Their newly accepted leader, Broken Stream, BS to his pals, a drunken House of Representatives member from Idaho (R). The man's name is really Ricky Chester, who as young man in Cheyenne, Wyoming was beaten senseless by the local high-school punks. The physical abuse involved small wood sticks, pieces of paper made into paper pipes, and baseballs being launched at him in the schoolyard in well-executed attacks by the school bullies. The brutal verbal abuse tortured him, calling him out as a "sissy, a fairy, someone whose mother wears combat boots." He used to walk home from the school bus stop with his head down, always looking at the pavement, never straight ahead or to the sky, past homes where people were smiling, cooking their hotdogs on the grill, drinking their beer, laughing amongst themselves. He would enter his home and slowly gasp for air. He knew that his next beating was mere hours away. So, patiently, he waited until his mother came home, drunk as usual, and after 15-20 minutes of tireless verbal abuse, the beatings would come. Would it be a belt, a rolling pin, a baseball bat, or a wooden paddle? The whole thing was like a potluck dinner at the local bingo parlor—one would never know until the next day what one actually ate. You see, his father was injured and could not serve in World War II, which destroyed his ego and horribly embarrassed his mother, whose father was a veteran of World War I. Her father looked down upon her husband because of this shortcoming, and Ricky's mother turned his father's failure and her subsequent rage on little Ricky. She also taught him how to shoot a gun at four years of age, which really came in handy during hunting competitions at Cheyenne Community College.

Ricky Chester now raises his arms in a mock victory. "From now on, you will all call me Broken Stream. It is my adopted name from the gang I (cough) grew up with, and you shall obey the will of my command."

"But Ricky, shouldn't we first..." The dissenter is instantly knifed in the ribcage by Gerald before any more words are spoken. This was more than enough of a message to anyone witnessing the statement, and enough for thousands, perhaps millions of others who ended up hearing the story as hearsay.

"I told you my name is Broken Stream! I guess you didn't listen to your mother either when she was raping you in the tool shed." BS immediately shuts up as if he's leaked knowledge of his own sad childhood to the rest of the group.

The group decides on the date of the next session while leaving the film room. They resurface in a central corridor in the Octagon. It is the newest and most highly secured governmental apparatus constructed on top of and beneath an artificial island located somewhere secret in Puget Sound. They head into the underground tunnels that connect their building and Seattle. A shuttle takes them safely through the miles of dark tunnels and filters them safely into another deserted church downtown. The streets grow dark and the new hip gangs filter in from their modern daybeds, Yoga classes, and homebrewed cups of strong coffee. The night has a different face. Entertainment is accessible to the public, but so is violence, and the danger far outweighs the excitement. All that remains in the major metropolises are live-in offices with networks of information interconnected between the toilet, television, computer, microwave oven, cappuccino maker, and the security system that protects it all for each and every household. People don't even reside in the cities anymore, except in New York, where the inhabitants managed to remain urbanized. A young man code-named the Pulsar, age 14, runs the security firm from his home in Tulsa. He told Bill Grate to screw when he personally begged him to head-up the operating system division at Macrohard. The kid is a billionaire now, and the highest paid employee the government has ever had.

The legion of power files out of the church's front gate and huddles together closely with one another as they approach the street corner. They hail a bus, and the bulletproof mass transport vehicle pulls to the curb. A device resembling a street lamp oscillates from above the door and locates the center of energy of the group. This is done rather quickly as the energy of fear bleeds from their souls as if from stray cats cornered in a dead-end alley with nowhere to jump. The beam of energy streams downward, engulfing the group and virtually lifting them off the ground. They enter the bus through a very wide door, which is half the length of the vehicle and slides open quickly, enabling the group to thrust themselves into the safety of the bus with all due haste. The shield reenergizes itself simultaneously and the bus pulls away quickly toward The Comfort Zone Phase One Hundred and Fourteen, the most recently erected planned community outside Seattle, a well guarded living establishment equipped with the most current security devices against thievery and violence, against terrorists and opposition thinkers.

Winchester Buckley Johnson and Jennifer flew in to Seattle to meet Broken Stream. Winchester racks his brain to recover memories of BS while at Yellow. He cannot recall if BS was in any of his classes, and since Winchester cannot recall if he ever went to class, his search for recollections was completely unsuccessful and did not take long. In fact, BS spent only a short time at Yellow and never graduated. He was a terrific son and needed to take care of his ailing parents, and so he moved back to Cheyenne to assist in the gracefulness of their aging. Of course, the fact that he failed his classes at Yellow had nothing at all to do with university officials asking him to kindly leave without dispute. In fact, BS and WB had no association while at Yellow, as they were too far apart in age. Winchester had to tell BS of his friend's strange disappearance back in Marblehead. He was hoping to discuss a plan of retrieval and the current issues of the day over a game of cards and some good single-malt scotch.

Winchester and Jennifer wait for BS outside his planned community. The highly modified public transit system bus arrives and they wait while passengers file off quickly. Since Winchester has not yet met BS but only heard about him from his father, and even though on the airplane he told Jennifer how he felt that he has always known him, Winchester wasn't sure what he was in for. BS arrives guarded by his newly elected submissives. They form a kind of circle around him to protect him from any stray bullets from the street. One woman getting off the bus behind his group is hit and instantly falls down dead, the bullet hitting her right in the ear. Ruby pellets of blood explode like tiny teardrops of acid falling into a river of lava directly on Winchester's shirt as he sits nearby, and he howls in fear, breaks down the front door of BS's condominium, runs inside, tripping over a stack of magazines on the floor, and makes a beeline for the bathroom. The trail of stench he leaves behind is outstanding! As the crowd disperses and each goes to their respective homes, a removal crew arrives on the scene to get the woman's body.

When Winchester emerges from the bathroom, Jennifer is seated comfortably on the loveseat showing Jener's animal herd photos to BS. They laugh and cry as if sharing deep emotional responses. Winchester notes that it is a tender and wondrous sight indeed. He thought she had lost the capacity for such interaction some time ago. The phone rings and BS answers. He is told that a "priest" has ordered a meeting the following morning at the church: "7:30 a.m. sharp and don't be late," says the caller.

BS lives in a wonderfully trendy loft-type condominium. Winchester makes his mind-set known immediately. "Stream, what are you a faggot? Don't faggots live like this?"

BS laughs and explains to Jennifer, who appears to be daydreaming, that Jener had humored him with stories regarding her father's mannerisms and the way in which he formulates sentences when they met in Bali. Jennifer asks if there are any old war memorials nearby that she can visit. BS finds this highly irregular for a child her age, but he informs her of a tribute to World War II artists at the Seattle Art Museum (SAM). He calls in his driver, Rocko, and instructs him to take Jennifer to SAM in his torpedo-proof Humvee. "And watch her closely. She's just a child," states BS, concerned with her well-being.

Winchester just farts his approval. Jennifer leaves with Rocko as Stream comments on her intelligence and her beauty. Winchester Buckley Johnson adds candidly, "Don't bother to try to engage her. She only likes the British Expeditionary Forces. I've even tried once or twice to get a piece, but no deal. She simply wants BEF soldiers." BS is slightly disturbed by his guest's behavior, but he says nothing more.

"So, exactly what happened to Jener that made it essential for you to fly to Seattle?" asks BS.

"Well, let me tell you, that asshole, a guy I used to share fraternity experiences with, took off with my wife. No, not just took off. I mean they left all together, evacuated like from a hurricane about to hit a less-regarded city."

"Hey Winchester, it happens—that Jener is quite a stud," BS states a blatant lie in order to make his new friend feel better about what happened. "He has been known to sleep with many a lady in his time, more than anyone I know, and you know his herd of little animals, I suspect that they ain't virgins."

"Yeah, I know. Wait, no, you don't understand! I mean that Jener opened up a hole in the wall, took Johnnie, and split, left this world! It was so strange that it made me very sad. I was impressed though! It was almost magical." Winchester's tone reveals that he is utterly bewildered.

"Sit down WB. May I call you WB? Sit down and rest yourself; you need to know some things. At the turn of the first millennium in the Christian calendar, Jener was actually idolized. People used to follow him around. He continuously told people that they shouldn't follow anyone that they have a freedom to choose their own thoughts and to follow their hearts and their beliefs, because that is what God wants them to do. On rainy days, when one falls deeper into contemplation, probably from a lack of sunlight or sex, who knows really, he thought perhaps that he was the reincarnation of Jesus, the Great One. He quickly got over his schizoid state and took off, left the cradle of civilization and ended up in the New World. He hit the road with a band of ancient Mexican natives, Toltecs I believe. He was really into the power of symmetry and magic, and so he found his calling with them. After years of transformations and retransformations between animal forms and human forms, he ended up where is now, northern Canada, living a somewhat normal life in semi-seclusion in Quebec at the southern tip of James Bay. He lived there, oh, about eighteen hundred years before the US government found that he was still alive. He even had the ability to make himself look younger because he found the fountain of youth, which is quite literally a small fountain built in 400 A.D. by a band of traveling Inuit outcasts living in northern Quebec. That's why no one ever really knew who he was. He was actually in denial for so long that he forgot who he was in the beginning, and in fact, he knew that this no longer mattered. He just went with the flow. Our governing intelligence body figured it out though— we always do. We have the technology. You see, when you have nothing else to do with your time and a solid bureaucratic foundation, you tend to figure things out. So, we gave him a full scholarship to Yellow University in order to help him help us develop a new wave of top thinkers, the kind that would be our top CEOs, Executive Branch leaders, and good conversationalists. He even kept his little group of animals in a local petting zoo."

Now completely convinced that Winchester, who is busy leafing through one of BS's magazines that he picked up from the floor, one called *Hunting and Human Game*, isn't really listening, BS continues. He is shaking his head in disbelief that Winchester could so completely lack curiosity. "After almost two centuries of keeping his identity concealed from the rest of the world, they led him into a training camp outside of Stone Mountain, Georgia.

They gave him a second small herd of animals and told him to do his thing with them. For them, it was about studying bestiality. Of course, at first, he had no idea what they were talking about, but then it slowly came back to him: the Roman treachery, the small rebellion, the missed apocalypse, the escape to North America and then Central America via what is now Siberia, the ages of darkness and unreason, and then the reawakening of humankind's sense of discovery and need to question life, to the increase of diseases and the discovery of travel using machines. He remembered trekking across what is now Canada to live with a tribe of natives, the only tribe for hundreds of miles around, where they refer to him as Contoogathe Kow Ikuoip, or extremely old dude. His sporadic points of remembrance are the key element to his longevity. At times, he remembers too much and begins to go insane. He told me this one night during a game of poker. Of course, I still don't believe everything he has told me—most of the stuff I think he fabricates simply for a good story. Then he breaks into this shtick about life as an illusion of some failed playwright's brain and informs everybody that we're all just parts of the ongoing joke the playwright tells to the drunks at the local bar. He says that eternity is merely a single moment stretched out for just that eternity, or at least, he told me that, for my purpose in life, this is reality."

"You mean, Jener really is... Wow, he blessed me with his presence and took my wife. Holy Cow, I mean, WOW!" Winchester was obviously listening to some parts of the story and is astonished by the news.

BS reveals a secret to him, for BS also has a plan that Winchester is not yet aware of. "Don't get too excited. There are many magicians in the world. Jener just lived longer than most of them. Actually, there are many in hiding in a trailer park in South Dakota with other very famous dead people. They arrived over time from China, India, New Mexico, Austria, Memphis, Liverpool, and, of course, Northern Quebec. Although the world knows of these people, their 'arranged deaths' isolate the masses' collective brain into forgetting about them in order to conceal current identities." BS begins growing weary of divulging this information. "I cannot tell you anymore, this is the top secret information that the CIB has, and you mustn't let anyone know, not even Jennifer, or your father will have no option but to have you killed."

"Dad? Well, don't worry about that." Winchester guzzles an entire 750 ml bottle of scotch, then rips a line of cocaine from BS's coffee table. "Wow, this is unbelievable. Wait 'til I... Oops, sorry, I won't tell anyone."

BS takes out his teeth and soaks them in a liquid solvent for the night. He proceeds to do a strange ritualistic circular-type dance around the table as the teeth in the solvent begin chattering. The teeth leap from the glass and on to the bamboo and walnut coffee table and sing some old Apache victory song. Winchester runs into the bathroom and lets his fears go. Broken Stream ends the dance with a raucous feverish foot stomp and goes to bed.

The clock strikes ten and Jennifer stumbles through the door and falls flat from art museum exhaustion. Winchester cries because he thinks she has been raped and wonders who could have done this to her—or more appropriately, how she let anyone get that close. He finds a picture of a soldier in fatigues in one of BS's American Hunter magazines and shakes her until she awakens to show her everything is all right as he dangles the photo in front of her. Winchester then stays up all night deciding what to do with this new information.

"How can I capitalize on this knowledge? Maybe my old company can take me back and we'll set up a secured, interconnected, facsimile-based site for 'very important historical characters' to chat as customer service representatives to keep consumers off-guard as I sell them energy products for the home or automobile!"

"WOW! WHAT IS BETTER THAN THAT?" he screams aloud. "We can invite consumers to have conversations about a whole line of great products with the greatest people the world has ever known..." His thoughts drift into a harmonious dream of himself, Jener, and his wife walking hand in hand through a garden with fiery red apples dangling gracefully from weeping willows.

The next morning, Winchester plans a trip from Seattle to South Dakota to find this trailer park. He knows a little geography and remembers that South Dakota is near Minnesota. He decides to fly into Minneapolis and drive from there. He also decides that he will leave his daughter behind. Broken has two daughters of his own, and one of them volunteers to take care of her as Winchester Buckley Johnson is on a quest and he needs to make this trip by himself. BS's wife, Licky, approves as well, for if she didn't, she would most certainly get shot or stabbed depending on what the nearest lethal weapon was. Broken drives his new mate to the airport and Winchester catches a flight to Minneapolis. At the Twin Cities' airport, he rents a car and begins his journey back to the west, toward this not so famous trailer park.

Act 6.

Fade to Blue: Zhu Zen Kow, The Keeper of Secret Places

"Now, before you go, you must remember the following: the Great Wall exists because mankind needs it there. It is not there for any other reason." These humble words spoken to Winchester from the lips of an old Business School Professor on graduation day ring softly yet precisely in his ears. He cannot fathom the course of events he has been led through, and yet he keeps going as if driven by an inner spirit. After driving almost four hours, Winchester finds himself at a diner in Sioux Falls, South Dakota. He is seated by a pool table and eating a rare cheeseburger so fast that it appears as though he is inhaling it through his nostrils. He is listening to a conversation between three men in the table next to him. They are discussing a ransom and taking care of needed business. He leans over to ask where Wall is. The three men remove shotguns and aim the barrels directly at his skull, which is now dripping with fear. One of the men tells him the tale of a small, rural upper-Midwestern town, weaving the tale like no other Winchester has ever heard, complete with police officers, business transactions, billiards halls, barbershops, and a Home Dreepo employee. Needless to say, Winchester knows the law and realizes he may be an accessory to some type of crime, and so he gets up and leaves at once. And furthermore, he also realizes, if he were to divulge any further information from this scene to anyone, he may be sued for plagiarism. While researchers and historians might be voraciously searching a similar scene in the Library of Congress, or searching some other futuristic place where vast amounts of data are stored, to uncover the truth about this scene in order to capitalize on it or to find fame from exposing it, they are clearly wasting their time. There are not enough facts divulged to accurately misstate what may have happened at that diner that day, nor is there any intention of misrepresenting possible facts that may or may not be true anyway. So, Winchester Buckley Johnson, for once in a short period of time in his life, may possibly rest his mind, and therefore, his colon. He has done no wrong and made a good judgment for his own safety.

Once in the rental car, he removes his map and finds the most obvious route to Wall. He hops on I-90 and starts his journey westward. In his mind, he recaptures a certain phrase over and over and over that was spoken to him from the dried, cracked lips of Broken Stream, who is now rotting in his brain like an antelope carcass in the heated sun of the Central Kalahari Game Reserve in central Botswana. These precise words were uttered in relative haste by Stream, as he did not realize their true poignancy, and now, amidst the dry terrain of the badlands, the words from Broken Stream could never ring more truly: "Remember, Winchester, there is only one way in but a thousand ways out."

Winchester thinks, then states aloud as reassurance, "I may meet some of the great men of the world." An erection forms a lump in his pants. "Like I'll get laid by them." He dreamily laughs to himself. "I wish I had a companion, one of the guys to keep my mind busy. Oh, but what if it was a nigger. That would suck. Or a chink-fuck or a Jew or worse, a Palestinian! Forget it!" He reaffirms his bigotry to himself for safety's sake.

A couple of hours later, he arrives at a familiar place, a gas station, and asks for the key to the rest room. The attendant obliges and Winchester finds himself in a dirty stall. The ceilings are high and graffiti covers them. He reads some of the prose on the walls. "Wow, this is my type of town!" He reads certain passages aloud: "I hate niggers and the Klan is my friend." He gives an affirming shrug. He really lets one rip into the dirty toilet water and it splashes back up toward the point whence the force came. "The French really do it right," he thinks to himself. He cleans himself up and leaves the restroom. He asks the attendant if he knows where to find a trailer park. The attendant laughs and points to a stack of trade journals and neo-classical type gossip collections. One journal catches his attention with an article entitled "South Dakota, Trailer Park Zone 23a of the American North Central Frontier: Houses Famous Historical Persons." Winchester reads on and finds this place to be near Wall. He turns to thank the attendant, but he is gone. Winchester then turns around again to see if there is any further information about Wall, but the magazine rack and the gas station disappeared and he is standing in the middle of a small barren field. There are no trees, just assorted twigs, sagebrush, and wilted roses by the side of the road and some strange rock formations in the far distance. Cars are driving by and honking. He sees the heads of dogs hanging out of the windows of most every car with drool dangling in the wind. His pants and boxers are down by his ankles and a pile of his excrement steams in the cool South Dakotan air. He hurries back to the car.

"This is so peculiar!" He begins crying, and all watching him from the theater audience feel empathy. An out of tune chorus sings out, "We feel so sorry for the crazy prince of the American Dream." Clouds part in the northern sky and a hollow tube of the most brilliant light conceivable is caressing the western land. His vision is temporarily disabled, and he feels the presence of a thousand birds carrying his spirit to the highest planes of the atmosphere. He now knows why he came here.

A couple hours later, on US Interstate 90, he sees the first signs for Wall. The signs are everywhere. There are advertisements of every possible consumer bamboozlement contained in Wall. As he approaches the town, there seems to be an air of suspicion hovering. People are wandering aimlessly around outside on the open empty highways. There does not appear to be any other life forms; even vegetation is nonexistent. Shadows appear on the ground with no solid matter between the earth and the sun to create them. Winchester begins to worry.

"What if I find Johnnie here? Will she want me to sleep with her?" He begins to cringe. Once again he pulls over and relieves himself on the street.

A voice rings down from the heavens, "You will stop doing that now!" Winchester quickly dives back through the window of the car, his pants loosely hanging over his shoes, his rubber ducky boxers slightly stained. The smell can be heard for miles. He is alone. He knows it. He has only himself to face in this middle of nowhere place. He continues onward.

A small roadside sign indicates that he has entered Wall town limits. He sees lights blazing across the sky as technology meets the Badlands. "Whoa, this looks like Vegas!" Winchester screams as his empty horror turns to excitement. I can't believe this! Wall houses the great persons of history as well as gambling casinos, fine convention halls, plenty of prostitutes, and a fine future basketball team for certain." But as he drives closer, he realizes how wrong his assumptions are. There are rows of dead persons scattered hastily on the streets. Decapitated children cover the land, their heads removed and hollowed out to be used as bowls for human stews. Skeletons of giant mammals and sharks line a translucent highway. Iron gates swing open and human waste flows through the streets into the town that is alive with former circus freaks and Enga-speaking Papua New

Guineans sitting in small circular groups playing card games like poker, gin rummy, and canasta. Dismembered lepers dressed in medieval robes wearing crowns and gowns and wigs walk or roll around briskly in rectangular patterns. Petrified trees sway in the motionless breeze. He has entered a carnival of irrational mirrors. Rows of severed feet make a pathway to a large steel wall in the center of the town. There are hordes of uprights trying to get in. The guardian cats keep them out by strict mind control. Winchester thinks, "I shouldn't be here!" A group of pygmy clowns remove Little Diarrhea from his adult body and carry him to the beginning of the pathway. His breath appalls them.

A young beautiful girl meets the now younger Little Diarrhea. She is wearing a black silk robe. Her golden hair appears as a mild flame growing wider and deeper, and her pure emerald eyes glisten in the mirrored insanity. He feels faint.

"So you have a pulse after all!" the young woman bitterly exclaims.

He stutters, "I don't know what you m..m..mean, you little bitch!"

She removes a small copper object from her robe and strikes him on the knuckles of the left hand with it. A jetting force of pain makes a beeline straight for his temporal lobe and he hits the ground screaming in agony. "You should see what happens when I kick you in the nuts." She laughs and the object disappears from her hand.

"What do you want from me?" He whimpers as he looks up at her, the sun partially blinding his slit eyes.

"We want you to be witness to, and play a part in, certain events in a particular light. I am not the one to tell you, but the information is critical. You may find great reward in it. That is why you have been brought here."

"Why me? I don't understand!" He awkwardly lifts himself off the ground whimpering.

"Please enter the temple and you will see."

"What temple? Where?"

A pathway opens to the great steel wall, which has many false openings that appear to be giant oval-shaped holes covered by thick glass windows. The windows have different designs etched into each one. A great light shining through the glass from behind the wall shows the etchings in full color and detail. Some appear to be scenes of great human battles, great battle scenes from Greek and Roman mythology, and some are images passed on from lifetime to lifetime from the Old Testament. Others are simple peaceful etchings of birds and trees singing to one another, waves crashing into white sandy beaches, and earthquakes destroying huge cities. Twenty-three large Cyclops' eyes, half open, are imprisoned behind titanium bars contained within a 32-meter high pyramid made of 46 billion color consoles winking at the unsuspecting Little Diarrhea below. However, despite all the amazing artistry on this wall, Winchester feels enlightened by the fact that he's about to transcend the path of most persons to find where in hell his wife went with his old college buddy. He turns to ask one more question, but the young girl is gone. There is nothing behind him anymore, no creepy carnival, no human waste, and no death looming ever-present on the empty streets. He knows where he has to go.

He arrives at the door leading into the great wall. It has a cross-shaped door knocker. He bangs the knocker and a rumbling echo is heard. After several minutes, a tall unassuming gentleman answers the door. He stands approximately six feet and four inches and is wearing a large black hat, bow tie, and tuxedo. He speaks with a deep, heavy tone. "Please enter."

The door swings open, and as Winchester walks through the door, it vanishes behind him. Little Diarrhea thinks how truly afraid he has become of the world, and how, if he ever had a chance to do things all over again, he would probably follow in his father's footsteps to simply join the CIB. As he is thinking of such things and considering his past, his conscience is recording carefully each and every thought he has, as it does with every living human being in order to help shape the decisions one will make in the future. Oh, the lack of care we place in our own thoughts.

Inside, or what was inside when there was a door, there is a huge open field with a coal colored smoke rising in the near distance. He walks carefully behind the tall man hoping to conceal himself in his shadow. Transfer in lush vegetation: A beautiful green landscape forms before his eyes, giant redwoods rise in the distance like tall fingers reaching out to touch the heat of the sky, and snow capped jade cliffs that seem to dive into beautiful open lakes spring up out of the eastern ridge. He sees the orange-golden M of MacDiddy's, and he is suddenly hungry for a Large Mick. He hears music playing, melodies from flutes and harps, and a giant supercomputer with every sound known to mankind is randomly playing three-second clips. A nanosecond later, he sees it fade in from another scene: a caravan of trailers forming a large triangle. He catches a glimpse of what lies in the center of the triangle, but what it is eludes him. He needs to get closer. The tall man has vanished now also, and Winchester hears his name called out. The music stops playing and voice screams in anger and disgust, "What is *he* doing here?"

A small woman clothed in a brilliant red silk gown emerges from the center of the trailers. There is a trail of smoke drifting away from behind her head. At first glance she appears to be ten thousand years old.

"Hush, hush!" she calms the angry voice. The woman comes face to face with Little Diarrhea. He has by now released several streams of liquid from his colon, but this does not seem to bother her. "Let me introduce myself."

Now, once again appearing older, Winchester tries to run but everyway he turns she stands in front of him. He closes his eyes but her image remains clear as recently cleaned toilet water, or so he imagines. He decides to face her. "I already know you, but how?"

"I was your Chinese history professor at Yellow University."

"No, that's not it."

"I also showed up as your first buddy in the oil business."

"No, that's not it either."

"I did a cover shot for a pornographic video. Don't ask why I did it. Let's just say I won the dare."

"I know you!"

"My real name, well, I mean the name given to me by my original elders, is Zhu Zen Kow. Although I have changed bodies and genders many times over the years, some of them actually overlap in your forced conception of time as linear, though in actuality time is a spherical entity. I hold the same capacitance of energy as I always have. At first this was difficult to keep under control, let me tell you, Mr. Johnson."

Winchester has a revelation and interrupts her. "In college, my buddies called me WB. You can call me B!"

She stands in silence for a moment, not allowing herself to react to the interruption, only to contemplate it briefly. She realizes that he is actually listening, and this is a very big step for him. She knows that she should be proud of his progress.

"Well, okay B. You see, it was pretty intense being in more than one place in parallel forces of existence simultaneously. And as I grow older, I am able to keep my self centered as growth enhances my memory, my ability to reason and find truth without fear and to work diligently toward what I already know will be my final departure from this dimension, which I now encourage you to define for all practical purposes. I also like to enhance my potential energy—it's so much more fun moshing when you don't get hurt."

"What in the hell are you talking about? Are you a pilot for one of those cheap airlines?"

Her disappointment, while hidden from view, charges a pulse of energy through her spine. "Hell? Sorry, my prodigal son, but you're not there except in your own mind. Or at least, that's the way it will be for you from here on in unless you open your eyes and your heart."

B turns to run but is stopped by a large wooden cork-like object. "Hey, I can't move at all! But I don't feel any pressure anymore in my stomach. Maybe my spastic colon is cured."

"Not a chance!" The voice comes up from behind him. "Sounds like you need a miracle!" A familiar face now stands before him.

"Jener! You sneaky bastard! Where's my wife? And who's this Chink lady telling me about her different lives?"

"WB, you always picked up on important insights well. That's why we all love you here." Jener points toward the trailer caravan. In the middle, Genghis Khan, dressed like a Las Vegas card dealer, is dealing cards to Albert Einstein.

"God doesn't gamble, but I'll try." Einstein sticks his tongue out at the Mongol dynamo.

Genghis bellows out in a drunken hysteria as everyone joins in a toast. Although Zhu Zen upholds very strict regulations as to who is allowed behind Wall's wall, Genghis Khan, one of history's most notorious barbarians, has proven to the parole committee in galactic prison that he can have supervised visits. Frankly, he is a big hit in the circle of historically significant peoples, his sense of humor an ongoing party miracle. Humor was always a way in. Wall sees several visitors regularly who have taken life on earth, and while they had been imprisoned for this already, some for hundreds of years, a detailed understanding of their crimes, a display of an expanded conscience and utter regret for their actions, and especially a sense of humor about what they have been through, can get some, though certainly not all, supervised visits outside galactic prison.

"Listen, B. You have been brought here via democratic process. All the elders in our group gather together and decide who should carry the torch regarding certain levels of thinking in the human-defined conscious dimension. You have been chosen on your level. The guidance you will receive is critical for many reasons, most of which you would not understand. However, let me just say that your presence in certain extremely relevant situations that most probably will determine the preservation of life, the future of ethical judgment and practice in the world's economies and political forums, and most importantly, the best way to help the people of the world persevere the unruliness of power mongers will prove most helpful. We have other as caretakers of existence who work on important matters like a comprehensive space program, controlling the manufacture of bacterial weaponry, isolating the destructive genes run amok in the DNA pool, finding cures for mental and physical ailments, and preserving the right to vote."

"Why me? I don't understand anything you are talking about. Oh please, Zhu Zen... May I call you ZZ? Please give me the strength to go on in this world. Everyone wants me to change into what everyone wants me to be. I only want a cushy life with nice homes, cars, boats and plenty of cash. And please keep the goddamned immigrants away from me. Why can't we build that wall between Mexico and the US? And Canada too! My daddy tells me that we should just annex them, and if we don't annex them—just make them believe that we like them— they need us badly enough that they'll do anything to be on our side—they'll even support those who will drop a little diarrhea on them now and then. But why me?" he whines.

"B, like I said, we will give you direction that will enable you to achieve peace of mind. You do not *have* to change, but as the rest of the world changes, what are you going to do, lie down and die or fight everyone or change as everyone else does? It is really up to you. There have been those who have tried to fight, and there are those who turn their backs and hope for the best, but they've been downright miserable and have never really succeeded. And furthermore, what in the hell do you think is happening in this world? Before you know it, your enemy will not be the so-called immigrants but your own children. Can you deal with that, Mr. Johnson?"

"Oh I want to change, but what happens if I lose my job? I'm so scared. I really have a good thing going. I don't really do any work. I spend all day practicing my golf swing, jogging, riding my bike, and insulting people—and I make millions. Well, of course I speak to my stockbroker at least twenty times a day too."

"Liar!" a voice screams out. A disgusted woman stomps toward him.

"Johnnie?" Winchester calls out in shock.

"No, Elvis." Her sarcasm gets a chuckle from the Memphis Wonder himself, who is drinking a beer and eating a jelly donut at a nearby table.

"Johnnie, how did you and Jener split like that?"

"Are you that stupid? Zhu Zen has explained everything to you and you still don't get it?"

"Hold on now Johnnie," ZZ interrupts. "I didn't tell him everything yet. Give him a chance."

"Why should I give him a chance? He litters his filth everywhere he goes. Nobody can take him anywhere, you know. At parties, he's a total bore, and at work, as he has just admitted, he does nothing. He cares about no one not even himself. He still eats pounds of pig meat, and not even the good parts. He farts to communicate, He invades many people's space with his stench, and he will someday, no doubt, invade everybody's space. His breath is unruly. He still refers to people of African descent as niggers and to Asians as chinks, gooks and slant eyes. He calls homosexuals faggots who deserve AIDS; and every woman is a chick, a beaver, a whore, etc., etc. He deserves to be incinerated and his dust launched toward the stars to litter the outer stratosphere. We don't need him here anymore." Johnnie is really heating up now.

"You make very valid points. We should just dispose of his life force once and for all. Mr. Oppenheimer, please join us here." ZZ motions the gathering crowd to disperse and get on with their partying as a slim unassuming gentleman wanders toward them. He is wearing a pair of overalls and moon boots with Manhattan Project stitched on them. "Mr. Oppenheimer, have you and Mr. Einstein finished the equations on demagnetizing the center of the energetic core? I would like to see it done on Mr. WB Johnson."

Old Oppy burst into a rhetorical rage, screaming about how he didn't know what he was doing and that military made him do it. It was that or the Alaskan pipeline, he screams, and he says he hated the cold weather and therefore he opted for potential earthly destruction. Of course, later, and he stammers this part, "Those bastards wouldn't let me through the doors that I built. Figures."

"Oh, cool off Robert. We didn't ask for your dissertation on military strategy, though I do agree with you in fighting for arms control. Once you have admitted guilt, you can move on."

"I swear they made me do it!"

"STOP! I'll do whatever you want," B screams. "Just shut him up. I have no idea what you're all talking about, but it doesn't sound healthy. What do you want me to do? I'll promise not to litter. I won't short sell stocks that I know will crash. I'll even be a vegetarian if you want—I don't really like tofu but I am sure I can learn how. I'll stop making racial slurs. I'll even pretend, I mean promise, to love my wife. Anything, I'll do it."

ZZ brings Johnnie, Jener, and the astrophysicists together in a small huddle-like formation. She speaks to them in some form of ancient Chinese dialect, a crude form of Cantonese, and as the words escape her lips they are instantaneously translated into the language the listeners understand best. They simultaneously laugh and disperse. Johnnie gives B one last angry look and walks away arm-in-arm with Jener as though he is escorting her to some special event.

"Phew," says B as he wipes his brow. "That was close. Thanks ZZ."

"Listen, B. You're not out of the colon yet, so to speak. I need to ensure that your trust is legitimate. The information I am about to give you will make you a marked man. True wisdom is not well liked in a world filled with hatred and differing points of view. You will be scrutinized, judged, made a fool of, and even laughed at."

"Oh, that's fine—all of that already happens to me. Almost every day."

"Yes, yes I know, but from now on, you will not want it to happen. After you leave here, B, you will gain an extra sense of subconscious direction in the form of a wave of force that controls your thoughts and feelings, of which you will not always be aware or even understand."

"Sure, sure. Just give me the info. I need to call my broker."

"Maybe Johnnie is correct,—you don't understand at all. Do you know what I am?"

"Yeah, you're an old chink gal."

"I am a mystic. Even Gods consult me when they're stuck dealing with modernity. I am keeper of another dimension. I am forced to stay here because there is so much work to be done. Do you think this is easy, trying to convince a mindless creep that terra incognito is not just some Latin burble?"

Outside the compound, Kra, disguised as one of the royal lepers, holds a remote control. On the remote control are three buttons: On, Off. and Self-Destruct. He presses the "On" button.

"I am beginning to understand. You do have secret plans for me." B's memory is activated, as he remembers Kra and the guard in Colorado Springs demanding the secret plans.

"Yes, B, I read your thoughts. As I stated, you will be a marked man."

"Oh damn, I don't know if I'm ready for this. Why me? Why me?"

"B, please listen. It is pretty obvious. You have learned great marketing techniques. You learned how to run businesses using very questionable ethics, even though all of those businesses went bust eventually despite your vast experience with free market trading. You studied, well sort of, at two of the finest universities in the world. Your father did, and still does, hold a very critical position of power. Do you know that the greatest, most influential works modern humankind has ever known have been marketed in a particular manner conducive to a lengthy lifespan and wonderful success and financial rewards? Besides the brilliance contained in all of them, the teachings in the form of massively condensed wisdom, well among other things, is the most relevant part for you. Look at the Holy Bible and its counterparts, the Qur'an, the Confucian writings and those of Buddha. Have you ever read any Roman, Greek, or Egyptian Mythology? These are the popular works, not as intellectually profound as some of the later Greek democratic papers written after Aristotle and Plato had set up their now legendary 2000-year camp in the Galapagos Islands. Find the scriptures of the Babylonian and Sufi mystics, the navigations of ancient mariners of the skies and the modern flight of software programming. If you're interested I can recommend some breakthrough works by medieval metaphysicists who were condemned as sorcerers. It's *all* marketing. Well, like I said, for all intents and purposes, as far as you're concerned it is."

"Wow, this is really intense. I knew I had some special gifts, but this is simply mind blowing. It's probably a good idea to learn how to read." B feels a stinging sense of pride, one he's never felt before.

"Well, B, I could have picked anyone for this expedition. Yes, please start reading; many more facets of life will make sense if you do. According to our information, you will soon represent a very successful family-run organization, and from what we are being told, you will be instrumental in bringing it to the top. Let me tell you something else, though. You were not our first choice. The other hundred simply refused to show up. I think they had the mental prowess but lacked any spiritual sensibilities. Remember, someday you will find yourself with power beyond belief."

"Wow, I am honored. Do you mind if I take this information to Bill Grate. I am sure he'll hire me based on this information."

"You can do what you like, but I must warn you that you will come to terms with *who* you are. This may be frightening, as you will find you are what you hate. People who do not understand what you are referring to will laugh you at. You may meet several of Wall's elite club members, due to timing and other issues that I cannot discuss, who will be allowed to freely associate with people in the world who are still alive. If you meet with them, please be subtle. Most of the world could never handle the historical elite coming back to earth to mingle with let alone to guide them. You'll be labeled a freak, a dysfunctional member of society, a raving lunatic, but you *will* have the goods!" ZZ walks away as though no words were ever spoken and fades into the center of the triangle, which while they were speaking, improved its volume and its shape, more clearly defined itself, and now appears to B as a pyramid converging into the mouth of a very dark cave.

"This might be the first step. I can see things more clearly," he thinks out loud. "How can I use this? I wonder if any companies traded on the NASDAQ already exist as secret mythological-type information-based data companies. New York would never have anything that risky. I think the Saudi stock market should be progressing fast enough in about a decade to entertain this type of a start-up." He picks up his cell phone. "Pops, get me the Sultan of Swing on the line. I have a *great* idea that cannot fail."

He then begins his long journey back, determined to use this knowledge in the best way possible. He begins playing out different scenarios in his mind, stumbling and fumbling about, but he clearly decides that this ultimately grand project must begin as something subtle. "I remember when I marketed low-grade oil synthetics for the first time. At first it was hush-hush, and then it became an explosion of profitability. I am very excited about this new venture. Maybe I'll be able to afford my dream island on that tiny stretch of jade mountain in the Tuamotu Archipelago."

He turns to thank Zhu Zen, but all has again disappeared like a faded dream and B enters a temporary state of depression. He begins to feel lonely. An air of emptiness surrounds him. He is back in his car. There is no Great Wall around. There are no cadavers littering the streets, and the lush vegetation has disappeared like everything else. "Where did everything go?" He sobs alone in his car. A sporty family-type ultra-luxurious raised sedan-like van-style wagon pulls up next to him. A man and a woman are waving to him. She is holding a glowing jar, and she and B exchange smiles and then the couple drives off.

"Wow, that was odd. I wonder what was in that jar. Probably their kid." He begins to laugh as though what he thought was somehow true, as ludicrous as it sounded. He is about to begin his trek back toward Minneapolis but stops the car. "Wait a minute! I think I am closer to a different city. He decides to continue going west and turns around. He sees a sign for Rapid City. "Rapid City. Hmmm. I think there's a monument there of some kind. It must be the Hoover Dam. The city's name reminds me of rushing water. I would love to see it while I am out on the road, and besides, might as well make a pit stop. Maybe I can take a piss in it."

"No, it is Mount Rushmore," a voice calls out in his head.

"Holy mackerel! It really works. Every time I screw up, my own subconscious will guide me and correct me."

"Not every time, you human waste," the voice rebuts.

"What in the hell?" B attempts to ignore the voice and continues on.

When he arrives in Rapid City, he decides the first thing to do is to get some money out of an ATM. He cannot find one, and so he pulls into a Burger Prince to ask a local. He sees a group of thirty year-old neo-Nazi thugs wearing three-piece Versace suits with swastikas on armbands and carrying alligator skin briefcases beating up on a twelve-year-old Nigerian vacationer. "I should ask one of these guys. They look like they know the area pretty well," B thinks to himself candidly.

"Hey guys, hold up there one minute. Where can I find an ATM? I need to take out a couple hundred bucks."

The leader steps forward. "Oh, we'll show you." He motions to the rest of the gang to follow. Little does B realize, but through his idiotic efforts, he may have saved that young man's life. They lead him to a machine and stand behind him with tire irons, chains, whips, guns, a bottle of stain remover, and a roll of extra-absorbent toilet paper.

"Hey guys, where can I find a girl for the night?" he asks as he punches in the appropriate numbers. "And do you know how much they cost around here? I may have to withdraw funds from more than one account."

"Oh, sure. We can show you. They cost around two thousand an hour here. Pickings are pretty slim and costly."

"Wow, two grand an hour? This better be worth it!"

"Oh, I guarantee it."

B removes cash from four different accounts in the British Virgin Islands, taking the daily limit on all of them. Just as the neo-Nazis in suits are about to jump him, a police officer approaches. He has a harshly soulless walk, pale skin that is almost completely colorless, and physically he looks like Apollo, that is if anyone knew what Apollo actually looked like, then they could visualize him properly.

"These boys bothering you?"

"Well, no sir. They're just showing me where I can find a good looking girl for the night."

"Oh really? I'd say that you look like a faggot to me. You like guys?" asks the officer of the law.

"I think so." B is having trouble remembering.

The policeman nods to the thugs and they all jump him, kicking him and beating him. They steal his money and run, except the police officer who remains standing over B's limp bloodied body admiring his work. B lies slightly curled on the ground whimpering. Everything has been stolen from him: his wallet and his keys to the rental car, his ego and his memory. The camera angle switches and slowly fades toward the sky. B is growing smaller and smaller in some darkening alley in Rapid City. People congregate around him, laughing at him, pointing and spitting on him. Television cameras then surround him like vultures, the photographers snapping images of the victim as he passes out. Fade to blue screen with image of a tall wild sunflower against a cloudless sapphire blue sky.

Act 7.

Identity Crisis

This would turn out to be the strangest of days in a life filled with a discernable measure of strangeness already. Johnnie has returned from her mystical sabbatical in South Dakota and is waiting for her husband to return home. Despite their differences, she has been reassured by ZZ that things will be different from here on in, and since she has placed an enormous amount of trust in ZZ, she will accept this as the truth. She has to admit to some doubt, however, for B has given her very few reasons to take such assurances on faith.

The alley in Rapid City is now a major crime scene. An anonymous tip led two CIB field agents here to investigate, and they have quickly whisked B back to the Octagon's medical facilities by private jet to ensure he is still in one complete piece. Although testing shows additional density in his body's mass, his primary brain functions seem to be operating at a similar capacity as previously, low. Once B is returned home to recuperate, Johnnie's maternal nature emerges and she decides to take care of her badly beaten husband. She feeds him and ooddloo him like a child, and they fall asleep in the same bed for the first time in a very long time.

Johnnie and B roll quickly out of bed to the sounds of muffled screams and other streams of unfamiliar noise deconstructing, of fragmenting audible dynamics, the impressionistic detail reflecting furiously eroding particles of sunlight passing through glass prisms. They both think they are imagining things and do not mention these effects to each other.

"I feel like I've been sleeping on a bed of quartz," exclaims Johnnie as she walks into the bathroom, half erect, holding her back in pain, and turns on the water in the shower. B sits up carefully to assess where he is, takes a generous deep breath, and smiles. His nervous system expresses gratitude in the rest he just awoke from, and he gingerly slips on a white robe with a Garden of Eden Flock Hotel insignia on the left chest. The smells of lilac and pine come back to him gently, and he recalls waking one morning to peer out across the cliffs of St. Barths at the rising sun, the breeze through the open window carrying the smell of crisp Caribbean air to his nose. He remembers seeing a small group of dogs below, running past a man dressed as a clown who was passed out on the beach, through the coconut palms, and down the white sand beach toward the sunrise. The dogs had quickly trotted out of view, and although that image was slightly odd, it remained a peaceful one for him. A kindling sparks his darkened heart reminding him of enduring beauty.

B proceeds down the stairs to the kitchen to get coffee from their very costly and massive Italian espresso machine. He pours himself a cup and pulls some papers and other materials out of a manila folder. He examines them while he waits for Johnnie to serve him his favorite breakfast, frozen sausage and organic eggs. He sips his espresso and listens to his wife cleaning herself and then fixing herself up. He looks toward the ceiling and smiles in gratitude for having a caring partner. He knows in his heart that he does not deserve such a turn of events, but he is convinced there is some greater purpose involved here. The beating really took a toll on him. It seems that after running away for so long he just got tired of running and is now facing certain truths in his life, and this alone is a huge step for B.

Johnnie comes down several minutes later dressed in a loosely fitting blouse and comfortable jeans, and as B finishes up his coffee, she begins to prepare his breakfast. Before uttering a word to her, B goes back up to shower. A sudden state of remembrance befalls Johnnie's sleepy brain. Quickly, images of birds in flight, mathematically scattered fish, as in an Escher sketch, swallowing lizards, variables of differential equations, and the motion of vibrating light like tiny exploding stars descend upon her. Johnnie shakes her head vigorously in an attempt to rid herself of these visions as though there are cobwebs in her eyes. She grinds the coffee beans, fills a small cup with espresso, and glances downward at the table where the papers B pulled out of the folder lie. She picks up the folder to take a closer look and a small bag of white powder falls out. Like a leaking faucet, tears stream down her cheeks onto her blouse. In a pseudo-schizophrenic moment, she immediately stops crying, and then becomes very angry. She remembers what ZZ told her about patience, and so she decides to handle this differently than she normally might. After a few minutes of brief meditation, she comes to her senses and her curiosity forces her to read the top page: "Rin Chin will be the next of kin and tomorrow we will die."

"What in the hell?" she thinks, and she decides not to read any further, for she needs to know what this cryptic message means before she ingests any more information. She washes the wine glasses from the night before and leaves them in the wooden rack by the sink to dry. She leans over the kitchen counter and tears a single sheet of paper towel from a roll, then sprays some wood cleaner on it. She bends down under the counter and wipes up a stain of red from the Santos mahogany hardwood floor. B meanders languidly down the stairs, and at the last step, he trips a bit but catches his footing before he falls. He sees her wiping the floor.

"What are you wiping?" he asks.

"A red wine stain from the party last night. I remember spilling something and not cleaning it up when it happened."

"Party? What party? I don't remember a party. Didn't I return last night half-beaten?" He is now very confused.

Johnnie changes the subject unsuspectingly, for her own memory is now very confused and clouded. "I thought you stopped using that nose candy after your father caught you and threatened to send you to National Guard duty!"

"Listen, Johnnie. I thought you put it there, as a test of my will."

"Will? Why would I test a junkie's will with a bag of coke? That's bold of you, but then, junkies lie when their will has succumbed to temptation. Let's forget about this for now and move on to these papers! What exactly does 'Rin Chin will be the next of kin and tomorrow we will die' mean?"

B begins explaining bluntly and very confidently. "I do not know. I vaguely remember someone handing me the envelope before leaving Wall, but I was too confused about what I had seen to pay it much heed. I didn't notice the bag then and am seeing it now for the first time." B has had a problem telling the truth to Johnnie for a long time because he fears her, and so she questions his response immediately.

"I didn't know that you knew the word heed! Anyway, I asked if we could forget about the drugs. How could you not fully examine an envelope that someone handed you in the middle of nowhere? That is ridiculous if not downright deceitful!"

"All right, calm down! I looked but it made no sense, so why bother bringing it up? I just put it in my bag and that was that. You know that cast of characters in the trailer park—there are a lot of jokers there."

"Jokers? I am not talking about jokers. I am talking about this 'we're going to die' statement!" Johnnie is heating up a bit again, ZZ's advice insufficient to keep her from this old habit completely.

"Listen," he rebuts, "it certainly was not intentional. I simply wanted to try to figure it out on my own before informing you, that's all. I think, anyway. There is nothing to worry about." B is now in very unfamiliar territory as he and his wife are actually speaking, attempting to work out a dispute. He thinks this is exciting. Maybe this new path will help him get laid more at home so he doesn't have to go out and search out some quickies and she won't have to find someone new in her life she can take care of and cook and clean and organize things for.

"Nothing to worry about?" She has decided she will not let down. "Today we are supposed to be adopting a child we have not seen but only read about, and you tell me that I should not worry when I read that Rin Chin is the next of kin and tomorrow we will die? Are you nuts? Do you have several screws loose? Did you check with security at your building? Did you ask your father? He must know! My horoscope says that something very strange will happen to me in the next twenty-three days and I'm beginning to believe it!"

B doesn't recall any adoptions, any new additions to the Johnson household. He wonders where this entire line of thinking is coming from. He is especially confused about the dying part. He really doesn't want to die. His father called him briefly during his flight on the CIB jet after his Rapid City incident and told him that he has some important work ahead of him and he needs for him to be healthy. Since maturing, in relative terms, into adulthood, B has looked up to his father. He knows that, if he doesn't do the job that his father wants him to do, his brother will, and that is not what B wants.

"All right, all right, all right! Let's discuss this rationally. Its probably one of the guys playing a joke, you know, to freak us out about the (gulp) adoption. My friend Kra is definitely a joker." This answer, though not entirely acceptable, is enough to suffice for the present moment. Johnnie has no idea who Kra is, but she knows her husband has many acquaintances and Kra is very likely one that he just doesn't speak about too often, if ever.

"Well, this is not funny!"

The phone rings and Johnnie answers, "Hallow?"

"Yes, is this the Chin residence?"

"NO! Who is speaking?" asks Johnnie.

"This is Harriet from the Transient Pilot Adoption Center. I am calling to inform you that your child is ready and can be picked up at noon."

"That's fine. We will be there, but where are you getting this Chin name from?" responds Johnnie, but apparently the caller did not hear the last part as she had already hung up the telephone. "That was the adoption center..."

"Chin? Are those damned Chinks after me again?"

"We can pick up our new child at noon."

For a brief moment, they forget about the envelope and its contents. Johnnie has waited a long time for this moment, and considering all the happenings recently, it is not surprising to her that B doesn't know about the adoption or remember if he once did. Nor is it surprising that Johnnie doesn't really care if he remembers or not.

Johnnie was told by a friend she met after leaving the trailer park that she should begin adopting infants from very poor countries to boost her standing among the Hollywood 'A' list crowd. And with the 'A' list crowd is where she plans to spend most of her free time moving forward. She actually went through intense bouts of depression and potential suicide before the idea of adopting a little person with no family struck her as the only way she could be redeemed for her sins, and only she knows about those sins, which she will keep concealed for her own safety until she dies. For she is a strict God-fearing religious woman and she felt that her lack of standing in the crowd was by her own doing and that God punished her for something she did, although she wasn't quite sure what that might have been. When Jener and ZZ came along, she knew that she was on the right path.

Failed memories and failed reasonable extrapolations of logic and rationality aside, B and Johnnie bubbled with excitement over the fact that they would soon be parents of a new baby. Their faces were dressed with sincere smiles—and a bit of white foam leaked from B's mouth—and happiness. Also, she had requested that the gender of the child be kept a secret for they both liked excitement and this was the best way she could think of finding it. Although the adoption center found this highly irregular, they obliged.

B calmed himself down and motioned to Johnnie to sit down, for he had something to tell her. The panic in her eyes was so great he could have climbed inside of her and been swallowed by the black emptiness in her expression. "Johnnie, honey, you were asking about the envelope. Well, I have something to tell you about a dream I had. It was a warm misty night. I know it was warm because

Dad's neighbor, Stan 'the Poodle' Ruffles, you know the CEO of Enstron, the guy with the long gray hair that doesn't move in the wind, stood in our driveway and, well, he was wearing nothing but a Speedo bathing suit and it was nighttime and his nipples were not erect. From the windows, you could see the rain moving horizontally in the windy streets through the bright street lamps. We were joined in our lavishly decorated living room by several couples, most indistinguishable one from the next, but one thing was clear. They all, I mean all, had beards and wore toupees, including the women. This fact was not that strange in its own right, but they all spoke backward too, and not just any words. Their speech sounded like they were juxtaposing passages from the Bible in an ancient tongue, probably Syrian Aramaic. Yes, I know it is fashionable today to say that people use this language that has been all but dead for 2000 years, but I really do think that they were. I cannot prove it, because I do not know Aramaic, and even if I did hear it at some time in my life, it would take hours of studying and translating even a few words to know for sure; but if I had to bet my life on it, I would say it was indeed Syrian Aramaic. Even Syrians never speak Aramaic, you know, but modern Arabic. How do I know this? Pops told Dad and Dad told me and Pops is never wrong."

Terror struck Johnnie with a memory interrupt: She, too, recently experienced Bible-like dreams—raging fires of the apocalypse, the judgment, the mass destruction. She was shocked and amazed with his sudden grasp of complex words and thoughts. She even felt the presence of her Lord in a truly moving experience of awakening. Yet the notion of complete ideological synergy with her present dilemma was far too great to comprehend, and so she simply sat and listened as B continued.

"Furthermore, the people were all facing a small glass object in the center of the room. I could not make out what it was, or maybe I did at the time but forgot, but I did notice an incandescent glow illuminating the room from what appeared to be that very glass object. And at once, in some bizarre flash of energy, the glass erupted into a core of fire. The force from the explosion felt like a nuclear weapon had exploded and the heat and radiation passed through all of us. The light emitted patterns and vibrations of color and sound. The room appeared almost cleansed with this strange occurrence, and in the corner I made out what looked like a mouth floating, and the intensity grew as I witnessed it opening with darkness inside—and the opening was covered by hair making it look similar to the beards and toupees on everyone else. Yet, this was only a mouth." The clarity of the story gave Johnnie a shiver and she asked him to not continue any further, but he interrupted. "I must continue. The last part was clearly the most bizarre. You and I changed. We no longer appeared recognizable to ourselves or to each other. We actually looked different. I mean our physical looks had changed and no one recognized us, not you me nor I you, and not even our own child."

"You saw our child?" asks Johnnie, unfazed by her husband's use of words that she wasn't aware he even knew.

"Let me think... No, I'm afraid I don't remember if I did or not. But I do remember being very hurt by this."

The clock on the wall strikes 11:00, and a small bird escapes a tiny door on the beautifully carved highly detailed wood clock's face. They watch intensely as the bird travels in and out of the door eleven times before taking refuge back inside the clock's body. They exchange confused glances and burst into hysterical laughter.

"Oh what in the living hell are we doing to each other? We always do this, whip each other into a frenzy until we actually start believing this bizarre stuff happens," exclaims Johnnie with a stern confidence that B cannot help but agree with. However, most obviously, their collective memories have completely failed them at this moment. The magical feat of physical regeneration from one point to the next, the time travel, the dream states, the hallucinations, the dead historical figures in the trailer park—they cannot remember any of it. However, they can experience this moment together, and they have a newfound faith in love and in one another and in their respective spiritual mother and father.

B stares into Johnnie's eyes, who sees into her soul. She trembles from this, and she reaches for him. He grabs her and they lock lips. She pushes her tongue into his mouth and closes her eyes. She is strolling down Rodeo Drive in Beverly Hills with shopping bags in hand from Prucci and Clartier. B is waiting outside Stiffany's in an idling Crazerati they keep at their beach house in Malibu. She gets a phone call from Scorsezhe, the famous revolutionary Kazakh film director, who asks Johnnie and B to his party in Bel Air. She opens her eyes and sees B in front of her. He is slightly trembling from excitement, fear, or a possible stomachache, or maybe she is standing on his bare foot—the probable causes are endless here. He has a tear rolling down his cheek. She licks it off. He is not afraid of her for the first time in years.

Time slips away as they stand glancing silently into the near distance. B glances then at his watch, which reads twenty-three past the hour. They seat themselves in the newly purchased sporty family-type ultra-luxurious raised sedan-like van-style wagon and find a road toward a new beginning. They flick on the radio to the oldies station, and U2's "I Will Follow," the country waltz remix, is heard through the vehicle's forty-four speaker audio system. Johnnie and B know this one by heart. They break into a very impressive vocal. B is in a sharp frame of mind after the kiss and after the strange incidents in the past few weeks and decides to delve into a topic often discussed but usually not with this clarity. Before speaking, he takes a gulp, one that is usually associated with nervousness.

"So what do you think about the government?"

"What do you mean what do I think? Do you want to know if it exists? That's stupid. Of course it exists. Or do you want to know how I feel about it?" Johnnie also seems to be in exceptional form.

"I feel like I have a new calling, and this calling might be to join the CIB or the government and get out of the business world altogether."

"Tough one, but I would say that, as long as it pays well, I think you should do whatever you want." Johnnie missed his point but made her own simultaneously.

"Okay." B responds without much further thought.

"I am concerned with the future of our child, and by the way, what are we going to name the little bugger?" Johnnie lets out a small chuckle, imagining what B's response to this statement might be. She continues, "Well, I thought we decided to name the little lady or little guy upon first glance. You know, like the Native American tribes used to do, or maybe still do," she announces with pride.

B has no idea what she is talking about. It seems now that Johnnie has had at least one conversation inside of her own head with B, or perhaps his memory is just so bad that he cannot remember anything she is talking about. So, doing his best to keep up, he stammers, "Which tribes?"

"I don't know. I read it somewhere, or maybe I heard it in a joke." Johnnie begins to back off with her righteousness. "I mean, I thought it would be better that way." B detects her angst and simply agrees.

They arrive at a small square building with a huge iron gate around it and people walking counterclockwise around in small circles holding signs that are indistinguishable at this distance. "Is this the place?" asks Johnnie.

"I believe so. It looks more like an abortion clinic than an adoption agency though."

"Oh don't say that!" Johnnie's fear of judgment takes over, and very possibly, the fear for her own life.

"No, I mean, why are these people picketing? Is there something we should know?" B's answer is very diplomatic under duress.

"Oh hell, I don't know! But we are here to pick up our child. So let's go in, and go in proud." Her phony confidence is amusing at best. As they make a left turn and pull into the gate, their car is pummeled with bloody eggs tossed by the angry mob. To their right, they see a group of wild dogs chasing two seemingly frightened people toward a car. As the dogs surround them, the man appears to be waving to B.

"Do we know them?" asks Johnnie, puzzled. B looks at his watch; it reads 12:06 p.m.

"Maybe I met him in Denver at the execution! Oh darn, I hope we aren't late. I certainly don't want to miss anything exciting!" B calls out half-confused and half-elated.

They arrive safely at the door and make it through unharmed. An older woman in a nicely worn casual business suit greets them. She has a look of sincerity about her, but they do not see this from their perspective. They are busy worrying about the mob and the wild dogs.

"Greetings! Welcome to our operation, the finest adoption agency in town! You must be the Chins. I recognize your faces." She ushers them into a waiting room and closes the door.

"Chins? Why does everyone think we are Chinese? This is madness! And she recognizes us? How? We've never met her," whispers B to Johnnie, who is too busy dreaming of hobnobbing with the Hollywood elite to pay attention.

"God, if I know what's going on... Let's just be patient. I'm sure everything will work out just fine," Johnnie weakly claims.

B rises from his chair after only a minute or so and pulls apart two blinds from the window. He sees the woman who has not revealed her name walking another couple toward a room on the other side of the main entrance. The room has a sign on it, but he cannot determine what it reads. B and the man make eye contact. The man has a horrible look of distress, pain, sadness, and fear on his face. The woman, who is carrying a blanket, is noticeably excited, her expression bleeding from her face. B thinks she looks like she's giving orders to a puppy.

"Oh look, honey. That couple just adopted a child. They look nervous. I hope they make out okay with that crazed mob wildly interrupting a very special moment in a person's life." Tears again interrupt Johnnie's stammering. B sits patiently and waits. She is obviously not as calm. Amidst the emotional confusion, all she can think about now is the dream B had and her own dreams, that they must mean something and how, if they don't walk out of here with a new baby today, she will not be invited to *the* Halloween Party in Bel-Air.

The woman reenters the room. "Sorry to keep you waiting. We had a bit of a delay with the last couple."

"I noticed that they appeared worried," replies B nervously.

"Oh, almost every couple leaves here a bit scared. You know, new beginning, new addition to the household. It can be a frightening thing. Oh, and by the way, my name his Harriet. Harriet Beecher."

"Harriet Beecher? I once read about a Harriet Beecher. Where was that? Oh damn, I do not remember. B, do you remember any Harriet Beecher?"

"I know of a Harriet Beecher Stowe, the author. *Uncle Tom's Cabin* was one of my favorite works in high school before, well, I stopped reading."

"Mine too," exclaims Harriet immediately, "although I never stopped reading."

"I think I knew a Harriet Beecher growing up. I remember the name, but not the face."

"I assure you that I am the only Harriet Beecher I know," Harriet replies with a giggle.

The three of then them laugh together, as if on cue in some poorly made 'B' movie, and skip the remaining phony pleasantries. Harriet begins explaining the operation to them.

"You see, our organization began a very long time ago. There was a time in history when adoption was not permitted by the dominant churches of the time, and although the government had a say in social issues, they were primarily the responsibility of the church and the religions they supported. Transient Pilot began as a social group, but after its leaders moved on, so did the group. It grew into a force of consciousness right around the time of Lincoln..." Johnnie and B begin to grow a little weary, as their preconception of the word consciousness is one of distrust, triggering words like failure, anti-patriotism, liberals and Commies. "And upon passage of the Thirteenth Amendment, our organization grew into an adoption agency."

"Oh, that's wonderful!" chimes in Johnnie. "I think the work you do is very admirable. When do we get to see our newest child?"

"Please be patient. You need to know more about our organization first," responds Harriet. Johnnie and B sit back and listen. "At the end of the 19th and beginning of the 20th centuries, the operation was in full swing. We were providing young couples like you with a family. I understand that you already have children, and it is wonderful that you have decided to help those in need by adopting a child. Over the years, there have been many reasons why women cannot give birth to a youngster..."

Johnnie interrupts. "Oh, I can give birth, but it's just not cool anymore to have a child on your own."

"Well," Harriet continued, "the church used to, and probably still does, make people feel shame for this..." Johnnie's face turns an ignominiously pinkish white and the flux in her blood flow causes time to invariably slow. Her pupils dilate slightly and her upper lip begins to twitch. She feels the stream of redirected blood go to her brain, where it meets a small positive ionic charge, rehabilitating the moment in real time. "But our organization is here to help those who have a problem coping with this dilemma. We provide the backbone for a step in a hugely gratifying direction." The words strangely tickle B's sense of sexuality.

"I understand your position here. But ours is a difficult one. We have tons of cash, and we desperately want a new child to flaunt to our friends. You see, our daughter is grown up already," says Johnnie.

B interrupts. "What she means to say is that our daughter is becoming a mess and we want to try again. Right, honey?" Johnnie is stunned by her loss of words; she just sits there in a fog. He continues. "We want to provide the best care and be good parents. We would also like to grow ourselves," proclaims B rather proudly.

That was the cue Harriet was waiting for. "I am so glad that you feel that way, Mr. Chin. Mrs. Chin, do you stand similarly?"

"Well yes, of course. I'm just a bit nervous. But why do you keep calling us the Chins?"

Harriet missed the last part, the question, as she was rifling through some documents on her desk. "What I propose we do is take the two of you to the selection hall. I know that our computer has predetermined a child for you, and you came here prepared for such an event; however, you may change your mind upon viewing the specimen. This may sound slightly odd, but trust me, it is the best way. On the wall leading to the Great Hall, you will find photographs of all of our recipients and their chosen new family member."

Harriet then leads them out of the room into a long shaded corridor. In the distance they can see the photographs lining the wall but cannot make them out. The revelation strikes B so profoundly, that he is emotionally moved: he has not sworn, farted, nor had the overwhelming need to release anything from his colon. He is amazed and dumfounded—it is as though he has been born again. In this moment, he doesn't even remember who Little Diarrhea was. He cannot think far back enough to remember Little Diarrhea, nor the Older Diarrhea who was just beaten up in Rapid City. Frankly, he is so surprised at his progress that he looks upward to the ceiling and quietly says a small prayer for not relieving himself in his pants.

"This is strange. From the outside the building looks small and square, but inside the corridor appears endless," Johnnie points out candidly.

"Looks can be deceiving," answers Harriet bluntly. She approaches a computer monitor and punches in several strokes on the keypad. From behind her, the Johnson-Chin couple observes the monitor flashing through several colorful screens, then going black. A relatively loud siren begins to sound, a large titanium gate closes the hallway off, and Harriet steps backward, then turns around to face the Johnson-Chins. "Unfortunately, my system tells me that the two of you are not quite ready for this. I am very sorry, but this is the way it works here."

"I will not leave until my child is in my arms!" Johnnie immediately bursts into tears. She knows that she will be outcast before she was ever truly in the mix, and since the only other way to get in is to sleep around, which is just not something she is willing to do, at least not in the public eye. At least, as far as this story goes, she is not willing to thus prostitute herself to achieve acceptance. She knows how cliques work, and she knows her doom is imminent.

"I agree. This is absurd. We are here for our child, and we will not leave based on that explanation," B answers calmly.

"All right. I can attempt to bypass the system's refusal, but I will have to get a manager's approval." Harriet hurries away to find the necessary personnel.

"Oh, I can give you plenty of hints on how to go around the system to get done what you need." B is quite proud of his exploits, but these thoughts give rise to a small grumbling in his stomach. He stops and thinks. "Oh, maybe this makes more sense now."

"I don't understand this. She went through that entire explanation for what, for our health? I simply don't get it," Johnnie bitterly cries out.

"Johnnie, I don't get it either. This is probably a test."

"A test for what, to see if we are ready? We're here, aren't we? Isn't that ready enough?"

"I don't know. I suppose you're right. Let's just wait and see."

They notice two chairs by a window and proceed to sit in them.

"This place is strange, sort of eerie in the way the lights are dimmed and the dimensions of the building are quite the opposite of what they appear to be from the outside. Maybe it's just me." Johnnie uses the pacification through ignorance approach to cope with the situation for her nervous system's benefit. B has known too many situations like this. He is unsure of how many of them relate to his cocaine problem, so he just allows the idea to die a natural death.

Like two shadows emerging from a pale light, two figures walk toward them. The person with Harriet is wearing a tall black hat and a bow tie with a black tuxedo, and he dwarfs her. B swallows a very nervous gulp. The man's appearance is impeccable, and he breathes deeply and carefully. Johnnie is shocked by his appearance.

The man looks squarely at B. "You again?" the tall man states.

"You look just like... Wait a minute. You know each other?" asks Johnnie.

"Yes, we met at the Wall," states B with some fear.

"Wall? I didn't see him on the inside," rebuts Johnnie with an aggravated tone.

"Well, the mystical elite don't like some of my choices, and so, you know, off to the abortion...I mean adoption clinic I go. Anyway, I won't complain. I understand you wish to take a big step. It is dangerous business, you know: Overriding the system. I may be questioned on the matter by my higher ups, and so I need to ask you a few questions about your perceptions of relevant issues."

"Sure, anything," responds B.

"Same here," answers Johnnie.

"Do either of you know of any severe defects of the nervous and/or respiratory systems in your families?"

"No," they simultaneously respond, puzzled and now seated rigidly in their consternation.

"Do either of you have a recent history of violence?"

They shrug their shoulders. "I don't think so, but I did get my ass kicked in Rapid City, and some Chink made my ears bleed in Colorado Springs," adds B, silently farting simultaneously as he becomes more of the man we know so well.

"Do either of you have any reason to hate anyone that is different from you physically?"

"What kind of question is that? Do we look like racists?" answers B, who is very annoyed and hoping desperately to conceal his past to help his wife ensconce herself among the social elite of her choice.

"That was not necessarily what I meant, but since you ask... I am quite aware of who you are, so let's not play any games here. There's a crease underneath your mouth that indicates to me..."

"Stop right there!" Harriet signals him to keep quiet with her index finger to her lips. "They don't know yet."

"I am sorry for that outburst. Today seems like it has lasted one hundred and twenty-three years for me." The unnamed man seems to be redirecting his anger in a positive way.

"What were you talking about? I mean the comment you started to make about the crease under his mouth?" Johnnie directs the question at the tall man in the black suit.

"Please forget it for now." Harriet is obviously trying to change the line of questioning.

"I believe they are ready. They seem to be adamant, questioning and sharp. I will override the system for them."

The man holds a staff with Chinese characters engraved throughout the middle portion. He motions to the characters and explains that they represent the kingdom that exists in the spaces between heaven and earth, the place where all humans experience their proper birth. He twists the top of the staff, which is an emerald eagle with a silver beak, topaz wings and rubies for eyes. The top of the staff folds open mechanically and the man removes a key from a small slot inside. He walks to the computer and places the key into a slot behind the monitor. Digitally produced photographs from mock Civil War battles in Southern Pennsylvania go blank on the screen and a cursor is left flashing. He quickly punches in his password and a small box rises out of the floor. Johnnie and B stand by in amazement. The man then reaches into his pocket and removes what appears to be a small hollow tube, made of plastic or some other clear synthetic, about four inches long. He places the tube into a small slot atop the box and a microphone ejects from the top of the tube. He speaks very softly into the tube. Johnnie and B cannot hear the words, but he speaks for at least four score seconds. The microphone slips back into the box and he removes the tube from the hole. The box disappears slowly into the floor and the same siren is heard as the titanium gates open. The tall honest man walks away, his mission accomplished despite his best judgments. "Orders are orders," he says.

"Should we thank him?" Johnnie asks Harriet.

"No need—he already knows you thank him."

B and Johnnie look into each other's eyes and shrug their shoulders as the excitement rebuilds once again. Harriet then ushers them into the corridor once again and they walk past the photographs, but the lighting is so poor that they cannot make out any of the pictures. They think they see famous movie stars in the photos, but they cannot be sure. At the end of the hallway, a light is emitted from beneath a large oak door with a knocker in the shape of an X, or perhaps it is a cross, depending on how you look at it. The light is brilliant blue, almost metallic sapphire. As they walk toward the door, Harriet is murmuring something but the words are muffled in this hallway. The vibrations of sound grow greater in volume and frequency. B unknowingly covers his ears and Johnnie is rendered zombified by the situation.

The door opens slowly and the glow transforms into a blinding light. A thin glaze develops over their eyes. Their vision is clearly affected. Harriet ushers them into a giant oval room with four levels connected by coiling stairways. The entrance is at the top level and the glow is much stronger as they approach a railing in the center of the room. After a period of adjustment, their eyes begin to refocus. B looks over the railing first and notices a big drop. He backs away and feels slightly nauseous.

"Sometimes I am afraid of heights," he proclaims insecurely.

"Oh we can fix that. Here take this." Harriet removes a small tablet from a pouch strapped around her waist and hands it to B.

"NO!" Johnnie screams. "Please, no drugs!"

Harriet responds in a calm manner. "Don't worry, love. This is not a drug, as you will see. Harriet takes the pill from B's hand and places it in his mouth, and he immediately feels a sensation in his brain and it is as if his feet were lifted off the ground and he were a spirit set free to run through the sky. He leans over the railing.

"I can fly!"

"Stop right there! None of that here." Harriet is unmoved by the sudden act of defiance. Johnnie shows little signs of life. She just can't believe that Harriet gave to her husband, a recovering drug addict, a pill to make him want to fly. "Come with me." Harriet again signals them to follow.

They find a staircase and begin climbing downward. Harriet tells them to be careful of their fingers so that the jagged iron railings do not penetrate their weak skin. The walls are engraved with images of individuals with notable historical importance, and at the top they see faces of great political leaders, scientists, philosophers and artists.

"Wow, looks like the Who's Who of Wall," states Johnnie as B shrugs his shoulders in affirmation. He is flying high as a kite right now.

As they climb downward, they notice images they do not understand: empty horrifying faces of a contorted nature, distended faces without eyes and eyes without faces, noses crooked, cheeks bloated, mouths twisted, teeth black from death. As they continue downward, B realizes that he knows this scene from the "other side" of Wall, but Johnnie has been exempt from the horrors up until now. At least they are able to experience some terror together, he thinks. Harriet beckons them to get off the staircase at a point where the walls begin to narrow and movement from dancing shadows bring them alive. Johnnie and B are now beyond fear. They feel as if they've been swept up by a tidal wave and carried to an exotic place where nothing seems real. While this is not an uncommon sensation for most, especially B, it is frightening for them now. Harriet again ushers them along the pathway. The walls are lined by large glass jars, each a different color of illumination. Most emit glowing shades of bluish gray. B feels like he is being watched, and Johnnie begins to snap out of her lost mental state and begins to shiver. Harriet, as if she knows exactly what is happening to her, places a ribbon in Johnnie's hand and her panic is driven away almost instantly. She thanks Harriet but remains completely baffled.

"All right, I've had it. Please, just wake up!" They both begin screaming as though this nightmare might end by virtue of their volume, "WAKE UP! WAKE UP!"

Harriet proceeds to calm them both down. "This is always the most difficult part. This is what we call the stage of realization, but it is a point of reference for future understanding, nothing more." Harriet's words sting like a snake's venom traveling through the veins.

"Harriet, we do not understand anything here. Can you please enlighten us?" Johnnie is attempting to face her fears.

"It is now time for you to choose your child." Harriet motions her arm in a circular fashion and points toward the jars on the walls. Johnnie faints in disbelief as B stands awestruck.

"You mean?"

"Yes, exactly. Please start the process of choosing your child."

Johnnie awakens smiling, but when she sits up, the terror strikes again. She screams, and B kneels down by her side and holds her as she cries uncontrollably. He asks Harriet to kindly explain what is going on for their patience is running thin just about now.

"But I already have. And Mr. Lincoln, he asked you very important questions. You answered them to his liking. If he did not deem you fit, you would have been released. You forget how anxious you both were to raise a new child."

"She's more interested in how this relates to her new social standing, but nonetheless, yes a child, not a jar. What's in these anyway?" B points to the wall of jars.

"Those are the selection of children you have to choose from. We have the vital statistics for all of them except this one." She points to a jar on the end. There does not appear to be any glowing light in that one.

"Okay, fine! Say we do choose a jar in here. What makes you think we can raise something in a jar? Is there anything alive in there?" B is remarkably cool for such a strange turn of events.

"Oh yes, and this is the finest crop we have raised so far. Each entity has great potential."

Johnnie removes herself from the floor and gathers her wits together at the wall. She leans very close, and as she peers into the closest jar, her eyes grow large and she turns very white as though she has seen a ghost. She sees a mouth, nothing else, just a mouth. Again she screams. B walks over to comfort her once again, but she has already moved forward to gaze dreamlike into the jars in an attempt to find meaning in this insanity. He catches up to her and they hold hands like young lovers out for an evening stroll. Each jar has a small hole punctured in the top, a small glaze of bland yellow liquid lines extending upward from the base of the jar holding, suspended and perfectly centered, an animated, human-like mouth. Some of the mouths suspended in some of the jars have hair and some don't; some are straight, some have teeth, some have one lip, some have two. The strangeness of these mouths begins to vanish for Johnnie and B, and they actually begin commenting on the shapes and attributes of each mouth in each jar.

"Now, before you choose a jar, I must ask that you see our fine selection of chins." Harriet uses the statement as subtle desideratum.

"Choose a jar? You mean this is it?" This time what is being asked of them hits B like an anvil falling on a cartoon character's head and his wits unravel.

"Why yes, this is it. Where do you think you are? Oh hell, this is pointless—you subscribed to us. We didn't come looking for you."

"Yes, but we thought you had children here. Not just mouths in jars." Johnnie is a bit more calm now.

"What else do you think there is? The rest of the body is pointless once the most outstanding characteristic of the anatomy is located. We've been wasting far too much space. We have documented proof of entire sub-societies existing coherently and cohesively in imaginary geodesic domes in simulated replicas of the Los Angeles basin, sub-societies made up entirely of mouths and chins in jars. There are some more experimental secret-type societies that contain only genital organs. They are a bit more difficult to keep under control, and they all seem to want to get into Congress, which I find very frightening for reasons I can't explain. Look, it's all here." Harriet points to a computer monitor, where a day in the life of a mouth in the dome is being displayed with imagery and soothing music.

"Harriet, how did you get this position? I mean, why are you here working on this strange escapade?"

"I was chosen. You do not think that everyone has the right tools and skills to work at a job like this, do you? And Abe, he is the most dedicated to keeping things in order. It's sort of the bipolar magnetic thing. What you did once, you now do the opposite in strict terms of perception, I assure you. The world is not a fair place, you know. Rules have been given, but very few people trust them completely or believe they are entirely true. And if rules are made by man, they will be broken by man— there are natural laws to balance things out." B and Johnnie listen in silence. "You," says Harriet as she points to B, "liked my book about the injustices that occurred in the 19th century."

"Liked it? I loved it! I don't understand now why I stopped reading. You really gave me a sense of life!" B exclaims excitedly.

"Follow me. You will want to see the chins."

Harriet leads them around the large oval to the left. She enters another room. This one is decidedly different than the last room. There is a feeling of great peace, and the couple embraces.

"This is the place where we will find our child!" calls out Johnnie exuberantly.

"B, do you feel the same warmth as your counterpart?"

"Yes, actually, I do. I am still taken aback by everything that has gone on today. You must excuse me." He seats himself and just drifts away in thought.

"Harriet! Over here! I want to know about this one," Johnnie hollers from up the way.

"Well, let's see." Harriet flips through her book and finds the correct entry, "this one is projected to have an IQ of 196 in its adult years. You know the average chin can live to be almost 92 years old. An IQ that high should not be passed up."

An excited Johnnie points out another. "How about this one?"

"This one does not seem to possess anything spectacular," Harriet says as she hands Johnnie the jar. "But it does appear to have a wonderfully defined cleft in the center. I don't..."

"This is my baby!" Johnnie begins to lose all semblance of fear and cuddles the jar.

"Now, hold on—this must be a rule made by committee." Harriet calls B over to join them.

"B, B, this is our baby." Johnnie picks up the jar and places next to her face. A loss of blood turns B's face a pale gray and he slightly loses his footing. Even Harriet takes a step back from astonishment.

"The chin, I mean that chin, our new child, has an identical cleft to that of its new father. In all my years, I have never seen anything as uncanny, I... I... I..." Harriet has trouble finding the right words.

They now continue their trek downward. At the bottom of the staircase, a feeling of emptiness overcomes B. He looks back up but a door has sealed them off. At the main doorway to the great Hall of Chins and Mouths, Harriet points to the ceiling then hurries away. A camera slowly moves down from overhead, its huge lens automatically focusing. A self-guided lighting system glides out of the top of the camera and shines a light upon them. The camera then takes three pictures of the new family of Chins. B watches Harriet leading a nervous couple into the same waiting room where he and Johnnie had been. Johnnie is speaking to the jar in a crude language. Her "words" are clicks and grunts and squeals escaping her mouth. B thinks, "How will they handle this?" The man in the waiting room splits two blinds and he and B make eye contact as Harriet appears in front of them again.

B has decided he needs some answers to very basic questions. "Are you familiar with the Wall in South Dakota? Is everyone really still alive, or is everyone dead? I don't get it. And if you are all dead, are we dead? And if we are dead, which now I am assuming is true, is this heaven? Is this what we have invested all of our hard earned cash in at our church?" B now begins to understand things a bit better.

"Wall? Yes, of course, I know Wall. I have not been invited yet, and I will certainly not try to force my way in—you can never get in that way. Abe will not discuss it much when I ask him about it. He likes to talk about the fights. He is always consumed with the fights. Although, I am not sure how he can speak about them first hand, as he is not allowed in. Maybe he sneaks in. Are you dead? No, certainly not dead. Heaven? Damn, is that old idea dominating popular thinking again? You'd think they'd have given it up by now and focus on something more meaningful, like a comprehensive world space program or organizing against the manufacturing of bacterial weaponry." Harriet shakes her head.

"They still have a monopoly on afterlife scenarios. It still brings in the big bucks." B shows a true flash of theosophical insight.

Johnnie is just concerned with her new child, and in a virtual fit of excitement she announces, "I want to name my child Rin Chin Chin." A canine howl is heard in the distance...

Harriet leads them into a special room. A sign on the door reads "Special Room." The door swings open and they browse even more photographs that line the walls, which are disproportionate, asymmetrical. "We are waiting for the new video equipment, and with some luck, we should get some technicians here soon to join our organization. We always seem to be a couple of steps behind. We would like to show our photographs in full motion, which will capture the reality of the experience a bit better. Also, a really good sound system would top it off just right. Has Frank Zappa died yet?"

"Frank Zappa? Reality? What in the hell is she talking about? Is she a Democrat? Holy Cow! She really isn't that bright, is she? She must be nuts, or a damned chink," B thinks to himself as he burps up some of his breakfast sausage.

"Please accept this invitation. You will meet a host of new parents and their newly adopted children there."

Johnnie reads the small slip of colored paper. It is an invitation for a party. Something quite peculiar catches her eye. The address on the invitation looks familiar. B notices the alarm in Johnnie's face and detects something is wrong. She places the invite in her purse and turns around. "Is this it? May we leave now?"

"Do you understand the regulations of the adoption? Before you leave, you must sign the papers. Did you bring the papers? Did you receive the bag of white powder? We had instructed the two of you in your pre-adoption briefing that you must learn how to sprinkle your chin with that specially made powder. You must fertilize your child with the powder and specially filtered water for the first two years before you can feed it with sunlight and the liquid, nutrient-rich formula your child needs to sustain its existence. You must feed your chin properly. His growth is organic but it is not accretive. He grows from nutrients, not by adding matter. Do you understand? These guidelines were laid out in the packet we left for you. Maybe you forgot. We can track patterns of viruses and natural mutations by examining the structural changes in its DNA. And have the two of you decided on a name for this child for certain? We must know. The center must keep track of the future and we do this by DNA strand and by name."

"Rin Chin Chin is our child's name!" Another howl is heard. The three of them exchange puzzled glances, and then Harriet reaches into a drawer in the desk and removes a stack of papers from a manila envelope. The name Rin Chin Chin is already imprinted on the top page.

"Please sign here. This clause states that you will care for your child in the best way possible. Also, you will not divulge to anyone what went on here. There are many other agencies attempting to steal our secrets. And furthermore, if you attempt to accept earthly or otherworldly possessions in exchange for information, the two of you will be put on trial. And you don't want that! That is all—please just sign." Harriet removes a special pen from her desk drawer. It is marked "Special Pen." B and Johnnie both sign on their respective lines and Harriet ushers them out.

"Good Luck!" Harriet waves them a hearty good-bye.

B looks at his watch: 12:05 p.m. "Damn watch must have stopped! Wait a minute. Didn't we come in here at...?" Johnnie is busy running toward the car because wild dogs are running after her from the right, apparently trying to outflank her. B catches up to Johnnie just as the dogs, snarling beasts with foaming mouths, surround them.

Johnnie and B are shivering. They notice a sporty family-type ultra-luxurious raised sedan-like van-style wagon driving past the front gate. As B motions to the car to turn around, the lead dog steps forward and begins speaking. "We would like to make an exchange..."

"Wake up! Wake up, honey!" Johnnie shakes B, who is sweating profusely.

"I had (yawn) the most awful dream. I never saw anything so scary," a semi-catatonic B wearily whines as he farts a few times.

"You had an awful dream? I feel queasy." Johnnie gets up and runs to the bathroom and vomits. B helps her clean herself up. The Johnson's then leave the bedroom and walk downstairs uttering little more than sighs and grunts. When they enter the living room, they see a jar in the center of the room that contains a bearded mouth. A large gathering of persons has assembled near the doorway holding jars with a variety of anatomical parts, party favors, wrapped gifts, balloons, and a large vanilla frosted chocolate cake with a picture of a chin on it. A clown sits by their fireplace. He is quite sinister looking. Johnnie runs toward the jar and trips, falling into the table where the jar sits. Time terrifyingly slows down, and in a single shift of motion, the jar rolls toward the edge of the table, falls to the hardwood floor and crashes. Like a solitary heart bursting in an open cavity, it begins spitting out precious stones through hollowed petrified tubes. Topaz, amethysts, rubies, diamonds, and emeralds spill out of it onto the floor. The onlookers gaze in astonishment as the bearded mouth bursts into flames, and the light passes through the stones and blinds them. The sound is deafening, like an atom splitting, and in unison, the guests shriek but only Johnnie's voice is distinguishable echoing into the narrow passages of air. "This is not my baby!"

Act 8.

Leaves of Sweet Grass Bending Like Memories on Rubber Stilts in the Soft Wind

Let us make no reference to the stability of the groundwork that we have thus far laid. Stability is extremely relative to many factors seen and unseen. So, let us see no forces outside time's steamy breath. Let us tire not, for the sun is our only star. Let the winds smile as the ground is swollen under its elder feet. In the near distance, one can detect a scent of smelted iron. The wind blowing from the desert carries the dry heat through B's body. It touches his oft-brittle bones which begin to crack. The dam breaks, and water rushes into the open fields, flooding the dry landscape—perspiration. He looks down and notes that his feet are moving faster and faster, gliding across the water, hydroplaning. The open landscape seems to widen exponentially. The sky is cloudless, a pale blue ozone-rich field of molecular movement. He visualizes the clouds forming in a static symphony. It is breathtaking. He begins choking, gasping for the silent air to breathe. He keeps running faster and faster. He looks behind. They are still chasing him. Three very large black panthers, like from his dreams during his final days in Yellow University, their strides like those of cheetahs and their force like that of lions and their fangs like those of Siberian tigers. B leaps from the ground and catches air, soars away higher and higher, and as he flies, he begins to lose his breath again. His skin no longer serving as a parasol, his flesh rips open and accepts the sunlight into his veins: Energized. He awakens in a hospital bed.

A short nurse in a terrible blond wig stands over him, injecting a shot of Demerol in his arm. The sensation rushes over him. "Thank you. I needed that. The cats were going to get me." His words are slightly slurred from the hypnotic trance the drugs have left him in.

"Just go back to sleep, Mr. Pubicle. After that explosion, you need the rest."

"Mister Pubicle? My name is Johnssson, but my friends call me Beeeeee—they callll me double-u-bee," he faintly stammers.

"Well then there must be a mistake. Your identification states your name as John Pubicle and that you are a Governor. We never had a Governor stay in our hospital, at least not one that I know of." Her concern with his temporary amnesia is slightly masked by her adulation from meeting a real-life celebrity politician.

B, although heavily sedated, has enough sense to decide that this is a dream and drifts away into a deep sleep. He awakens several hours later. There is a tall thin man dressed in a very ugly gray suit standing over him. He has the strange mannerism of biting his upper lip. He keeps doing it. B stares and stares and stares at this strange man. "Who in the hell are you?" B has awakened with a resurgence of energy.

"Just calm down, Governor. You've had a nasty experience. But don't worry. Everything is being taken care of. Your speech on environmental mismanagement in the nuclear medicine industry is going to be postponed until Monday next. Your doctors told me that you would be released tomorrow but need at least three days of rest. Oh, and that damn Democratic asshole, Franz from Massachusetts, keeps calling. He wants you to sway your opinion on the gay marriage thing. He's such an asshole. Just because you're a moderate Republican does not mean you will buy into his left wing Commie bullshit rhetoric."

"Oh, what in the hell is going on? Democrats, Republicans, gay marriage, environmental what? What in the hell has happened to me? Where's the chin kid? Who in the hell are *you*? Who in the hell *am I?*"

"The doctor told me it was quite an explosion. They're doing a recount though. Your challenger, G. Sport, that young independent righteous fool, had his people stuff the electronic ballot boxes in the primary run-off. We don't know how, but since voting is done electronically, anything can happen nowadays. I reiterate sir that you should consider getting some of these alternative fuel companies in your back pocket. Never put all of your eggs in one basket, right?

"Oh yes, and your father's stockbroker called me. It was the strangest call as I was forced to answer many questions about my life in order for the call to be transmitted. I could hear the wind whistling very loud on the phone, and the broker complained about the dry heat of the, and I quote, fucking desert. He expressed concerns over the stability of the groundwork we are laying, and I asked him what that has to do with Governor Johnson. He's just a Governor? 'Governor?' he questioned. 'He's the damned President! Let's not worry about Iraq so much— they're toast! We're not letting that son of a bitch get away again.' Those were his precise words. He also said that the timing just couldn't be better as more enemy OPEC nations are about to get what they deserve. Both crude and natural gas will certainly become more scarce and much more costly, and after we topple their sorry pathetic asses, then we can own it all. He said, and again I am quoting, 'Those pussy former Soviet republics are already eating from our hands. How else can we convince Congress to invade? If the people speak, Congress listens.'

It just so happens that we can determine what the people speak. Right, sir? That's what your dad told me. Good old Gerry, he used to say these funny sayings all throughout our tour of duty in WW-two."

"Just go away."

"Uh, sure, sir. I'll come back later. Especially if I hear any news about the recount."

B is sobbing uncontrollably. When a voice in his head begins singing a lullaby, he sucks his thumb. He fades in and out of consciousness.

"Your mother and I will not allow for our son to suck his thumb." The words of his very famous father, Gerald Johnson, thunder through Little Diarrhea's ears. Gerry cracks an empty scotch bottle on an antique oak lateral table and swings the jagged bottle in front of young Diarrhea's face. Poison berries. Little Diarrhea and his neighbors, the Jockliquer twins, are running through the woods behind their homes. They carry BB pellet guns that resemble shotguns. Little Scooty Jockliquer aims the barrel at a young sparrow whistling a magnificent song through the leafless thin autumn branches. Fire. Death. Instantaneous death like that of a plane crash victim or a school of fish in the Arabian Gulf as oil dumped into the waters are suddenly set ablaze. The earth's multiple suns darken behind low cirrus in a mostly cloudless sky. B picks up a poison berry and tastes its succulent juices, immediately feeling the skin of his throat begin to swell. He is losing precious oxygen, swirling, falling. The young boy cries and starts sucking his thumb again. The drunk picks him up by his head. His little neck stretches out, way out like a caricature of a slinky with a human head attached. His thumb remains lodged in his throat. He takes him into the bedroom and lays him on the bed and strips his clothes off him. The fear bleeds from young Diarrhea's anus. Scotch drunk goes to the closet, a place where Diarrhea usually hides, and removes a thick cowhide belt. It has a solid gold four-leaf clover buckle. Little Diarrhea has never been less lucky. The whipping begins. At first the pain is unbearable. The shrieks explode from his tiny mouth. But then he begins to see his visions, an old Chinese woman appears from nowhere, her hands waving slowly downward. Her image is swaying, almost fragmented. She is letting him know that everything is all right. He smiles.

His face is visible in the mirror opposite to his father's, "Oh, you like this, boy?!!!" his enraged drunken paternal figure screams at him as he beats him until his skin is chewed up as by a rabid dog. Little Diarrhea imagines someone else must have actually been his father. It cannot be this beast. His father's mouth is foaming with pleasure while electricity is being generated within his body. What emerges are all of his failures projected downward like a lightning bolt onto his small son.

"You think that just because my father is a Senator that I want to be one too? You think that I can't be President some day? Screw my father! And screw you and your brothers and sister too! I should kill you all and your little faggot friends, especially those Jockliquer twins. The whole lot of you belong in a dungeon, tortured and mutilated and coerced to change your faith. And your villages should be plundered and your Jap wives and children raped!"

His eyes are flaming now and he is obviously screaming at someone other than his son. He finishes several minutes later and leaves Diarrhea on the bed. Little Diarrhea's physical presence is completely numbed. His eyes are wide and alert in a tired, frightened, emotionless stare. His now very pale face appears plastic, like a mannequin's. He hears more screaming from downstairs, coming from the family room by the marble bar next to the staircase. The sound echoes a certain way when reflected off the bar, and Little Diarrhea can detect that echo a mile away, and the echoes are interrupted by a physical presence. There is someone coming. He is unsure if it is his father or his mother. He is not ready to take another beating, and so he dives out the open window and does a perfect somersault onto the back lawn. He runs down the street naked, screaming. A young couple walking their dog finds the young, physically destroyed boy curled under a street lamp in the fetal position. The glow of the light on his young skin poses an Angelic aura around his body. They carry him inside their small home. They know who he is and they are aware of his father's reputation as quite ruthless when he wants to be, despite his almost comically whimsical personality, so they do not want him to go home just yet. They feed him and clean him up the best they can given all the blood and bruises on his small body, and they give him shelter. In the morning, they telephone the police but ask them not to reveal to his parents where the young frightened boy is. Within minutes, five cruisers are at the door. Little Diarrhea's famous parents sit in their respective limousines next to one of the police cruisers. Both are pointing inside of the house. Little Diarrhea sees the police and screams in terror.

Brother Jack, a now quite tall but frumpy, simple man, speaks very poorly of everyone, including himself. Distant blood, genetic formations like blistering skin inside of a cave, the apple falls where it may, but never too far away. He bends his mind over his recollection of his brother, Little Diarrhea, sitting alone at a small child's table placed on the floor by an old Italian lambskin sofa while he and the other children were forced to sit at the adult table and listen to the adults' ramblings about politics, economics, secrecy and control. A stream of vomit forges a thin film of odor in the room. Jack is drinking his liver into oblivion. He is dancing in front of a mirror. He is adorned makeup and wearing a now terribly undersized and old Boston Police uniform he stole from the Salvation Army when he was 16 on a little summer road trip with some friends while his family vacationed up north at their summer cottage in Maine. He says that the world has gone to hell and that his oldest brother has a lot to do with it, and the world needs a *real* police organization, but it must start with a mass support module. Every time he becomes angry in any way, he puts on this uniform. It gives him courage.

Their mom, Betty, used to sing to Little Diarrhea. "First comes love, then comes marriage, then comes Little Diarrhea in a baby carriage." Then Little Diarrhea is grown up. He dresses in finely tailored clothing and is sent to the finest schools, where he is called WB by his fraternity brothers, handed the keys to all the family assets, given his advanced degrees on a crystal platter until he is ready to be thrust into the limelight to hide the real ongoings of the world as directed by the elite. "Keep them off guard," Dad used to always say—he learned it from his grandfather. Brother Jack swears revenge on B for the pain he has caused him and for his lost love, his recently departed third nanny, who he has been screwing on the side. She has proclaimed her allegiance to the Green party, and while Jack and his wife, Jill, knew nothing about her politics, the family fears that she could seriously destroy him in a federal public office. Furthermore, his wife caught them in bed in a motel in Jacksonville because of an anonymous tip by someone in Seattle. Dad's plan is to include Jack, but he keeps him positioned in lesser roles. Jack just can't keep it in his pants. But the fact that he can't be the one who is always in the spotlight is what really pisses Jack off.

The young neighborly couple was arrested immediately for kidnapping, and after a brief interrogation, they went on a permanent vacation to Rwanda. Little Diarrhea went home.

B awakens again, still in bed. Jennifer stands over him. He has a warm towel on his forehead, and she begins to cry. "Dad, I thought you were gone. I was so worried."

"Where am I?"

"You're home."

"Where's that damned chin? And wait, where's home?"

Jennifer loses control. Her tears run like from a ruptured water main. The bed becomes a sink. He reaches up and pulls her close. "I will never treat you poorly again. I am so sorry for everything that has happened. Let us start anew together."

Jennifer and her twin have been waiting for these words their entire collective life, or at least since her fifth birthday party when Dad showed up with cocaine all over his face and blood on his pants. It appears now that B might be coming to terms with things, especially since he seems to have a handle on his problematic colon. She has always loved him, but now a lot of her confusion must be dealt with. There is confusion about her grandparents, mostly related to why they will only see her by appointment. There is her intense desire to join the military, why Mom took off with that crazy animal herder, and what to do next summer vacation. Jennifer leaves for a short moment to get him some water. Drifting in and out of consciousness, he half-opens his eyes again and sits up and turns on the television by remote. He sees a person on the television that looks like him. It is a debate on environmental mismanagement in National Parks being broadcast from the Garden of Eden Flock Hotel in St Barthélemy. Contestants this evening are two of the United States' foremost voices in state government, John Pubicle (D-Minnesota) and Jack Johnson (R-Florida), who are here in support of their party's views on subjects that are most concerning their constituency. A bonus of $600,000 extra PAC dollars for every answer that causes a conspiracy of some sort will be given to the lucky contestant. B thinks the debate is about mismanagement in the nuclear medicine industry not in the National Parks, or so he heard somewhere. Time's spherical presence bleeds posthumously from Diarrhea's stressed colon. He has absolutely no idea why his brother is on television as Governor of Florida against some man from Minnesota, whom a nurse in his dream thought was him. But his main confusion is why the bathroom seems to be on the other side of the room while he is relieving himself where he sits. The room gyrates and he passes out.

He awakens again several hours later. Little Diarrhea rises like gas from the bed. He wants things to be ordinary again. He wants no part of any additional madness in this life. Jennifer comes back holding two plane tickets back to Boston.

"Jennifer, how did I get here?"

"I think you were born, Dad. Don't be so silly."

He realizes the question deserved that kind of an answer, and he laughs aloud. Perhaps this is the first sign of his recovery from the delusional course his mind has taken. However, he remains extremely confused. His memories of the events that have taken him to this point are jumbled. He cannot even keep them in line to make sense from any of it.

"How did we get back home after the explosion? I do not remember much."

"Dad, you're being silly. We're not home. We're on vacation in St Barths again. Uncle Jack has an internationally televised debate with that weird looking guy from Massachusetts. See, it's on television."

"Uncle Jack? Why is Uncle Jack debating anyone? Why in the hell are we in St Barths? Where are Mom and the chin kid?"

"Dad, you need some rest. A man named Kra called. He told me that you guys had some issues to discuss. He sounded very sad."

"Kra? Holy cow! How'd he find me? Listen honey, Mr. Infinite and I go way back. We need to resolve some issues with each other. That's all."

"Way back? He told me that you guys just met and he forgot to give you something. He believes you need it." Jennifer goes to the blinds and pulls them apart. From the window, the view of the Caribbean Sea is breathtaking. Across the tranquil sea, dozens of dolphins play as the sky stands placidly subtle through the low thin white clouds. The ocean is sparkling in the sunlight. The smell of island palm and lilac blows gently into the room.

B has leapt out of bed and is staring down onto the beach. "Where's that damned clown! He's down there somewhere!" Linear time has failed him. It no longer serves as a basis to measure his life's moments. In a state of panic, he telephones his broker. "Pops?"

"B? Is that you?"

"Oh Pops, I really do exist. I was scared for a minute. For some reason, I feared the total destruction of every truth I have ever believed, but since you remember me…"

An enormous build-up of static filters into their conversation, Pops' words are meshed somehow with commands of some sort. There is a long silence followed by a click.

"Pops! Pops? Are you still there?"

"Darkstar. Darkstar. This is Jess. Do you read me, Darkstar?"

"Darkstar? Jess? I'm B. This is crazy! Stop it!"

"Solution TT6.3.11 GHAT has been located. Downlink must be expatriated from site QQ8 on frequency 8.01E. Sub-coordinates follow twenty-third tone. I repeat, twenty-third tone. Agent ATZX must be located prior to identification of satellite core magnetic isolation. Agent ATZX must be located at once. Civilian interrupt. Civilian interrupt. ABCHAWMAU at zone 2, sub zone 334, division 5, room 340. Jess: infiltrate and detain. I repeat, infiltrate and detain."

B hangs up the phone and lets loose all over the room.

"Dad, I thought you had controlled your bowel problem. Are you wearing your padded undergarment as prescribed by your proctologist?"

"Mr. Johnson, Dr. Whitman will see you now."

"Doc, I don't know what in the hell has been going on, but I am afraid that I simply never learned how to control my bowels. It began when I was a baby, well, I mean as an infant, a newborn, and that was just the beginning. Everything in my life went astray from that time onward."

Doc Whitman, MD, who is a proctologist and poet, says:

"These tumbled rock-piles grim and red,

These reckless heaven-ambitious peaks,

These gorges, turbulent clear streams, this naked freshness,

These formless wild arrays, for reasons of their own,

I know thee, savage spirit, we have communed together!"

"Hey buddy, I ain't communin' with no crazy doctor!"

Dr. Whitman removes his skin from his face, and what is underneath resembles an insect with large concave eyes that glow like black pearls. His hand is gloved and swishing around in Diarrhea's anus. The sacred drums of Burundi playing songs requiring incredible talent and skill resonate in the white room.

"Yes, when the stars glistened

All night long on the prong of a moss-scalloped stake,

Down almost amid the slapping waves,

Sat the lone singer, wonderful, causing tears."

Winchester Buckley Johnson hallucinates formations of planets dancing in the sky as though in a ballet against a cosmic azure sea. He deems them moments regained that he thought were eternally lost and now magically showing in multiple spheres of rotating color and texture. Splotches of sound and light cover his being.

"Low hangs the moon. It rose late,

Is lagging-O I think it is heavy with love, with love."

Doc places the skin back on his face and bids B a hearty farewell, his orbs like distant planets in our visible sky. He disappears behind the silk screen of rising stars, and B thinks of Johnnie, of how they met for the first time since childhood just off the first tee at the Weston Golf Club. He was sporting a new suit, she a new bonnet. Their eyes met. Well, actually their eyes met each other's new outfits, and both became very excited. He immediately imagined her cooking and cleaning and taking care of his home, while she imagined herself being showered in jewels, long lines of paparazzi waiting outside costly boutiques to catch a glimpse of her. His thoughts switch back to the moment, and he thinks, "Everything began on such solid ground between us. How did everything get so screwed up?"

Outside the window, sirens blare like timpani accompanying a thunderous, low-decibel tuba solo. B peers from the private balcony, toward the roadway to his left that winds around the cliff. Twenty, maybe thirty tiny Fiats quickly approach the hotel. The automobiles jam into the valet parking area. Three men leap out from the first car, and the other vehicles sprint in opposite directions, creating a guarded perimeter around the hotel. The occupants of the Fiats are all wearing golf shirts and khaki pants and some type of designer looking tennis shoes. They are carrying small video transmitter/receivers with a very fast CPUs, probably Mobile MMVII 23,216, 400 Gigabytes of RAM, and 400 Megabytes of Cache (2.23 nanoseconds), a removable 10,009.1 GIG HDD (swappable with an optional $2.3_{x10^{44}}$X CD recorder/CDROM/DVD+/-RW, LW, CNW), a 14,117.96 GbPS satellite modem with Purple Iris technology, a 3.14159267" full color active matrix display with a 900.46 GIG video module. They are pointing to his room. There is an immediate knock on his door.

"Room service."

B cannot handle the pressure any longer. He tries to release anything he can from his colon but can't, and so he pushes harder and harder. Nothing happens. Could it be true? Deep inside of B, Little Diarrhea, is constipated? There is another knock, more insistent this time.

"Room service! *Votre petit dejeuner:* your breakfast monsieur!"

As Jennifer approaches the door, time slows nearly to a halt and the room begins tipping to the side. B has seen this before. The déjà vu is frightening. She swings open the door, then turns to face him. There is a cut under her eye. B can see the blood dripping slowly down her cheek, each small crimson bead an enormous collection of molecules and liquid reality. The blood appears closer and closer in front of his eyes, so close he can reach out with his tongue and lick it—he tries. From Jennifer's perspective, it appears as though he is sticking his tongue out at her. She thinks it is a game and does it back. The phone rings, waking B up from the strangest of dream sequences.

B reaches for the telephone by the bed and places it to his ear as his eyes look upward toward the ceiling. "Hello?"

"Son? Is this you, son?"

A voice arrives in B's head just in time, right before the thumb is lodged into his throat.

"Dad? There's a Mr. Infinite at the door. Is this your friend Kra?"

B opens his eyes once again. Or so it seems. "Goshdarnit! I'm sick of this diluted paranoid nonsense!"

"Diluted paranoia is not nonsense," says the voice in B's head.

Another voice from across the room says, "Hello, Deej. Remember me?"

"Kra? What are you doing here? How did you find me?"

"SON! SON! Don't talk with him, he's the enemy!" says the voice on the phone he still holds to his ear.

"What, Dad?"

"I have my ways," continues Kra. "Do you have the secret information yet? I need the secret information. Hurry up, for I have little time."

"Kra, I really don't know what you're talking about. I am so sorry, but we did have a wonderful night together. And I do care about you, but..."

Kra abandons the attempt and sort of waddles like a penguin, which seems to be his top speed, down the hall to a staircase, then toward the beach below, where he has a bag of clothing waiting for him, a clown suit, which he places over the clothes he is wearing as quickly as he can while still waddling over the sand, a small pack of homeless dogs now chasing him down the beach. Diarrhea stands in the window, eyes wide, mouth gaping open. Lines of filth stretch across the room around him, making figures and symbols he does not notice and so fails to read.

The men in the golf shirts and khaki pants and what B now recognizes as white Ralph Klauren tennis shoes enter and place him under military arrest. They tell him they are with Interpol and that he will be detained until 1600 Zulu when the CIB jet arrives. "Infiltration uplink site disturbance sealed. Jess out."

On the other end of the still open phone line, Gerald breathes a sigh of relief that B's hallucinations have not led him into a state of complete breakdown. The envelope has been pushed far enough, however, and it is now time for a different course of education, the next level, that is, his reeducation just the way it was done to Gerald. It is time for his Little Diarrhea, WB, Deej, B, to learn a thing or two about the CIB, what it means to be part of such an elite organization, and how, through every means available, one always wins no matter what the rules are supposed to be, not matter how gentlemanly one is expected to act in love and in war. Gerald knows that in either there is no option but to destroy the enemy. B is whisked away to the newest detention center the CIB has constructed inside the Decagon's hidden right of center wing.

Meanwhile, back at the trailer park, Doc Whitman is playing cards with Uncle Bill Burroughs outside the Old Saloon façade, giving him lectures on spatial freedom even as Bill loiters in the doorways of death. Uncle Bill is laughing as he reads the New Testament backward aloud for Khalil Gibran and Wystan Hugh Auden.

Brother Jack just wants to take his own ego and hold it up and look at it for a while until Gerald decides what to do with him. He imagines someone, it could be anyone, making breakfast for him; and he calls out to his new maid, his lover, or his wife, whoever is more accessible at this moment, to come and clean up his messes.

Act 9.

G. Sport Magupati: Magic and Assimilation

The planets were aligned for maximum magnetic strength. Fresh water pumping into the world's oceans from melting polar caps has begun to desalinize the world's salt water supply, and this interaction with the atmosphere creates havoc on the unknowing victims below the surface. What this may mean now, in this time, is nothing compared to what it may mean in the near future. Mankind must learn to adapt, as always, to his new environmental conditions, but the fact remains that, as long as people do not have enough food to eat or enough money to buy that heavy winter coat in the wintry months, what good is topographic knowledge? Why did the strategists and architects deliver a new federal government compound below the surface of a giant sea? Why was the Pentagon remade as the Octagon and why was the White House reconstructed in solid gold and renamed the Gold House? The top minds of the CIB had determined this as optimal strategic positioning and accurate symbolizing, but were the decisions of construction optimal for the longevity of the species?

Was he dead? Was he carried away by close friends and taken far from the point of initial impact in order to save his life? Or was one confused for another? For there are many posing as G. Sport Magupati in this day and age, and for that reason, the real G. Sport Magupati often conceals his identity. Mass appeal was always the way to people's hearts, at least as far as iconoclastic methods go, but survival has always taken precedence. Being in the spotlight was never necessarily his greatest desire, but dictating the flow of life was and still is, and one must take extra care if working behind the scenes of the big film plot, of a top publicly traded company, of a heartily wealthy religious outfit, of any governmental organization, or any monarchy, oligarchy, or democratic autocracy. The great behind-the-scenes artists will attest to this: the bottom line remains the desire for real power. Real power, as most have of said artists have gathered in their quest for knowledge and history, is the power by which one moves mountains and creates worlds unto their own desires. Wait a minute. Alexander is yelling something over here, but he is drunk again so forget it. And while some might argue that this is complete and utter nonsense, well, prove it to be wrong and Rembrandt will paint your portrait for free—at least this is what he is saying he will do.

Nestled in the forest on the surrounding edge of the Cascades, Mount St. Helens, the American Fujiyama, in the distance, the moonlight shining through the thick arms of the old elm outside the well maintained and completely technologically updated mountainside cabin of G. Sport Magupati created enough of a magical undertone to the night's calming breeze to summon the animals in the area to join in a potentially uplifting evening of ritualistic frolic.

Mr. Magupati enjoys the finer things in life. He, in most meanings of the word, lives as a Shah might have in modern times, not the contemporary Shahs but the ones from ancient Persia. He is adorned in finely knit clothing. He has great tastes and insists on style and comfort in his surroundings and intellectual pursuits to fill his time. He also enjoys the finest technological gadgets. He uses creature comforts as forbearance against his very intensely lived spiritual existence, but he does not take aim at anyone or anything, unless, of course, they first took aim at him—and in such cases he can be downright brutal. As he slowly meanders down from the high loft upstairs bedroom to the cabin's lakeside entrance, G. Sport gives a hearty chuckle. Something crucial could happen at any moment, and he can decide something crucial if he so wishes, which gives him incredible power. Most of humanity would not know what to do with such power, let alone know when to use it and when not to.

He opens the cabin door, and the wild animals sit in a semi-circle at the bottom of the stairs. He removes a hand carved scepter from a tall cabinet built into the porch. Then he removes a small medallion from the front pouch of his poncho and fastens the medallion securely to the top of the scepter. Some of the animals gasp in awe and others merely growl, sing, whistle and groan. He then places the scepter in a small hole on the porch. The moon is shimmering overhead, dancing as though in preparation for some kind of event. A small beam of light catches the medallion, and it begins to glow. The outlined shadow of the medallion creates a black hole-like penumbra on the doorway of the cabin, which frightens some of the younger animals. After several minutes, the entire scepter begins to glow an opalescent orange with a metallic gray tint. Small images are projected outward to the grassy knoll by the side of the home opposite the lake. The images show, in vivid detail, a group of young suited professional-type persons with wireless headsets and a small silver microphone extending toward their mouths from an earpiece. The entire contraption is permanently sewn into their heads. These people appear to be cutting deals of some sort as they are excitedly exchanging high fives. It would be difficult to say what type of business they are engaged in. Nowadays, mostly everyone has headsets permanently sewn into their heads, and people give each other high-fives for most any reason thinkable. Although only military applications typically use wireless signals, it is not impossible to imagine this being done on a commercial or consumer level in the near future.

Actually, one of them is giving a high four because she lost her pinky finger in a tragic boating accident in the seventh grade. The clarity of the images grows stronger as the bodies twist and turn in the night air, their holographs morphing into skeletons by way of a bright reddish-orange glow. Their bones show cracks from decay, and the collective, singular organ that joins them together appears as a liver but is beating like a heart with a slowing monotonous tone.

"There is very little life left out there," states G. Sport, and the animals nod in agreement. "Let's say we have some fun here. Our time is very limited, so let's hop to it." The animals dance in small circles around each other in their exuberance.

G. Sport removes a book from the cabinet on the porch. The illustration on the cover is of a small diamond packed into a field of coal. There is no writing on the cover. He opens the book carefully as though not to discharge anything unwanted from the pages. He finds the correct page (Chapter 12, page 23, paragraph 7a). The animals brace themselves on the ground below their small feet, hooves and talons. The moon is in full bloom. He reads aloud from the page:

How terrible it might be

If the animals are all set free;

And the scribes all agree

For a very small fee

The land can merge with the sea.

And fatefully decided on a cold bitter frost

That some of us are united against any double cross,

And Hercules may find the strength

Of a million bulls to dance

On the heads of the doctors of trance.

But ritual by design

Is dead by 23rd at nine

So work we must in keeping with our sine.

The animals immediately dash into the forest, and G. Sport Magupati retreats to his cabin to remove a golden harp from the closet. Silently, he meditates, and then he begins to play Handel's "Concerto for Harp." The animals again emerge from their wooded kingdom, now appearing as humans dressed sharply in the latest fashions by French and Italian designers. After several moments of listening, they speak in a very fluid English tongue, each with great command of the language and its syntax. G. Sport smiles as they gather in his cabin. There are twelve of them: six brazen women sharply modified carrying the fiercest stares Wall Street has ever seen and six lanky yet strong men, a look of subtle ferocity blending neatly with their finely cut jackets and pants.

"We have exactly twenty-three days before the spell is to wear off. In this time, we will quickly and methodically take over the planet, but not in order to enslave man, rather, so we can set them free. I am guiding you on a spiritual journey in which you will play a part in liberating mankind from his promises of suffering to a greater power. This is no prance through the wood, mind you. This is dangerous business. Humans are, by nature, the most ruthless and cunning killers the world has ever known. If death by physical force is not possible, or not intelligent, death by other means executed quickly and efficiently, takes its place. We will provide humankind with the ability to overcome death of the spirit, death of the heart, and of the mind; and in doing so, we shall overcome this destruction of life." This quote was extracted directly from G. Sport Magupati's book, *Wowing the Crowd with the Right Thing to Say.*

The newly formed humans are touched by the moment in a Byzantine sort of way. The eastern and western skies part simultaneously to reveal two distant stars radiating powerful light upon the darkened earth, and in a flash, the sadness caused by the suffering of humanity is joined by the joy of existence and the energy becomes complete—one. However, this joy does not last very long because magically induced moments tend to vanish rather quickly.

Those gathered join hands and have a strange power orgy-like dance as they complete a series of circular turns around a virtual pig-pile. Gathering together in geometric formations and performing domination-like dances by means of subtle gestures, all flaunting their new genitalia. They parade around exchanging partners in a dance as they grope at one another. This practice of sex magic ends unexpectedly, as anyone approaching the use of magic without proper meditation and training will fail, and sometimes with great tragedy. The session ends with a cry of pain by all. The pain came from learning how to see, which can be very painful.

However exciting this magical enterprise might be, it is raw fact that the coming battles between real powers on earth will mean more to humanity than any battle of the previous six thousand years combined. The battles will be part of a stunning conclusion, as the foreshadowing has been cast and the plots, already very thick, are continuously thickening, and the playwright is busy drawing the final scenes for something truly unforgettable while his ghostwriters make frequent edits to keep the storyboard clean and fresh.

G. Sport Magupati knows that he is merely a cog in the wheel, but his powers are nevertheless very wide ranging; and he believes that, since he has such powers, he should certainly use them. This road, as you will find out shortly, is not always the best one to take for it often leads one into territory where no man, woman, child or magician should go. For years, Mr. Magupati studied the various rituals and practices, including philosophical studies and metaphysical rites of ancient cultures. However well practiced, no one is well practiced enough to play with such magic using broad careless strokes. This territory belongs to the Gods, and according to some whining voices of certain foreordained fake mystics and sinister sorcerers, apparently this territory belongs to them too. This latter assertion, however, is their false impression and ridiculous interpretation only, as logic and reason tend to lose their place in areas of magic amongst the uninformed, and this is a territory in which no human being belongs, at least not in this story.

Act 10.

Saint Helen the Compassionate: Deconstructing the Center

Set inside the halls of relative absolute power, a terrific stylistic thriller awaits magnification. All of Hollywood's best are at this convention in the Entertainment Wing of the Octagon: prominent members of the screenwriters' guild, the great action heroes from the past and the present, the lovers of triangular love affairs, the most influential and most powerful media gurus. The Octagon itself is shrouded in some kind of mystery. The parts known to the general public as the undersea apparatus, which houses the American federal government, is inaccurately called the Octagon, for there are two supplementary wings just to the right of the center wing that are kept a secret. Only a few people in the world know they exist, but the existence of the two additional mystery wings makes the Octagon, in all reality, the Decagon. However, since the secret wings are unknown to humanity at large, the Octagon is what it will continue to be referred to in our story.

The thrilling revelry on this exciting evening is in celebration of the legacy of the existence of a very powerful and very relevant governing body. There are bodies of this nature in the world, but none other quite like this one. Martinis are served in sapphire rimmed crystal, as crates of 80-year-old Burgundies and 100-year-old single malt scotches are unloaded. Evangelical ministers are mixing olives with translational reason as a bland convolution of pale light and sound is projected over the heads of the important people, who we understand to be utterly misinformed, as they mingle or give their blessings to human physiology by forming lines outside the bathroom waiting to release waste from their respective bodies. B watches from a small room above the main floor, wondering why people wait in line to go to the bathroom. Future methods to capture the imagination of the viewing public are debated heatedly by the attendees standing at the urinals and sitting in the stalls. Arguing the use of a more finite sense of mind control is a favorite topic.

"We can do just about anything we want. I mean, look at how popular Gilligan's Island was. I mean, WOW, that is amazing."

"Yes, and consider all the stupid game shows. Do you think that people will one day want to watch these television shows again and again and again to remind themselves of where they once were?"

"What did you say? Sorry, I wasn't listening."

A small glass cubicle descends from above and stops falling approximately ten meters above the diamond shaped stage. Neon blues and reds line the cubicle. A platform rises up to create a winding walkway from the glass cube downward to the main floor. B emerges from the cubicle sporting a terrorized expression. Gasps arise from hideously jealous crowd, and a handful of attendees call their secretaries to fire their stage directors.

Following a terse introduction, all in attendance begin to laugh, then cry, and finally, as if on cue, to feel severe stomach discomfort at the smell that has erupted from the glass cube. The secret agents of fashionable brute force through mathematical conquest come forward from the crowd and encircle B as he stands on the winding walkway. They articulate in unison as though they are robots. Actually, it is quite compelling to the ear, as they break into a beautiful a cappella version of "God Bless America," the six men and six women alternating words while maintaining complete rhythm. The highly emotional crowd cheers and cries simultaneously as the newly transformed wild animals finish with a resounding, "White with foam, God Bless America, My home sweet home. God bless America, My Home Sweet Home."

"Did you hear that? I want them on my network! Sign them to a deal today! Don't give up the fort though— they're no Def Leppard!"

B feels displaced again. For him, this setting simply isn't right. He was never meant to tread lightly amongst the media elite. He is too brutally honest in a subjugated world where every angle of an argument is well conceived and sugar coated. He realizes in an instant that he could never exist peacefully in such a lifestyle, but he knows his wife could, a realization that causes him great stress. He passes out, and the crowd quickly disassembles. The Hollywood elite go back to Tinsel Town to contemplate a rebellion against Seattle. They feel as if they have been cheated.

"What kind of party was that?"

"Party? You call that a party? It ended before anyone could have sex with his or her best friend's wife or husband or part-time lover. That's no party."

"Well, nonetheless, I am really angry because my time is being wasted."

"Who invited us anyway? I want a word or two with him or her."

"Who? That is a great question. I have no idea."

"What made you decide to go then?"

"I don't know really. I just knew that I had to attend."

"Funny. Me too."

Meanwhile, as the new acts are being written, G. Sport's Clan slips past the guards at the entrance to the passage-like tunnel between the Octagon's Entertainment Wing and the Prison Wing. They employ a secret hand gesture they use in delicate moments, pulling the trigger on platinum encrusted special edition model 92 Berettas. So much for setting humanity free through relatively peaceful means. And because a force that resembles the old Magus, Magos, Maga and Magauuan Clans of the past guides them, the dream interpreters, the modern version of said Clans is able to change their identity at a moment's notice, to take on the identity of the guards of the White Wing. Soon enough, they reach B by following the trail of his smell. He is hiding deep within the Prison Wing, as his all-access retina scan gives him complete and unobjectionable access everywhere within the decagonal Octagon. He sits not so quietly in an undersized cleaning room closet filled with disinfectants and air fresheners, which do not mask his scent. He may have been snorting a couple of lines of laundry detergent while hiding—this is being investigated.

He is brought into a mirrored room kicking and screaming like an infant whose pacifier was forcefully removed from its lips. He is forced to sit in the cold under very bright lights and put in a straight jacket and fed some horrible tasting cough syrup.

"Wait! Stop! I'll tell everything I know!"

"Go ahead," states the leader calmly.

"My memory is a bit sketchy, but if I can just think for a minute, I will be able to put it all together for you."

"We're waiting..."

"Let me start at the beginning." B looks around to see how alert his interrogators are. They stand erect, almost robotic. He thinks, "Well, they are certainly agents of the government—their demeanor gives them away." He pretends to gather his thoughts as he really lets one rip. The gasses are visible to the naked eye, as though his fear from being detained added an adrenaline-rich substance that smelled of six-month-old breakfast sausage and had sufficient oomph to reflect light. The smell was so terrible that one of the agents, a rabbit before being magically transformed, quickly swallowed a pill to self-destruct. The other eleven agents quickly removed the body, flew him to Alexandria, and buried him with full military honors. A small parade was held outside Tyson's Galleria in Tyson's Corner where about 120 people watched in wonder as the remaining dozen-minus-one marched in circles around the mall's parking lot wailing like lost children in a theme park. They then hurried back to Seattle and found B still sitting there, staring at the mirrors with a comically sinister smile, gloating over his ability to make people sick.

"We want the facts. NOW!"

"Okay, here it is. The first memory I have of all of this nonsense is practicing my golf swing in my office. Next thing I know, my old school buddy, Jener, takes off with my junkie son." At this point in the story he thinks they are not really listening to them, and so he begins to bend the facts—at least his remembrance of them. "And my wife goes out and becomes a lesbian, and I get roped into this bizarre situation involving a bunch of hoodlums in Fort Wayne and I wake up in the Fantasy World Hospital in Kissimmee. To make matters worse, I had met this guy Kra in St. Cloud and he finds me in between dream states while I'm in the hospital in Tulsa. Now, if that isn't bad enough, I am given some weird liquid from a cactus in central Mexico, and all I remember is how I longed to have sex with my father, a jackal scrounging for a tasty insect lunch. You tell me what this all means!"

An uncomfortable silence ensues, uncomfortable for B, that is, because he still can't tell the truth to anyone. He is so afraid of everything that he cannot fathom the notion of revealing anything that has damaged him over the years, especially the time when that Pakistani man took him in an oil deal back in the early 70s. He looks at his watch, which grows like a skyscraper on his wrist, reaching higher toward the ceiling, and breaking through and reaching into the sky and toward the sun. This monument of man stands alone against the chaos below, the object of time contained in a glass encased medallion worn on the wrist of virtually every human alive, a symbol of mankind's hypnotic servitude to production, the tireless effort to reach further and further until all else is insignificant. A Samba rhythm begins to grow in B's head, and he envisions Brazilian dancers marching in Rio de Janeiro's Sambadrome adorned with precious gems and tall headdresses and singing, beating drums, and dancing in unison, pulsating through the caverns of time.

"We are still waiting Mr. Johnson."

"That's it!" The realization strikes him like a wild card in a game of chance. "We are waiting. That's the truth I can tell you. That's the only truth I know. Everything else is just motion relative to a motionless object."

"That is brilliant Mr. Johnson, but we need the secret information."

"What secret information? Why does everyone always ask me for this information? I'm just a fucking marketing master."

There is a fierce rumble coming from beneath the building and squalid looking man in military fatigues enters the room unannounced. "St. Helens blew her lid again, but this may be the big one. We have to get out. It looks like the entire state of Washington may be covered in lava and we'll be nothing but a memory of a distant civilization if we don't get out. NOW!"

Within moments of this interruption, B is picked up in a jeep and driven at high speeds through a tunnel that connects the subterranean mega-complex with the airstrip at Bremerton Naval Station. Small groupings of anti-nuclear weapon protestors are kept at a safe distance from the airstrip with leftover M60A1 battle tanks borrowed quickly from a nearby used arms dealer. A CIB jet waits for Winchester on the tarmac, and he is quickly flown to safety. A hole has opened in the ground where Mount St. Helens once resided, until it blew a funnel of lava two miles wide and six miles sky high. While the lava could be seen from as far as 500 miles away, no one present at the naval base knew of the catastrophe approaching. The devastation would eventually eliminate 97.6% of the topical life within 300 miles of the volcano in one direction, but surprisingly, Portland, Oregon, sitting less than 60 miles from the eruption in the opposite direction, had escaped devastation. Aside from a half-inch thick blanket of ash that caught the jet stream and ended up south of the explosion, no sign of the lava ever went south. The winds were blowing from the northwest that day, but the funnel of fire seemed only to travel north and northwest, clearly against the wind. It was as though Mother Nature pointed a huge cannon from beneath the earth's surface, took aim, and fired north, shooting pyroclastic flows and ash toward Seattle. As the ash, pumice and gasses were discharged from earth's cannon, gravity took hold and swept the flow under the jet stream far above.

Like streaks of lightening, G. Sport's agents bail out and are never to be seen again. From the roof of his cabin, G. Sport is carried away in a Vertol CH-113 rescue helicopter as his home melts into time like his magical master. The lava had invaded the hills, the towns, villages, and cities as additional land along the Pacific coast is forged. Puget Sound fills with hot lava and cools instantly, forming a fortifying landmass where an enormous sea had just been for tens of thousands of years. It not only created new landmass, but it changed the atmosphere. Instantly, Seattle's weather became similar to that found in Las Vegas. City planners got right on this. The planning for reconstruction was complete just weeks after complete annihilation, and shortly thereafter, the digging out began.

Like a body with malfunctioning arteries, the bloodstream that is commerce and other comings and goings is slowed but does not stop. A voice of panic rumbles low and long for days among the people as they go on with their routine to the degree they are able, as if awaiting the inevitable flow of disaster to make its way across the nation. Television sets, all tuned in, cover every angle with photographic brilliance, and every possible expert on volcanic apparatus is busy informing the intelligent public, "Do not worry. Next time, we'll know what to do."

The Federal Emergency Mismanagement Authority, FEMA, is very quick to respond. They and the CIB had been using this scenario as a model for future emergency management training courses, and so they are better prepared than they might have been otherwise.

"Senator Chafedskin, we need 450 billion dollars to dig the Decagon out from Puget Sound and another 1.8 trillion to move it back to Washington, and then, an additional 16.6 trillion to rebuild Seattle."

"What's in it for us?"

"An extra month in St Barths and a monument named after each of you on Lava Boulevard in the new downtown Seattle marketplace next to the world's largest casino.

There are rumblings that this could be the next Vegas. The Giant Condom Hotel and Condominiums will replace the Space Needle, and it will be the world's largest building. The penthouse will have the ability to expand and contract depending on the weather. The Spanish architect who won the bid is hell-bent on using this new material he discovered in an abandoned laboratory outside of Nairobi that not only has the physical capacity to change shape but also to change color, or so he claims. We think it will make Seattle the number one American tourist destination after the Fantasy Kingdom."

"What does the President think?"

"He's too busy running guns to both the Contras and the Sandinistas so they can kill each other off to comment. You know, just like in Iran and Iraq. Furthermore, it's only Seattle that was destroyed. If it were Los Angeles, you can bet your cowboy hat he'd be on the crisis like a fake six shooter on the hip of an actor in a spaghetti western."

"What does the Vice President think?"

"He gave the order."

"Oh. Okay, of course, let's do it."

B arrives just in time for the USS Constitution's visit to the small port in Marblehead, arriving from just downstream in Charlestown after generations of visitors have reminisced while gazing at its hull about this war and that war, this President and that President, this memory and that memory. Could it be that B's path is different than even he imagined. His father calls him on his enormous and heavy mobile telephone. He tells him that there is something he needs done and he only trusts one man to do it.

Meanwhile, high in the bureaucratic heavens of God, Gold and Glory, man is being reconstructed into half machine/half muscle by ex-NASA scientists who have been covertly employed by the CIB. Synthetic masks of plastic and carbon monoxide emissions are replacing the human brain. Computers are busy making poorly conceived predictions about the probability of sightings of everlasting life in distant lands where mystics are given free reign. Even the general systemic processes are different where oxygen is the most vital element of nature. Some humans still hold on to the land, fight for every square inch of it, while the machine tramples everything in sight underfoot.

B wanders through the streets of Marblehead, past the old homes of long deceased fisherman, the boutiques, the restaurants, the BMWs and the homeless people in the streets. He sees timeless pleasure in ignorance in the faces of the tourists here to witness the historical event. He watches generations merge into a large electrical apparatus of communication, its synergies of spirit lingering alongside it as if waiting to make contact with the elders of the ancient tribes of wisdom. As he waits to make contact with the physical world, the duality of life comes to form before B's eyes. He vanishes as though his life were just a speck of nutrition for the earth.

The tunnel he passes through is wide enough for his body but narrow enough to see that no tributaries exist. He looks at his hands in front of him. Like shiny steel they reflect the glowing light energizing the route from the source. The sounds are whole and dynamic, and there is a feeling of instability as he floats through air. Hearing voices of torment, he lingers for a while before disregarding them as anything serious, and then he approaches a gateway. Golden arches formulate a doorway and iron bars with gargoyles perched atop each pinnacle stare fear into B. He is greeted as the door opens.

"Hello again B," his guardian calls to him. She is a spirit now. Her physical form appears as a red silk gown cascading like a waterfall.

"Holy Cow! Where in the hell am I?"

"Relatively close on both accounts."

"What am I doing here?"

"At last, a relevant question escapes your mouth. I will now call you Wild Card, for that is the name the playwright has given you at your rebirth, and before I answer your question regarding why you are here, you should first know where here is."

"Am I dreaming again?"

"Wild Card, you are an interesting person. When I first received the assignment, I was skeptical about how long I could withstand the degree of insanity you represent. However, I am glad that I persevered, for I have been ordained a dimensionless mystic and no longer have to wait on earth for my next lesson. I may now travel to gather strength through wisdom, gain it from visiting other realms. Although I am frightened, I have the knowledge that I will always fight for my survival but will always remain alive. This freedom I have attained can no longer be taken from me, for I have passed every test presented to me. If I make mistakes in the slopes around my sphere that is my existence, and surely I will, I can only lessen my degree of freedom in my travels in intervals of conical time, where I must re-energize myself with a method of centering you do not know how to use yet and most likely will never quite understand. And if I make it far enough, my destination will be to exist as a star, alone and brilliant, like our sun, though I would have preferred to be a comet—you cannot always get what you want."

Keith Richards, who often hangs around the trailer park and is considered a halfling (half alive and half dead), gives Salvador Dali a high-five because, well, he told him so.

She continues, "But more importantly, you will take this wisdom back to the conscious physical plane on earth with you, where you will be punished by humanity for the way in which you mistreated everyone in order to protect yourself. I am very sorry, but this is the way it must be done. If this were not the case, I would not have gone this far. I can only imagine what life would be like if we had some choice in this matter."

"ZZ, I have traveled further than most mortals, and yet I remain completely ignorant. Do I really have to change? I like my scotch, but I cannot foresee drinking it forever. I like chicks, and I, like my brother, especially like to dress up like them. I do not like drugs too much anymore, and I don't particularly like the military, but I love my daughter so I must at least recognize the fact that being a soldier is something that some people want..."

B wakes up lying on his back with his entire body wrapped in a crusty cloth. He cannot breathe. He starts feeling around desperately with his tightly restricted fingers. With some effort, he is able to break through the cloth and tears it from his entire naked body. He slams into the walls around him. The sounds are loud and panic stricken. He hears screams and a light appears as the cloth on his face is torn off. A small group of Ukrainian tourists holding lanterns begin to gasp for air as B is released from the tomb. The room is dark and dank and smells of death. He is led outside and stands in the hot Sahara desert. The Great Sphinx grows eyes that are alive and glow a fierce red. The tourists and the guide are busy praying to their newly found human demigod, to B. He announces himself as Wild Card, and a 99th Pyramid is immediately constructed with a profitable casino, showgirls, free liquor, prostitutes, and the world's best restaurants. Two rows of neon-laced 66.6 meter Malaysian palm trees are planted along the 2.3-kilometer strip all the way from the left foot of the Great Sphinx to a singular point on the West Nile river bank where, if standing under a full moon in October, one can see, on the star map, a large American made toilet in the sky.

Wild Card sits in his penthouse office hoping this will never change. A number of personal slaves are at his disposal, including large Canadian Royal Mounted Police eunuchs flown in especially to be his private guards as tourism and gambling become Egypt's second and third most important industries behind storytelling. The guards are introduced to Wild Card as emanating from Canada, but there is no indication of how they had been chosen and what testing they had gone through to determine their reliability. There is also some indication they are not actually from Canada, but a background check is being conducted. Meanwhile, Wild Card sits in absolute bewilderment because of the completely unclear facts surrounding this newest turn of events—he is now the figurehead of an immensely lucrative empire. The parts of the empire are connected like minuscule points on an intricate impressionistic painting resembling an enormous electronic stock exchange board. Renoir was asked to fashion his ultimate masterpiece using all the information given, and he said that it might take him a while, much longer than we have to tell this story, he is afraid, but he has begun. He does inform us that the finalization of this masterpiece should coincide with the grand opening of the new fine art museum and beer hall being constructed behind the wall.

Scanning the landscape of desert and pyramids and hotels and restaurants and bustling tourist, tiny teardrops roll down Wild Card's pinkish cheeks. He feels exceptionally fortunate. He thinks that his father would be very proud of him in this moment. This is a moment of rebirth for him similar to moments he has already experienced in his past, but this is the first of its kind while he is sober. Inside the energy created by the winds in the land of the pharaoh is certainly a good place to find oneself, but Wild Card has no idea why the winds have blown him here or which way the winds blow.

Act 11.

Pyramidal Deconstruction:
Wild Card's Revelation

The southwestern entrance of Wild Card's great gaming establishment was forced to undergo frequent physical restructuring due to an increased probability of terrorist attacks against tourists, varying management theories, and theistic sensibilities. When built, the original entrance was constructed to simply maintain stability as one entered the lobby. Giant marine mammal replicas made of solid ice lined the walls of the Great Galaxy Entrance, the décor Indochinese overall. The ice sculptures are contained in 500 gallon refrigerated tanks to keep them preserved. However, upper level management of the Pyramid decided that the ice gave an inappropriate sensation of visitors being kept cool in a very hot place, and that was clearly not the mood they were attempting to set. For to cool off potential bettors is a maneuver that is quite intelligent once some lucky character gets on a roll, but to cool them off before they even lay down their money is, decisively, a very poor business decision.

To counteract this supposed sensation, they decided to deconstruct the entrance and rebuild one with a greater sense of openness and with more actual airflow, letting the warm desert air roll consistently through. However, it was later decided that the passage was far too large, and being at the edge of the desert, showed no respect for the extreme heat. Besides, such a large entrance insinuated disrespect and a lack of humility. The passage was torn down again and rebuilt as a crawl space. Each person wanting to enter the casino would first be required to kneel down, answer a few fundamental questions about autocracy, and crawl through. This brilliant strategy lasted only a few days, however, and although this spectacle received great media coverage and positive feedback from the ruling governmental party, the casino was losing way too much money, and very quickly. The original edifice was reconstructed and instead of using ice-encapsulated sea mammals, management brought in live animals from the Serengeti along with the best animal trainers on earth. Although this move drew very little press coverage, the strategy proved to be the way to go.

Wild Card sits high in his elevated office. The very top of the Pyramid was severed from the rest of the building visually and placed on hundreds of thin steel support beams above the structure. A giant bloodshot eye is illuminated in neon lights on each side of it. Wild Card spends most of his time giving instructions to his eunuchs on how to cheat the players in the most congenial manner possible. This is when the attack came. This is also when Wild Card found his soul, which, as one might imagine, was shrouded in confusion.

In a concealed location somewhere between the east and the west, somewhere between the north and the south, near a desert, a river, a mountain, a stadium, a shopping mall, a fast food chain restaurant, a meeting was taking place that involved three very important criminally minded people. While the identities of these three persons will remain anonymous for now, Wild Card was clearly the topic of discussion, as was the immediate future of life on this planet, which was being methodically planned. These three were orchestrating a series of events indeterminably linked in methodology, yet somehow seamlessly tied together in abstract thought, all involving

Wild Card, who had proven to them, following a series of tests, that he was probably the right man for the job, *probably* for no one can be completely confident about this fact, especially considering the circumstances, but it is the assumption that matters. This series of cataclysms, tragedies, and formulaic ideals of physical destruction were mapped out on a timeline in order to give maximum fear to the maximum number of human beings in the shortest period of time. While this feat had never been attempted, the powers making this ruthless decision had a sparkle in their eyes, a jump in their step, and a grin on their faces as, one by one, the cataclysm, the tragedy, and the destruction were executed and, quite honestly, mastered.

Evaporating from low levels of dawn's early mist arising from the Nile into the hot, dry air, the particles of energy morphed into a hallucinogenic portrait of a suffering mermaid stranded on a bed of rocks with little more than an isolated imaginary droplet of water fading toward the sky in the distance, her scales peeling and muscles swollen. The news came like a flash of terror from the desert sky. The time read approximately 3:30 a.m. (GMT). As the sun rose over the land of the Pharaoh, some distance from the Pyramid Casino Hotel, there was a very loud explosion followed by gunfire. There was also screaming, and then came a mesmerizing and deafening silence from the angels as encrypted messages were contractually destroyed in pools of swaying fire. Japanese drums beat feverishly inside the minds of the audience, and the walls of doom opened as, like a tidal wave, earth was submerged in historical self-annihilation. Wild Card met his opposite. Like a great secret unraveling before one's senses, the great limiter of expanse, internationally acclaimed best selling writer on business ethics and university professor, Ka Zin Flow, appeared and disappeared in a moment. His brief encounter with Wild Card was very compelling and quite interesting, but the facts are rather sketchy as there were no witnesses to the encounter. Considering the elements of these two personalities, interviewing them for the details on the encounter is a waste of time, and hence, any further journalistic integrity regarding said meeting is moot. Nonetheless, regardless of the content of their discussion, the result is what remains important. The flow of life shifted on this planet. The flow of life shifted inward once again, until of course the second coming of the mysterious and sublime truth of eternal type destiny and all that.

In that same brief moment, Wild Card found his roots and quickly became Diarrhea. He rolled down his pants to his ankles and really let one rip. The steel beams suspending the giant bloodshot eye-top of the pyramid gave way and crashed through the glass ceiling, crushing unsuspecting onlookers as they held golden handles in their weathered hands. Wherever there was silence, noises would erupt like highly pressurized fountains. Across the planet, in three simultaneous moments of disaster, thousands were crushed by the pinnacle of the pyramid, the tumbling of steel and glass, and the shrapnel from exploding devices. Wild Card fell unconscious as people were filed into two distinct categories of thought and feeling that would come to be called the great divide: those who believe that what happened was random and uncalculated and those who saw the wings of angels and the horns of devils locked in battle through faded mists as sacred scrolls dictated the direction of the universe over the centuries, through great gaps in space and in looping waves of motion. And when Wild Card awoke, he was faced with the most eerie sensation, one that told him that this is merely a precursor to something much worse, much larger.

The sensation that someone was clearly watching him, and only him, hung languidly around his trembling body like a giant, loose Christmas tree ornament. Despite his faults as a human being, he was blessed with a balanced inner conscience that had somehow been given to him, or so he thought, a conscience that dictated clearly that he shall not take sides. His opinions would clearly matter, but only from his perspective, and although he was not quite sure what that meant, the word "perspective" that is, he was given a true gift: He shall not have any beliefs or any ideas or any arguments that would lead him to corrupt his balance. Of course, this is until a couple of hours later when he remembered that he thought he saw Jesus playing black jack in the casino and ordering a Sex on the Beach, at which point B decided that he would be a religious man. Although he did not quite act on his religious meanderings until some time later, he knew deep down that this was his calling. He had never had any thoughts of depth until this moment, never searched into the meanings of things, and so he decided that he could never share this insight with anyone who might understand and would hold onto it as tightly as anyone holds to a revelation or a miracle that changes one's mind, changes one's life.

Like a solitary Wild Card in life's deck of cards, he stood alone, standing hard and tall against his deeper inner-feelings, ignoring the messages and separating himself further from the direct signals given to him from a greater plane of existence. Despite this newly discovered self-awakened strength, Diarrhea could not shed his roots, however, and he continued on the other Wild Card's path, which was now giving him more power than he ever conceived existed, and this path was clearly related to an unknown someone who was always standing behind him, always lurking in the shadows making his decisions appear as though they were his own. Alas, history will teach that his decisions never were his but only appeared to be if one were really not looking out the clear glass windows separating the ongoings in the world from all the modern caves that dotted the mindscape of humankind.

Act 12.

The Speech Near to the Bazaar:
Incidents and Accidents

As if fate played out an interesting twist, Wild Card does not actually become a man who is knowledgeable of his place in the world. He is no longer the puppet that we know him to be, at least in the eyes of many, but he is clearly much more of a puppet than ever imagined as a select few very relevant people continue to pull his strings without much thought regarding the notion of complex consequences. Their only consideration was how the string-pullers would benefit financially. Furthermore, what can be considered a degree of intelligence has not made its way to his conscious thoughts. He does not appear to have the ability to be even somewhat reasonable or clever in the public eye. This is what his father, Gerald, had been hoping for but never received for all of his efforts. After all of his training, Gerald knew that, with the right amounts of physical and emotional abuse, the fear would create precisely the man he wanted to create; but, he wonders, why has his plan failed so miserably? What better type of man to be used as an instrument than one who has learned to operate from fear? In the creation of such a man, the world has given birth to, coddled and pacified a man to be looked up to because a man who fears life because he was raised to do so is perhaps the only kind all of humankind can relate to. So, despite his father's failures in raising him properly, the end result may still be the same. What is simply astonishing is how, following his multiple transformations, clever Little Diarrhea had become Wild Card. Unbeknownst to the man himself at this time, his relevance will become far greater than he ever wanted or understood.

A caravan of bulletproof stretch-Humvees lines the streets of Cairo. Inside one of those machines is Wild Card and inside another is his entire band of eunuchs dressed as French fashion consultants. The rest are just empty, except for drivers, and stocked with fine champagne, caviar and pornographic videos. People stand on the street's edge and watch in wonder. The caravan enters a private tunnel and arrives at the rear entrance of an open-air modern convention center. Inside the convention center, which is adorned as an ancient amphitheater, albeit with Michelin three-star, chef-owned food kiosks that line its front entrance perimeter, is a crowd gathered for a speech by one of Egypt's newfound sons, a friend to all Egyptians, even those who oppose his points of view according to the public service announcement given over Egyptian state television the night before. The entrance fee of 850 Egyptian pounds enables the power elite to gather together under a bright sky without the inconvenience of having to mingle with those who do not have such disposable cash to spend.

Wild Card is led to the podium and handed a speech printed on slightly discolored and decaying papyrus. The ink displaying some kind of signature has bled slightly, and the only visible letters are *e Crao*. The crowd hurries to their seats and quiets down. Wild Card gives a quick glance at the papyrus, which is written in perfect modern English, clears his throat, removes a small flask of scotch from his pocket and bends over to take a generous slug. A small buzzing in his ears gives way to a voice. The voice begins reading word for word what is written on the paper. Wild Card murmurs softly to himself that, since he cannot read, he should simply repeat the words spoken to him. The voice tells him, "Good idea." He turns to see if someone is behind him, but there is no one standing near him and so he decides that it must be his conscience. He begins speaking:

"Like an ancient sore on the Achilles heel of man, a young frightened New World boy failed to learn from his mistakes; and the age-old repetition continues onward until the end of our cycle. And as ZZ has been told from beyond, the end has come as our ellipse has found completion. Five thousand four hundred and thirty-two years ago, a prophecy was made that the floodgates will open for all unrestrained behavior. Deception will no longer coalesce the underground senses. The rivers that flow beneath are alive and momentous and quite transparent, and the people who live there are shouting upward, causing vibrations inside every soul that walks the earth. From what transverse wave will the next modus vivendi arrive? From which planetary system does the next vessel land and spark consciousness into change?

"And back on earth, we simply wait and often we sit around and yawn. Perhaps the truth is that no one has the answers. Hath the roads that converge into one now split at the end after all, or do the ones that split eventually converge back into one? And when in time do we think we are? Do we give a moment's thought to the notion of 'when' in this refuge of vast space and infinity, to when we might possibly wake up and feel the pressure that has been building from below for thousands of years, from the earth, as a raised jewel lying immobile for millions of years? This stone contains the only perceptible signs of life on this self-destructing planet. Visible colors and streams cover us. We are bathed in moments of lucidity and tormented by empty vast openness, and we seek retribution in the finalization of our cycle, but with the ending of the cycle, do the gauges reset? Or like anything else, do the memories leave only traces of understanding, fading in and out of our consciousness like scars that reopen and close only after the shock regulates the flow once again. And when the poles depolarize just enough to make a significant difference, what happens to our lands? Are they lost forever like Mu and Atlantis, like Baghdad and Beirut, and like Sea...?"

The only man seated in the audience with a Mohawk hairstyle removes a small remote control and stops him from speaking further.

Wild Card shakes his head as though his ears were clogged and continues, "And in this perseverance, did we, as a species, ascertain anything at all? Are all the secrets kept in tombs protected underground? Better look up, better look down, better look ALL the way around, and do not sleep! Oh, by the way, does anyone know where I can find the nearest Turkish bath?" Wild Card backs from the podium and bows.

The crowded amphitheater erupts into gasps and whispers. This is a truly random audience. The only element that connects them is their ability to pay for the ticket. There has been no commercialized marketing scheme to prey on a certain behavioral type or utilizing certain consumer criteria to determine a sense of "freewill" in spending habits. The attendants have merely found their own way here; of course, the small implants may have helped a little bit. They have simply converged into a monument of human development and understanding.

Keynote speaker Wild Card is instantly hailed as a philosophical genius. The event, billed as *Say It Ain't So: The Next Stage of Human Development*, was a resounding success as the hordes of victims to this inconspicuous mind trick file away from the amphitheater discussing the speech and what is for dinner. Victor Hugo, joined by a parade of Russian writers from the Golden Age led by Gogol, Tolstoy and Turgenev, set up a tent by the Nile's east bank where they give free consultations and pass out rather well illustrated novel-sized pamphlets on *Using Constrictive Politics and Wartime Propaganda to Forge an Ideological Enterprise*. The illustrator was unknown to the ghostwriting editors, and so he or she may still be alive. Only a few visitors understood enough world history to show up at the tent, but those visitors, at least those not seeking autographs, those who were actually inquisitive, walked away with a wealth of knowledge.

Kra Fere Infinite raises his glass to the sky, for he hopes that his next order will come soon. Jener Shoke's presence still protrudes itself into time like a spike in the ground of a recently decayed ancient Rome-like Seattle. Blood spills into the streets as explosives detonate in Belfast, Algiers, Srinagar and Khartoum. There is more silence as Wild Card re-approaches the podium, albeit a little late as only a few lingering bodies still litter the grounds.

"Fight for your minds. They are not your own," Wild Card says and is immediately pushed from the stage by a guard who is watching for signs of trouble as bullets shower the stage from the seats in the upper right corner of the grassy knoll laid out neatly across the upper rim. This was not something expected of Wild Card. Indeed, he spoke out of line.

Wild Card finds himself being led into a mud walled tunnel hundreds of feet below the surface of the wildness above. Skeletons of the lost dead line the walls. Sounds of water are heard dripping from unseen caverns. Wild Card removes his mask in these tunnels that connect the amphitheater to the riverside village below, and he once again becomes Deej. His guide, whose identity is unknown to Deej, tells him where he must go next. Deej, of course does not question why but simply knows he must follow the instructions. He exits the tunnel through a secret basement door in an old bakery where an elderly man wearing a dusty whitish-gray cloak and skullcap is kneading bread dough. He spots Deej coming through the forbidden door, nods to him, and lowers his head once more. Deej lets a good one rip, and the man chuckles as Deej makes his way up the stairs to the sunlit streets above. He is now in a bustling bazaar, people rushing around this way and that, and getting lost amongst the faces in the crowd is very easy here. There is no chance that he will be found.

In these streets, humanity is animated with colors and the ebb and flow of consumer excitability, yearnings for one more piece of bread, one more section of cloth, one more mutual fund or stock option, one last whisper before their words fade into the night's silent repose. People exchange ideas as they exchange money, share stories and laugh and cry and hope for a better tomorrow as Deej slithers his way through the bazaar with a pocketful of knowledge and no place to spend it.

An eager vendor peddling sweet sugar candies catches Deej napping as we walks. The peddler strikes up a conversation with the unsuspecting American. "How much you give me for my sweets?"

"I don't want any sweets. I'm looking for the Babylon Club."

"Babylon Club is close by. I can tell you how to get there if you buy some of my sweets."

"Screw your sweets, but I'll give you some dough, you pathetic beggar. You know how much money I made when oil prices skyrocketed in '80? I can buy your whole family!"

"I do not understand sir, but my sweets go very well with the best Arabian coffees."

Deej's thoughts shift back to the moment he and Johnnie misplaced their sensibility and ended up with a chin in a jar, the moment that changed the direction of his life.

Deej then farts some coins from his ass onto the peddler's cloth and snags one of his sweets, pops it in his mouth and begins to feel a bit strange. "Must be the heat and the sugar," he stammers to himself.

Back at the amphitheater, the local police are questioning the witnesses. "What did you see before the bullets were fired?"

"A spirit formed this whole scene. The reckless ambitions of the modestly adorned saw a flash of white light followed by the birth of a universe and the formation of an intense black hole-like vacuum in the center of it all. Stars began to explode into existence, and as time grew further into the reaches of distance, the center began to evaporate into a core-like tunnel, a tunnel like this river, with it's turbulent past and naked future," says Doc Whitman, who has joined Victor Hugo and the Russian writers because he loves to impress the world's police forces. He continues, "And with all time concealed in a single thought, the motion of planets breaks waves unto the earth and sends entertaining spirits downward to feed the hungry lost souls with a divine connection."

"What in the hell are you talking about it? Take this one to the station. I think he may be on drugs."

Doc Whitman begins to laugh as the police officers chain up the legendary poet and toss him into the back of a military Humvee. "You think I need drugs? You think I care whether you lock me up? Do you know that all modern thought started from my brain, you stupid halfwits?! And furthermore, do you know how many inmates will love my services? Hell, I am a Doctor!"

Deej wanders for most of the day, and as sunset illuminates the muddy river by this quaint old village within Cairo's city limits, he finds the Babylon Club. He is supposed to meet a business contact there. And, as things go, he really doesn't know why. For isn't that the nature of loosely translated allegories? His contact is completely alien to him. He knows not what he or she looks like or anything about the character at all other than the contact's name is Green Fever. Inside the Babylon Club, the lights are dimmed and small tables surround the mural-covered walls. In the center is a waterfall looking apparatus with a green and black tiled floor carved in swirling patterns. Deej stares at the floor and it seems to move on its own.

"Get me a drink!" He screams at no one in particular. A small olive skinned man approaches with a ridiculous smile and offers him a towel to clean his fingers before partaking in spirits. "Shove that towel up your little brown ass! I need a scotch." The young man appears to be confused but keeps the smile on his face. He places the towel in Deej's hand, bows and walks away. Deej throws the towel on the floor and screams, "Where's Green Fever and where the hell is my single-malt?"

A woman approaches from his left side and seats herself next to him. "You're looking for me?"

"Hey baby, if I wanted to get laid, I'd call that little brown faggot over here."

"Oh, you must be Mr. Johnson, American. Little Diarrhea, isn't it?"

"My good friends call me WB. Everyone else calls me Deej."

"Well you are an interesting creature. Kra, I mean Jener, told me you'd be a learning experience."

"Did you say Kra?"

"Ugh, no, I meant to say that, for crying out loud, this may be interesting."

"Yeah whatever, I was told that you could help me get out of here, help me get far away from this nonsense. Do you know I have a penthouse office in the new glass pyramid in Giza? Well, I did, it sort of took a tumble."

"From the sounds of it, your nonsense is partly created by assholes like yourself."

"What did you say to me?"

"I said that it would cost you."

"That's why they call you Green Fever? Sounds like you're nothing but a high class whore."

"You are a bit more intelligent than you appear to be, Mr. Johnson, but no, that's not it. I spent years in east-central Africa studying the behavior of governmental agencies and studying ancient sorcerers to learn the secrets of the universe. What a waste of time. Actually, I got a fever from an exotic leaf I had used by mistake in a hot tea. It made my face turn green—I had a green fever."

"Sounds like you got fucked by a faggot and got AIDS."

"This is no use, you ridiculous man. No deal." Green Fever stands up to walk away.

"Wait!!! I apologize. Sometimes my name catches up with me. I desperately need to go to the Far East. I'm not sure where, but everyone in the Western Hemisphere is looking for me. I was able to get out of the country at the last minute, although..." He searches his memory. "I really don't remember how I got here, but undoubtedly the entire trip was first class of course. But now, they're on to me. I need out. Help me out of here."

"Who's on to you?"

"How the hell do I know? All I know is that this strange journey of mine keeps taking odd turns and I find myself doing things I never would have thought of doing when I was snorting cocaine in my college days."

"Sounds like you're on a mission of sorts."

"Call it whatever you want, you stupid bitch... Sorry, call it what you want. All I know is there are things I have to do."

"Meet me tomorrow at Fritz's Gothic Bakery by the Obelisk marked Aziz 23. It is on the West Bank by the main bazaar. You'll never miss it. A street performer who has a snake suck on his genitals stands right in front of it. Try not to get caught up in the frenzy though. Most of the French nationals congregate there about an hour early to get ready."

"Should I bring anything?"

"Just a pile of cash, USD please, and I'll provide the rest. Do me a favor? Please try to keep your mouth shut as much as possible. You may offend the wrong person and, instantaneously, we'll have to find another goat to finish this mission... Uh, I mean, we'll have to find someone else to help."

Deej slips out the back and ends up, after wandering for quite some time, in the bar at the Golden Tulip Hotel. He sips Singapore Slings and dreams of treading the streets of the Orient, where he can really behave foolishly and no one will give a damn.

Act 13.

The Kingdom of Fantastical Things: Turkey Legs and Infinity

"When in the hell do they serve us food on this damn plane anyway?" Deej is busy harassing a young stewardess.

"We will serve dinner in two hours," the young woman states, and she gives him a courteous, but obviously phony, smile as she continues down the aisle.

"I hate these goddamned chink airlines—everyone is so stupid!" Of course, Deej doesn't realize how loudly he is speaking and everyone on the plane instantly appears to be of Asian descent, and clearly, many of them understand English.

On longer flights, he has much time to think. Giving Winchester Buckley Johnson too much time to think is usually a poor idea as the same thoughts repeat over and over again in his mind until he verbalizes them. Usually, the results are rather malicious or contain some type of negatively rooted idiosyncrasy. This time seems to be different, as his hypnogogic thoughts turn somewhat constructive. Drifting away, he wonders how he can possibly rekindle a spark with his wife. He remembers the torrid love affair when they first met, and also after he purchased her second automobile for her when she became a virtual dynamo in bed, asking Winchester to bring home different costumes from the local Halloween and Party Store so they could role-play. His daughter's story is a bit more bewildering. Her immersion into the darker realms of military strategy and history at a very young age is something that still eludes him. He sees no direct connection to her behavior and anything of his own past. She knows that he avoided military duty because he always brags about it. Perhaps, as her psychotherapist pointed out to him in a group session, she is compensating for his lack of interest in patriotism and the like.

"I am patriotic! I am patriotic! I am patriotic!" he repeats loudly as his bulging retinas twitch. One can only imagine what his dreaming might entail as his left hand is rammed down his pants rubbing his genitalia while he is screaming about patriotism. He awakens quickly with some turbulence and grumbles about the stale peanuts given to him by the flight attendant. "I told you I only eat salted peanuts. This unsalted crap is for coach—this is First Class! I'm fucking hungry! When's a guy going eat here?" He quickly changes the impressions of those around him. They no longer consider him a perverted traitor, just an asshole.

He quickly falls back asleep, and his memory takes him in a different direction: Lake Buena Vista on New Year's Eve in 1984. He brought his family there to have a nice family vacation. New Year's Eve in the Fantasy Kingdom is a special trip for a consumer advocate like Deej, who beheld a sense of spirituality in that place he had only dreamed of as a child, a longing for fantasy and participation in an allegory representing all that is and all that can be. It is the possibility of time that made life interesting for so many people, for so long, which for Deej, came to culmination in Snow White's Castle, in the bathroom to be precise, as he was releasing gallons of enriched fluid from his enflamed rectum. The time was 11:03 p.m. and the park was the filled with the greatest number of visitors ever to enter its gates in a single day.

A show was being prepared for performance on stage in front of the Castle, and many people were exhausted from an entire day of being pushed and prodded like cattle adorned in American-currency-colored hide on the special day that marks the end to each year. And as Deej emerged from the Castle, he was given a vision, in a long line of many more to come, of the death of consumer-driven humanity. And in that same moment, the same thousands upon thousands of people he had left wandering about the park lie dead on the ground, each holding up for all to see, clutched in hand, a maggot infested turkey leg bone that had been cooked on Thanksgiving Day the year before, 1983. That fateful Thanksgiving Day, the feasting of the harvest in congruence with cultural splicing and gathering, the number of turkey legs cooked exceeded the number consumed by 130,000 as the result of some very poor planning.

"We can't waste 130,000 roasted turkey legs! I'll lose my fucking job! Find a place for them, and we'll work it into the books later," barked Jack D. Fromensetter, Director of Operations in the Food and Beverage Division of the Friends of Lake Buena Vista Department of the Magical Theme Park Bureau of the State Department's Foreign Relations through Brainwashing office at the food distribution manager dressed as Goofball, the famous fox character.

Goofball called in the forces on call for clean up, and they arrived in a tractor-trailer truck with a badly spray painted charcoal colored eyes in a big yellow smiling face imprint like a mask on the cab. The four men unloaded themselves from the cab of the rig and made an assembly line formation into the trailer. They did not speak. They simply executed commands given to them. In about two hours, they loaded the truck with 130,000 hot roasted turkey legs and started off toward the woods in the campgrounds surrounding the park. They were not seen again for over thirteen months.

There was much speculation as to their whereabouts. The headline in the *Orlando Times* read, *Four Men Disappear with Turkey That Probably Could Have Been Used in Soups for the Area Homeless*. The popular opinion was that the four men had eaten so much turkey they went into hibernation, but others thought maybe they had sold the turkey legs to Third World nations or traded them for nuclear arms, biological warfare components, or secrets to the Illuminati's whereabouts, or possibly donated them to charity, but no charities could confirm or deny these allegations.

On New Year's Eve, 1984, all speculation came to a close. The executors of commands arrived with a strange twinkle in their eyes, like they had been hypnotically induced into a different agenda or turned on by remote control, or perhaps it was their own agenda they were following. Again, there is no confirmation one way or another as to their motivation. The arrival marked a special celebration, the New Year, with one of Lake Buena Vista's greatest and longest running mysteries coming to a climax at the same moment.

For on New Year's Eve, at around 5:00 p.m., these four men, brought an Apocalypse of sorts to the Fantasy Kingdom. They arrived on white horses and were dressed as knights in shining armor. They were hauling 125,000 turkey legs behind them.

In a swiftly executed donation to all patrons of this theme park on this special day, everyone made a toast at 11:00 p.m. with a reheated roasted turkey leg in hand. They toasted in the New Year. Deej had been eating so much during the day that he asked his wife and daughter to wait by the Castle door while he took care of business as the turkey legs were given out by Fantasy World characters in uniform. Since Jennifer was in the phase where she hated anything that wasn't a Twinkie or a Ring Ding, and since Johnnie didn't eat Turkey, ever, for it reminded her of badly chosen window drapes, the Johnson clan (this one anyway, for there were 4,600 or so Johnson clans in the park that day) was spared. By 11:03 p.m., as Deej cleaned himself up and reentered the Kingdom from the Castle, 124,997 people lie dead, littering the ground with their rotting flesh and decaying bones. Fifty-seven minutes later, the fireworks, which were automated using the best robotics available at the time, were erupting into the sky. The Johnson clan stood in awe as the Fantasy Kingdom was a landscape of human waste and consumer destruction under the most spectacular celebration of exploding colors and lights in the sky above.

Back on the plane, Deej orders a Bloody Mary and a turkey leg.

"Sir, we will not be serving food for about 1 hour and 15 minutes. Please be patient. I will get you your drink though."

"Hurry up. I don't have all day."

The other passengers grow more impatient with him as he begins to fart uncontrollably.

Deej stares into his small cup of tomato juice and vodka and swirls his fingers around in it, carefully watching the patterns and formations the liquid makes around his finger. His memory once again uncovers times of pain. When he sold oil futures and cut his hand on a staple remover, that terrible pain forced him to cry, and he remembers how his coworkers chastised him for months. He remembers getting into a fight with a coworker, a large, former enlisted army man who had been back from the Vietnam War only three years—two of those years were spent in jail in South Carolina for fighting an entire squadron of police officers with his bare hands.

"You pussy! Oh, did Little Diarrhea cut his finger? Why don't I suck the blood out of it for you and then you can suck my dick!"

"Fuck you, Reed! It hurts."

"I'll show you pain. I'll rip out your eyeballs and piss on your skull. How's that for pain?"

"You, uh, want to take this outside." Deej's rebuttal was very powerfully stated.

"No, pussy. Let's keep it in here." With that, Bob Reed, this enormous hulk of a man, planted a fist into Diarrhea's face so hard the he shattered Diarrhea's jawbone. The crack was heard all the way to Houston. Diarrhea passed out from the intensity of the pain, and fear showed its ugly self as he soiled himself on the floor.

Years later, the large man would work for Deej selling oil contracts to the very gooks he had been killing 15 years earlier. "May I please take your order, sir?" he would say, over and over, day in and day out.

"What the fuck is wrong with you, Reed?! You suck! You couldn't sell a fucking hand grenade to a Gook in a war."

"Yes, Mr. Johnson. I have not been performing to the best of my abilities."

"Fuck your abilities, Reed. You don't have any. You suck. Why don't you get down on that floor and shine my fucking shoes."

"Yes, Mr. Johnson."

"Do it now, Reed!"

"Yes, sir."

"And while you're down there, why don't you suck my dick!"

After many more hours in flight and a satisfying meal, the airplane touches down in Hong Kong, soon to be, once again, a part of China. Deej, although claiming to hate the "little yellow motherfuckers," has never felt more at home than he does here. He is mesmerized by the intensity and bustle of the streets, the passionate flow of people moved by some force that is beyond them.

"You can't fake it, can you?" Deej asks a fish merchant.

"What did you say?"

"You can't fake it, can you? I mean, life carries you places. You just have to go with it. Just make sure you stay on top."

"Wise words, sir. Would you like to buy some cuttlefish?"

"No, not hungry. I already ate."

"Try the Palace of Arms on Hennessy Road, next to the electronic stores building. You may find what you are looking for."

"How the fuck do you know what I'm looking for?" Deej is back in form. "And furthermore, if you did know, you little yellow bastard, why should I listen to you anyway? Communism is dead, you stupid bastard. DEAD! Your system sucks the very dirt from my toenails." The merchant slips from behind the fish-lined table and begins to walk away. "Where are you going, you little yellow asshole!" Deej screams, but the sounds are muffled by the chaotic flow of bodies and mingled voices.

Another merchant appears at the same table. "I eh so sorry I had to step away. Would you lie to bie sothin?"

"Uh, wow. Hell, no."

"Goo day, sir," the elder man stammers with a sincere grin on his little face.

"Yeah, uh, goo-day to you too."

Deej walks toward Hennessy Road. He picked up a street map in English while in the marketplace and is maneuvering his way around the city, soaking in the sights of a land recently dominated by small fishing villages and warring tribes that now consists of 50-60 story skyscrapers and lavish hotels. He enters the Palace of Arms, a small antique arms dealer. The walls are lined with swords and guns rummaged from small battles won over the years with the Japanese and traded weapons from pirates that sailed the South China Sea for centuries. A small woman stands behind the counter. She wears a red gown and looks very much like Zhu Zen, but she is much younger.

"How cah I hell you?"

"I was sent."

"I do nah understahn."

"I was told to come here."

"Would you like to puhchase gun or sword?"

"I don't want your fucking swords, lady. I was told I would find something here." Kra Fere Infinite steps out from behind the silk screen in the back office. Deej farts. "What do you want from me Kra? Yes, I had a wonderful time with you, but what do you want from me? How did you know I'd be here?"

"I have informants everywhere, Johnson. As I told you before, I want the plans."

"I still have no damned idea what you are talking about!!!" Deej screams as mock tears roll down his slightly sunburned face.

"I know you are not that stupid, Johnson. I know you much better than you think." He pauses as if maybe he does not want to reveal too much. "I heard your speech in Cairo. You are clearly concealing something that you will not give up. I have wealth behind me, and you must share what you know. I will give you land, women, men, cars, a lifetime supply of beer—whatever you want—but I need the secret plans!"

Deej, feeling trapped, begins to release the most hideous odor from his body. The young Chinese woman and her five year-old son seated next to her faint from painful pleasure. Kra simply coughs a bit.

"It's not going to work, Johnson. I had my nasal passages surgically blocked so that I can finish what I need to do for my superiors."

Deej begins to explore his inner self. Perhaps he has once again rediscovered Little Diarrhea. Does he house the ancient wisdom of the keepers of great secrets? Does he have access to the most critical information known to all people who know things, or does he in fact know things that no one else knows? Clearly, he does not know the answers to such questions, otherwise he would have stopped running away years ago and just given the information up. He is not sure how to answer. He stands, dumbfounded and unaware of what to do next, but in the back of his mind, there is a voice telling him to trust his instincts. So he waits and he waits, and finally he decides that he should say something.

"Kra, if I did have your secret plans, do you know for certain that you would comprehend their magnitude when I reveal them? I mean, how do you know that the secret plans are not so obvious that, when you hear them, you will say to yourself, I already knew that? Does that make you a little leery? Haven't you ever thought of such a possibility, or are you so busy taking orders that you have no way to think for yourself? Not that I am a serious candidate for self-reliant thinker of the century, but do you only follow orders?"

"I do what I am told. And that is all."

"Well, Mr. Infinite, let me tell you this. One secret that I can tell you right now is that you are standing on a self-perpetuating node of falsely justified allegory, and this strange dream we all exist in will implode into itself someday. You better hope you're there—you don't want to miss it." Deej scares himself with this statement of detached philosophical beauty. He had never heard the words that just escaped his lips before, never mind spoken them, and to put them together with some clarity was a feat hitherto unknown to him.

"I just want the plans WBJ, just the plans that are concealed in the colon...I mean, the spaces between..."

"Sorry, Infinatum, no dice."

Deej walks out the door into the hot afternoon sun, and he hears drums beating on the streets as a troop of Hong Kong teenagers sit in a semi-circle in the marketplace a few blocks over pounding on plastic cans with elongated chopsticks. He realizes that one confrontation, the one with infinity, may be over for now, for Deej must close up the caverns in his mind and let the medicinal traits of non-philosophical thinking clear his senses so he can get some dim sum before he starves.

Kra slips into a state of euphoria as he slides the opium pipe into his tired mouth. His deed is not yet complete, as his agenda has a much larger purpose, and because Winchester Buckley Johnson has yet to reveal anything significant to him, anything that he can use in his quest.

But now he must reach back out into the outer realms of space, open himself up to the sensation of infinity, the one that he has run from for so long.

Act 14.

Peer Gynt In The Kong

He was watching the Hong Kong dawn, but it was as though he were staring into the sea of false promises. The ground practically shook beneath his feet as millions scurried around chasing their dreams of wealth and power and success. The mist that swung downward like a vine over Victoria Harbour was thick enough to conceal a poorly conceived lie. The view to the west was as pellucid as Wild Card's mouth vociferating something idiosyncratic. It was as though the fog and mist hung only on one side of the mountain, a half necklace of pearls around woman's gently sloping neck. The partition created a very surreal image, even for the unimaginative Wild Card. While Diarrhea still existed behind this mask, the one that the rest of the world saw was Wild Card. At least, for now, he had this going for him.

"Yes Dad. I will do it. What? I don't think that is possible right now. No. Okay, I will try. You promise? Oh boy, Jack is going to be pissed, well, who cares though—he is a moron. I know he's my brother Dad, but what can I say. I think he's rather stupid. Who? No! Wow. Okay, as soon as I am finished here, I will meet you in Washington. Oh, okay, I will see you in Boston then. What? I am never late." Wild Card hangs up his rather large and weighty mobile telephone as he wanders to the greater heights of Victoria's Peak.

"Wow!" he stammers to a Norwegian man next to him. "These little yellow bastards have quite an impressive place here. I really do love the little yellow bastards, but we definitely should have nuked their asses too." He was eagerly anticipating some type of condolence from the man next to him.

"I am sorry, but I do not understand. Little yellow bastards?" asked Edvard, the Norseman.

"Yeah, you know..." Wild Card lowers his voice so that others standing nearby on the mountain's summit cannot take notice of what he has to say. "These little chink bastards are industrious sons of bitches, eh?"

The Norseman, who had bent over slightly to listen more attentively was completely horrified, straightened upward again and looked at Wild Card squarely. "Mister American. You are obviously a very dimwitted man. Have you ever heard of my *Peer Gynt Suite*? You are standing in the Hall of the Mountain King. You are in my hall, sir. You will not speak of the resident folk like this. Take this back or I will have you sacked."

"Sacked? What the hell are you talking about? We, of European descent, have to stick together. Of course, I come from European stock, or so my grandfather used to tell me, but I am a full-blooded American." Wild Card pulls off a thick layer of skin that had been grafted from his ass, which was now covering an old scar on his face from his "fight" with Bob Reed years before. He places his hand over his heart and begins singing the national anthem of Canada: "O Canada! Our home and native land!"

Edvard Grieg walks away laughing gently as though he was a witness to some moment of pure bliss, staring a madman in the face, one who is madder than he. "Okay, Mr. Canadian. I will let you finish your song."

"I am an American! You dumb German! I am not Finnish! Do these idiots ever listen?" He tones his voice down as Mr. Grieg meanders down the mountainside toward the tram area. "Oh damn, I am late again. My business contact might not like the fact that I am late. One minute too late and they are insulted." Amazingly, Wild Card becomes aware of important facts sometimes, as though a button is pushed from somewhere afar and he grows a conscience like a third eye. He hurries down the mountainside and passes Grieg, who is strolling casually and whistling the demonstrative melody from *Dawn* in his *Peer Gynt Suite #1.*

Wild Card takes the tram down to the depot in Hong Kong Island Center. Then hurries to a taxi and goes to Wan Chai. His client is meeting him at Joe Bananas, an "American" bar in the very heart of this massive Chinese wave of humanity. Some early 1980s synthesizer "new wave" music is playing in the bar, the song "I Ran" by Flock of Seagulls blaring very loudly from the music system. It is only 6:00 p.m. and there are very few people loitering around. "Damn, I figured this place would be packed, especially with Phillipino and Ukrainian prostitutes," Wild Card says aloud as he whirls around to find a six-foot Chinese man with small round spectacles standing in front of him.

"Hi. I am Terry."

"Terry, hi, Deej here." Wild Card sticks out his hand to shake Terry's but notices that Deej still has some brownish-colored stains on his fingers. He forgot to use toilet paper again. He retracts his hand.

"That's okay. I know who you are. My friend Kra, I mean... Ahhhh, I figured you were an interesting guy."

"Kra? How do you know Kra?"

"I did not say Kra."

"Yes you did. I heard it. Look, Mr. Infinite and I have some unfinished business, I know, but he doesn't have to continue sending his henchmen after me. I have nothing to offer. I swear it." A strange ringing goes off in his ears and Kra appears in the doorway. The sunlight from outside breaks through like funnels to create the optical illusion of a man with wings in the doorway.

"Hey WBJ, guess who again? How's it going?"

"Uh, hi Kra." WBJ is feeling a bit uneasy in his position. Terry walks to the bar and orders a couple of iced green teas.

"Look WBJ...I am not here to pressure you into anything. I just figured after that wonderful night we spent in Denver, we could be friends, you know, the popcorn, the family-type movies. You were so gentle. I don't meet many guys like you."

"What kind of a sick and twisted human being follows someone to the Kong just to be friends? You are psychotic!"

"Well, I am a bit eccentric, I admit." Kra laughs to himself and bends over slightly as he looks down smiling. Then he straightens back up. "That's not the point!" His words come at Wild Card like Kra is throwing a punch into the thin air. "I think you and I have some information to share. To keep relations good, you know. I did some serious thinking about our conversation in the weapons shop. I am ready to accept infinity back into my life."

"You are ridiculous. I have no idea what you are talking about."

Kra is angered by Wild Card's insistence on keeping his usually free flowing trap shut, and his eyes begin to pulsate a rhythm that reminds WBJ of his old cocaine dependency. He breaks down and cries. Kra's face lightens up. "I am sorry, Little Diarrhea. I did not mean to make you cry. Look, I am staying at the Peninsula. Come to my room later—I'm in 2125. Make sure you knock three times or I will not answer. I will take you out on the town, and I'll even take you to Temple Street in Kowloon where most Westerners do not venture out at night."

"Okay, Kra. I will come to your room later, but promise me please, no more anger. I am a pretty happy-go-lucky guy who likes a good bottle of scotch and a couple of nice prostitutes on my arms, that's all. I don't need more than that. We can discuss business tomorrow."

As Kra leaves the bar, Terry returns with the iced teas. "So where were we? Um, yes. Mr. Johnson, I think you are a funny man. Go clean yourself up and we can discuss the trades."

"Trades?" WBJ says to himself as he walks to the bathroom. "What does he mean the trades?" There is a drunken United States Navy midshipman passed out on the floor by the urinal. He has a bloody tattoo half finished on his forearm that says "KR" only. His Hawaiian shirt with horses on it is covered with blood and there is a note sticking out of his shirt pocket. Wild Card removes the note and begins to read it:

"To all Hands on Deck: Rendezvous in Jbs at 23:30 on 7 April. Disguise level Delta. This is critical op. RPT, Critical Op. Wild Card must be dealt. I rpt. Card must be dealt. He is elusive but all eyes are to stay on the Card..."

Winchester has no idea what this was about, but since his alter ego, Wild Card, is mentioned, he momentarily becomes quite scared. But his sense of denial, always very strong, steers him out of any serious paranoia. He washes his stinky hands, leaves the Banana without telling his new acquaintance, Terry, and takes the ferry to Kowloon where the mad bustling of humanity continues. He walks to the Peninsula, which is not far, and stands outside gazing across the harbor toward Victoria Mountain on the Hong Kong island side. He notices a light reflecting, which looks like signals being sent between confidants. He steps backward for about 50 feet and looks atop the Peninsula, where he sees a man with a large mirror also reflecting light toward the mountaintop. Wild Card screams, "Mobile telephones would be much easier. HEY! Ever hear of technology? What an idiot!" The man disappears into the roof entrance of the hotel.

Wild Card enters the hotel from one of the rear entrances. Without any sense of humility, he begins stammering, once again, about "the little yellow bastards." Most simply look at him and shake their heads in disbelief. He stands alone among six million Chinese with no visible protection and fires insults like bullets at anyone who passes by. His inflated ego is at an all-time high. He imagines himself on the fairways in Augusta, playing side-by-side with the great golf icons. He begins practicing his swing in the lobby. The concierge runs over and asks him in very good English if he needs to know where the nearest golf club is.

"Yeah, right, like you chink bastards know how to play."

The concierge, being a man of human services, simply shakes his head and walks away.

"These dumb little fuckers think they can get on the links with guys like Nickraus and Playmer. Damn, they are egotistical little yellow twisted bastards. Damn, Augusta won't even let white *women* play in the Masters." He repeats the last part screaming, "NOT EVEN WHITE WOMEN!"

Wild Card feels a sensation come over his stomach like its being eaten from the inside out and makes a beeline for the restroom, which is actually only a janitorial closet next to the restaurant Gaddi's and he relieves himself amply. The odor is outrageous. It empties the lower level of the hotel as most patrons filter out onto Nathan Street to wait for the firefighters wearing gas masks to come and check the hotel's ventilation system.

Once again, a voice arrives in his head. "Will you please stop. You are really making me look bad here." He nods as though he is having a conversation with himself.

He comes out of the closet and sees the hotel is empty as though a neutron bomb explosion ended all advanced forms of life and he were the only one left. He finds himself in a lingering moment of complete isolation, which is death for *him*, a feeling of complete emptiness. He wanders outside and the streets are empty. There is no one to insult. The cars in the streets are abandoned, the doors ajar and the alarms ringing. The buildings and sidewalks are empty. No one is in sight. It is as though, in a flash, six million people vanished. After wandering for much time, Wild Card finds an old man sitting by the harbor next to an old rowboat. He asks him, "Where did all the yellow fuckers go?"

The old man points to Victoria Mountain. The mountainside is teeming with people and resembles a giant anthill. The man takes him across the harbor that now has a Styx-like haze to it. The man is rowing slowly and Deej can no longer see his face. The thickness of the newly formed fog keeps noise to a minimum. He can only hear the water rippling gently against the oars as the old man rows. Images begin to appear before his eyes from his past. At first the images are playful like his time as a child before the beatings began, but then they transform into nightmarish symbols, devils from every known belief system dancing around him, a metamorphoses of all the memories from all of his ancestors at their moments of death. The gripping nature of this transformation is more than any human should be equipped to maintain, but Deej miraculously cracks a sharp whip-like fart from his ass and the images vanish. As they approach Hong Kong Island, he hears the *Peer Gynt Suite* playing, growing louder and louder. The mountain is now in full view. The hordes of inhabitants are climbing over one another as the sunlight at the top is beaming people up toward the heavens. Edvard Grieg is standing with his arms raised toward the universe. The notes are now visible to the naked eye and construct colorful waves that fill the sky, the flutes and oboes and violins and cellos carrying each note to its apex of beauty. As they approach the shore, Wild Card glances back through the mist at the back of the old man who is still rowing.

The streets on Hong Kong Island are empty. Wild Card reaches into his pocket and notices that he has no money. The old man holds his arm out, the palm of his hand is up and his fingers, with long dirty fingernails, extended. Wild Card thinks for a moment, then scribbles some notes on a dirty napkin in his pocket. He gives it to the old man. It reads, "Call my broker—Pops. Tell him that I instructed you to buy 1,000 shares of INTC with funds from my account and to sell it when it when the millennium changes. You will be tempted to sell it sooner, I know, but trust me. Buy it back in 2003. Then hold it again until early 2008. Then sell it all and cash out. You will put your entire family's children, whatever's left of them, through college." The old man nods and accepts this as payment.

Wild Card meanders toward the mountainside. There is a procession of taxicab drivers waiting to take those with money to the peak where the road ends. The exodus of people climbing the sides of the mountains in the tens of thousands is like a dance to the heavens. The cars can barely get by. Wild Card cannot stop staring at the faces, all the faces struggling to get to the top. He shrugs. He notices the children especially, the pain in their faces, their bare feet bleeding. He sees the hunger and the hopes of millions. Edvard Grieg still stands at the top raising his hands toward the sky. Wild Card is now in the Hall of the Mountain King. The strings are chopping away in rhythm, the horns blowing in syncopation. Wild Will Shakespeare is there. He is wowing the crowd with a new rendition of "Hamlet" entitled *Claudius: Man, Myth or Chinaman?* Nietzsche sits by reinvestigating his postulates on man while a lit cigarette dangles from the cracked lips of Hank Chinaski as he smiles at the madness.

"Wait a second!" screams one of the ghostwriters. "Is Chinaski dead yet?" No one responds.

Chinaski is carrying a ham and cheese sandwich in his right hand and holding a beer in the other. A choir of doves rises and falls like they are puppets on a string. Wild Card gets to the top of the mountain. There is a line five thousand people wide crammed together, waiting to be carried up into the funnel of light.

Wild Card sneaks around the side where the road ends and scales the side of the hill. At times, the way is very narrow as its drops down toward the sea. Much of the haze has lifted, except in the distance where it was still very substantial. Battleships sit in a row in the South Sea behind the thick-as-pea-soup fog. The radar devices are spinning wildly atop each battleship. Down on the seaside piers, fights are breaking out like wildfires in Florida during dry season. Lorca and Hemingway are exchanging blows and verse—Hem decks Lorca easily at 5 o'clock. Faulkner takes a swing at Brodsky while Elytis laughs madly at his bleeding fingertips. Henrik Ibsen is furious at how much attention Grieg is getting with no homage being paid to the writer of the play that the *Suite* was based upon. Van Gogh is mocking the ability to "hear" as no sounds are attainable except those escaping the wild brawls from dead artists, and nothing else rises above the visible notes from the *Peer Gynt Suite.*

The Master Kong, Confucius, can be seen hovering above the mountain top, smiling as he drifts in and out of focus. Not everyone can see him as one had to look very carefully to spot him, and most simply never looked up as humans mostly only look down. His words and thoughts are still revered by billions of people. The light passes through him like water through an aqueduct. There is a cry like nothing ever heard, a lament for the departed channeled through millions of voices simultaneously.

Wild Card closes his eyes, and for once, he imagines himself to be a man of importance, a tool in the hands of God. He reopens his eyes only to see himself back in Joe Bananas staring down at the drunken sailor. He begins to weep. For once in his bizarre and miserable life, he has found something of meaning. Zhu Zen's words glisten like snowflakes falling on the Arctic tundra in the brightest sun in his mind: "You will be a wanted man."

He thinks to himself, "Damn, I better get out of the Kong before they get me." He has no idea why they would want him in the first place, but he knows he must flee. He calls the airline and books an earlier flight back to Boston. He wants to go home. He wants to see his wife and his daughter and their chin, and he wants his mommy and daddy. He stands before the entrance to the main terminal at Kai Tak airport reading a sign about the plans to build a new International Airport on a soon-to-be reclaimed island. The sign reads:

Chek Lap Kok International Airport

Construction to begin in 1992

Make Hong Kong your destination and make Chek Lap Kok your return from The Arabian Dance.

"What in the hell?" Deej shakes his head to make sure he read the sign correctly. "I wonder who this Chek Lap guy is—must have been a Chinese porn star. They actually named an airport after his dick. WOW! Now he must be

GOOD!" Wild Card imagines all the people Mr. Lap must have had sex with. "DAMN! I wonder if he plays golf," he murmurs as he begins humming a song from his childhood softly through his excited lips while practicing his golf swing.

Act 15.

Mucho Mengele

It can be said that crimes of the mind and crimes against humanity are much different than crimes of passion and of the heart. It can be said that, in this era of information, we are becoming increasingly aware of other people's actions, and we know immediately, not minutes let alone days or years after. Moreover, judgment is passed immediately. It can be said that perpetrators of crimes in previous times are slightly innocent because they were not fully aware of the extent of their trespass. Actively permitting the pacification of this kind of thoughtless man in the face of the recurring disturbing occurrences of human history is an acknowledgment that modern man is no different than those who have come before him, and yet, humankind seeks to expunge this type of thinking. At least some do thus seek to expunge this type of thinking, those who have thought about it anyway.

And crimes, both known and unsolved, big and small have been studied forward and backward, inside and out, and it has been determined that crimes are an intense alchemic mix of terribly reckless behavior, a little bit of bright sunshine, a mockery of rational thought, and poisons of all shapes and sizes, volumes and imaginations—all shaken together in a tall crystal glass for everyone to see, and the result poured slowly over a canal of glaciers found rippling gently along the currents of the oceans.

Take the case of a one Josef Mengele, a man, if he can be called this, guilty of the highest crimes of humanity, his so-called experiments on human beings for the sake of his so-called science. But like most perpetrators, even of the highest degree, he skates away on the thin ice of mankind's shaded future, with moments of being browsed upon by the masses. There are a few individuals in the crowd who would die to crush these monsters, lurking behind old typewriters and canvasses and violins and podiums and keyboards and movie screens. They close their eyes in the sunlight and feel the warmth massage their eyelids. No one else dares fight these monsters among us. They are the keepers of light. They are also partly stubborn, partly ignorant and partly insane before they awaken to discover the true discourse of their undertakings. However, by then, it is too late. It is their life's mission. And they follow this mission with bravado and a greater sense of inner strength, one that is understood only by those who see the truth of existence, whatever form it takes in that volume of space called home.

One of the keepers of the light is not Winchester Buckley Johnson, nor his alter egos, Little Diarrhea, WB, Deej, B or Wild Card. This is a man of no cares and no hopes for humanity. His only concerns are for his wallet, his decreasing ego, and his sense of self-righteousness, which is usually quite wrong, and his templates of delirium and anxiety, which coexist with his motivation: Pure greed, in short.

For the first time in months, Winchester makes it back to Boston to report his findings to his boss. He was supposed to be doing some deals, conducting business, and if not conducting actual transactions, at least setting up future transactions by creating trust between himself and his contacts. The Chairman of his fine organization, one fine man indeed, brings Deej to his special office to associatively and indirectly remove the findings from

Deej's memory. Diarrhea walks into the fine ornament disguised as an office, the furniture mahogany and teak, the walls adorned with original artwork by masters Klimt and Miro. It can be said that the office itself is worth more than the company, but money was never a problem for the Chairman. He has lots of it and knows where to keep it. He also uses men like Deej as pawns in a larger game, a game of humor and disgust. As Deej regains his sense of space, he sees a picture on the wall of the Chairman and Kra posing before a trophy-sized black marlin. Deej's stomach is thrown into an upheaval and he beelines for the Chairman's private spa, apologizing vehemently to one of the Chairman's bodyguards on the way as he leaves a small trail of brownish colored liquid strewn across the marble floor.

Outside, the voices are muffled but there is clearly more than one. Deej wonders if the Chairman uses the same stockbroker as he, Pops. His feeble attempt to spy is destroyed by the sounds he is making in the bathroom, but his fears are quickly confirmed that this might not be a broker call. He clearly hears the Chairman use the name Kra, and he hears this as though it were the only sound in the world, as if the words were being spoken directly to him. Deej thinks to himself that he is truly afraid of Mr. Infinite by now and that he is no different than many before him. What he does not realize is how truly frightened Mr. Infinite is of himself. Kra cannot comprehend his own role in this life, and so he seeks out the extent of that role, firmly and assertively, as he is engaged in his parallel quest.

Flashback: When Kra was in prison in the late 1960s for possession of LSD, he met the person who might possibly be the single most influential of his life, a man with only one name: Zim. Zim was imprisoned for multiple crimes against humanity. He was a sex offender of all kinds—he raped children and adults alike and both men and women. He embezzled money from the bank he was a security guard for, and he ran guns and drugs to Nicaragua before the CIB ever did and well before the notion became a serious pop-culture phenomena. Zim was a man feared by most, feared by everyone in fact except Kra. Kra was too busy "tripping out" to know where he was or who he was with, but Zim had never quite met anyone like Kra either, a man at the ripe age of 44 who seemed to fear nothing. Zim did not want to recklessly destroy this man's body for sexual gratification. He wanted to talk to him and learn from him. Everyone else who had come into contact with Zim was petrified upon initial contact. He simply had that way about him. But Kra saw images come and go like phantoms of some mastermind's imagination and he failed to comprehend the monster that was Zim. Or at least this is how it appeared. Of course, nothing in life is ever truly how it appears, except for the few who have experienced a singular moment of true clarity, and for most experiencing such bliss or torment, the enhanced perceptions resulting from such singular moments tend not to last too long.

In the case of Zim, monstrous acts were what he lived for, and the basic fact that Kra seemed to accept him was enough to inspire Zim to take him into his world and show him a way of existence like few others have seen. The one and only Dr. Josef Mengele was Zim's instructor in philosophy. Although, he only met Mengele very briefly at the Alvear Palace Hotel in Buenos Aires' famed Recoleta neighborhood, after Mengele fled Germany for Argentina, this moment would assist in changing the course of civilization. In a parallel study, it is clearly obvious that all moments assist in the movement of civilization, yet only a few recognizable root moments dictate the change in flow. This was clearly one of the latter.

It was in Argentina and in Brasil that Mengele was able to keep up his harmonization with evil by trading secrets of his medical findings with others hot on the trail of having some "biblical significance" in the way of Mengele's boss, Hitler. Zim, being from Buenos Aires, met Mengele one morning when Zim was a young man and overheard Mengele on the telephone. Zim was waiting for his best friend Diego to return to Buenos Aires from a trip to Patagonia with his parents. This great hotel is an exciting meeting place and an even better place to watch people, and Zim and Diego always spent time there, hanging out, watching people, and laughing like the children they were. Zim approached Mengele and asked him for the time, as any child would, out of curiosity. Mengele looked downward, and what happened next would change Zim's life forever.

Mengele was not a terribly fierce character to behold. In fact, he was, relatively speaking, sort of weak looking— until one peered into his eyes. It was only then that something significant that existed in his mind became extremely apparent, and this significance happened to be of a destructive nature. He was hell-bent on proving that men and women from other races and cultures and histories had less-powerful genes than he did, a notion that he held bone-deep until the moment he died, when, actually, his spirit turned to a vaporous gas that emitted a nasty odor for months. Little Zim peered carefully into Mengele's eyes and was raped of all his senses.

"Do not bother men of importance. If you want to know what time it is, go to Auschwitz."

Zim later became one of the most notorious criminals in South Florida. When Kra reached his 44th birthday, the FBI busted down the door in his friend's Key Largo estate thinking he and his friends were trafficking marijuana against the ordinances of the US Congress. In fact, Kra and his friends were committing the most disturbing of criminal acts known to mankind at the time, dropping acid while listening to the Beatles on vinyl and having a naked pool party. All the partiers were naked that is except Kra, who was very modest about his body and therefore refused to strip in front of anyone. The FBI was a little embarrassed, and for publicity reasons, they arrested Kra anyway and sent him to prison. Kra had no defense as he was so tripped out on acid that he told the judge, "Whatever you do, man, don't let the acid rain on your justice parade." The judge, being a man of courage, immediately sent this perpetrator behind bars.

It was then that Kra learned of his own quest for secret knowledge and one in which time was of the essence. Kra's real name was Robert Kragon, or at least we think it is. There is more research going on at this moment to clarify this fact. But Kra retained his new name because Zim told him that Kra was a biblical name and that Dr. Mengele would have wanted him to change his name in that instance. Robert, not having much of a handle on current events, surmised that Dr. Mengele was a man similar to a Dr. King, who he had heard about in the news. So Robert became Kra. And in a wildly hypnotic night of blotter acid and, loosely characterized, meditation, Kra stared helplessly into the abyss, the void, the end of the tunnel. And when he awoke from his subconscious state, he told Zim that he feared the end of life, although he had discovered there was more lurking behind the curtain: "It's like I fear the Infinite."

Zim aptly sent him on his way—Kra Fere Infinite—to find the keepers of secrets and report them to him, and Kra went happily for Zim was a chosen man. Kra knew it and Kra dedicated himself wholly to Zim's quest. Zim gave Kra complete access to his bank account and told him to use all the money he needed to spend his life finding the secrets of the chosen ones because Zim was going to gather these secrets in a diary and make them a Neo-Testament wherein everything goes, wherein there are no rules or commandments or conscience. There is only chaos. And although Zim would never be released from prison, he would be the purveyor of this new way. And it would be called Zimmydom.

And so Kra continues finding his way into the most influential of people's lives: going fishing with them, golfing, elbow-nudging, art gallery hopping, museum tracking, island bopping, dancing, feeding, swimming, and so on. He is being used ceremoniously as a pawn in a game, and he is completely aware of this fact. Zim receives frequent updates from Kra, however Kra has grown quite beyond Zim in secrets-gathering techniques, and the actual information Kra has received, albeit none of this has been from Deej, is enabling Kra to build a case of his own, a case to prove that he can become someone important.

Helen Keller is informing us that we are way off base about Kra, and she will not say any more about it. She informed the ghostwriters that they should stop looking with their eyes and begin looking with their brains, and then maybe the truth will come like light emerging from the shadows in a cave.

As most of us already know, Deej has nothing particular about his character or personality to offer humanity. It can be said that he who does nothing but shout obscenities and unforgivingly condescends to others with luminescent clarity followed his instincts to the corners of the earth, which tricked Mr. Infinite. This is important. Infinity waits for nobody and often follows everybody, sometimes in circles. Even those who speak loudly and say very little cannot hold up the infinite, although they may continue trying to stop time.

Zimmydom would eventually catch on. His disciples are seen everywhere: Oklahoma City, Afghanistan, Tokyo, Tanzania, Sana'a, Panama City, etc. The word *chaos* has become popularized through the movement upstream by the underground countercultures and is sold in bookstores and music stores and used in conversation between mere acquaintances. Friends, lovers, drugs, relative stupidity and bravado quickly push those teetering on the edge between organized reform and full-blown rebellion against any perceived establishment toward chaos. Zimmydom is not known as Zimmydom, but it is assuredly known as evil. Evil has many faces, some of which actually hide goodness. Imagine for a moment one thought of goodness amongst a fire of hate. The good must keep up the mask to survive until the mask is sufficiently unnecessary. And, similarly, imagine a good deed amongst men of evil. The deed must be concealed, for if an evil man's good deed becomes public knowledge, he is no longer part of the inner circle.

Frank Carboni of Brooklyn, New York, known to his friends and associates as Frankie Gold Tooth Carboni, is a perfectly workable analogy to represent the need to conceal one's identity on numerous levels. His two upper front teeth were solid gold, a present from Tony "the Overripe" Marinara after a mistaken identity dispute relating to a billiards game. Tony used his favorite pair of brass knuckles as dental floss in Frankie's grandmother's dining room during a traditional Sunday dinner with La Famiglia Carboni all present. Tony, of course, being a good boy in the neighborhood, apologized to Frankie after learning he was not to blame for his brother's loss of $500 to a pool shark who had come to the neighborhood seeking his fortune ripping off the locals in their pool halls. The shark, aptly named for the tattoo on his back of "Doc," from the television dramatic comedy series known as "The Loveboat," spearing a fish, took Tony's younger brother Louie for the cash. The shark quickly disappeared but he resembled Frankie, at least his face did for no one ever saw what Frankie looked like without his shirt off, and Tony had to take revenge on *someone*—Frankie was the logical choice. Frankie showed Tony his shirtless torso with no ink stamps and the apology came in the form of two solid gold teeth and the cost of the dental surgery.

Tony makes his money trading currencies in the Asian Currency markets. From his tiny apartment in Brooklyn, he makes more money in one night than his grandfather who smuggled olive oil from Sicily to Middletown, Connecticut did in 20 years. But Tony's goombahs cannot know what he does for a living, for anything that does not involve the physical assertion of his will is simply not "cool," not "hip." And any kind of intellectual enterprise would alienate Tony in a way that he is ill prepared for. Unfortunately for Frankie, he did cross one of Tony's cousins by accident, stepping in front of him in line at a local delicatessen, and this cousin happens to be connected to some very important people. As a show of his machismo, Tony removed one of Frankie's gold teeth with a pair of rusty pliers as revenge. And in order to keep his identity concealed, Frankie just took the pain. So now Frankie is known as Gold Tooth instead of Teeth.

But this portrayal has another side to it. Frankie is not just an ordinary neighborhood boy. He is a foot soldier for the CIB as an intelligence gatherer. Frankie spends most of his time making links between people of relevance and people in the organized crime racket. He knows that Tony's stockbroker happens also to be Pops, but Tony is not directly acquainted with either Winchester or the Chairman, for Pops has countless clients. Frankie knows this and is still trying to make some kind of a connection between them. His cover is so well masked that even his superiors do not know who he actually is.

Frankie's ardent mission: To determine the root cause of chaos in order to protect his nation from it, or at least, to protect the federal government from it. Frankie spends his evenings in the neighborhood in Brooklyn. The precise location will remain anonymous for purposes of his family's safety. But during the business day, Frankie puts on a different face and spends all day on Wall Street. No one seems to know much about him, only that he is well suited and well mannered and that he does a good job of sharing profitable information. What they do not know is that he is serving another purpose: that of the Bureau of Intelligence. It has been hypothesized by some of the CIB's higher-ups, key-people, and people in the know that the whole Wall Street franchise is a cover for big money lobbyists looking to disenfranchise the government by convincing everyone to stop paying taxes. The members of the CIB with true power, of course, stay out of this debate.

The CIB sent in Frankie to find out if there was any truth to these speculations, but Frankie has been on this circuit for five years and all he has discovered is that people on Wall Street like to make money and they like to flaunt it by spending it. He still has not found that man beneath the covers pulling all the strings. Perhaps he is not looking in the right places.

So Frankie masks his intentions by associating with his coworkers on a friendly level, and they do not mind. He's from Brooklyn. He has a degree from Hunter College and he's made it big. They're all from Harvard, Yellow, Princeton, Brown, NYU, Columbia, Stanford, Penn, Wesleyan, Williams and Amherst, oh and according to a whining Hawthorne, also from Bowdoin. They all consider themselves humanitarians, and accepting Frankie into their clique is their gift to society. This alleviates any guilt they might feel regarding their collective greed and provides a modicum of humor between the office walls.

The case of Frankie Gold Tooth Carboni has relevance of a different nature as well, relevance directly relating to the rise and fall of Zimmydom. Zim has a son, Jim. Jim also works on Wall Street. Jim is the one who made all the money for Zim, and hell, he did make a LOT of money in the junk bond market. Jim is a dedicated son, raised by his single mother in Tuscaloosa, Alabama after she fled Miami once Zim's antics spun wildly out of control. She raised Jim to be loyal to his family and lied to him about why his father was in prison. People in Alabama did not know much about Zim, as his identity, at the time, was kept hush-hush in the media because the CIB feared the rise of Zimmydom. So Jim thought good ol' dad was behind bars for tax evasion, and he being economically minded and somewhat rebellious, cherished good ol' dad for that. So after playing football for the Crimson Tide, he went to Yellow to receive his Economic Doctorate. Once in the exclusive company of men in cliques, he would never return to Tuscaloosa. He sent his mom money and secretly set up an account for his dad. His father's monstrous acts remained a secret to Jim for many years, until one day, he met the woman of his dreams who happened to be the daughter of one of his father's many rape victims. Jim learned the truth during a period of courtship, and although she was his half-sister, he still married her out of pity but kept her true identity and sad past concealed from the men in the clique. Jim and his wife have three lovely, healthy children and they live in the Upper East Side of Manhattan. Only their eldest son shows any signs of having been produced by half-siblings, a strange growth on his left femur.

Immediately, Jim stopped sending funds to his dad's bank account and sought to have the funds removed by court order, but Kra had already begun working for Zim and had drained the funds before Jim could take them back. Now, Kra who has learned that Jim is a hotshot at J.P. Noonans, the big investment firm, coddles Jim. He follows him around from time to time, showing up at the same parties, kisses his ass at functions and events, and even has a spare key to Jim's beach house in the Hamptons. Kra does not know how Jim relates to Zim, and Frankie has been spying on Jim for quite a while. Kra and Frankie have actually had coffee together in Drunkin' Donuts in Brooklyn recently. Frankie has not yet uncovered the true link between Kra, Jim, Zim and Mengele. But he is certain one exists and is still searching.

It now seems that the metamorphosing story is a vulgar attempt to arrange a geometrical relationship between human experimentation, drug usage, secrecy, physical violence, big money, fear and infinity, but this simply is not the case. Everyone connected here, with the sole exception of Zim, just went home, lit up a big fat cigar, drank some bourbon, put on the golf highlights and went to sleep. Zim simply went to sleep, and of course, Mengele is only a vaporous memory.

Act 16.

Back Bay Freedom Fighter:
Atop the Tower of Truth An Icon is Born

It became very apparent to Deej, squatting in the Chairman's private office spa, that to make the slip once and for all from Kra and everyone else who seems to be chasing him, his actions need to be more carefully thought out. His running has truly led him nowhere, and now is the time to make a more difficult decision, one that might lead him directly into the heart of danger, or might lead him completely out of harm's way. For in this moment, it is clear to him that his life is no longer light and without at least some rudimentary understanding of consequence. While he remains almost completely disconnected from the overall idea of cause and effect, he very faintly senses that the notion of consequence is indeed real. It is becoming apparent that, without the frequent resolve of his physical needs, he would be no different than most. If he were to keep his mouth closed, on both ends, he wonders while sitting in an Italian marble decorated toilet room in the Chairman's private spa, if he might be a less easy target.

This is the day that he decided to confront danger. This is the day that he decided to take his life into his own hands and, no matter the consequences, be brave enough to make this step. He would not run any more, at least not now. He was no longer afraid of what he was to discover.

Emerging from the private spa with the Chairman's half used bar of soap hanging out from the pocket of his pants, he marched briskly to the Chairman and took the telephone from his hand. With an air of authority, he made his demands. "Kra, I know you're there. Why don't you come out of hiding so we can have a nice three-way chat."

"Wild Card?"

"ZZ?"

"Wild Card, listen, I have some unfinished business with the Chairman. Do you mind giving him the phone back?"

"Uh, sure."

Wild Card makes his way right back into the Chairman's private spa. His stunned physical state has overwhelmed any ability to think. He turns the heat on in the sauna, removes his clothing, and gets in. His body temperature really heats up while he bends forward crying profusely. His own spiritual guide is now on the side of the enemy. What can he do? He is completely lost and now feels alone and isolated. He looks up to see the Chairman, Kra, and ZZ all standing in the small window of the sauna's redwood door. He blacks out.

He awakens stretched out on the Chairman's modern Italian black leather sofa. It has the form of a giant U, and the track lighting on the walls shine off the stainless steel feet giving the impression of streaks of light on the pinkish-blue marble flooring. Wild Card looks down to see his own reflection in the shiny floor and sees pockets of burnt skin hanging from his face. He is wearing the Chairman's white Garden of Eden Flock Hotel robe, and he now feels the blisters all over his body from overexposure in the sauna's intense heat. He hears more sounds coming from behind the Chairman's private office. Focusing in on the sounds, he hears several voices.

As the door to the Chairman's office opens slowly, Wild Card's perception of time completely slows to a halt. His heart beats low and deep like a bass drum, and his vision is slightly blurred from the ringing in his ears as Gerald walks slowly from the office door toward Wild Card. The Chairman, Kra and ZZ are standing behind him, and now, he thinks, that he has misunderstood his entire existence. He quickly assesses the situation: "Could it be the drugs? Could it be my upbringing? Could it be my brother, the idiot, always wanting what I have? Is it the way I treated my wife? Maybe it is that damned kid in a jar. I am so very, very wrong about everything."

"My son, please sit up. We need to talk."

"Yes, Dad, we do. I am so confused. What in God's name is going on here? I simply do not understand."

"Well, you have undergone your most difficult exam. Since this is the only exam you actually took on your own merit, I have to give you some credit. We never thought you would make it all the way through."

"My own merit? I have been chased and I have been tricked and fooled and spied on and laughed at. I don't know who I am or where I have been or if I am dreaming or if I am even alive. I converse with the deceased. I hear voices when clearly no one is around. My wife loves me but took off with Jener only to come back and adopt a chin in a jar. My son is a special forces tactician at age 7, yes tactician, and my new best friend, BS, wants to hire me for some construction company somewhere in the desert that he plans on taking over after he abandons his seat in the House of Representatives. Dad, please help me."

"BS already talked to you about the construction project? I better have a word with him later. You are helping yourself just fine. Are you ready to get into the public eye? Do you think you have experienced enough to handle yourself properly under daily scrutiny? We really need you, Little Diarrhea, to be more like Wild Card and less like Deej. Can you do this? Can you live up to the task?"

"Dad, I do not know what you are talking about. Don't tell me that you want me to be the Governor of California."

"Close. You will govern the state of Texas. California is for someone else."

"Me? Really? Why Texas? Oh, I don't know."

"Well, I have my reasons. Just tell me if you think you can handle it. We will get it done. Until then, I have another venture for you, one that will make you some good money, not this million here and million there nonsense."

Gerald turns to look at ZZ, who is whispering something in the Chairman's ear, and motions for them to leave. Deej notices that Kra is now wearing a gray and white woman's business suit. ZZ and the Chairman disappear from view. Deej farts in fear. Kra approaches and sits down on Deej's right. He places his left hand on his right knee and slowly guides his hand up to Deej's genitals. Just before reaching, he looks him square in the eye and then grabs his testicles, squeezing them tightly. The pain goes right to Deej's stomach and all the blood drops from his face. Just before he passes out, he releases his hand as Deej blows out a gasp of air. The amount of air he released was enough to fill a hot air balloon. He looks back at the Chairman, who reenters his office and closes the door. Gerald lifts Deej off the floor. "That was your final test. We call it the 'Riding of the Gods into Valhalla.'" Wagner cheers and pours a stein full of Wall's homebrewed hefeweizen.

"You are now ready for your public career," Gerald states as Kra removes his mask and costume, and Deej realizes that it is his mother, Betty, who lurks behind the shadowy wall that formed quickly in Deej's mind. Sophocles arises briskly from a prolonged slumber and begins doing cartwheels all over Wall. He receives appropriate congratulatory gestures from everyone for making the right call except a disgusted Joseph Conrad who contends that it has been a Heart of Darkness that has led the cast to this point.

The shriek that escaped Deej's lips would have shattered windows had the glass not been one inch thick in the Chairman's office. This was far too much for him to handle, that Kra was really his mother. He leaves a pile of waste on the floor like the effluvia from a very sick elephant.

"But she spoke Chinese?" Memories have a way of concealing true fear, as he clearly does not remember having sexual relations with her in this moment.

"We weren't sure how prepared you were for real pain, tragedies, and fear. Look son, we needed you to understand how difficult this task is."

"You're in on this too, Mom?"

She laughs. "In on this? Who do you think orchestrated this whole traumatic comedy? Do you think it was your father? Yes, he can tie his shoes okay, but you think that he's the one capable of such a brainchild as this theatrical event? C'MON! I thought you had more sense than that."

"Wow, Mom, I really should have known. All the trailer park activities, the chin in a jar, the anthill on Victoria's Peak, the room full of Chinamen in Colorado Springs— you did that! Wow, I am impressed!"

Betty and Gerald look at each other in alarm, and suddenly, Deej's stomach turns in knots. He realizes that they had absolutely no idea whatsoever about the moments of divine significance he mentioned. This is when the fear came back, and this is why it would stay. The moist smell of fear sweetened the air with its pungent inclusion. Early explorers seeking to discover new lands never encountered smells such as this. It was simply unnatural. Deej's guard is let down for an instant, and in this instant, his fear is greater than all the fear that he ever felt combined. Without time to consider further consequences of his newfound knowledge, he jumps up and runs down the hall to the staircase leading to the main floor of the edifice. His robe is half open, his blisters are open and bleeding from his burns, and his mind is racing in a thousand directions. His mind screams at him to imbibe an entire bottle of single malt scotch, his body to score some nose candy, and his feet tell him to just run, run away as far as he can go, and with some luck, all of this will simply vanish.

So he runs and runs, all the way from his Kendall Square office building in Cambridge and across the Longfellow Bridge toward the heart of the Back Bay of Boston. A news helicopter spots him from above and broadcasts this live on the midday local news. The camera pans in closely. The determination on his face is unlike anything the news reporters have ever seen, which makes the need to follow his journey paramount. He darts onto Charles Street, running through the backside of Beacon Hill, through the Boston Commons, past the George Washington monument to the center of Commonwealth Avenue, the dog mall, and then he takes a left onto Clarendon Street and runs past Newbury and Boylston Streets right to the John Hancock building. He is dripping with sweat and tears, and his bare feet are bleeding profusely. A land-based news crew having lunch in Skipjack's restaurant just around the corner is summoned to pick up this story immediately. The producer gets stuck paying the bill while the reporter and cameraman lunge for the door and bust out toward the John Hancock.

Deej finds the roof access and climbs out to a ledge. He stands atop the ledge, the wind blowing violently, and loses his balance a couple of times, but he catches himself. A calming of the wind is accompanied by the parting of the low clouds to reveal a bright sun. Just to the east of the sun, Venus is almost visible to the naked eye, and Winchester can hear more passages from Holst's "The Planets," specifically "Venus, the Bringer of Peace."

Back in the trailer park, Mozart is whining. "Any number of my symphonies could have been heard here! Holst has TWO looks already! *Dieses ist nicht angemessen!*"

The real ZZ assures Wolfgang that his moment is coming shortly.

The news crew climbs atop the roof and captures Winchester Buckley Johnson, the son of the Vice President of the United States and ex-Director of the CIA and current Director of the CIB—however they do not know this is the man before them due to his horrifically mutilated skin—in a robe, suicidal, about to jump. Suddenly, without warning, without premeditation, a seemingly lost very young white tailed kite falls from the sky right into Winchester's hand. The bird appears to have been wounded by air turbulence from a low flying plane. Deej's heart stops for a moment, and this moment of heroic beauty is captured surreptitiously on film. He climbs down from the ledge and looks at the bird's features, its brown head, back and nape, its slightly broken wing lying limp in his hand. He looks into its grayish white face to see the eyes, as the injured bird is squeezing its little eyes shut as if in extreme pain. He looks directly at the camera and screams, "Is this what you want from me! Is this it? Am I supposed to save all the injured and help them fly again? Help them find freedom? Am I supposed to take the dispossessed and give them back a safe place to live? Fine, I will do it."

The cameraman drops the camera down by his side in emotional flux. The reporter, a woman of Arabic-American descent in her mid-thirties, senses the poetry of the moment and she looks to the sun as tears roll gently down her countenance. As he walks to the doorway, he viciously throws the bird down to the concrete on the rooftop. Its little head makes a sound like the commonly expressed word "splat." The cameraman and reporter didn't see this less than sympathetic gesture—the injured bird being hurled to the ground like shares of a bankrupted airline stock due to unruly rising oil prices—and later that night they report his heroics on the news. Prior to the live local report, which went national, the news team was given a "tip" from the Network's Vice Chairman. The benevolent Winchester Buckley Johnson, the world's next icon in training, was in the Copley Plaza Hotel giving a speech on combating poverty in East and Central Africa when he was given a sign from above that he needed to save the broken winged lost bird and set it free, give it back its flight. The facts were never checked and the resulting report sent Winchester's hopeful idyllic future into the approaching tornados.

Soon, billboards all over Boston, New York, Chicago, Los Angeles, Houston, Philadelphia, Miami, Wall, South Dakota and many other cities displayed a giant image of slightly blurred Winchester holding the broken-winged bird as tears rolled down his face with his robe half-open, his eyes squinting in the sunlight atop the modern edifice, the tallest building in New England. The photograph captured perfectly the way the light was reflecting off his blistered skin like a war hero coming home from the front. His bravado would serve him perfectly as the newly discovered savior of the wounded and weak and lost. He would soon rise up to give greater promises to the idea of freedom, promises that would surely end more gracefully than the lost white tailed kite on that poetically just Boston afternoon.

Gerald's private jet takes off from the Air Force base in nearby Bedford. He calls a meeting of his closest friends and allies in Congress as well as the top CIB officials and those in military intelligence.

"It is time to place him in the next level," he informs all in a conference call. "It is time to make him a managing partner in a major organization. He has some decent press coverage at the moment, and we *have* to run with this. We have few choices left. We need to see how he really handles himself under serious pressure in the media spotlight.

"What type of organization?" replies Judge Louis Bangkok Webster, acting CIA Director and Deputy Director of the CIB. "Some of the boys are concerned about his willpower."

"I have some friends ready to buy a baseball franchise. If we make him managing director, he can profit from it and we will all get a cut. He can remain as director for as long as I want him to. And his will power his very little to do with anything. I tell him what to do."

"Does he know anything about baseball?"

"Does he have to?"

"Which franchise?"

"His old favorite, the Texas Air National Guard Special Forces Rangers."

"You sure we can get a cut."

"Are you sure that I just did not decide to cut you out of the picture."

"I hear you. We'll get everything prepared."

"You don't have to do anything except coordinate this properly across all channels, especially with the FCC. I am owed a couple of favors, but we'll have to keep the whole deal under wraps. We're going to make a killing on this. I'll be there at 2200 Zulu."

Act 17.

The National Pastime: Deciding Things Over A Round in the Desert

After a six-month long tour of duty, Winchester Buckley Johnson is exhausted. He has been kissing babies, coddling immigrants, and helping the homeless find shelter all over the continental United States. His wrist has gone limp and his fingers are in constant pain from signing so many autographs. A New York newspaper's front-page article showed him in his Yellow University days at a fraternity party drinking a funnel of beer. The article entitled *Once a Man of Drunkenness, Now a Man of Greatness* comically portrayed the "Great" Winchester Buckley Johnson as the new savior of the human race. In a National Pubic Radio commentary, thus renamed for the numerous uncovered sex scandals from the 1970s, an acclaimed writer who will go unnamed stated that, although men and women alike must rise above their weaknesses and vices, making this man an icon was "simply ludicrous." The writer was later whisked away from a candlelit dinner in his Manhattan apartment with his wife, detained for some time, and sent to Angola "on assignment." Unfortunately, not many readers understood the breadth of his message, for if they did, perhaps what would later become a very sad and sinister course of events may have been avoided, or maybe not. The jury is still in deliberation as regards this question, as the readers of said New York newspaper are a minority of the population at large. The Great Winchester Buckley's face is selling on T-shirts, he is being idolized on popular daytime television talk shows, and local networks paste his face nightly on their "around the nation" news reports. He was invited to the Waldorf Astoria in Manhattan to give a speech on displaced refugees in the tundra of Southwestern Asia. He was a no show.

"Johnnie, I am so tired of this politicking. I just want a drink. Just a taste of the scotch."

"Winchester, I have told you over and over again that I will not watch you piss your life down a toilet. You have come so far, my baby, so far. Don't forget where you came from. Now hang up your expensive cellular telephone and get on that airplane to Tucson. I have you set to give a speech at the University of Arizona on the freedom and future of flightless birds."

"That's right, I do have an expensive cellular telephone! But Johnnie, I don't know anything about flightless birds."

"Just read the cards and leave. You don't have to answer any questions."

"But Johnnie..."

"Shut up and stop being such a pussy. Do you want me to call Bob Reed?"

"NO!"

Winchester was met by Broken Stream in Tucson. BS was sent by Gerald to give WBJ some words of encouragement. The autograph signing was simply overwhelming him, and there was a growing fear amongst the power elite that Winchester just might not be the right man for the job after all. Gerald, wholly unconvinced of this, was not ready to give in to the negative attacks against his son.

BS agreed to take the reigns of this wild horse. "Gerald, I can take care of this, don't worry."

"Ricky, if you don't shape him up, I will kick your ass back to Idaho."

"Sir, I am Broken Stream now."

"Shut the fuck up or I'll have you removed from the Gold House and sent to Venezuela to serve the revolution we have brewing down there."

"Yes sir."

The University of Arizona lecture had the makings of a phenomenally successful stop on the tour. The fourteen lifetime members of the University's Flightless Bird Society were there. Unfortunately, a pep-rally for the school's nationally competitive men's basketball team in the auditorium near to the courtyard where Winchester was to speak was filled to capacity and the cheering in unison by the school's happy faithful drowned out any hopes for Winchester's attempt to read his cue cards. He had been studying with a real reading professor, and this was a huge step for him. Winchester was very upset by this, but mostly, he was tremendously disappointed by the pep rally. He used to be a cheerleader at Yellow University for the women's intramural tennis squad, and he slipped into momentary euphoria remembering his days with fellow Yellow University Pitbull students. The post-match tea parties and the late night cocaine fests with the men's diving team and the intramural women's rowing team were moments of his life he would never forget, and now, being back in a university setting, these memories came flooding back. He was booed and jeered by the flightless bird people as he stopped reading and walked away from the courtyard half smiling, half crying. He turned to them and cried out, "Go Pitbulls!" as tears rolled down his swollen eye sockets.

BS arrives in Tucson to meet Winchester at the historic Arizona Inn. This is a brief get-together with the real meeting to take place on the links, at the TPC at Starr Pass, a well-regarded golf course in the Southwestern US. There is a third man to be present at the meeting, however, neither BS nor Winchester have met this man personally, though both know of him through acquaintances, business partners, and his dealings with Gerald.

A waiter is carrying two glasses and a carafe of orange juice to an isolated table in the Inn's restaurant. The eunuchs surround the perimeter of the hotel to ensure no one unexpected gets through. BS is explaining to Winchester why the autograph signing tour is so important as the waiter pours a glass of fresh bright orange juice for both of them. The waiter glances at Winchester, who has his right hand shoved into his pants and is fondling his genitalia. He subtly laughs and walks away.

"Do you have a problem, you faggot?" Diarrhea blares after the waiter, who turns around and shakes his head, half in wonder, half in disgust.

"Everyone is becoming familiar with your face."

"BS, I know this. I am not an idiot you know."

"Well, anyway, the next step is an important one. Your public image is as important as what you eat for breakfast. Speaking of breakfast, I was made aware that ex-NASA geochemists are working on a special filtering device that will turn your unexpected discarded waste into solids that appear to be rocks. All you will need to do is shake leg and all of your waste will fall from your pants on the floor as rocks."

"Wow! So, I can stop worrying about letting it go, just, basically, let her rip!"

"That's what I am saying, but until then, please do your best to keep your bowel composure, especially around our guest on the golf course. And, please, we are really gunning to get the support of the homosexual community for the next election. If you continue to behave like that, we'll never get that vote."

"Yeah, sure, whatever. Those damned chinks, niggers, Palestinians, faggots—who needs them anyway? Listen BS, I am really, really hungry. Do you mind if I take a bite of your sausage. Thanks."

"Palestinians? I didn't even know that you knew what a Palestinian is," says a bewildered BS as Winchester inhales the breakfast sausage with his nose without the aid of utensils.

With the sausage half-lodged in his nose, he responds succinctly, "Yeah they're towel-headed Jews, right? Hate them too."

BS stares at Winchester as though he were being tortured. Before Broken Stream's eyes, Winchester's wardrobe suddenly changes. A long red robe with a white collar adorns his body, and he wears a black knitted skullcap and his face appears somewhat pinched. He motions with his right hand to one of his eunuchs, who picks up BS and slings him over his shoulder to carry him from the table to a door opposite the front door of the dining area. BS is then carried down the dark staircase by several of Winchester's eunuchs, who are now dressed as medieval executioners in dark cloaks and badly stitched cloth masks with uneven cutouts for the eyes, nose and mouth, like one would see in a bad horror movie. Gerald stands at the bottom with pale light emanating from several candles scattered throughout the room. Gerald is holding an iron device in his hands with four prongs, and he places the heretics' fork around Broken's neck. The fork basically connects the bottom of the chin with the base of the Adams apple. If Broken were to drop his head down, out of fatigue, the prongs on the fork would pierce the flesh and perhaps cause asphyxiation and subsequent death.

It is no secret that Broken Stream's past is somewhat shady, but there is nothing like having breakfast with Winchester Buckley Johnson, which he finds comparable to torture used during the Spanish Inquisition. The experience is a combination of visual absurdity mixed with hideous odor splashed with a profound sense of the insane. The mere fact of being in the presence of Diarrhea humors him and frightens him in the same breath, and he wonders if Winchester can see this at all. And while he chose to be here, he clearly does not know why he made this choice at points in their exchange. This is, of course, until he considers the opposite: Working at Burger Prince in the drive-through window back in Boise.

As the limousine approaches the Tournament Players Club main entrance, a line of black Strange Rovers stretch across the driveway. BS is concerned that someone else important might be there that day, and so he calls Gerald. Winchester sits by and daydreams about Johnnie, and about his chin and his daughter growing up in a safer world while staring at the fluffy clouds in the sky above the Sonoran desert. Gerald informs BS that the man they are to meet, Nasim bin Lafouz, travels heavily guarded and hence they should not worry.

Mr. bin Lafouz is a member of an illustrious family, one that is one of the wealthiest families, if not the wealthiest, in the Arabian Peninsula. And although the family's beginnings were modest for they are not part of the Royal line of successors, their business dealings have ranged from energy companies to privatizing public gaming to satellite and telecommunications to political meanderings and special forces training units. And, although, he is considerably younger than BS and slightly younger than Winchester, he is clearly more mature, more intelligent, and more able to conduct himself as a professional.

On the 1st tee of the front 9 known as the Rattlesnake, a man wearing a pink oxford shirt, bright yellow twill pants, a lime green beret and gold golf shoes is waiting for them. He calls out to the two Americans walking toward him as four Apache helicopters circle high overhead keeping the perimeter covered.

"Fellas! Let's play some Gopher ball!"

"Gopher ball? What are you some kind of chink sand nigger?" asks an energized Diarrhea, now coming back to life.

"I like this guy! Chink sand nigger! That is very funny. Your father told me that you were a funny man. He did not explain the claim very well, but now I understand."

"Oh that's right, you know my dad. Well Mr. Bib Lala, whatever your name is..."

"bin Lafouz."

"Whatever Mr. Been There Done That—let's put your money where your mouth is! Let's play some golf!"

"Want to play for money, you stinky American?"

"Hey, hey. I don't stink," blares BS.

"I wasn't speaking at you. I would not insult you sir."

"Yeah, I'll play for loot. Let's say you win, I get your shares in Hack Energy Co., and if you win, you can have my stake in the baseball team I'm about to take over," rebuts Wild Card.

"Although my shares in Hack Energy are worth about 400 times that of your share in whatever American baseball team you have your dirty little hands in, I am so sure I will beat you that I will make that bet."

"Oh boy, this is trouble." BS is shaking his head as he watches the two immature bullies stand face-to-face, invading each other private breathing spaces. He spots two blue winged teal dabbling ducks flying low overhead, and he quickly takes out a Dan Wesson tactical revolver and blows a three inch hole in one bird's belly. The duck falls to the fairway as an Arizona black rattlesnake slithers by and quickly scoops up the carcass. Winchester and bin Lafouz saw none of this, but BS is gloating about his kill.

"And, if I win, you have to sing the National Anthem at the home opener in the Ballpark of my choice. And you have to botch it up and sing half of it in French!"

"Whatever. I will win, and after I do, I have a little surprise for you. I will enforce a secret desire of mine, one that you will not know about until I say so, and when I say so, you oblige. Deal?"

"Deal!" Winchester is really excited now. He can taste victory, and he can taste the humiliation of his Arabian golf partner on the rim of his desalinated lips. Winchester's seemingly fortuitous position here in the desert this day has given him all of the confidence of a professional athlete. What he does not know is that his opponent is one of the better golf players on the Arabian Peninsula and has had private matches with Nickraus, Playmer and Waltstone. Galbladdesteros has dined at his seaside palace near the Asir National Park on the Red Sea. Winchester's experience with professional golfers is zero. He has played some pickup games with some of the boys from Yellow and Harvard, and once, he was able to watch most of a PGA event in person before being asked to leave by Tour security for "obscenities, vulgarities and physical ailments." Truth be known, he had his colonoscopy the day before, and so he was mostly empty of anything in his digestive tract.

After the first nine holes, it is clear that Mr. bin Lafouz is a superior golfer. BS measures the situation from a discrete distance as bin Lafouz does the Safety Dance, taunting Winchester who is crying like a baby because he is losing, because he always wanted to be a baseball team owner, and because he is stuck. He has not soiled himself since the green on the third hole, but he does not know why. In times of trouble, he can often count on his incontinence to give him a way out. In this circumstance, there is no release and, therefore, no way out.

"I quit! I'm not playing with you anymore! You cheat!"

"I do not cheat, Mr. Stinky Pants! I just whooped your behind like a baby sucking his thumb in front of illustrious company." Quickly, he shuts his mouth, as though he revealed something of relevance.

"Well, I'm calling Daddy! He'll straighten this out!"

"Do not bother calling Daddy! I do not want your stupid baseball team, but what I do want is for you to make good on the favor you now owe me."

"Sure, I'll do anything, as long as Kra isn't involved."

"Who's Kra?"

"Thank God! Someone who doesn't know Kra! Yes, I'll do it."

BS has had Gerald on the telephone for quite some time, and he is shaking his head in utter disbelief at the antics before him. He had been making some notes on the scorecard and stuffed the scorecard into his pocket.

"Join me in the clubhouse! Lunch is on the US Government!" states BS, who is excited now beyond words because the baseball team plan is still a go.

"A sand-nigger's got to eat!" Diarrhea bluntly states, thinking he is being funny as bin Lafouz glares furiously at him. BS leans into Winchester's ear and tells him softly to keep his mouth shut, that he will do all the talking now. Winchester farts in response.

Meanwhile, back in the District of Columbia, construction crews have rebuilt the entire center of the Beltway. The estimated time of completion for the project was to be four years, but with the help of a very wealthy Riyadh donor, the project was finished in a mere three months. In a telephone interview, a *London Daily News* reporter asked the donor, who was vacationing on Lake Geneva, about his financial assistance in the rebuilding of Washington. He stated, "Yes, Americans are my friends. I want to ensure that the people have complete confidence that their government is housed in top quality buildings and are completely safe."

"But how could you afford such a huge donation? Basically, the city with arguably the largest buildings in North America has been rebuilt and stylized and restored overnight thanks to your generosity."

"Oh, I own about 4% of the US real estate market. It was really nothing."

All the famous memorials, which had decayed slightly with age, were given complete facelifts, and the hundreds of empty Beaux-Arts buildings were demolished and then reconstructed from scratch. New architectural methods ensured the longevity of the governmental housing for centuries while preserving the same look that everyone was accustomed to for the better part of the past 200 years. New memorials, new airports, and wider roads were also being constructed simultaneously. The

Presidential palace was rebuilt as the Gold House using real gold imported from China, as opposed to gold dust created in a Northern California fake factory tourist trap since all the actual gold in California was pillaged long ago. A more advanced subway system was ordered, and some of the best hoteliers and restaurateurs were flown in from Europe to upgrade the District's core, which was handsomely transformed over night. What was recently the murder capital of the United States, well, remained America's murder capital for many years to come, but the center was safer. To put it poetically, the cream in the center of the giant Oreo cookie was safe from being licked by unwanted dark tongues.

At the lunch table in the Clubhouse, bin Lafouz, BS and Winchester discuss the plan to unify the United States' energy needs with the Saudi energy supply. The only questionable and negotiable element to the agreement was the length of time this agreement would stand. Gerald and the Saudi King had already mapped out the details over the telephone, and the overall plan was to be finalized by a handshake and couple of rounds of golf. The likelihood of either of these points of finalization gave way to an agreement in person between BS and bin Lafouz, as the Arabian delegate refused to touch Winchester's hands in fear of bacterial infection. Moreover, he was appalled that Winchester was such a poor sport that the game ended after nine holes.

As a parting wish, bin Lafouz asked to be taken to a professional baseball game, and the team from Arizona, the Snakes from the Desert, had quite a following back in Riyadh. Although the team was only in its first year of existence, they had the fourth largest foreign fan base of any team in the major leagues. Following a swift phone call to the owner of the team, Lafouz, BS and Winchester were seated in front row box seats at the next game in Phoenix. Winchester was boasting to one of the players taking practice swings in the on-deck circle that his

Special Forces Texas team was going to beat their Snake-like asses to a pulp. The player graciously informed him that the teams are in different leagues and they would not play each other unless in the World Series.

"Shut up. What do you know? Fucking baseball players think they know everything."

BS sits by, quietly wondering how long he will have to endure this level of madness.

During the 7ᵗʰ inning stretch, bin Lafouz asks Winchester to honor his end of the bargain. "You must make good on your deal."

"Yeah whatever Balalalou."

Out of a small black leather bag, bin Lafouz removes a formal white thobe and places it over Winchester's clothes. On Winchester's head, bin Lafouz places the white ghutra headdress with the black agal ring resembling a headband. The agal has the letters KRA stitched onto the front of it. Finally, the black bisht, which resembles a lightly threaded cloak, is placed over the thobe. The large video scoreboard shows Winchester adorned in traditional Saudi royal garb turned around facing the crowd as he is screaming some obscenities at a fan sitting two rows behind him and to his left. Holding a pair of high zoom binoculars, Kra stands in the media booth next to the woman who controls the scoreboard functions. He whispers something in her ear and she laughs. He hands her a wad of money rolled up with an elastic band around it.

An announcement comes over the stadium loudspeakers that Mr. Winchester Buckley Johnson, famous American icon in training, has just been named Managing Partner of the American League's Texas Air National Guard Special Forces Rangers. Winchester stares into an ABC Sports camera positioned directly in front of him. His eyes are as wide as a deer's in headlights, a glob of mustard is on his right cheek, and a half eaten hot dog in his right hand and a cold beer is spilling from his left. A mild mock cheer from the crowd turns into very loud boos. He turns to wave, and someone throws a dirty baby diaper at him. The offender is quickly removed by Winchester's eunuchs and driven to Area 51 in the Nevada wasteland, dumped from the moving vehicle and left to rot. Hungry vultures circle the carcass, casting shadows on the desert landscape. Luckily for the man, this area is quite a tourist trap and he is picked up only 22 minutes after being left to die.

Winchester is now the managing partner of a major baseball franchise, and he is happier than he has ever been. He loves baseball. He loves hot dogs, beer, and cracker jacks. He even invites his brother to a couple of games. Perhaps they can rediscover a common bond of brotherhood, one that will carry through the rest of their lives. Unfortunately, Jack arrives at the baseball field on opening day the following season only to find that Winchester has left no ticket for him, and then he is not allowed in through the team gate. Jack settles for a scalped ticket in the right field seats.

For the next five years, Winchester uses his position as managing partner to really impress the people he likes to impress. And his wife uses this opportunity to vehemently search out deeper links to the Hollywood A-list crowd. Moments were defined over these five years, then lost as time wore away years of their lives. Their daughter is now a teenager and shows all the physical signs of becoming a beautiful young woman. Her relationship with Broken Stream is becoming deeper, as though Broken's maturity replaces the lack of adult leadership from her own father. Rin Chin Chin is growing into a remarkable character. Often funny, sometimes depressed, but never dull, their adopted child is something of a party favorite as well and Johnnie takes him everywhere she goes. The chin kid often jokes about becoming ruler of the Free World one day. Winchester always likes that joke the best.

Ex-NASA CIB geochemists did develop that promised technology, and everywhere that Winchester goes, he drops some rocks and just keeps going. People no longer laugh at him as much in person as they used to, which has clearly affected Winchester's growing ego. With fewer people laughing, and because he is being placed in higher positions, he is really getting the bug now, the fever to go all the way to the top. He really wants to be Commissioner of Major League Baseball.

Rin Chin Chin's prophecy of being leader of the Free World would never quite come to fruition because any semblance to a Free World remains only incidental. However, the world would eventually certainly appear to be a freer place in some regards. Gerald was elected President of the United States, replacing the one and only Randolph Ulysses Rabbit as he finished two very successful Presidential terms, successful in the sense that R.U. Rabbit moved the country closer to where Gerald certainly wanted it to be, and when Gerald took over, he did not lose a stride. Winchester gained his first real political experience during his father's election campaign. He was able to see firsthand how the buffet table was set up at each stop on the campaign tour, witnessed the artistry of applying makeup to his father's face, and even saw how the camera worked and how people behaved in front of it, while it was on and while it was off. In watching carefully, he noticed the ability to read from the teleprompter was critical. He maintained that he would have to brush up on his reading again, and so he ordered his wife to buy a bunch of books just in case. Rin Chin Chin actually read all the books, and interestingly enough, he did it without any eyes.

Act 18.

Governor Schmovernor

"Don't think, you dimwit! Just read!" eagerly stated Gerald moments before the announcement of the winner came on local and national news.

"Dad, I am not your puppet. I can *think* you know."

"Don't let me down, boy. You'll have that thumb back in your mouth faster than jack rabbit slim had a pound of cabbage shoved up his ass in the cabbage patch."

"What?"

"Exactly, my dear boy. Exactly," stated Gerald as he backed away slowly, a huge rather sinister smile plastered on his smirking well-worn face.

Gubernatorial election winner Winchester Buckley Johnson removes some pieces of paper from a folder as he stands modestly erect behind the podium. He reads over the papers very quickly. It does not appear as though he is actually reading, more like he is scanning the pages for recognizable words. His gut tells him to say something from his heart. Although his father's words always terrified him, he knew that he could not always live in Daddy's shadow, and for years the struggle between opposing forces, becoming a free man or living and breathing everything his father told him to, terrified him. His soul consistently ached, day and night, and his mind just shut off when his father loomed closely by. But this step he was now taking was a brave one and his budding audacity would later prove to help him conquer many demons.

"First, I want to thank you, thank everyone who voted today, for there is no other possible way that I would have received two million three hundred thousand percent of the vote if you did not vote. So, I accept your vote to be the Governor of the great state of Texas. I will do my best to make your lives better than you ever thought they could be in your meaningless jobs earning useless wages. Thank you all for your support." Winchester breathes deeply as he stands before the stunned faithful who just helped vote him into the top political and legislative seat in the state of Texas. He can barely hear himself think. He was instructed clearly by his campaign manager and his father to just read from the paper. He smiles and waves to the stunned crowd. Some mock cheers followed, but mostly there was utter silence. Johnnie stands by his side just out of camera view at this moment, and Gerald and Betty are to her right. Gerald gives Johnnie a little nudge, and Johnnie holds up an "Applaud Now" sign. The obedient crowd erupts into wild cheers, which instantly gives Winchester a boost of confidence, one that will not stop swelling until, well, until later.

Gerald approaches the podium and gives his son a nationally televised paternal hug and whispers in his ear. "I'll send you to boot camp in Kuwait if you don't just read from the damned paper." Smiling, he withdraws again and lets his son speak. And, as luck would have it, since Winchester could not read, and since his father needed him to be the Governor of Texas rather than exiled to the desert, there were no exhaustive boot camp regiments for the Governor-to-be. Instead, his assembled family gave him a pat on the back and giggled nervously.

After a wild night of partying by all, and a party it was—booze, cocaine, Liquid Drano, pills, frills and wills being rewritten, there was sex, rock and roll, good old fashioned country music, lines of drugged and drunken cowboys and cowgirls doing the single shot, the two-step, the three-fall and the four on the floor in front of the toilet, and they were joined by plenty of Texas' finest prostitutes sporting ten gallon hats and overalls—the newly elected soon-to-be Governor retired to the library in his father's lavish estate just outside Houston the next day. He had declared his domicile to be in Texas just one week before the election to forego any possible complications regarding this potential legal issue. The public found this out many years later, and the one person who knew at the time is no longer an American citizen. He is leading eco-environment tours in Patagonia now. Texas law regarding the issue of domicile relating to holding public office is now permanently locked up behind State Supreme Court doors and can never be reopened except by court order and with the consent of Governor Winchester Buckley Johnson. Winchester knew nothing about this at the time, of course, but his father's attorneys set up the paperwork and Winchester just signed the bottom line, where the little red sticker shaped like an arrow with the words "Sign Here" was placed.

Johnnie's first order of business as First Lady of Texas would be to shed her daft image and replace it with one that was much more conservative and much stronger. After her trailer park hiatus close to a decade previous, she learned many things about the human race, at least about those elements of life that make sense for her, and it was there that she found Jesus. Well, he never actually came to the trailer park despite the hysterical reactions to the possibility that he might be visiting from time to time. The hysteria was especially strong with the Spanish painters and the Greek philosophers, between whom discussions would lead to arguments that would lead to brutal fisticuffs regarding his potential arrival. Johnnie had settled for a personal journey through the tenets proffered by the Tao Te Ching and Gautama Buddha, Zarathustra and Abraham, Martin Luther and John

Calvin, and many, many others—a journey led by Jener. Jener had studied with Jesus' disciples in the old days, but he took a different path, and his wisdom, while it could never match that of a very powerfully wise Jesus, was valuable in its own right. Jesus Christ's wisdom was unmatched, however, and over the course of time, few would truly understand the complexity of his existence. His full comprehension of every religion that came before him was held deeply in his soul, and in many ways, of those religions to follow.

What Johnnie is able to decipher from her experiences would ultimately set her on her own parallel journey. While not everyone has sufficient sensibility to seek out wisdom, Johnnie's teachings would lead her to a different place. Her journey landed her inside the Governor's Mansion in Austin during the all-night rave following the election, and the subsequent five years were filled with raving, raving madness mostly. Sometimes raving lunacy would prevail, which is usually one in the same with madness, but sometimes not even on the same map. This is the same journey that would help her construct her own points of view regarding politics and socioeconomic philosophies, and of course, how to manage a big ol' Texas kitchen. Previous to this, she had the latest and the greatest—cars, technology and new acquaintances begging at her doorstep. She caroused with some of the Hollywood 'B' list crowd, as she was never able to penetrate the movable feast that is the Hollywood elite. Slightly disgusted, Hemingway sees the merit in the analogous statement and keeps his mouth shut. He grumbled a bit while he petted one of Wall's many cats lounging about, but he didn't utter any noticeable words of dispute.

Johnnie knew changes had to come. Sufficient modesty was in order as a counterpoint to her husband's wildly conservative demeanor, the one that got him into trouble so many times and got him out of trouble so many times.

For her husband's image was critical and she knew this all along. In fact, Betty was so sure that Johnnie would fall into place that she made a deal with Gerald to not have Johnnie "reeducated" at their ranch in Midland, the same town where Johnnie was born and where Gerald and Betty had mostly raised Little Diarrhea. Midland was the place that ultimately connected the two of them, more than the electrically charged first adult meeting at the Weston Golf Club, more than their Marblehead home for years, and certainly more than any theosophical beliefs they might or might not share—no one is quite sure what they talk about behind closed doors or out of the range of the CIB's listening devices.

But Johnnie is certainly no intellectual slouch. ZZ and the guardian cats don't let just anyone inside the walls of the Wall. You have to be able to deal with it, and she can deal with it. She gets it on many levels. She would not likely be a Professor of Art History from Antiquity to the Renaissance at Princeton or a leading candidate for the Nobel Prize in Physics, but she understood what she learned well enough to organize information well. Her organizational abilities would play a much larger role in things to come. However, her role is never quite apparent to the masses because Gerald and Betty keep her quietly preserved behind the electronic tentacles of a continent-sized octopus. And there she will stay until, well, until Betty says so.

Johnnie's role as mother has not been clearly defined until now. She is a very loving mother to their daughter, and she seems to have grown quite fond of Rin Chin Chin, though she does not interact with him too much. Despite her mystical hiatus that one crazy autumn, it seems that she has a maternal instinct that is second to none, except maybe that of Mother Nature. And their well adjusted First Daughter and First Chin of Texas are happier than they ever could have imagined to be living in the mansion on the hill. Rin Chin Chin has begun to really enjoy contact sports and likens American football to a visit to the Orthognathic surgeon's office. Most everyone except Broken Stream likes that joke, whose displeasure when he hears the joke will remain a mystery until the end of time.

Johnnie's whole story is really a story in its own right, one that could be told from a hundred different perspectives, maybe a thousand different perspectives, and still not paint a moving picture like the one painted here. Her combination of feminine austerity and subtle wit, combined with the absolute dedication to her ridiculous husband, is something that future television shows might make a mockery of; but the story that is not told here is the one that shows her clear sense of judgment for the future of her family, the judgment that may come into play some time in the future and that places her loved ones in a strategy and a belief system that may or may not win out in the end. Alas, the end will show the truth of all things merely the subject of speculation at present.

This is all very difficult even for Rin Chin Chin, and perhaps especially, for he, beyond all things, is a symbol of their love for each other and their love for humanity and all of its pursuits. He is the solitary ring visible from a million miles away from Saturn, the Bringer of Old Age.

"NEIN! Dieses ist lächerlich!" Beethoven screams in a rage. Soon, the other Western classical composers join in. A revolution is on the brink of outbreak because Gustav Holst got his third look, while Mozart and Beethoven, Berlioz and Bizet, Mahler and Liszt have received no looks, not even one. ZZ calms them down. She claims that they will get their fair shake, but they have to be patient. The finale will be something unlike anything that has ever been seen, heard, smelled or fought about. However, as sad as it is, Holst had paid a certain someone off with promises of a future piece dedicated to one of the ghostwriting editors for the extra looks. The "Unknown

246

Planet" will be ascribed the ghostwriter's name, as soon as it is discovered by humanity and inhabited by human consciousness. Alas, a favor is a favor no matter the dimension contained therein.

Still unsure about anything relating to law, politics and economics, Winchester Buckley Johnson takes the stage to lead the people of the State of Texas and sit at the head of the Texas State Legislature. He will remain there for several years, and in those years, some things will change, some will not. But, like anything else that his geologically challenged human form gets involved in, there is a story to be, and if it fails to be told, the truth will never be revealed. It will be swallowed and directed into the category "unknown," like the aforementioned planet to be named later.

"Fellow Bostonians, Governor Waldermar, Speaker Kra, my wonderful wife and daughter and chin, and many, many acquaintances and business associates." Winchester is practicing his speech in front of a mirror just 30 minutes before his Inauguration Speech in January of 1995. He is very nervous about this moment. The facts surrounding his arrival as Governor are unclear to him. It is as though he is unsure about which of Holst's planets he is on. He was never comfortable with speaking in front of crowds, and if those geochemists had not developed his special diaper, he would certainly have emptied the room prior to uttering a single word. He remembers his father's strictest instructions: "Don't think you damned idiot, just read!" He begins repeating this to himself: "Don't think, just read. Don't think, just read." Soon, a voice arrives in his head.

"Don't listen to your father all the time. Yes, he was President of the United States, but he does not always know what is best for you. I suggest using your guts. Why can't you think? Why do you have to read? Forget about reading. You have done so well up until now by following

your innards. Just stay on your path. You will not regret
it."

Winchester is quite happy that his conscience has sided
with him and believes in him. Sometimes that is all
Winchester Buckley Johnson needs, a little positive
support from his conscience. Support is often an
emotional need and rarely does it relate to anything even
superficially logical, and since his deeper thoughts and
feelings are not based on any particular set of laws or
logic, often he needs only to hear his conscience speak to
him for it to be supportive of him, no matter the words,
big or small that his conscience conscientiously or
unconsciously conscientiously uses.

His first major decision as Governor was made after an
all-weekend binge thrown by Broken Stream in a
Houston dive-bar. Rin Chin Chin and Jennifer joined the
party at the end, mostly in a capacity of intervention, to
help their father sober up. He decided that he wanted to
change how people saw governance and government in
general, and he garbled something to the effect that the
people have the right to elect a "regular" guy, not some
Harvard brainchild or some ex-cokehead Baylor student
turned Governor, but someone with real guts, real
pizzazz, someone like him, someone who fought for every
inch of every victory. And while Jennifer listened to his
slurred tirade in a somewhat confused manner, she
understood what he meant and that is all that mattered,
for he was her father and she loved him dearly no matter
how irrational he became after he blew some lines or hit
the sauce hard after his beloved Yellow rowing team
continued to lose to the boys across the pond from Oxford.

Winchester's office was pristinely decorated. Johnnie
really helped him with some finer touches. The historical
paintings on the walls were evenly hung, and no dust
laden books lined the shelves as the illegal Honduran
cleaning crew kept the library spotless and even, at the
instruction of Johnnie, moved a book now and then to

make them appear used. The library in the Governor's office did not use the Dewey Decimal system, a method of organization that was popularized during the 1970's Great Dewey Decimal System push in the nation's educational system. And being a woman of great organization, she made sure that her husband could at least stumble upon a particular book if he needed to illustrate to a news camera that he does, in fact, read.

"Look darling. I said, LOOK darling. Thank you. Listen carefully while I point, okay? Remember your time at Harvard, my darling. Will you pay attention to me! Remember Harvard, where you bought, I mean where you received your MBA. Some of this should make sense. Melvil Dewey would not be happy about this, but I could not use the Dewey Decimal System to organize your books. I bought you the "How to Read for Dummies" book so you can remember what a joy it is to read. See those shelves of books? I placed only history and law books there. They are organized in chronological order from left to right and from top to bottom. The sections are then organized alphabetically. But chronology, do you know what chronology means? Forget it. Listen my darling, my little stinky Governor, coochie coochie coo," she says as she tickles him, and he begins to giggle. "Do you understand anything I am saying?"

"He, he, he, yeah, sure. Hey, when's dinner? A Governor's got to eat!"

"Not until later. Speaking of dinner, we're having Broken Stream over for some good Texas BBQ. He has some kind of special announcement for us. He's been on a hunting expedition in Thailand and probably bagged the big one. Licky told me that he has always wanted to shoot an elephant then bring it back to life. Maybe he just shot it then blew it up. He likes explosions. Licky told me that they make him horny. You know, your father's Presidency had its many ups and downs, but one thing is for certain. BS is still really, really pissed after letting that Sad-Ham guy go. And your father was so angry, that, according to your mother, he stayed in bed for a week after finally deciding to pull the arsenal out of Iraq. I felt so badly for him that I bought him the VHS tape of *Terms of Endearment* so he could let it all out with a good cry."

"Terms of what? Hey, I was looking at my calendar and I noticed that I still have, like, 330 more days in my term as Governor. How cool is that?"

"Very cool, sweetheart, very cool."

"Speaking of cool, I was thinking of making some new laws."

"B, are you sure you want to be treading in those waters? Shouldn't you leave lawmaking to legislators and judges and people who really care about the law?"

"I care about the law. Officer Dooley in the Marblehead Police Department makes sure that my Driving While Intoxicated blunders remain off record. That's law well served!"

"Seriously, baby cakes, I think that perhaps you should just let this term run its course. Let's go sign autographs. You know how much you enjoyed meeting regular men and women and holding the babies. You had so much fun those months, remember?" After not receiving a response from Governor Johnson for 90 seconds, she walked out of the room. He was staring at a book lying on his desk. His deeply inquisitive facial appearance summoned her to leave him in meditation.

"Wow! Did you see this book that someone put on my desk? *Ho-Lee Bi-Bill.* Wow, it's a *Ho-Lee Bi-Bill.* Who is Lee? What a whore, Lee the Ho! He must be Chinese. Maybe he was that transvestite I picked up in the Kong. Who is Bill then? Maybe it's that guy who beat Dad, Bill Clifton. Maybe he's a faggot. It says here that he is Bi. I wonder who he sleeps with. Maybe that Chinese porn star, Chek Lap Kok. Wow. That is impressive! Probably a murder mystery. Maybe it's a good old-fashioned spy book. Maybe he's like a Chinese James Bond, a fucking chink 007! Honey? Johnnie?"

Suddenly, the fear struck. Did she leave again with Jener? Tsar Alexander I thought Winchester's diatribe so hilarious that he punched Napoleon Bonaparte in the arm hard enough to make Nappy wince from temporary shock. The blow sent tingles like small electrical currents shooting right down his arm, which was tucked neatly into his jacket pocket as always. Surprisingly, his 12-inch long fingernails had always been fondling his genitalia while his hand was tucked into the side of his coat. Apparently, he is the most prolific masturbator in Wall. Of course, Stalin and Hitler often complain that they can never get into Wall's elite club, and so why should Napoleon? ZZ never answers. She does not have to, for she has her reasons and receives her instructions. Moments of realization are always complicated for Winchester. Discovering new things makes him very insecure. But, like a child, he wants to share everything new with everyone in sight, just as when he first discovered the moon in the sky. He quickly scans the room, looks in the closet, and starts screaming like a depraved infant. "Johnnie! Johnnie!"

Jennifer arrives in the library holding Rin Chin Chin in his jar. They are laughing and speaking to each other in Spanish. Maria, one of the Honduran cleaning women, is not far behind. Her extended belly is jiggling from laughter. It is this moment that Governor Johnson thinks of his brother Jack. He immediately picks up the telephone and calls him to apologize for not leaving a ticket for him at the baseball park on opening day several years earlier. Jack is still very bitter but accepts his apology, albeit with a certain lack of enthusiasm. Jack quickly hangs up the phone and begins taking off his old

Boston police uniform. Jennifer and Maria sit by the window in two antique hand-carved wood chairs, and Rin Chin Chin's jar is placed in the mahogany windowsill. Rin asks if he can take a nap in the afternoon sunshine.

"Rin?"

"*Si?*"

"Rin, can we speak in English? You know I am not practicing my Arabic yet."

"Okay, Dad. What is it?"

"I am very concerned about my stay as Governor. I really don't know much. I believe that I can be truthful with you. Quite honestly, I do not have any idea what I am doing. I want Texans to be very happy. I want them to make money and have nice cars and guns and stuff. Do they want anything else?"

"Sure, what about healthcare?"

"Health what?"

"Dad, come on! You know, hospitals and stuff—medication, doctors, nurses, crutches, lobotomies, places to go when they are feeling sick."

"Oh yeah, my grandfather told me that I would be better off with a labota-whatever."

"Presley? Your grandfather was quite a humorist."

"A what?"

"This conversation is going nowhere, Dad. You should read a little, brush up on your vocabulary. Try using words that you have never known. Trust your mind. It holds words in there. They are buried, but they are in there."

"Oh my dear son, how do you know so much? You are so smart."

"Dad, just try reading. Start with Dr. Seuss—his material is fun to read."

"I like *Green Eggs and Ham*! I love the pictures! Okay, but I really don't think I can handle big doctor's words. I can barely spell my own name."

"Oh Dad! You are so silly!"

Rin Chin Chin dozes off in the sun streaming through the window, exhausted after reading *The Brothers Karamazov* by Dostoevsky in Sanskrit translation from cover to cover in one night. The afternoon sun sits low on the western horizon. The hackberry and sycamore trees on the ridge above the Governor's mansion dance in a light breeze. A wild rabbit sits in the grass nibbling on a scrumptious snack. Winchester stares at the rabbit and realizes how lucky it is to be a wild animal, to live in a world where only nature's laws preside. He realizes that he is the Governor of one of the largest states in the country and he must act as such. He has no experience in running and managing people. He has been in positions of power, but actual management skills or leadership were not required. He knows how to market things, and despite his hideous smells of the past, people tend to like him. They forgive him for his trespass because they are taught to and believe that it is right to forgive those who intrude.

He remembers a conversation with Jener during a fraternity party at Yellow: "WB, the finer things in life are found in the soul. Sometimes great confusion drives one to find answers, but true solutions to life's problems are answered in searching for truth. And this, if acted upon accordingly, can become wisdom. It is up to you."

"Jener, shut up and roll up this tenner for me," he had said as he handed Jener a ten dollar bill. "I want to roll hard tonight. Cocaine and vodka for everyone!"

The wild animals in the frat house proceeded to set a record for the most cocaine consumed in one night in Yellow. Or so one of Yellow's famous secret scrolls stated. Winchester was fortunate to have contributed to this legacy, which will remain enshrined in the lore of the school's mythology. Albeit one of the darker elements to the mythology, it is firmly planted there. Jener happened to be the author of many of the secret scrolls hidden in Yellow's hallowed vaults. Some of this lore is based around the legacies of Winchester, Gerald and Presley, an illustrious line of Johnsons leaving indelible marks in the classrooms and lecture halls, fraternity houses, laboratories, and lavatories of Yellow's New Haven, Connecticut campus.

Governor Johnson set out to make some changes in his state. During his State of the State address in 1997, he made an appeal for people with less wealth than himself. He made appeals for education. He told the good people of Texas that he thinks people should have the right to go to school and pray. In truth, he has learned lots of "valuable stuff," as he would call it, from his *Ilo-Lee Bi-Bill,* and he learned that reading is important too. He now realizes that repeating himself over and over gets the message through clearly to people who are not listening to him, or at least to himself, as he never listens to his own words. This will become somewhat annoying later to anyone who hears it, but he uses it like a weapon when he needs to. Since it is clearly not in Governor Winchester Buckley Johnson's interest to learn anything that would confuse him, he sticks with what he knows. He likes to play darts and make telephone calls. Calls on his mobile cellular phone have become less costly, and he is especially happy about that. He has stopped using his emotional crutches, like alcohol, drugs and overt vulgarity, and he has replaced them with searching for new ways to make laws. Despite his virtual illiteracy, he is quite a creative man when he needs to be, but the motivation has to be there. A muse is a muse no matter the quality of the artist or the merit of the subject matter.

A conversation with Johnnie was overheard once in the Sam Houston bedroom. Winchester is quoted directly. Although the Mexican gardener who was tending some of the flowers in the mansion could not understand English perfectly and he only understood the gist of what was said, the wire he was wearing that the CIB taped to his chest picked up the dialogue with perfect digital clarity.

"Sweet cheeks, I think that Texas should secede from the Union of American States or something like that. I heard that word and I like it. I heard House Speaker Jack Haney tell a visiting federal court judge that Texas law is clearly separate from the federal law in many regards. Do you know what this means? Maybe Texas can be its own country! How cool would that be? President Johnson! President of the Country of Texas! You can be the First Lady! Jennifer can be the First Chick and Rin can be the First Chin! What do you think? I have really thought about this, and I have actually prepared a speech."

Johnnie sat bewildered. In all her years with Winchester, she has never heard him use so many big words at once. She was never present at one his many speeches, especially the one in Egypt when he repeated what he was told. Nor did she join him on his "autograph and handshaking" tour as she had remained behind, although like a good secretary she made all necessary arrangements for him. While his thoughts regarding secession were clearly without fundamental grounding and unintentionally logical, he had no possible way of staging a political upheaval. He simply did not know anything in relation to law, politics, economics, social welfare, or anything at all for that matter. And rebellious leaders can usually read well—at least in modern times most can.

The days passed by rather uninterestingly. Winchester hadn't heard from ZZ in several years now, and it seemed that everyone was happy. His conscience interrupted him only on rare occasion. His brother Jack finally succeeded in something on "his own merit," winning the Gubernatorial election for the State of Florida in 1998. To no one's surprise, Jack received an overwhelming number of votes to win easily. After spending time in Latin America, Jack had married a beautiful woman from Belize, and they had several children together and adopted many more, which angered Johnnie a little for jealousy is a harsh burden not laid down easily. Jack's wife helped him gain the vote from the Latin community in Florida and was heavily involved in grassroots campaigning. She went door to door and passed out small plastic cups of Cuban coffee and some documents to unsuspecting illegal Latin Americans scattered all over South Florida. Clarification is being sought as to what was in those documents she passed out. The ghostwriting team is working on it. Jack even helped Winchester get some Panamanian teenagers to serve short internships as a cleanup crew, removing the rocks he left strewn everywhere he walked. So, both Johnson's were Governors of largely populated states, two very important states for the political and economic health of the United States of America.

Winchester's bodyguards were very aware of his idiosyncrasies now, so they did not let him stray too far without "accidentally" pushing him back into the proper place. They had the strictest instructions from Gerald, and BS was always hanging around somewhere nearby. Everyone was careful not to interfere too much, at least not in a fashion that could be interpreted as interference, for soon, the next election would come and this would show Winchester's new potential in stronger leadership roles. They did not want anyone asking the all important questions, like: can Governor Johnson of Texas show strength without all the "help," or would that be just too risky a venture considering what is at stake?

Despite some of his smaller gaffes, like trying to shrink educational funding by 110%, his term was run with relative smoothness. After the Speaker of the State's House explained to him that reducing spending by 110% was mathematically unfeasible, Governor Johnson's reaction was, "So what! Unfeasible, flam-sleazable, I call it a good Governorial move." After Rin Chin Chin explained to him what the word unfeasible meant in terms that he could understand, he just stated, "Oh, fuck it then."

He was proud to have overturned gun control. And his new "Roman Law Program" was new to any state government. He could just "call out" a new law and it would instantly be law. As he told everyone he knew, "It can be just like in the Roman days. I say it is law and it is law." In effect, however, he made no serious changes that might affect the daily lives of Texans. Most illegal immigrants would be allowed to stay as long as they kept their mouths shut, and his ties to the Republican Party, Pseudalopex News Network, and the United Methodists, the Episcopalians, the Lutherans and the Baptists became stronger. They were seeing him as a perfect man to be the voice of their respective causes, a pioneer in the frontier, conquering ideals and giving a face to carrying forth faith into the future of human growth, a man with not much on his mind but a determination to prove otherwise.

Winchester was living the high life. He dined with his father and the supremely wealthy. Foreign dignitaries trying to establish business bases in Houston and Dallas visited him in Austin. He learned to play H.O.R.S.E. with Rin Chin Chin, who always managed to beat him despite not having any arms to shoot the basketball. Winchester set up a miniature golf course throughout the Governor's mansion where he and Jennifer would play like children together until the wee hours well beyond bedtime when Johnnie would finally have to yell for them to come upstairs. He was truly happy and wondered if he could just be President of the country Texas until he died.

His second term as President of Texas began seamlessly. It was clear to those following his public career that he was becoming much more spiritual, and it appeared as though he had developed a penchant for reading, at least reading one particular book, for he found immense pleasure quoting it everywhere he went. Perhaps the conversations with ZZ became part of his life to a greater degree than he had suspected. He really enjoyed meeting "regular" people in their daily routines. Some of his aids in the Governor's office added that he felt like "one of them." He always said that people who judged him for his family's wealth and his business successes really did not know him at all, for they failed to see the true Winchester Buckley Johnson hiding behind that mask. The "regular beer drinking backyard barbeque guy you would tailgate with at a Cowboys game." And he was proud of the "real WBJ." Sadly, more regular people like himself could not find themselves as President of Texas. He attempted a "Be President for a Day" campaign, which would have run his entire second term as Governor so he could play golf daily, read his book, and not have to concern himself with legal matters and party politics. His campaign for this new program died on the State Senate floor by a 31-0 vote, however, but he took the loss rather well. He remained gleeful for a couple of months, until the day Gerald, Broken and Ka Zin Flow showed up for a "private meeting" when Johnnie, Jennifer and, especially, the Chin kid, who always happened to be hanging around during important meetings, were otherwise occupied.

Act 19.

A Confectioner's Delight

It is duly noted that the persistent squabbling between the ghostwriters and the elite journalists present in Wall is beginning to annoy the playwright and, in turn, the narrator. The narrative is becoming burdensome to the journalists, but deemed necessary by the ghostwriters. Edgar Allen Poe refers to this as his "Journalistic Eulogy". He makes claim to the notion that in creating a transition from dialogue to narrative, the bridge crosses over the river of death into the realms of the unknown. This drives the journalists a bit mad.

Henry Jarvis Raymond, founder of the New York Thymes newspaper often raves, "We have been quoting here! This will destroy our integrity!!!"

Bram Stoker responds with the echoes of Poe's argument, "Without this bridge, there can be no resolution between the losses that humanity has suffered at the hands of few and the possible outcomes resulting from the actions of these mentioned few."

Eating a ceramic bowl full of mandarins, Mr. Raymond replies, "Poppycock! By quoting directly from the conversations between characters, the story remains more honest!"

"We are to be reminded that measuring elements of such things as piracy, secrecy and shady stock transactions, we have to consider the positive ramifications of narrative versus dialogue. Yes, dialogue can transport the reader through moments of pure bliss or pure disgust with ease, but I must agree with Mr. Poe, as a narration will transport the reader across the bridge over the river of death with unbridled clarity, the one we all seek to cross." This claim by James Joyce would appear to be the final word on the matter, but the journalists simply will not shut up.

"Henry said POPPYCOCK! And I say DOUBLE POPPYCOCK! You are so cynical Jimmy! The very fact that you are quoted directly here refutes your argument!" Harry Reasoner aptly replies.

Intently listening, Jack London sits back with a wry smile on his face as he sips a strong espresso while staring at his half-eaten chocolate-covered hazelnut biscotti.

At the time of his death, James Lick was the wealthiest man in California. The year was 1876. Twenty-eight years had passed since James W. Marshall found that bright speck tangled up in the gravel of the rocky cragged streams flowing into the American River in the Sierra foothills near Coloma, California. Claiming to seek a utopian ideal to set up his agricultural empire, John Sutter and his band of scavengers hopped upon the discovery of the century and began what would later be described as the next stage in piracy. Captain Kidd, the notorious 17th century pirate, was not allowed behind Wall's wall for reasons not wholly known, but he could not defend his own legacy. Recently, the Captain sent his best, regarding the socio-economic development brought by the gold rush to the area and its people as an attempted buy-in for occasional visits, but ZZ remains unimpressed with his decision-making over the years, and so he remains permanently on the outside.

His bid is not the first by a pirate to get into Wall, and indeed, some forms of piracy are less forgivable than others. Although the influence of piracy was never mentioned bluntly in this historical chapter, the mere mention of it in our story carries forth a degree of relevance unlike most categorical changes in the great files of human history. In the future, the telling of history will be less reliant on actual fact and more so on supposition, and this will create many problems for historians and historical persons alike, the latter attempting to fortify their respective places in the spaces of "real history" as recorded in time like a stamp—the history that *always* reveals itself in some way in the end.

Piano maker, explorer, land baron, patron of the arts and sciences, socially astute humanitarian and politically active entrepreneur, James Lick wanted, among many other things, his legacy to be forged in chocolate. So he convinced his Peruvian neighbor, Italian confectioner, Domingo Ghirardelli, to move to San Francisco shortly after gold was discovered in those California hills. Why San Francisco and why chocolate? Well even in the 19th century, a high was a high, and sweetness is an ancient delight and business is always and forever business; but more importantly, the wave of humanity that had a foothold in San Francisco in the years that followed the initial strike could be likened to the wave of immigrants who came from Cuba to Miami in the early 1980s. The predications were different, but the result was the same. San Francisco grew to be one of the great hubs of commerce, culture, and overall socio-economic relevance. Since those days of the gold rush, Miami has become something similar. The business climate in greater Miami derived from a meteoric rise in immigrant population, and the city quickly became something of a pirate's land. Shady real estate practices paved the way into a new dawn as drugs and guns were run up the Miami River to awaiting perpetrators from established New York, New England and Chicago mafia families. In many ways, a new culture had begun. A self-contained Latin American escape pod landing pad served refugees on the run from their military dictatorships, corrupt economic policy makers, and social and political guerrilla warfare, mixing with the locals, who were typically retired persons from America's Northeast who were no longer working but seeking quiet refuge in the twilight of their lives. Day by day the swelling persisted. The largest wave was from Miami's immediate neighbor to the south. Waves of Cubans, hopeful of finding safety from a hellacious existence under the regime of Fidelity Castrate, the former Philadelphia, Pennsylvania used car salesman and dictator of the island nation of Cuba, inhabited the Florida peninsula. Within a decade, the Cuban population far outgrew the established population in metropolitan Miami, and while many of these new citizens were lawful, happy, hard working people, many of them very well educated and some very wealthy, the "old Cubans" that arrived in Miami far before the wave of thieves and others that were the worst derelicts from Cuban prisons. This latter fact would later play a critical role in the development of the socio-political landscape, and furthermore, the elections of high ranking state and federal officials.

In the Yuba goldfields, area miners panned for gold using old tin pans until industrial technology mongers swooped in like vultures hovering over a dying carcass. Soon the hills were dotted with smaller industrial mining units and hydraulic mining production began to take shape. Blasting jets of water into the hills allowed the sediments to flow downstream. As quickly as it began, hierarchical arrangements formed that were brutish and rugged like the terrain, as Barons ruled over the land and gave orders to the serfs, many of them immigrants from Mexico and further south. San Francisco's population grew from 1000 to 25,000 in less than two years due to the economic boom in the nearby hills. Crime was on the rise, and a form of Western vigilantism was molded from the ensuing chaos. In order for the powerful of the young nation to capitalize on the project, California, without any compromise, was admitted as the 31st state of the Union enabling the federal government to legally tax the barons and the gold enthusiasts. At the same time, the nation-state of Texas received financial support from a Congressional order to relinquish lands west of the great Rio Grande to the territory of New Mexico. This angered hard-line Texans more than anything, as this was a clear indication that the Union was not recognizing the significance of their hugeness, their bigness, their gigantic relevance. Plans to secede would come and go for the next one hundred and fifty years or so, but once statehood had been established, none of these movements got very far.

Back in San Francisco, immigrants began streaming in from Latin America and Asia, and the developing port city was the likeliest place to establish a stronghold relative to commerce. Controlling the shipyards and docks meant controlling the trade. The word spread so quickly of the gold in those hills that a virtual war took hold between the government, landowners, and immigrants. Men jockeyed for positions of power, and those already holding seats of power knew instinctively that the path to more power was through self-preservation, preservation of the status quo.

Broken Stream is naked, kneeling in a large golden wheat field. From above, the field appears as a golden brow stretching across the earth's face for miles. A salsa rhythm moves him from within and he imagines giant cranes and cargo ships and raw steel manufacturing facilities with small ants wearing white turbans scurrying around carrying his orders to and fro across a vast desert expanse. A light appears, as though the dawn of industry is upon him. He is transported to a room far beneath the Colorado plateau listening to code breakers intercept complex signals between opium growers and kingpin drug lords. He knows his time has come.

It was not until 1942 that the United States government had its first official Intelligence Agency, the OSS. However, since the Revolutionary War ended in 1783, spies were not uncommon anywhere that the nation's changing flag was flown. In establishing statehood, state by state, an integral part of this expansion of governance was ensuring that the American way would be preserved, and via this spy game and its attendant arm-twisting and other forms of manipulation, well-placed men in leadership positions were always running everything from behind the scenes—this element of so-called American democracy never changed. The Central Intelligence Agency was founded in 1947, after World War II had been brought to an apex by dropping two catastrophic bombs on Hiroshima and Nagasaki, Japan, which signaled a new generation of spies, spying, and espionage technology. The National Security Agency was formed shortly after the CIA and was largely responsible for technologically challenging intelligence maneuvers, such as code-breaking and eavesdropping, and more formative measures such as teaching children in poor neighborhoods to abandon long lines at the polls on Election Day. Prior to World War I, the Bureau of Investigation, the BOI, was established. Leading investigators hired by the Department of Justice formed an agency that would later be renamed the FBI, which grew into a formidable outfit, as investigating crimes related to the US government and federal law was blossoming into a growth enterprise. In short, as the government grew, so did the intelligence communities as a necessary safeguard against risks to the American way of life.

On a brisk spring day in 1972, the great President of the United States, Chester Toxin, in a subterranean chamber deep beneath the Pentagon, signed a secretive ordinance combining the FBI, CIA and NSA into one cohesive unit, the CIB. The CIB would exist outside the realms of the fringe organizations it stemmed from, and its physical location was mobile. This was the first time in history that a major intelligence organization had mobile headquarters. The CIB runs a parallel government to the government of the people and in its brief past, very powerful men have led it. When the Decagon was built beneath Puget Sound in 1984, the CIB occupied permanent space in the federal government's quarters, holding two clandestine wings and leaving operations in the other eight, the Octagon, transparent. That is, of course, as transparent as operations buried deep beneath a sea can be. So, while they became immobile in regards to where they kept their offices, their invisibility enabled them to behave as if they were mobile. Since the NSA, CIA and FBI would all occupy one of the Octagon's mammoth eight wings, intelligence outfits would occupy 30% of the entire Decagon in reality, but as far as public opinion went, they only occupied 12.5% of the Octagon. This helped keep the informed and uninformed public off-balance, and this was the beauty of intelligence. Although connected, there were no direct entrances to the CIB wings from the other wings. Access was so well guarded that, on occasion, even CIB members would get lost trying to find the tunnels and doorways.

The CIB exists completely off the radar and only a few know of its existence outside its lifetime members. The FBI, CIA, and NSA still exist as such, but they are merely shells concealing the dark pearl in the oyster's center. This parallel governing body grew well beyond the realms of intelligence gathering, per se. It dictated political and economic development, particularly of Third World nations, for decades, and no one can stop them. They have money, personnel, and global influence beyond most anyone's capacity to understand, and they have managed to remain completely invisible. The key to the CIB's success is guarding information, and while leaks of their actions are frequent, a governing body plans them accordingly and releases the information to the world's media streams. Planning and coordinating the release of information was always a strategy of the CIB upper echelon. However, the CIB, like the three branches of the United States federal government, has its internal checks and balances. This is the beauty of it. The CIB internal divisions keep a check on one another. If one division becomes too powerful, the others quickly take clandestine measures to keep the balance of power. These measures have run from publicly issued scandals and bribery involving federal government officials to foreign relations sabotage. The federal government has existed like this, in balance, for years. However, the state of balance is no longer in check as one of the three branches has run amuck.

Gerald was a key player in the development and organization of the CIB, and eventually, he rose to the top. His ties to world leaders and men of incredible wealth made him a logical figurehead for military strategists sitting lazily around the large oval table in the CIB's command center. He would come to sit in two head-of-the-table chairs, which made him the most powerful man in history: President of the United States and Head of the CIB. The head chair in the command center was specially design and built by renowned architect Peter Stork. It is made with stainless steel legs and back and has puffy gold velour fabric cushions covering the entire structure. It appears to be a giant H from the distance, but the closer one gets to it, the appearance shifts to a K. Gerald liked the K chair. He dreamt of it one night while bathing in the Adriatic, imagining a modern king would sit on it. There could be no greater man of power imaginable than the dreamer himself, for in all respects, Gerald could be considered the king of the planet. He was very clever in keeping a core group of faithful loyalists by his side through the years, his court, his senate, his soldiers. He knew how to gain favors and when to use them. He was so masterful playing Capitol Hill games, knowing who to divide, who to keep on board, when to split ranks, that the process was named after him—

Gerrymandering. Hold on, there is an interruption. Oh, Katherine Graham is informing the team that Gerrymandering has nothing to do with Gerald Johnson. Sorry about that, Kate. It is admitted that the ghostwriting team does have the leeway to write from instinct when deemed fit. What? She asks to give her best regards to Ben, Bob and Carl, if they are reading this.

Gerald would outgrow the walls of the Capitol. The Gold House was no place for the likes of him. His no-bull approach in dealing with people was too harsh for the public eye, and so he surrendered his position as President after his first term. Stand by. There is more misinformation according to the journalists in quiet confidence. Okay, well, he did not surrender in actuality. He lost the next election. This is being rechecked, and perhaps the point will be clarified later. Often, when transcribing history, one must be cautious of one's intuitions as well as the information being reported, which can conflict, and sometimes, the conflict is so strong that historians have committed heinous crimes following such intensely deep struggling. In 2000, a Polish historian attempting to solve the riddles of the French, German, and Russian occupations of his homeland brutally murdered several wild dogs barking in the middle of the night while he was trying to work. For while his disgust with the surrenders of his peoples were imminent, the more research he conducted, the more he realized that his people were a mixed people, and Poles as such were Slavic, Prussian, and Franco mutts blended over time like a DNA potato-based vodka martini. His sense of Polish nationalism was so strong that the canine murders were a metaphorical and literal result.

Whichever the case, having lost or surrendering the top post in the federal government, the indispensable truth is that there did exist someone from whom he received his orders, and this person was very difficult to pin down for an interview. This is no conspiracy theory but fact relative to the human mind and human spirit. Whether such facts can be recorded as facts will cause great distress throughout the accurate writing of history. Whether this unknown person pulling Gerald's strings was capable of determining the fate of the human race, as someone in that position has the power to do, we may not know until the final scene. The playwright's ghostwriting team is, only now, editing that last scene.

Membership in the CIB's illustrious company is determined by a fundamentally sound selection process. One cannot join but is invited and must pass tests. This is the most critical element to membership. An indicative behavioral element is having an insatiable hunger for knowledge, wealth, and power. A typical CIB secret handshake involves striking left elbows against the right palm of the hand in unison, then grabbing one's genitalia with the left hand. If it is a man, he grabs from beneath, as if clutching his testicles, while making small upward thrusting movements with his wrist. A woman would slide her hand downward over her groin area, starting just below the belly button and making a circular rubbing-like motion. If this secret handshake is ever viewed in public, the issuing members are immediately killed. Often, members are issued orders to assassinate each other to see who the better agent is.

Gambling is also a huge problem within the walls of the CIB's wing. To keep it from growing completely out of control, a small casino was built inside the wing next to the four star steakhouse to assuage the desire of diseased gamblers to return to sea level to bet. Betting above ground became forbidden, in fact, and those who attempted to head to Vegas for a weekend were tracked down and poisoned. As each member's every movement is electronically tracked like animals in a zoo, their whereabouts are always known.

Winchester Buckley Johnson has an insatiable hunger for wealth and a moderate appetite for power, but he completely lacks the first element, knowledge. Gerald was always distraught by this. They could have been the greatest father and son team the world has ever known, but instead, Gerald was forced to settle for a mere shadow of greatness. But family is family, and Gerald believed that to preserve his own power, he could use someone to dangle in front of the world like a carrot on a string hanging before a caged rabbit.

Winchester, on the other hand, could not be happier. He is on the Republican Party ticket to run in the 2000 primary election for President of the United States. The likeliest candidate for the Democrats to survive the primaries was Senator Calvin Impale. Winchester and Impale do not go way back. They do not have a history of disliking one another. However, Impale made some very clear judgments about his potential counterpart. This is mostly related to geologic conditioning. With biodiverse geologic technology behind him, Winchester leaves piles of rocks wherever he goes, rocks filled with a nutrient rich molecular structure. The rocks are claimed to be porphyry, or large grained crystals. Porphyry is volcanic in nature, and while Winchester's intensely insubordinate digestive system could imply surly volcanic activity, Impale doesn't buy into it. He, without any substantive argument, claims that Winchester's strewn geologic waste is nothing more than a metaphor for his disregard for everything including our own planet. While Senator Impale appeared slightly insane when making this argument in the beginning, the ghostwriters believe that he was closer to revealing the truth than anyone else in this scene.

In a whirlwind tour prior to the Iowa Caucus, most Republicans vying for the top seat dropped out of the race because of the enormous wealth backing Winchester's campaign. Senator Ore-Ida ran a marvelous campaign, however. His credentials as U.S. Naval Academy graduate, Vietnam War veteran and prisoner of war, and

U.S. Senator, coupled with his family's frozen French fries operation, launched him as a front runner in the early stages of the campaign before the primary. Party insiders felt that, although Winchester was backed by big money and power, more individuals could connect with Senator Ore-Ida. His sometimes modest demeanor, and sometimes nasty one, coupled with a dogged work ethic made him a man of the people, or at least a voice to represent something tangible to connect with, like the crunching sound of biting into a well-done frozen French fry. Worthy accomplishments that set him well apart from Winchester included the ability to read. To further compare levels of literacy is entirely unnecessary, but for the record, the following illustration can be made. He could write more than his name in crayon. While he could similarly color a sketched butterfly in a coloring book, staying within the lines of course, he could also read the words that accompanied the picture. In fact, any factors relating to basic human intelligence could be listed.

Interestingly, another U.S. Senator had ties to the Ore-Ida family, a marriage to one of Mr. Ore-Ida's daughters. And while this could be viewed as mere coincidence, it is no coincidence that family members of food production companies have never fared well on the path to the White House, which of course, was later reconstructed as the Gold House. Beltway think-tankers consider it likely that Gerald and company have placed Winchester's opponents in both the race for Governor of the Nation State of Texas and in the primary election to be the Republican nominee in the 2000 Presidential Election. Winchester's opponents were in fact formidable, but the transparency of the conspiracy would be insurmountable if his opponents were less intelligent, less qualified, and less likable than his son.

Senator Ore-Ida was smeared publicly so often that his demise was imminent. His heart was not yet dark enough to play that dirty. It is repeated—not yet dark enough.

Once the primaries were settled and the respective parties selected their candidates, Winchester's place in human history was well on its way to be written. BS was to be Winchester's running mate, his Vice President-to-be. While BS would have preferred the top slot, his determination to not fight the system was a wise strategy, one that would get him as far as he could go in the power scheme. Besides, Gerald had a strong hand in developing the system that is in place, and so to buck that system would be committing political suicide. His favorite behind-the-scenes power player, Grigori Yefimovich Rasputin, the Mad Monk, always said, "My penis is enormous, so I do not need the top position of power. I have real power." Of course, he stated this in Russian, but BS only knew the quote in English, and so he speaks it often. He especially finds use for it at parties, on the House floor, back home in Wyoming at the local strip clubs. BS carries this uncontested mythology forward, whether or not his penis is actually enormous or not. Most in the trailer park consider this to be a metaphorical assertion, but his wife Licky will not comment on its actual size. Rasputin's legacy, of course, lies rooted in his incredible power over Tsar Nicholas II, leader of Russia during the time Rasputin sat behind him, whispering in his ear—power by virtue of mind control. His poor relationship with the Russian representative assembly was no secret, and BS considered Rasputin's rebelliousness to be forthright and quite essential in the need to exercise true power, for like the Russian Duma, the United States Congress would certainly stand in his way, and he being a former member of the House of Representatives knew of its bureaucracy and its disliking of rebel factions within the Executive and Judicial branches. This understanding would later be critical in his grasp of the roles to be played out by those involved, especially his role relative to Winchester.

Prior to the year 2000, Winchester's life had been a tumultuous experience. His childhood was filled with angst and turmoil, and consistent public humiliation. His teenage-hood was filled with less than spectacular achievements, the days at Yellow University too, and so too his war time days as an ace jet pilot. There were also the difficulties in maintaining actual attendance in Harvard Business School classes, the subsequent years of partying, the drugs and alcohol throughout, the erratic behavior bordering on schizophrenia, his business launchings and subsequent failures, his transparent idiocy, the obviousness of his weakness and shrinking ego, the time traveling, the conversations with apparitions and former dead historical persons. His ability to guide large corporations and franchises despite being illiterate alone had indicated that he might somehow end up subsequently in the top seat in the Texas administration and eventually running for President.

Carlos Rangerover, the mad genius behind the election stagecraft, could be deemed one of the most dangerously inhumane criminals to ever be seated so close to the nation's top seat. His team was so clever that his not so secret dedication to Zimmydom was well hidden. When it did become public knowledge, however, the assertion was quickly dismissed as mud-smearing rhetoric on the part of the Democratic Party. He brilliantly turned all political contests into the slinging of feces back and forth until the entire campaign resembled a day at Deej's house after an all-night rave pre-ex-NASA geochemist diaper technology. Winchester was ultimately comfortable with this approach. It was like falling off the wagon or blowing a few lines. During one of the pre-election debates, Winchester was in the process of removing the Velcro straps from his diaper to solidify his victory. Rangerover, while thoroughly amused by this potential strong suit move, with Broken Stream's consent, whispered his disapproval directly in Winchester's ear in mid Velcro tear, stating, "While winning the debate, you might turn off the voters if you actually emptied the room from your horrendous odor." Winchester simply nodded and retightened the straps.

The more liberal wing of the Democrats stood by and commanded, "Don't play that game; we are above that." Apparently they were not above that sufficiently to win the popular vote in the election. What? Hold on? Are you joking? There is a newsflash that will shock the world. Apparently, the election of 2000 was *not* fixed as had been understood and reported. Conspiracy theorists take a hike! Go have a picnic under a shady oak in rural Kansas. This misreporting was a terrible case of "intuition vs. historical fact," and it seems that intuition will win this debate regarding why Winchester Buckley Johnson beat Senator Calvin Impale to win the Presidential election after all. Obviously, Winchester had better attorneys, this much is known with absolute certainty.

Rangerover's approach was simple. "Stick to what you know and what you are good at."

"Like what?" Replied an oft-confused Winchester.

"Speak from your gut. You have an instinct to win. We are always behind you. So, trust yourself. Whatever happens, the team will clean up after you."

And so it went, "cleaning" became the buzzword of the campaign. This strategy so altered the face of the campaign that instructions were constantly given to guarantee the cleanup was spotless. Winchester's tremendous ability to make people cringe when he spoke allowed Rangerover to see ahead. The predictability of WBJ's weaknesses made setting the stage for cleaning up after him a virtual breeze. Winchester became so confident in his approach he really sounded genuine. No matter what words escaped his lips, his team would mold those words into something brilliant, something patriotic, something worth defending. This knowledge proved to be the right formula for letting Winchester run from coast to coast boasting about this and that, letting his mouth and ass run as it always has. Combining the resounding effects of Zimmydom with the technology to metaphysically transform the effects of Winchester's odd digestive system woes into something invisible, off the radar, his power to influence the masses was highly unique. It was like having the ability to conceal the largest diamond in the world in a tiny room filled only with black wallpaper, a black-carpeted floor and bright spotlights. Rangerover and his squad had real talent. It was as though destiny ran through these streams, the same destiny that ran through the American river, the same destiny that brought Kra and Carlos Rangerover to a Zimmydom rally outside of Belize City in 1989.

"Hi, I'm Kra."

"Hi, Kra. I'm Carlos."

"Want to have sex with me?"

"I don't think so, but thanks for asking."

"You know Zim?"

"Not personally, but I am a faithful follower of his enterprise. Do you know him?"

"Yes, yes. I know him better than any man or woman on this earth. We were roommates, and we spent many a night planning out the next 30 years."

"Wow. How do I get in on this?"

"I will speak with Zim directly. He gives his orders only to me."

"Wow. I heard that he is quite an artist. Do you have any of his work?"

"I sell his coloring books at a small boutique in Wichita. Sales are slow, but it's not about the money. I have plenty of money already."

"Can I buy some of his coloring books? I really want them for my collection."

"Sure. What else do you have in your collection?"

"I was able to pick up some audio tapes of conversations with Charlie Monsoon at an estate sale. I have some paintings of the court jesters by Jack Willie Grocery. I have others, but those are my favorites."

"Wow."

"Are you sure you don't want to have sex?"

"Yes, Kra, I am certain."

"Well okay. I will see how Zim wants to use you, if indeed he does want to use you. I will get back with you."

"Great!"

Governor Jack Johnson's face is red as a baby's spanked bottom, "I am not going to help him! He is a prick! He never respected my family or me. I studied at my University! Did he? No! I carved my own path! Not by Daddy's help! NOT BY DADDY'S HELP!"

Carlos calmly listens to a fiercely angered Governor Jack Johnson. "Just calm down, Governor. I am sure we can work something out. How does 2012 sound? I can get you on the ticket for 2012?"

"The ticket?"

"*The* ticket."

"Damn, I can't pass on that one. Well, I always read that sacrifice can lead to great things. Okay, what do we need?"

"When the time is right, I will call on you for your help. Hey, how's that vixen who is your Secretary of State? I hear she's quite a tiger in bed!"

"Oh, Carlos, Carlos, you have no idea, my man. No idea."

"Well, keep her on a tight leash. Don't let her get away."

"Get away? I am thinking about leaving my wife for her. I mean she does things with a cantaloupe that you cannot even imagine."

"Wow. Get it on film. I want to see that."

"Sure thing. I'll do my best to hide a camera in my office, but if I'm to do that for you, I want a guarantee that I'll be on the 2012 ticket, and maybe 2008."

"I can't guarantee 2008, but Gerald has already agreed on 2012. It is against my nature, but you have to keep it in your pants. Your brother is on the wagon, you know. Otherwise, he wouldn't be where he is. If he can give up hooch and coke, you can bypass a little poontang."

The last part of the conversation really got Jack thinking clearly. If he can find the fortitude to dump his mistresses, he might be President some day. This is very exciting for him. He has always wanted very badly to play a larger role in family affairs, the affairs that run the federal government and the intelligence community, or at least play a part in his family's oil companies or numerous investment firms. But, Gerald never saw that in him. Perhaps this is his big chance. He decides he will desperately try to show his worth to his father, who is always looming nearby, in order to gain his acceptance. Standing before a mirror in Florida room in the

Governor's Mansion, Jack removes his jacket and tie, loosens his white collared blue oxford and runs his hands through his hair. He gives his body a ritualistic shake, perhaps a ceremonial maneuver to get ready for the next stage of his life.

"Mirror, mirror, on the wall. Who is the fairest Johnson of them all?"

As he stands waiting for an answer, he dives deeply into his soul as he peers intensely into his own eyes. He has done good deeds for people. He knows that, in doing good deeds, he has made friends in important places. However, he never finished constructing that bridge to the other side, the side where his older brother Winchester has always seemed to be, the side where Gerald smokes a fat cigar and dictates the ebb and flow of human traffic. While he cannot completely assimilate his brother's experiences, his mouth produces a slight metallic taste of iron. He thinks that maybe it is about chemistry. Perhaps his way of being just does not suit his father's needs. Well, he can be anything he wants to be, and if that means being more like Winchester to make Gerald happy, he will do it. He wants to please his father, and he desperately wants power. The difference, for him, is that he always wanted to do it *his* way, not Gerald's way. He had made it on his own for years, or so he thinks. The first order in changing his strategy is to carry laxatives at all times. Perhaps if he were as freewheeling with his bodily functions, like his brother, he could get the respect he seeks.

Thirty minutes prior to a speech in the Manatee Gardens outside the Governor's mansion, on a typical bright, sunny Tallahassee day, Governor Jack Johnson ingested three helpings of a powdered laxative mixed with gin and lemon juice. His breakfast that morning consisted of four blue corn tortillas stuffed with poblano chili peppers and Manchego cheese, a favorite way to prepare tortillas by his newest maid and lover, an Aztec descendent named

Mayra. He slugged down two cups of strong black coffee and a glass of freshly squeezed Florida grapefruit juice, then mixed the laxative with the gin martini. Before the speech could begin, as the media crew was assembling their equipment around the perimeter of the garden by the podium, Jack was busy soiling himself inside the mansion. He simply couldn't hold it. Soiling himself in public was simply out of his reach. He didn't have the goods, the know-how, and the make-do.

The mirror subsequently answered after taking a short nap, but no one was in the Florida room to hear the answer as the Governor's mansion was emptied out from the smell: "Why, you are, Jack, the fairest Johnson of them all." When Jack asked who is the fairest, he meant who is the best looking, the most well maintained, but the mirror mistook his question as one relating to justice. Alas, there was nothing to be misinterpreted, in reality, as the response was not heard anyway.

Ernesto "Che" Guevara de la Serna is often considered one of the great revolutionary thinkers of the 20th century. The Argentine born Marxist lived an extraordinary life. He essentially wrote the manual on guerrilla warfare, helping to lead social revolutions in both Guatemala and in Cuba, and later in Bolivia before his untimely death. Some say his ideas about revolution figure in the Congo-Kinshasa situation as well, but the facts are still in dispute. While some Belize counter-culturalists tried to run with Che during the social and political changes sweeping Belize's neighbor Guatemala, most citizens were comfortable with the transition between British Crown Colony and independent nation. So, the movement died in its early tracks. However, some followers of Guevara's teachings eventually helped organize with other revolutionaries throughout Latin America in an attempt to battle the imperial power of the United States. One of those young, impressionable thinkers was Jill Rossi Mendez, a young idealist who left her homeland of Mexico as a teenager to fight Britain's imperial hold on the citizens of British Honduras. As a young revolutionary thinker, it was her responsibility to help free the citizens from the wrath of capitalism in order to establish a social and economic fabric of equality. Che was her philosophical leader. It was not until she met her future husband, Jack Johnson, a wealthy American teaching English in Belize City, that her views would be slightly altered and, eventually, her rebel ways give way to wanting only to pop out a few puppies from her womb.

Her connection with radical philosophies was never abandoned completely, however. It was during her courtship with Jack that she was introduced to the world of the CIB. Belize City had been a giant centrifuge for clandestine operations for all of Latin America. Some CIB members were already posing as Marxist revolutionaries. These Marxist fakers, while frequently turning up across the world as pop-culture enthusiasts, had no relation to the CIB spies, who were in fact lifetime spies and did not live to be recognized for their coolness.

Her bank-owning father and Florida State Legislator as well as cattle and citrus baron grandfather had paved the way for the future Governor Jack Johnson's Secretary of State, Nancy Hardon. Little Miss Hardon spent some time in her youth on an exchange program in Belize City. It was during that stay that she befriended another teenage revolutionary, Ka Zin Flow. Mr. Flow could have been a caricature from a comic book. His physical features were dramatically chiseled as if made of steel. Miss Hardon, a very impressionable young teenager, was so overwhelmed by Ka Zin that she dedicated her entire existence to his desires. And a dedication like that does not die so quickly. Ka Zin was the nephew of CIB deputy director Johnny Waltrip. Ka Zin's parents were extraordinary fans of the Surrealist movement and his odd name was a mere reflection of this fact. Waltrip spent several years running the CIB operation in Latin America out of Belize City, and it was here that Waltrip and Gerald became very close friends. Gerald enjoyed the spirit of Ka Zin, who reminded Gerald of his own youth. The younger man's drive, his dedication, his chiseled features brought joy and happiness to Gerald. Gerald's offspring were too busy lacing themselves with drugs and alcohol, and so, to see a fine young philosopher-in-training was a joy for Gerald.

It was here that Gerald first met young Miss Hardon too. This relationship would sporadically develop throughout the years until Miss Hardon eventually became a full-fledged member of Gerald's team. The CIB needed some insider theosophical thinkers to head up anti-Muslim operations, and Miss Hardon, who was studying in a Christian Commune in Switzerland in 1997, was the choice deemed most fit. Extreme Muslim groups had been operating out of Europe since the early 1970s, and the CIB and Interpol are forever hot on the trail of those looking to exterminate themselves in order to enter Allah's good company. Miss Hardon was persuaded to abandon any former philosophical deviations to dedicate herself completely to the notion of global undertaker, to the CIB.

Since their days in Belize, Ka Zin Flow had become one of the great business ethics philosophers and taught at globally prestigious universities. He holds honorary tenure in New York's Columbia, Paris' La Sorbonne, and the American University in Dubai. Interpol never had enough evidence regarding his pedophilic crimes to formally imprison him, and his outlandish personality made him a pop culture hero, especially in Scandinavia. Despite his negative publicity, the CIB held onto Ka Zin like a black marlin holds on to an eight-inch hook eighty kilometers east of Miami, near Bimini. Ka Zin Flow was deeply rooted in the CIB and all of its operations, and although a much younger Ka Zin and Jill Rossi Mendez had a short fling in the fall of 1973, no connection between Governor Jack Johnson and Ka Zin Flow existed. Jack and Ka simply lived on separate planes of existence. And although Belize was a center point for everyone involved here, Nancy Hardon and Jack Johnson had no contact either until much later. It was the relationship between Jill Rossi Mendez and Nancy Hardon that caught the fancy of most. Some have even claimed to be witness to overt lesbian behavior, but nothing has ever been proved to the effect. Nancy's dedication to power and Jill's ability to hold power between her teeth without clenching would constitute a formidable relationship in the early years but become quite a problem in the latter years.

As part of his secrecy, Ka also became a Swiss chocolate confectioner in Geneva. While teaching at La Sorbonne in the mid 1990s, Ka's true talent was setting up businesses using his exciting algorithm-based sliding "consumer scale of excitability," a tool that he teaches as part of a fundamental class in understanding global economics. His true passions lie in setting up businesses that would cause great excitement, then become a global smash, use shady accounting practices to avoid taxation, convince investors to take the company public, use complicated schematics to move the company into failure, sell his shares out, short sell additional shares through invisible organs worldwide, then publicly criticize the functionaries running the operation in order to drive the company into public scrutiny and subsequent failure, buying back the shares he short sold to make a killing in both directions. Consumer excitability has since become a corner stone of the advance econ program at the American University in Dubai.

In a very hostile takeover, Ka swallowed the Swiss confectioner, Vindt, then brought it to new heights of profitability. He then sold the majority shares of the company to the Vishnaivas, an Indian family from

Mumbai who owned a competitor to Vindt in Asia. Then he staged a huge coup d'etat by declaring the business practices of the Vishnaiva family unethical and coercing another Swiss giant among confectioners, Presle, to buy American confectioner giant Ghirardelli in order to completely demolish the Vishnaiva Chocolate Group. Presle never did buy Ghirardelli, but Swiss confectioner Lindz did, despite the hundreds of patent infringement lawsuits brought against Lindz by Vindt because the name is so close to its major competitor. Being a paid consultant by both Presle and Lindz, Ka successfully orchestrated one of the ugliest maneuvers in the history of the sweets industry. The confection turned a virtual blood red as heads rolled onto the platters of shareholders in the Zurich stock exchange. Shares for Presle, despite the amazing takeover, plummeted, especially in Zurich. Just weeks before the takeover was complete, Gerald sold 400,000 shares in Presle short through his broker in Riyadh and then closed the short sale after a 26% drop in price. And likewise, the shares in Lindz skyrocketed, and he similarly made a killing on that. He, of course, split the profit of both transactions with Ka Zin. This is very important to know. Ka Zin Flow could dictate the future movement of commerce. Despite a very complicated global economy, he knew what to do. And Gerald being Gerald, was not blind to this fact.

On election night 2000, Governor Jack Johnson sat in the Governor's mansion nervously eating a box of Presle truffles given to him by his dad's good friend Ka, which had been hand-delivered from Secretary of State Nancy Hardon. It was an entire box of dark chocolate truffles, his favorite. He was nervous because, although he hated his brother to the bones, he wanted to see victory because that meant his chance of making it to the Gold House in 2012 was very real. Standing before his reflection, admiring his boyish charm, he once again confided in the sacred mirror, "If my idiot brother can get there, I can do it too. I just need to convince Dad that I will do whatever he wants me to do. But I want guarantees. O mirror, mirror on the wall, who is the cleverest Johnson of them all?"

Gerald monitors Jack's every move, indeed all of his children's moves, with special tracking devices surgically implanted inside of their chins that detect their voices and relay what they say with perfect pitch and clarity with data concerning their precise location. Winchester's device often malfunctions and Gerald gives blame to the high levels of acid in his body due to his malfunctioning nervous and digestive systems. Gerald, in conjunction with Ka and Nancy and using tactics employed by Che and Kra, and therefore Zim, pulled off the greatest invisible operation known to all inside of Wall and outside of Wall to steer the election to his son. The problem is, as history will show, facts cannot be found to prove that the election was rigged. It is mere speculation. Until the facts are actually found to prove this, intuition is what history is based upon. Wall's two finest historians, aside from Herodotus, Colin Macfarquhar and Andrew Bell, claim that facts must be based on real fact and not intuition. This has been overridden by the playwright's ghostwriting team. The facts do exist but have been misplaced, and therefore, intuition is a sadly imposed replacement. A replacement that is necessary, however, for logic must still hold true. A proof is a proof despite "losing" the evidence.

After the victory parade held in Midland, Texas for the new President of the United States, the former President of the Nation-State of Texas, Winchester Buckley Johnson, his Vice President-elect Broken Stream and Rin Chin Chin sat patiently waiting for Winchester to return to the Governor's mansion. He had a surprise for Winchester, a gift that would later prove to be somewhat dangerous for Rin. But being a chin inside a jar, he assumed that he had very little to fear. The gift was quite odd by any measure. It was filled with layers of meaning and purpose, yet it was like a toy for a child. A water-filled snow globe, the ones that, when shaken, typically resemble fake snow falling over New York City, the World Trade Center buildings in the center, was waiting for President-elect Johnson in a silky silver gift wrap. Like a child at Christmas time, Winchester opened his present with great excitement. This particular snow globe had a gold Sinterklaas, or Santa Claus, his right hand raised to the sky as he rode upon an Arabian horse that was standing on its hind legs. It was inscribed, "To My Dad, the Great Winchester Buckley, President of the United States." When Winchester shook the globe, it made a sound like an alarm, the kind of alarm that is similar to the National Broadcasting System performing an audible test on a radio. The snow that swirled around the globe, around the golden Saint Nicholas and horse, was phosphorescent, as though nuclear fallout was swirling around inside a thinning atmosphere.

"Rin?"

"Yes Dad."

"Why does the snow look like a neon sign?"

"Why do you think, Dad?"

"It looks like *nuculer* rain."

"Good guess Dad, close enough."

Act 20.

Freudian Isometrics: The Replacement and the Replacement's Replacement

The playwright gave his first directive since Act 1, but he still remained out of sight. The directive arrived in a crude form of communication, a telegram sent from an unknown location. In order to guide the ghostwriters properly, the telegram indicated how he wanted to handle the Presidential election fiasco.

"Mull over the impasse of an electoral recount. This particular recount is the process needed to determine if the popular vote in the Presidential election was valid. If the voting process was tainted, and therefore the vote failed to represent the will of the people and the process to protect the rights of citizens, may or may not be the root issue here. For if the process was tainted or a proper recount necessary, indeed whether the avoidance of a recount was something legal, is largely determined by popular opinion. As it is, the legality issue was never argued well enough to matter, and an ensuing public outcry was never quite strong enough to force additional action into being. What exactly happened is very complex and quite tedious, and in many ways, the actual facts are unimportant. What is important is the matter itself, and this matter is categorically misunderstood. The reaction to the matter remains most important, for it forged a very deep cavity between American citizens depending on the political party they support. Stop."

The meteor that hit the United States, the one that began at the state of Florida's voting booths then went careening across our galaxy only to return like a sling shot from a distant star's gravity field, left the ensuing crater deeply embedded in our memories, a crevice so deep and wide that a Civil War was, and still is, a very real possibility to some.

So it goes. So begins the new adventure that Americans face, Americans who live in the United States and Americans who live outside its geographical boundaries share a common bond. The bond is not one of geography, nor is it one of philosophy, nor is it one determined by a belief system or by a non-belief system. It is a link like a well-marketed pop star placed on a shelf for the world to consume. It is a link that is shared without choice and without a fight. It is a link to the men and women who govern and the choices these knights of governance have made. Questions linger in the minds of those who have paid attention to all significant occurrences since mankind has come together in an information-condensing machine. What choices have American citizens made? What choices have they failed to make with clear minds and clear hearts? What choices will continue to be made? What does it mean to have had a President who was mere moments away from achieving peace in the Middle East by mediating the crisis facing the Israeli people and the Palestinian people by bringing the two leaders together, behind closed doors, making a leap of political faith, blurring the lines of political boundaries to shed hope and peace for the future of humanity. What does it mean to have a new President who cannot read, a President, who will sit on his throne, like an old king, by birthright, without any valor or sense of duty to his post or his people, an autocrat placed by a puppet master in a highly skilled regime, an amateurish leader of no hope for his own people, and no hope for the agreements that can bridge the gaps between peace and all-out destruction?

The recounts never mattered. The determinable vote subsists in the fabric of mankind's existence. The chosen candidates run against one another, vying for the nation's top political spot, the one that largely determines the very direction of the world's political, economic and social direction, but was the choice entirely the people's? Skeptics win here, as the truth lies somewhere between forced public appeal and mass marketed brainwashing. More specifically, the recounts mattered and yet they did not matter. The vote matters, but to vote with one's conscience means to vote with knowledge, and so, the vote itself, largely does not matter as most people act without thought or conscience. This particular bit of knowledge, who *really* won, is in hiding somewhere on a shelf in the J. Edgar Hoover Library in the Gold House not to be touched again for years.

"I just like the way he looks on TV!"

"What about what he stands for?"

"Oh, well I heard that he stands to protect all of us against our enemies."

"Who are the enemies?"

"Well, there are lots of them, and all I know is that he will protect me from them."

"Is that the reason you will vote for him, the only reason? What about the other candidate? Could he protect you equally well?"

"Well, I have never heard the other candidate on the radio station that *I* listen to. I have never seen him on the television station that *I* watch."

"Try changing stations once in a while—it might help you see both sides to determine who is better qualified to lead us."

"What did you say?"

"Forget it."

"President-elect Winchester Buckley Johnson, the walking geological wonder, the man who derived his sense of urgency from his disastrous nervous and digestive systems, the man who, despite his weaknesses and failures and inadequacies, is the man we will support unconditionally because, if we are to survive as a nation, we must stand behind our President!" stated Senator Impale calmly and assuredly after his second and final speech, after foregoing any further challenge to the election results and the legality of the voting procedure. A small handful of supporters cheered loudly as the rest just listened to their fallen leader.

"I will certainly stand by him, for that is the way of our country. I am not bitter. I accept the loss, albeit with a heavy heart. I accept it and I will do everything I can to help this country move to a brighter future."

In an unprecedented move, Winchester escaped the grips of his father and his new circle of campaign tacticians in order to give the speech that *he* wanted to give rather than the speech that was ordered of him. Moments before speaking, he located the device implanted in his chin and removed it with a razor blade and a pair of rusty tweezers he keeps safely in his underwear drawer, the same tweezers that removed a splinter from Deej's finger years ago, the one that reminds him of men that are stronger than he, the same tweezers that remind him of when he lost the election for House of Representatives back in '78, when he declared across the airwaves in a debate before a roomful of Vietnam veterans in a Moose Lodge: "If you elect me to be your representative in your house, I will do everything I can to keep oil prices high so that I can make sure that I have enough money to still do the things I like to do."

He left the tracking device sitting on the rich cherry end table in the Governor's office as he darted out the door with blood streaming from the cleft in his chin. A limousine sat waiting to whisk him to a local brew pub in Austin's warehouse district, where the band playing that night was to take a break so that President-elect Johnson could take the stage and join with the men and women that *he* connects with, the ones passed out by the bar or lingering about while the bartender pours shots of ice cold Jagermeister, not the voters watching television, patiently waiting almost a month and a half after the election to have a victor declared, to know definitively who will lead them into the future.

With his face bleeding and his clothes covered in his own blood, he looked like a man returning from battle, and all of those present to see it were moved by its symbolism. "I, Winchester Buckley Johnson, your new President, will now take the pole position in this race to make America the best again."

Ferdinand Porsche smiles gently as he receives a soothing neck massage in the physical regeneration tent in Wall.

"I want to make some promises to you."

"Yeah! Promise to get me laid tonight!" spouted a drunken sophomore from UT Austin with a fake ID and a pocket filled with ecstasy pills.

"Well, if I promised you that, I would have to promise that everyone here would get laid too."

The bar goes crazy and starts chanting "Winchester! Winchester! Winchester!"

Winchester observes the crowd, which is ferociously supporting him, and he feeds from these people's wildness. He never had a problem feeding from a crowd.

"Fuck it then! Let's party!" Winchester wildly reacts to his new faithful crowd. "Drinks on the federal government! Let's get rocked!" he screams into the microphone just before he does a stage dive. Dozens of young energetic students and young professionals catch him and pass him around their upwardly outstretched arms while he mimics his favorite body surfing poses in the process. Within thirty minutes, the entire bar is full to capacity as cell phones quickly notified hundreds of acquaintances that free drinks were on offer. Drunk, staggering, happy as a bull in a crowded narrow Pamplona street, Winchester takes the stage again.

"Hey! Quiet down!" He sticks out his tongue and gives the University of Texas Longhorn salute, the one that is virtually identical to the devil's horns salute given at heavy metal concerts, only the hand is in reverse. "I know that now I will be President! But, we all know each other here pretty good. I want y'all to call me by my new nickname that I just gave myself! Call me Great Winchester Buckley! Or, if you want to visit me in the Gold House, like, just call me GWB!"

Back at the trailer park, Zhu Zen is becoming very weary. She knows that a battle is being written into this play, the battle between heaven and earth, the one linking men and women from the afterlife to the men and women in the conscious dimension. She knows the very balance of existence hangs on the words of an illiterate, out of control, childish rebel with a drug and alcohol dependency, a spastic colon, and incontinence. She knows this, and yet, she cannot do a thing about it. Her guidance has failed him. Moreover her better nature was abused. Zhu Zen Kow, the keeper of secret places and consultant to the Gods, is forced to play a hand that she did not want to play so early in the game. But now, throwing her cards on the table seems her only available solution after years of keeping a straight poker face.

Working in conjunction, the CIB and the Pseudalopex News Network were intercepting any video feeds of Winchester streaming across the airwaves surrounding planet earth and its upper atmosphere, where satellites twist and gyrate in technological wonder. The feeds were immediately routed to the CIB's tracking station where teams were ready to re-release the feed after being edited for mass consumption back to the earth's common airspace. Except for those present, Winchester's foray at the bar was never seen by anyone, and most present that night were far too intoxicated to recall if the incident did actually happen. Back at the Governor's mansion, Winchester's clone was taking the podium. Luckily, Gerald's top scientific staff had been perfecting his muscular movements and the greatest plastic surgeons had perfected his expressions with real skin grafted from a recently slain 55 year-old man who died of heart trauma. They learned how to keep the skin alive by feeding it certain nucleoproteins to keep cells healthy, even though they were only loosely connected to his quickly conceived stem cell grown muscular system, similar to the powder given to Rin Chin Chin for the first couple of years of his life. The computer that is the clone's brain was taught to speak precisely like Winchester, using the same intonations and reflections and methods of expressing grins and grimaces, smiles and looks of terror. The computer was well constructed enough to learn the most important element of thinking like Winchester, the ability to repeat the same word or groups of words and ideas despite its desire to speak fluidly using complete ideas and then move on to the next thought without repeating itself. The disappearance of the new President turned out to be an excellent test of the plan to replace Winchester with his clone. The clone's repetition of certain phrases was the primary method by which they intended to convince the listeners that he was the real Winchester, not an imposter. In order to divert the attention of those paying attention, these repetitions were intended to frustrate the listener until he just shuts out the message from absolute frustration. The same groups of words repeated over and over created a diversion enough to allow the listeners to pay less attention to the message, and psychologically forced the listeners to listen more to their own brains telling them that "he just said that a second ago, didn't he?" The computer's regeneration was so well done, that often, later, when the real Winchester and his clone sat side by side in the Rectangular Office in the Gold House, no one present, except Rin, could differentiate the two.

"Thank you very much. Thank you. Thank you very much. Good evening, my fellow Americans. I appreciate so very much the opportunity to speak with you tonight. Mr. Speaker, Lieutenant Governor, friends, distinguished guests, our country has been through a long and trying period, with the outcome of the presidential election not finalized for longer than any of us could ever imagine…" GWB's clone unearthed a well-groomed and well-thought out acceptance speech.

In fact, many clones walk the earth. Most are small animals that escaped CIB laboratories, but there are a few select humans who have been cloned. The CIB keeps the media on the chosen trail of truth and fiction related to how they want people to understand cloning, or anything else for that matter. Disinformation has become the most relevant form of journalism unknown to modern man. However, the notion of reckless cloning upsets some of the scientists in Wall so much that a meeting is held to determine potential action. Among the participants at the meeting that went on for days at the trailer park, a new sense of enlightenment has been overtaking the "let's go crazy because we can" mentality of the historical human elite. Small groups have been forming to discuss the future of the human race, and this, while not relevant to humanity at large just yet, may actually play a part in the direction that humanity goes. The secret lies in memories stored in DNA. Knowledge is dangerous, for as human consciousness grows, so does the collective memory capacity, and therefore, so grows the influence of past generations on our daily activities. Despite how much we may or may not want this knowledge, it is injected into our brains, like force-feeding an infant with an upset stomach. Even isolationists have an impossible time keeping out of the flow of the traffic jam on the highway of consciousness. While this might seem to be a theoretical stretch of the imagination, the same rules of logic apply to what has not yet happened for the memories are already present.

"People need to readjust their minds. Time is not a linear concept. We have known this for a very long time. But how can we help people understand that to travel through time one simply needs to look in that direction and set off." Leonardo da Vinci was pushing his hands toward the sky, his fingers flapping like a bird's wings, mocking a flying gesture with his fingers. "During my final days in Amboise, I was certain that I was not only going to die, but that I was also becoming a child once again. I know that my good friend Albert will argue this point. Al? Al? He was just here."

Albert Einstein is busy running around in circles like a madman. "Turn off your television! Turn off your radio! Close the doors, pull the blinds, remove the listening devices, any form of radio or microwave that can contain transmitters, and talk to each other about everything until the root memories are dislodged and new thoughts arrive. Head back to the cave! Time will wear a dirty ugly old waistcoat that begs to be worn, but do your best to ignore it. It will only destroy your ability to stay alive. And whatever you do, retain all thoughts as though they are like steps in a ladder, to help you understand where we are going, and I predict we are going up. I hope this place is far away and a more forgivable planet."

Plato was able to catch him and hugged a very excited Albert Einstein who loves bantering about this subject, especially with Marie Curie and Charles Darwin, who really get into this with him. "I say that if things do not change, we demand that our most famous theories and public knowledge of our most practical experiments should be removed from the history books. That way, those with the knowledge already will be forced to talk about it amongst each other, as though they are lunatics, and this might give credibility to the knowledge, like the old histories of previous civilizations that were burned or purposefully lost during the darker moments of the human escapade like during the crusades and the periods of inquisition and witch hunting. As a matter of survival, that information became part of an oral tradition, never to be lost and reaching mythical status."

"Sorry, Al. We're not going to remove theories from the history books—nice dissertation though."

"Come on, ZZ. You above all people must see the merit in this proposal."

"Yes, well, perhaps, but it is not wise."

"Do you know how easy it would be for people to accept the removal of my general theory of relativity from history's files? Remember, I am Jewish, and many people would gladly forget me for just that reason."

"I appreciate your intentions Al, but I don't fall for racial and political satire to shape my actions. Tough luck."

"Damn! Okay guys, how about a beer!"

They join arm in arm and converge toward one of the beer tents where a small group of Belgian monks are busy pouring homebrews at the busiest bar behind the Wall, where the patrons sing and dance all day and night. ZZ sits quietly considering how she can stage her move without causing a riot within the trailer park. Her move must be subtle; she must reach out gently to silently topple the wall that separates the historical persons from the living persons. If the methodology is too violent, people will repress their desire to grab hold of it. A struggle between living human beings and their illustrious past is not what she wants. "The Balkan mess is the clearest proof this must be subtle," she thinks aloud.

What purpose can her action serve so that it is heartily accepted? ZZ knows the consequences of this maneuver, and yet she searches the deeper realms of her being to find the secrets among the secrets, the ones that ancient sorcerers use like weapons when fighting unwanted guests or interruptions from the spiritual world. In those secrets, she hopes to find the reason why it may not matter if she removes Wall's wall gently or blows it to kingdom come.

At South Carolina's Buck James University, BJU, a sinister side plot is making its stomach-churning underbelly known. University officials, teaming up with new members of Winchester's cabinet, who were appointed by Broken Stream with Gerald's advice, are plotting the demise of the American educational landscape. Superficially, it might seem like quite a paradox for a university to plot the takeover of intellect and replace freely thinking human beings with automatons constructed from living matter using assistance from Macrohard's newest brainwashing program, which was developed specifically for the CIB. In intelligence circles, this plot is known formatively as *The Great Dumb-Down of the American People.* Several critical factors contribute to the relevance of this side story. One is the fact that BJ University is not accredited as a university or recognized as such by the Department of Education, and while school officials would argue that they are a candidate for accreditation, this does not mean that they will be accredited. What does this mean? A university claiming to be an institution of higher learning cannot be recognized as such without accreditation. Many companies, state and federal institutions and boards of education, science and arts do not recognize a degree from institutions like BJU. But this is just a single underlying current in the river of significance. The real force of the stream is conducted by the sinister minds gathering here, which is the real significance, and while many others attempting to battle the dumbing-down of American culture and educational growth attempt to use legality as their main weapon, one will eventually see, if they look hard enough, that legality is controlled by those who interpret the laws, and therefore, can often be tossed aside like unwanted garlic croutons on a simple garden salad.

The mostly unreported purpose of this university and the tremendously patriotic group of deep humanitarian thinkers who run it, besides helping to make Americans dumber by design, is the industrious on-campus development of sex toy technology. The secret chamber within the university President's office, behind the library of unread books, is a virtual kaleidoscope of colorful gadgets, bondage apparatus, lotions and potions. University President, Sven James, is notorious in the underground network of BDSM establishments, where he is revered for his two-fold existence, preaching complete religious conservatism and displaying the most liberal of sexual behavior. For this, he is regarded as a true revolutionary even by Wall's elite standards. His great new inventions are marvels of orgasmic delight. The Arabian Horse clippers and the Westover Bendover are two fundamentalist favorites. Despite the occasional flack he receives, he continues to work with Japanese electronics manufacturers in the design and implementation of new toys, which he tests thoroughly on himself and others and then distributes through his website. (URL removed due to a patent infringement lawsuit.)

Terry Gay, the Majority Whip of the House of Representatives, and Justice Preevins of the Supreme Court sit in on the cabinet meetings. Through the MacDiddy's phony Foundation for Educational Enterprise, the group decides to coordinate the effort with a ceremonial kick-off, a planned parade through the streets of Los Angeles that will include floats expressing themes related to the world's most well known people who never received an education from an accredited institution. This plot humors some of the elite thinkers of the trailer park, but others are infuriated. The division seems to be related to, but not exclusively derived from, whether or not one has had the "college experience" or not, and, of course, this relates mostly to how much partying one did while attending each person's respective university.

Broken Stream, who, himself, had a miserable experience at Yellow and then at Community College, demands that Congress curb funding for America's overrated educational apparatus in order to beef up the military's might and provide additional funding for oil drilling in America's protected National Park System. Most in attendance agree, but not Secretary of State Plower. However, he is so heavily in the minority that he does not last a moment. This is to be taken very literally, as Gerald has already constructed Plower's clone, which is waiting patiently on a peaceful sabbatical in Uganda. Plower was named to the post by GWB, which went completely against Broken Stream's orders, and more to the point, Gerald's orders, before Winchester's clone was in place. GWB liked the way Plower looked in a suit, so he always wanted him around. Plower, already highly recognized as a solid strategic thinker and humanitarian, was the perfect man for the job, assuming the job was what it was cut out to be, which is mostly keeping his mouth shut and is usually a given for he literally fears for his life. Gerald's great fear, of course, is Plower disobeying Winchester's clone, and being a smart clone,

Winchester's clone may see merit in his disobedience, and as a result, the cloned President might make alternative decisions that are unmistakably against what Broken and Gerald want from time to time,. This is not a group that considers open mindedness a virtue. Despite the university President's sex toy operation, the mindset of this crew of virtual modern Argonauts is clearly fundamentally closed shut, tight as a vacuum-sealed lid on a jar. Jason, who comes to the trailer park to dine from time to time because of its list of timeless French star chefs headed by Marie Antoine "the Crèmeiest Brulee of them All" Carême, is humiliated that the ghostwriters have made a metaphor of his Argonauts, who many think to be true heroes of humanity as some of the earliest traces of true adventurism began with his illustrious Hellenic crew.

"Our goal for this parade is for all Americans to quit school for one year and donate their time to the Republican Party."

"Can that work?"

"How can it *not* work? All we need to do is advertise the parade right."

"Sure, sure, but will it reach *everybody*? If we want it to reach everybody, we have the tools, we have the resources, and we have the staff of millions at our beck and call. Trust me, we can do it."

"I see convincing everyone to drop out of school as a choice might be an issue, so why don't we just enforce it?"

"That's a good call. Let's make it a law."

And so they did. Winchester's clone submitted a bill to Congress making a law entitled "Dropping Out of School For a Year" to support our party. Since the Republican Party controlled the Executive, Congressional, and for all practical purposes if not legal ones, the Judicial Branches, passing bills through the federal government became a joke. While many might have complained about stalemates in Congress, not being able to push through important legislation due to policies set and voted upon along party lines, not having a stalemate can be far more dangerous at times, especially during times of disunity, and of course, the danger lies in the moral fiber of the decision makers, however thin or thick or even present at all this fiber may or may not be. This enactment would be celebrated with a parade, not only in downtown Los Angeles but also in New York's Times Square. This law would go into effect on September 10, 2001; and every September 10th would be known as Dropping Out of School For a Year Day to commemorate this valiant effort to craft American society as less intelligent and more apt to follow orders. The Republican constituency was so pleased with this idea that they devised a Winchester Buckley Johnson Day, the next newest national holiday. After a brief deliberation, it was decided that this day would coincide with the other new national holiday, and the subsequent commemorative parades would make the perception of this holiday's importance, like Independence Day and Thanksgiving, huge and complete, and so the new law was quickly enacted. Therefore the official title of this new holiday was as follows: President Winchester Buckley Johnson's Dropping out of School for a Year Day. Soon, children and teenagers began dropping out of school ahead of the law, as a matter of obedience to their nation and its fundamental operative agreement with its citizens to follow the lead of its governing body; and to show true patriotism, they acted expeditiously. Of course, it was also a year long vacation from any school. So, obviously, not many youth objected and the overwhelming majority of them celebrated. The real power of this enactment came in the form of terror. Similar to the 'Red Scare' of McCarthyism in the 1950s, one utterance of the word Harvard or Yellow or Columbia or even the University of Iowa, or mention of the respective university mascots, like Crimson, Pitbulls, Lions and Hawkeyes, meant instant CIB involvement in one's life: wiretapping, video surveillance, traffic light fixing (this is very uncommon knowledge) and other forms of control.

Eventually, the parades that were planned in Los Angeles and New York were scrapped due to lack of support, and although American citizens knew that they would be forced to leave school for a year, new replacement schools were being formed daily to counteract this law in practice. True renegade journalism served its philosophical roots by exposing the connection of the new law with the crooked minds behind it, and while it is uncertain whether one of the original law-baby makers leaked the information through safe media channels so as to not be intercepted electronically or it just slipped by the censors, the connection became public knowledge. A rising force of criminals determined that forming other non-accredited institutions would be a way to avoid having to drop out of school per se, but major and renowned universities were the first to act with guerilla warfare tactics. By changing the name of the university and shutting down their current physical address, they could continue to operate from remote locations, or even from mobile locations if needed. The shadowy halls and old brick buildings were mere edifices of a structural regime, for the true strength of a university lies in its people, the professors and the students, and their interaction with wisdom and history, with historical persons as it were—and of course its endowment. Books were swiftly removed from the libraries during all-night packing events and transported safely to hiding places. Harvard renamed itself Harvord and was found in remote locations throughout Cambridge, Somerville, Allston, and Brighton, and Boston's South End. Yellow renamed itself Yalow, but they barely moved as they simply occupied some deserted industrial buildings in downtown New Haven to show their allegiance to the cause, and more so, not to stand out. Columbia and New York University officials fought over the name Central Park University, but NYU students, who found intellectual refuge mostly scattered throughout the East and West Village, Chelsea, SoHo and further downtown, even in Battery Park, wanted nothing to do with Central Park so they protested and officials quickly decided to go with Union Square University instead. These non-accredited megaliths of learning and teaching remained alive alongside the law. For, as long as BJ University remained in existence, which really meant as long as the sex toy industry was flourishing, non-accredited universities were safe havens from the law.

Sometime in late-February, just a quick month and a half after Winchester's clone took to his throne in the Gold House, the first human clone to be President of a country, he had a major malfunction in his nervous system, which began spewing gasses from his skin just before his State of the Union address. GWB, who was vacationing deep undercover in Phuket, Thailand, was called back to duty. Johnnie and Jennifer had been tricked for almost two months leading up to this. The clone would sit in his study and read law books and history books, and he would perform like a voracious sexual animal, bringing all sorts of sex toys into the Gold House's rooms, the virginal ones as well as the overused, and Johnnie was exhausted daily as the clone really gave her what she wanted all along, a firm and rhythmic Presidential screw. Jennifer and Rin used to sit in the Purple Room and chat with Winchester's clone about public policy and the like. In fact, Rin was very concerned with his father's new sense of intellect, and from the beginning, he did not entrust any private information to him by virtue of a clearly active survival instinct. Rin's first clue was the missing illegal Central American geologic cleaning crews scurrying around the Gold House. There were no rocks, and Rin had not heard anyone speak of his dad being cured of his systemic ailment. While this went completely ignored by everyone else, as busy as everyone is running a country, Rin's powers of observations were too keen not to notice.

The day that the real GWB returned, the Gold House was virtually redecorated as volcanic stones were piled in seemingly every corner of every room, under every desk, and waist high in the bathrooms and kitchen. His former sedimentary deposits were replaced with plagioclase feldspar and microcline deposits due to very high levels of stress and pressure within his body, and he left trails of sulfuric stench in every corner of enclosed space. He knows what is at stake. He is the President of America and he feels the pressure like an unarmed bandit at an Old West saloon.

Zhu Zen Kow summons a meeting with Sun Tzu. She is seeking advice, not on war theories or stratagems, but how to approach Chang Showmin, the leader of China's Communist Party and President of the People's Republic of China. Zhu Zen has access to rough drafts of the play, even while the ghostwriters are busy editing, and she has determined that there is a very slight chance of intercepting trouble before it arises. Despite how small the chances of success are, she decides to gamble. She knows well the care she must take in her approach, for if she changes the course of events unwittingly, she will be forever outcast from Wall, and this is not what she wants for her future. No matter what earthly plans are held for living beings, those in Wall are safe, except, of course, from all-in nuclear war in which radiation completely annihilates the top layer of molecular life on earth. Thus it is written in the natural laws of Wall that special treatment must be given to nuclear annihilation. Although all behind Wall's wall are dead already, with the exception of a few visitors, such nuclear destruction would even destroy the trailer park and its inhabitants for the simple fact that this would represent a collective failure by those admitted into the elite club. Hence, changing the course of the future might mean sacrificing her own admittance to the greatest after-life club going, but she is willing to take the risk because she has a sense of responsibility to the others. This makes her a valiant leader.

Sun refuses to speak unless he is ordained and let behind Wall's wall. Against her better judgment, and against the advice of some of the Roman and Hellenic philosophers, and against the usually placid moods of the guardian cats, Sun Tzu is allowed into the trailer park with free and unlimited access rights. Sun Tzu instructs her that the best way to a Chinese man's heart is through his penis. So, she calls upon Sigmund Freud for some assistance.

"Siggy?"

"*Ja.*"

"English please, Siggy. We are in South Dakota. Please speak English."

"Okay. How may I help you o' wondrous mystic leader."

"Oh Siggy, you always were a player. I need some advice."

"Twelve inches is the most you can probably handle."

"Sigmund! *Anschlag!*"

"*Ja,* okay."

"I need your advice on how to win over a Chinese man's heart through his penis."

"Ah, *ja.* This is easy, *mein dame.* What does this man do for a living?"

"He is the President of China."

"Oh, a man of power, of politics, and no doubt of a small penis."

"Just help me out, Sigmund."

"Go to him in his sleep. Ask him if he would like to have a larger penis than the President of the United States. He will, of course, reply with affirmation. Go to BJ University in South Carolina and pick up a new product in the development stage called a Pocket Missile. Jam this missile into his rear end while he sleeps. He will undoubtedly form an erection from this as it massages his prostate gland."

Oscar Wilde molds himself into his character Dorian Grey, appearing young and beautiful, takes off his clothes and runs through the center of the trailer caravan screaming, "I always knew Freud was queer. I always knew!"

Doc Whitman joins him, and they do a dance around a newly formed totem pole and a bonfire, where several Native Americans chiefs drop from the sky and join the performance. The rest of the camp gathers, chanting and clapping, while Whitman and Wilde dance and sing under the Badlands' clear blue sky. Proust, still somewhat morose, sits alone in an enclosed black painted, cement walled cell yawning from boredom, clearly unmoved by this showmanship.

Sigmund, unfazed by Doc Whitman and Oscar Wilde's antics, continues. "Anyway, once this has happened, and it will happen nightly, as he dreams, he will come back to this moment of euphoria, the moment of bliss. Give it about a week."

"Make it two!" shouts Tennessee Williams who just joined the trailer park recently, thanks to write-in votes by Whitman and Wilde who both hold decent clout in the group.

"Okay, two weeks," Freud continues. "Then wake him up while he is fully erect and tell him that if he wants this to continue, night after night, he must join you in conversation about very important issues."

"Thanks, Siggy. I can always count on you for a solid earthbound psychological approach."

"Sure. Hey, by the way, when are we going to let in Adolph? I have some questions for him and I think that, if I can just get him to sit down, take a deep breath and relax, maybe I can get through to him."

"Adolph? Forget it, Siggy. No such luck."

"Damn, maybe I'll try to meet him in purgatory; but I'm afraid once I get into the purglands I'll never get out."

"Don't do it, Sigs." Dante feels the need to put in his two cents. "That place is over-hyped, and furthermore, Adolph will NEVER make it to purgatory."

Zhu Zen sets out to meet Chang Showmin in his dreams, for in his dreams she can get to his conscience. Fear is her largest obstacle, hers. She is afraid that, as a man of the Communist Party, like a man of the Republican Party, this man has no conscience and his sole focus is power and how to preserve his power through any means possible. While he might think of his own people from time to time, he mostly thinks of himself, his ego and earthly relevance, and apparently, despite his tremendous efforts to convince everyone otherwise, his penis.

Act 21.

9.10, 9.11
Quitting School and Origami

"Who in the hell is bothering me *now*? Doesn't everyone know that I am on vacation! This is impossible. I just want a little rest and relaxstation."

"Dad, I think the word is relaxation. You are the President, Dad. You have only been in the Gold House for 11 days, and you are expected to lead the people and run our country," stated Rin Chin Chin candidly from a bright, sunny windowsill in the Gold House during a videoconference call with his father. Winchester is complaining from the Gold House West, his ranch in Texas, while his father sits in the Rectangular Office with Rin. One could say that Rin is a lover of nature, and while Rin does not think in these terms, he does feel a deep connection with the earth, and despite his small size and utter lack of all organs in his body, his fondness for Gaia is unmistakable.

Rin adores the panoramic vision laid out before him through the windows of the Gold House. The sparrows perched in the white mulberry trees and singing, and the way the branches leap to the sky on an English oak, how the sycamore maples spread their girth and their arms in all directions to absorb even the worst city's pollution, the people bustling about. Anything that is organic, Rin connects with both ideologically and metaphysically, and although GWB begged Rin to join him at the ranch in

Texas while he vacationed, and indeed Rin loves the ranch and its wildlife, he decided to stay put in the Gold House to watch over things. The strange relationship between man and son, between man and isolated body part in a jar, between illiterate buffoon and genius is often indescribable. Perhaps the most notable point of interest is the incredible emotional support Rin gives to his father, and while this might not be all that uncommon, it is especially strange for a chin in a jar to give emotional support to anything or anybody, especially the President of the United States.

The telephone rings and Winchester picks it up. He yells to one of his maids. She scurries in and helps Winchester utilize the multi-participant videoconference function—his Chief CIB contact needed to get in touch with him.

"Mr. President there is a very serious and continuing threat to the safety of the people of our nation. We have very credible sources, and we have confirmed this with many others in the intelligence community, especially MI23, which has been keen about this as well, that something is about to happen—to us, to our country. Certain American landmarks have been mentioned repeatedly in electronic chatter, and we believe the threats are real and we should deal accordingly with them. I advise a very high alert be declared, especially for the parades next week on your new holiday, sir."

"I don't think the Democrats have the balls, the cohoonees, to try and organize around my parades. What are they going to do? They're going to convince everyone to go back to school. HA! What a joke. Just ask BS. He'll tell you how much he likes this holiday," President Johnson replies to his Chief CIB contact. "Stop worrying and let the people celebrate. This is a day to celebrate! Right? Come on now!"

"Sir, did you mean *cojones*? Anyway, I don't think you understand. We briefed everyone at the Gold House, and even BS has been placed in a highly secured cave already. At a moment's notice, he is ready to be moved to Camp Daniel to resume authority away from potential targets."

"Whatever. You're all a bunch of pussies."

President Winchester Buckley Johnson, the Great Winchester Buckley, GWB, began his speech before a crowd of tens of thousands in downtown Houston. It was the morning of Winchester Buckley Johnson's Dropping out of School for a Year Day and the faithful had braved some very hot weather to come out en masse to show their support for the fearless leader of this intellectual enterprise. "There is a sense that everything and everyone are unified. This country is amazing. I never thought that this could happen here, all of you joining hand in hand, showing us what a great country we have, standing behind the only party that matters in this country. My party! And, if everyone is lucky, what a party it'll be!" He is quickly removed from the podium by one of his eunuchs, who are now his secret service agents. BS has given strict instructions to all of his security staff. Any mention of partying by GWB and he is to be removed from roving eyes of the media. The eunuchs are highly trained and good listeners and know how to act swiftly and without forewarning.

September 10th, 2001 turned out to be a very funny day, funny in an obtuse sense. It was the culmination of great effort to make the people of the United States feel categorically intelligent, so much so, that they convinced themselves that learning was overrated and support for Winchester's political party would help them understand things like freedom, democracy, and the power of faith. It was quite an effort that cost somewhere in neighborhood of $400 million in publicly siphoned monies, otherwise known as taxes. As one might assume, the categorical intelligencia, like their fearless leader, does not read a newspaper, a magazine article, a book, or even their breakfast cereal box, but they do in fact watch television and listen to the radio. They have been told day after day for months how overrated learning is, and, of course, they believe it whole-heartedly, as the Gold House controlled media spin the brainwashing tactic, reporting in every direction but the correct one, the one of true journalism.

September 11th will be a sad day for Winchester. He has to fly to Sarasota, Florida immediately after the speech in Houston. Anytime he has to go to Florida, it bothers him. Florida is his brother's state, and so the visit reminds him of his past, which in turn reminds him of what would happen if he continues to screw up. In many ways, he understands that his exalted position has been achieved because he knows how to take orders like a good soldier. And since he never really served in the military, this was his opportunity to be patriotic, something he longs for. Furthermore, and most importantly, he really wanted to stay and get loaded with some of his new friends from Couscous University. His main problem seemed to be that some elementary schools figured out how to bypass the new law like the universities did. Party officials and his cabinet believe that a visit from the President will help the rebel youth understand how important it is to quit school for a year, and although the students are all between the ages of 5 and 12, quitting school helped so many important people in illustrious positions throughout the federal government that, it is believed, they just need *to see it to believe it*, which became the new tagline for parade organizers.

Broken Stream had planned on making this trip with GWB to visit the growing educational rebel alliance base camps, but BS was called into the revamped North American Aerospace Defense Command headquarters in Colorado that morning and placed in a secure cave deep underground. After the state of Washington all but disappeared by Mother Nature's edict, NORAD was relocated back to Colorado. The place was given a huge facelift first, and although it lies beneath the earth's surface, out of sight, top architects were called in to give it great aesthetic appeal. They designed it to resemble the new Octagon building in Octagon City, Virginia. This factoid is not important relative to other facts being noted as sidebars; however, the implications of wasted federal tax dollars cannot be understated. Taxation has been proven by history to create stability in the minds of citizens. Subordinating a level of their income to their respective governing bodies, entrusting a portion of their livelihood in the powers that be, can be soothing for the mind, like a lost sheep finding the flock for protection. And taxation well spent can do marvels for the infrastructure and social welfare system. Wasting tax dollars in the United States can be likened to people suffering from bulimia nervosa—the emotional desire to suck in more than is needed for comfort's sake is usually followed by the need to purge the intake. Purging money is something that is ideologically linked to liberal economics, but if one were to dig a little deeper, it becomes obvious that tax dollars are redirected, in many ways, to the bank accounts and tax-free shelters of those standing atop their soap boxes preaching against liberalism. Albeit not an unobvious fact, it is a dubious hypocritical modus operandi.

The CIA director, oddly a member of the Democratic Party that Winchester decided to retain for his team and the son of Greek immigrant parents, Yiorgos Tenedopoulos had been working painstakingly for several years to filter through the very high levels of anti-American sentiment being reported by different field offices around the globe. It was impossible to answer all of these purported threats, as they were so many in number that even thousands of additional field operatives could never sift through the maze of information. Recently though, CIB field members had warned of a very serious threat of numerous terrorist attacks in the weeks prior to the holiday, attacks against national landmarks and places with high concentrations of people. It was largely assumed by the Gold House Politburo that the intelligence gathering was falsely infused by well-staged leftist spinning, in short by the Democratic Party, including the CIA director, whom BS regarded as someone dangerous. However, firing him outright would set back intelligence gathering several years, and so Tenedopoulos retained his position. An alternate theory, as posed by Goethe, was that Tenedopoulos remained in office by BS's command in order to raise the level of fear of the spin-happy Gold House cabinet members, to keep them on edge enough to supply victory during the next election. The reality is most likely largely misunderstood, for the most overwhelming hypothesis by political scientists in Wall is that, since Tenedopoulos is Greek-American, BS may have been hoping for a secret rendezvous now and then, similar to those found on the battlefronts during antiquity. Applying Occam's razor suggests this is the best possible explanation.

It was becoming very clear in the days leading up to the big holiday that trouble was brewing somewhere, the kind of big trouble that changed things in a big way. BS listened carefully to the CIB chiefs—the heads of the CIA, NSA and FBI—who always seem to be at war with one another over methodology. He held closed meetings with them and several well-regarded field operatives. BS consistently informed GWB of what his policies should be, and he did this in very creative ways, always doing his best to enforce his own will and sense of power but so as not to damage GWB's ego, for this was a delicate time. GWB's ego was very much in a strange state of being. He completely avoided the Gold House, and although many of his inner-circle found humor in this, the power structure must be maintained in the public eye.

Gerald held the notion that, although the separate intelligence agencies still held a degree of institutionalized importance, and while the CIB was an amalgam of the three, for all intents and purposes of practical execution of bureaucracy, the agencies were to be left intact. In these days, GWB never called upon Gerald for any fatherly advice. He was determined to show his strength as a leader and be a powerful man in his own right. For GWB, an illiterate and a fool, BS was a savior for his own public image, and especially his image relating to how his father saw him. However so, Gerald and BS knew all that was at stake, and if ever GWB were to make moves to undermine their ultimate goals, he would be cast aside. No one knew this except Gerald and BS, and one unmentionable other, a clandestine character who will remain invisible for now.

BS's moves were known as policy making—he declared it and it became official. It was simply accepted that his voice from behind the curtain was the true voice of power. National Security Advisor Candy Couscous and Defense Secretary Pat Ramrod would sit around doing bong hits from a five gallon water cooler bottle transformed into a huge water pipe with four different intake tubes allowing four different Gold House officials and/or staff to get high at the same time in the rectangular office while listening to Pink Floyd's *The Piper at the Gates of Dawn* compact disc and laughing about the stupidity of the Democratic Party and the people who stayed in school. This was especially interesting coming from Candy Couscous who, prior to being appointed National Security Advisor, was a high level university official at an elite institution of higher learning (the name of the university has been removed for purposes of anonymity and in keeping with the law). They were very careful not to insult the President too badly despite everyone's natural tendency to want to, but they could really let loooo much of the time because Winchester was never really in the Gold House.

However, simply because one is physically present, this does not make one available. Availability of oneself, to give oneself wholly to an enterprise, human relations, a belief, concurrent actions, deliberate intentions, is to give oneself for all to see. Sunlight, crystal, clarity are words that, throughout history have represented metaphorical meanings of being able to see through a situation, to see things outside the cave without shadows draped over what is despite the effort of the interested parties to conceal themselves or their actions. These words had recently given way to a more relevant term, one that relates not only to behavior, but now, also, to intelligence gathering, message formulation, and edicts of state: *transparency*. This word was never used by GWB, BS, or the rest of the staff, however, for why would they wish to tip anyone off that they were being anything *but* transparent. While hypocrisy was not something that GWB cared much about, thought about, or even understood the definition of, he was steering himself, at all times, away from this word—transparency. Even he intuited that, hidden inside this word, is a responsibility to honesty.

He was on permanent vacation, so to speak, and as a matter of fact, he was overheard frequently ranting about obeying the law himself: if kids didn't have to go to school, why should he have to go to work. While some thought he was joking and just laughed at him, he did actually stay away from work, all the time. He would call in sick to the Gold House switchboard, disguising his voice to sound like he was bedridden or dying. Then he would hit the links for a round of golf with visiting Yalow buddies and old oil company executive cronies. On occasion, he would take his daughter to see a movie. GWB was never happier than he was in those months following his cloned replacement's inauguration as President of the United States. Even when he returned to the Gold House and had to actually perform some menial tasks, his usage of the Gold House was so limited that he had to ask where the liquor cabinets were.

He rarely does anything stressful, and consequently, his geochemical diaper is almost unnecessary. His life has become a stagnant breeze with no gusts of wind in the forecast. Broken Stream, who is clearly in charge of policymaking anyway, is often traveling either with or for Gerald. The two of them have a very healthy enterprise going, including a global business in energy related companies, investment and finance companies, and also construction and real estate projects. However their asset diversity was somewhat lessened as they temporarily and systematically transferred most of their assets from real estate, stocks, and bonds directly into gold futures. This was done silently for weeks in boutique financial chop shops all over the planet.

BS only comes to the Gold House during critical moments. His staff has been adequately trained for whatever he tells them to do, and communication is so tight that he is notified immediately, wherever in the world he may be, by satellite. He wears a com link in his ear at all times so he may hear any pertinent news and give further instructions. He knows that Ramrod will follow his orders and that Couscous is just happy to be in the Gold House fulfilling her childhood dreams of social importance, which means she goes about her job with great fervor. Plower, of course, petrified for his own life and the lives of his family members, never opens his mouth.

Back in the trailer park, the ghostwriters receive an important communication tip from the playwright. Again, it comes in a crude form, a telegraph: "Be careful how you interpret the next part. The moment is delicate and the emotion is strong, and if you confuse things with your own thoughts or feelings, you will make some people very angry. While in some textual moments this is the emotion we are going for, anger is not appropriate now. People need to know that emotions are healthy. Instigating people emotionally is no way to get to someone's heart, however. I have no problem engaging the reader with intellectual debate. It is up to them to decide what is considered right and what is not, and allowing them that ability with a clear heart is the only truthful way to approach such a thing. I wholly support the endeavor. Beware of the human heart for it is a fragile organ. Stop."

Among the ghostwriters, especially between the English playwrights, who always seem to be arguing about style, a feverish debate ensues. There is intense deliberation regarding the methodology of the narration. French philosophers want the next moments removed completely aside from a quick mention. As Sartre says, contradicting his own usual methodology, "By minimizing the verbalization regarding the incidents to come, the emotion can be more accurately depicted." While the merit in this argument was clear, it was decided upon differently. Camus and Voltaire think that absurdity still reins supreme; and many others join them in that assertion, and in particular Aristophanes, Samuel Clemens and Jonathan Swift join the Frenchmen. But it is the Russians, especially those who had been imprisoned and exiled, who really took charge here. This was territory they were collectively familiar with, the territory of fear and persecution and of high levels of anger and the overall emotional tidal wave. Many ghostwriters succumbed to this kind of political and social pressure during their respective lifetimes, as most artists have, in some way, felt the persecution of those in power. So, after much debate, days and days of endless banter without a single word being written, it is decided to abandon, as a primary motif, the colorful absurdity depicted and replace it, albeit temporarily, with some seriousness regarding the human soul and the effects of tragedy and a pandemic sense of doom. However so, the desire to remain mildly humorous was always present, for even the Russians could not completely escape the need to laugh on occasion. The absurdity motif would be restored, but only after a short rest, for during moments of impending doom, often it is humor that shakes the clouds from the minds of people to see where it is that they have actually been and how they arrived there. Franz "Big Bad Bug" Kafka argued his point well, and this seemed to put consensus regarding the issue over the top.

"Ladies, gentleman and terrorized thinkers, I want to begin by saying I agree with the direction we will take, but should it not be more morose? The horrific moments to come are something that can best be described by pure suffering alone. But I want to reiterate that, through all unbearable likenesses to the mutilation of the human spirit, complete synergy with our own experiences must be understood, not as defined from isolated perspectives, but collectively, for therein lies the truth of the story. So whatever we collectively decide, I will accept wholly."

As Kafka's mouth was moving and the words dripped from his tongue like a waterfall of clear, crisp mountain water, a young boy appears, a saintly glow surrounding his small body, his eyes welling with tears. Kafka closes his lips and the waterfall of words freeze in mid-drop. The boy speaks softly, almost inaudibly. "Please be careful in this moment, for this is a special moment in the new direction of mankind, as you all will see clearly, and it is up to you to decide how it is told. I beg your compassion for the weak and suffering, for they feel real pain, and I beg your empathy for the less intelligent, for they know no better. Please be cautious with your words—be firm but be considerate." The boy disappears as a phantom, and the ghostwriters, busy taking notes, are moved to tears.

Nathaniel Hawthorne is the first to speak and he is trembling like a hummingbird. "I vote that we take a break and get some air, breathe a little, feel our senses regenerate, that we rest our minds, if only for an hour, to walk alongside a brook, to bathe in a crystal sea, to hike a jade peak, to sit beneath an old tree and ask for peace, or maybe hop a train to a distant land." Who could possibly disagree with that? While some of the Russians were a bit anxious to get moving, stillness gave way and all in attendance stood and walked in separate directions to allow their minds to settle back to a place that is serene, if only for a moment, for in the subsequent moments, everything changes, and movement, if not orchestrated properly, will miss the mark...

A thump in Winchester's heart causes him to frown before a small rebel faction of second grade students at a Sarasota, Florida elementary school. He fears that he might be having a heart attack, and he wonders for a moment if maybe Johnnie has run off again with Jener. There is no pain, however, and so he dismisses the heart attack theory and begins to go over the scenario in his mind: Jener arrives at the Gold House gate with a pass to enter issued by Johnnie. He slowly walks toward the side entrance, where he winks at one of Winchester's eunuchs standing by the doorway smoking a clove cigarette. He enters the Rectangular Office, where Johnnie awaits dressed in a scanty cowgirl outfit, complete with a feathered white Stetson and white tasseled boots. Jener waves his hands in circular motions, as to cast a spell, and Johnnie instantly appears nude in front of him. Rin spins around within his jar to face outside, so as to not be witness to anything compromising as he sings the song "Anything Can Happen" from the children's TV show *Barney*. Jener begins to kiss Johnnie, slowly and deeply. Winchester is very upset now. He is making a face that looks like he has been shot.

One of his eunuchs approaches. "Sir, I have some very, very bad news." He pauses, and as he pauses, Winchester fears the worst. "Sir, the World Trade Center has apparently been attacked by terrorists. Both towers sir, both Towers have been hit by commercial airliners."

Winchester sits in awe. His face shows anger, shows defeat. There is a spark in his eyes but no fire. He sits as if the geochemical diaper he wears is made of lead. He cannot get up. He cannot think. He is frozen in time as the entire world's eyes focus on lower Manhattan.

The moments prior to this one and immediately following would define the future direction of the United States, its governing body and its people; and in many ways, those moments would redefine how people communicate and understand one another. The reasons for the attacks are many and too complex to delve into completely here, but for the purpose of understanding the collective human heart contained in human bodies across the world, it was as though, all at once, that collective heart welled up in pain and screamed in agony. The American dream, the one that forbears all other dreams, the one that combines freedom, prosperity, passion, individual thought, domination, expression and love all rolled into a single morphing ideal of the way in which humanity can be lived and enjoyed at its fullest, came crashing down within seconds. Perhaps what remained in those moments— besides courage, hope and fear—was the overwhelming sensation that someone was capitalizing on this. Someone somewhere was gaining something from this, and this notion alone terrorized humanists everywhere, whatever lot of them still exist. The act itself was well planned, and the acts that followed showed what the human spirit is made of, showed what true leadership is made of. Sadly, for the American people, and ironically, for all of humanity, the true leader was not the President of the United States, but the mayor of New York City.

"Winchester, I need for you to stay away from New York."

"But BS! I am the President!"

"When the news broke, the cameras trained on you were not filtered, the images not run through our media filters. They managed to catch your real expressions, and the world knows how you managed yourself in the moments following the attack."

318

"BS, I was having a bad moment, just a little insecurity—don't worry about it."

"Even if your clone was healthy, we can't even use him! We need real emotion, not your pathetic groveling or the robotic nature of your twin. We need someone who will really take charge."

"Can I at least tell the mayor how to handle this?"

"Are you fucking kidding me? When you were informed that terrorists attacked our nation, you just sat there, not moving a muscle. We cannot afford another brain fart fuck-up like that again. Sir, no disrespect. You are the President, but you really fucked up badly!"

"Damn my clone!"

"No my friend, damn you!"

In one of the CIB's two hidden wings in the Decagon, all *relevant* personnel met quietly to discuss the nature of what happened, to decide upon a response, and to call in some of the former hit men of federalism's industrious and complex recent history. Ramrod and BS could not agree on any of the old bulldogs. The two of them were the most qualified, the least dignified, and the nastiest men anyway, and they had a long history in the Gold House and in its predecessor, the White House. One of Winchester's father's men came in through that closed door, and he was welcomed with openness, as much openness as one might expect in an airtight bomb shelter anyway, but openness nonetheless. Barry Snowcrop would prove to be instrumental in aiding the mindset of those gathered more than anything.

"We have to make the CIB and the Executive Office one," Snowcrop said in a casual conversation with BS, Couscous, and Ramrod. "Perhaps this will truly expedite decision making and we can funnel a TON of cash into the Gold House and into Intelligence, and once Congress has appropriated the money and we can do whatever we want with it, well, hell, let's go to town, boys!"

As he spoke, Ramrod began massaging his own testicles. BS proceeded to get down on his knees in front of Snowcrop and was about to unzip Snowcrop's pants to take care of him orally. He had never heard something so compactly beautiful. It was the newest sermon, the equal of the one on the mount that Jesus gave for all to hear. These too were words from God after a fashion, at least from deep within his own humanist soul, and delivered in a windowless closet deep within the hidden part of the Decagon, the part of the Decagon not hit by the commercial airliner on 9/11, the part that is deep underground, or a few blocks away, or perhaps in a small office behind the kitchen of a fancy French restaurant in Georgetown, no one is sure except those present. This edict could change the very nature of the federal government. A bill was quickly drafted, and GWB was able to get involved, finally, against BS's better sense of reason and beyond the reach of his father's distant but still powerful hand for GWB had to sign the bill. The Great Winchester Buckley Johnson was still the President, no matter how much of a buffoon the rest of the bunch thought him to be. He still had the power given to him by the Electoral College (cough, cough).

The CIB immediately corralled all of the important Saudi nationals and sent them back to their home country. The swift act was so well managed and secretive that the world had no idea what happened. Gerald's business contacts' sons would not have to face the imminent interrogation of all Arabic peoples in the country or Arab-Americans with ties to any kind to any outspoken or militant regime. They would not be included in the harassment of anyone of Arabic descent, or anyone who had at one time or another traveled to an Arabic speaking country, or anyone who had used the word Allah or the word Al, or Qaeda, or the phrases "bad president" or "bomb explode" or "airplane crash." The state of Michigan became a giant detainment center for guilty people, potentially guilty people, and potentially potential guilty people, especially those whom others now called "towel head, sand nigger or falafel-brain."

The Saudi players played a role that was unthinkable by casual glance alone but entirely understandable with a modicum of thoughtfulness. Throughout the entire process following the attacks, as any valued businessman would attempt to do, the idea was put forth that relations must be kept open and remain transcendent of the attack, for while many of those involved in the activities of doom were from Saudi Arabia, the Saudis regarded business relations far above other issues. Therefore, they offered to help in any way they could, in the U.S., in Europe, etc. They offered to share information and gather evidence against those seeking to destroy the fundamental roots of capitalism and to thereby destroy capitalism's effects on people around the world. Clearly, this was a major goal of the destructive acts, which were not just against the targets and the people in them but against the principles and the fabric of existence that was lived by those who held these principles, albeit that most who lived in the US only understood said theory at a trite level and indeed most don't capitalize on much of anything while inside the bubble of comfort created by a multi-level social class system. In short, this was not an attack on people per se. As a matter of fact, highly questionable characters across the world were given almost instant immunity against further pursuits by the CIB if they were willing to cooperate, and this included those who committed atrocities in the recent past.

Hope can sometimes carry an entire people on its weary shoulders. Mayor Randy Gallarotti of New York City, beloved by millions, now respected by billions, single-handedly carried the fears of billions worldwide on his rejuvenated shoulders. He would stand and fight with tears in his eyes, and he would guide the people to feeling they were safe again in a place where safety had become part of everyday existence. Fear was created by the destructive act and worked its evil magic, but he vowed to destroy that fear. His heroics would later be overshadowed by theories of conspiracy relating the terrorist attacks to the President and his family, which was ludicrous overall, but the fundamental truth that lead to such conspiracy theories lie in the very notion that Gerald, BS and GWB had much to gain from their ties to the Arab world. Another compelling argument for a conspiracy is the fact that Gerald and BS's gold futures skyrocketed as they literally doubled their money within days of the attack. Is this coincidence or just smart investing? However, the notion that they orchestrated the attack is fundamentally stupid, and Mayor Gallarotti's legacy will live forever because of this. Even Wall's elite applauded him in private behind the all-seeing eyes of the afterlife.

Zhu Zen Kow quickly assembles a team of military thinkers. She fears more horrific moments are about to come to light, and she wants to be ready if she is to, in any way, interfere with the potentially destructive course of events. General Douglas Macarthur and the great Prussian military theorist Carl Von Clausewitz sit at a small table with ZZ to help her construct possible hypotheses. Despite Macarthur's questionable past, sufficient to put his admittance to the greatest afterlife club of eternity into question for a very long time, it is now clear that ZZ let him in for instructional purposes. Most famous historical characters of such notoriety, of any kind, with the exception of a few select monsters, would be given a free pass to get in on this particular discussion if they had anything at all to contribute. Seeing the gathering of history's great warriors, leaders, and strategists in one sitting made some of the artists very uncomfortable. Perhaps their legacies of power and brutality frightened the artists, for while the brutality of artists is in the creative revolts they have led on paper, canvas, stage and screen and in sound, the ones which shed actual blood are far more distressing, and perhaps most distressing to folks of their artistic ilk. For this, in a relevant way, separated those who lived out their fantasies in their minds from those who lived by action in the formulaic world of matter. As civilization grew, the two separate ideals merged into one, approaching the form of a single entity. Many hands and many minds constructed the bridge that crossed this river, but as the inaugural caravan of vehicles to cross that river was about to commence, the attacks came and halted the caravan from crossing that bridge.

"How close we were to complete physical and ideological synergy?" Marcus Aurelius asks of Ayn Rand.

"So close, I could almost taste it."

Chang Showmin calls GWB on Air Force Winchester, the new highly modified force field of a flying Gold House that is now hovering somewhere above the Continental United States with a squadron of Air Force fighters escorting him. "President Johnson, I want to tell you that China is behind the United States right now. We support your needs in any way."

"Thanks Chang. I want you to know that every time I called you a chink whore I did not really mean it. I love you yellow bastards, really."

The connection was cut instantly by the CIB monitoring the conversation. Ramrod and Couscous quickly summon BS to call Chang Showmin back to apologize, but President Showmin is livid at what GWB said to him and refuses to take Broken Stream's phone call. Gerald attempts to step in, sending a plea to President Showmin to forgive his son's behavior, but Showmin was already in conference with his strategists. Gerald is at odds with himself as regards what to do next. He knows that GWB's clone is still in a state of relative malfunction, and he knows that GWB will have to go before the people and before Congress to speak about leadership and about times of trouble—and he is dreadfully afraid of what his son might say or do. Tension between China and the United States, despite its inevitable past and certainly inevitable future, is not what Gerald wants right now. The pieces are not in place yet on his giant human chessboard he keeps stashed away in some readily available corner of his mind.

Inarguably, the men behind the planned attacks, at least philosophically, are Origami bin Louis, the Saudi born militant, and "The Doctor," Ayman al-Zawah-he-don't-like-anyone-who-isn't-Muslim, the Egyptian intellectual who lured many young, bright Egyptian men into the enterprise of giving their lives to destroy the Great Satan from the West, the United States of America. Origami stands with a small group of rogue intellectuals, all well trained fighters, a couple of sushi chefs, and some Swedish masseuses in great barren deserts of the South Asian tundra. The cold wind whistles through his not oft-washed hair and long beard. This man, once backed by the CIB during the Russian invasion of Afghanistan to fight back the Communist regime, is now one of the most dangerous thinkers on the planet. His orders are sent to his minions via many low-technology means, and the CIB's high technology simply cannot keep up with the speed at which things move on foot. The Doctor ensures that the orders are carried out and he does this with great precision and very careful planning. He and his followers move as invisible men from place to place, in and out of caves and villages, some say in Afghanistan, some say in Pakistan, some even think that he ended up safely in Nigeria or maybe even Indonesia, and some other rumblings were that he ended up in Midtown Manhattan driving a taxicab. Any place where he could disappear would be the place for him, and to continue moving, as to elude any possible CIB tracking of his whereabouts, was imminent in his plan. There was a great hope among the CIB and the Gold House that the Doctor was killed while performing some very quick surgery, a kidney removal for a Dutch businessman kidnapped in Baku in a basement of an Afghani safe house. They had hit the house hard, dropping bombs from low flying jets, and later the purported head of the Doctor was given to the CIA for a hearty reward. It turned out not to be the head of the Doctor but of a goat killed by accident in a local police raid. Origami would have been forced to face the next legs of the battle without his trusty sidekick, like the Lone Ranger without Tonto, like Batman without Robin, or like Gerald if he lost BS to a mishap during a hunting trip in the Bayous of Louisiana. For now, these latter two remain a pair made in heaven.

Origami bin Louis is one of history's more interesting tacticians. He is purported to use his extensive mastery of creative paper folding, kamikaze pilot training with several Japanese regiments that splintered after World War II and ended up in Pakistan, and suicide bomber instruction. However, this last tactic is questionable, as he, himself, would never kill himself or die for any cause, let alone his own. What is known for certain is that he maintains a militant army across the world. In every corner, on every hill or mountain, in every cave, there exists one of his many disciples, ready to die for his words, awaiting his orders to destroy the enemy, anyone trying to take their land and their desire to pray away from them.

Origami launches a disinformation campaign to frighten the people of the world on two levels. One is to strip them of their freedom through fear. The result of this is transparent. But, how is this done? The execution of the plan took years to conclude, for in order to take personal freedoms away from an individual in any nation, the governing bodies of that nation must be granted more power than they know what to do with and isolate that nation's people within their own borders. The ways are many. Attacking within a nation's borders is the best way to secure complete control of a government over its people through fear. The second, and perhaps more puzzling tactic of fear, was to become the world's most renowned Origamist. This was a departure from logic, as understood by most, but Origami's plan was simple: to confuse the people of the world as to his real plan, to become, like the great Grand Masters of chess, the great Master Origamist. Eventually, he sought ways to fold things other than paper to make cute creative designs and shapes. He would sit for hours, alone, hidden in caves, talking to himself about Allah and about bombs while he figured out ways to reshape rocks and reshape fibers into little animals, mostly pets, but also of some wild creatures like boar, grizzly bears and ostriches. As his skills improved and his methods were perfected, Origami set his sights much higher. Deep in the caves of central Afghanistan, Origami bin Louis learned how to make small detonating devices out of rocks. He then learned how to make guns, knitted caps, and financial documents out of the rocks from these caves. He refused to make anything that involved "high technology" for that would go against his principles. This may be his ultimate feat or this may lead to his eventual demise. Once he learned this trick, he convinced himself that he would, some day, make an Islamic prayer rug out of Winchester Buckley Johnson's volcanic rock waste piles. This dream foreshadowed all else that he set out to accomplish, and this sad and sadistic dream, unfortunately, helped change the world.

The CIB sought desperately to track Origami and his team of bearded hit men and find them before they committed a Jihadist act, so as a matter of remaining incognitos as well as a matter of cleanliness before Allah, they must shave unwanted hair from the face and body, becoming no longer bearded. GWB was busy making speeches before the American public and before Congress, and since he could not read his teleprompter, his speeches came from his guts. He was calling to the people of the world to join him in war. Gerald developed an ulcer because of this, and BS was nowhere to be found. He was apparently was drinking himself into oblivion somewhere in his own cave beneath Colorado. He drank not out of fear of further acts of terrorism, but because GWB had to speak publicly to the world in a time of great emotional pressure after being on vacation for months.

"Fellow Americans, I ask your understanding and patience in this delicate time. I ask that every American and everyone in the world who supports my cause to come together to find this murdering towel head and bring him to justice. We will find a way to rebuild those wonderful buildings and, if we are lucky, the baseball season will continue without interruption. We will find a way to get that son of a bitch. I will personally smoke him out of his cave if I have to. I will go on foot, with all the soldiers of America, into every cave of Pakistan and Afghanistan to find this devil. If he thinks that he is going to falsify energy documents using my volcanic waste, he is insane. I'll kill him first."

All of President Johnson's speeches were emotionally charged with threats and calls for solidarity. Quickly, the spin-doctors of Pseudalopex News Network took his words and created a new-fashioned way of reporting. All PNN journalists were now required to speak like President Johnson. They were to use incomplete, fragmented sentences. They were to repeat certain lines and phrases over and over again until those phrases became part of the lingo spoken by every American who watches television. No news organization aside from PNN was to be allowed inside the Gold House for conferences, and all PNN reporters were required to place small American flags behind their left ear to show patriotism. In fact, in the coming months, more than 100 million

Americans, on any given day, walked around, drove to work, and sat at the dinner table with small American flags behind their left ears. Incidentally, Ka Zin Flow owned the small flag manufacturing facility in Taipei where all these flags were produced. BS and Gerald surmised that, if GWB has to be in office, they would make him sound exactly the way they wanted to. Even if the most insane phrases and thoughts came out of his mouth, the words would be molded quickly by tacticians into fortifiable political and militaristic strategies. How, one might ask, is this done? The answer is so simple. Feed the people what they want to hear and they will forever keep their eyes closed and their ears sealed tightly shut, and tell them how to vote for that is the most important element, that is, until elections become obsolete as all Americans will eventually be disenfranchised, not just the African-Americans. Then, voting itself is just a matter of history.

Act 22.

Kra: The Trickery Unmasked

In January 1988, the Superbowl of American football featured the Redskins from Washington, D.C. and the Broncos from Denver, Colorado. The game was held in San Diego, California. A game of American football, in many ways, resembles war game strategy. Offensive and defensive maneuvers are planned out, and these strategies are often altered using audibles in mid-play. Strategy was always a game, like playing chess or planning a divorce battle. As with any modern commercialized professional sport with billions of dollars at stake, the teams represented on the pitch, the playing field, the court or the ice rink are the final product of hundreds, and in some cases, thousands of employees of the corporations that run the teams; and these corporations, for all intents and purposes, resemble small armies strategizing, maneuvering, plotting and planning. This final game of the 1988 season had more ramifications for the future of humanity than any one single person present at that game or watching on television could ever possibly imagine. A wager was made between then United States Vice President Gerald Johnson and Iraqi dictator Sad-ham Husselini. Sad-ham was so sure that Denver was to absolutely destroy Washington in that game that he made a bet with Gerald with the following stakes: If Sad-ham lost the bet, he would give Gerald a 1000 square kilometer slice of border land between Iraq and Saudi Arabia of his choice; and if Sad-ham were to win, he would get Kuwait and Bahrain, and maybe, if the spread were large enough, Israel. While the actual spread was known to only one select bookie in Las Vegas, the details of the bet were known throughout the gambling underworld.

The Redskins clearly and decisively won that game, which is obviously far different than what happened when the European colonizers arrived in North America at the end of the 15th century and proceeded to kick the hell out of the locals. Gerald was the happiest man on earth in those days. He was to receive an enormous parcel of land on Iraq's Southwestern border to be placed in escrow in his real estate trust company located in Dubai in the United Arab Emirates. Sad-ham, as history showed clearly, was not a man of his word, nor was he a man of faith in anything besides his own ego, which is a deadly combination of character traits for a person of power to have, especially one who controls land and the most valuable of natural resources directly in the middle of the most volatile political and economic hotbed in the world, the area nestled between the Arabian Sea, the Caspian Sea and the Mediterranean Sea. All of the signs were given to Gerald that he was never to see that parcel of land, but he had had decent relations with Husselini in the past, funding Sad-ham in their CIB orchestrated war with neighboring Iran for the previous eight years.

The Iran-Iraq War was a bitter border dispute among warring radical Muslims in both nations, and also a battle between Sad-ham Husselini and Iran's supreme leader, Eye-At-Olah Khomeini—the two literally hated each other beyond words. They had no ability to see eye to eye even though their fundamental method of exercising power was so similar in nature. On the surface, however, their methods were night and day, one religious and the other utterly secular. Each leader claimed the disputed region belonged to their country dating back to the 7th century, but the real reason for Sad-ham's invasion was the $15 billion US dollars transferred to his Swiss bank account. This was a result of the extremely angry United States government following the kidnapping of Americans from the U.S. Embassy in Tehran by the radical self-imposed leader, the Eye-At-Olah, out of fear that the coup staged by the CIA in 1953 in Iran was about to be reenacted following Iran's recognized, more secular leader, the Shah, going to the United States to undergo medical treatment. The Eye-At-Olah quickly took a militant stand and kidnapped unsuspecting Americans, burning the American flag, shouting death to Americans. The CIB, which backed the Shah's Iran prior to this, was very angered by this move and immediately switched allegiances to the horrible dictator and monster next-door, Sad-ham. Sad-ham found the perfect opportunity to expand his humongous ego yet more by marching across the border into a fragmented and splintered Iran to annex the disputed territory. Sad-ham did not expect to run into opposition as such, but the war lasted eight years with over one million people finding themselves buried or dissolving like liquid dust from explosions, chemical evaporations, and barbaric mutilations.

During this time, Iran called on its allies, all known enemies of the United States: China, Syria, Libya, North Korea. Iraq also called upon China, as its leaders sat upon the fence in this war, the United States, France, Great Britain and Egypt for military support, weapons, and for strategy. This was the first time since World War II that so many nations backed one party or another in a major war, so many nations that did not have to necessarily commit people, only words, but these words were enough to set the future stage for dramatic tragedies and comedies, one after another, like no other time in history.

After supporting Sad-ham's war against Iran for years, and simultaneously supporting Origami for years against Russia, the two would become the number one-a and one-b enemies of the United States. Gerald was so angry that, once he was elected President, he began planning an attack against Iraq, finally seizing the opportunity with a full-scale commitment after Sad-ham decided to annex Kuwait as well, another of America's allies. But what really angered Gerald beyond all other things was that Sad-ham did not pay Gerald his parcel of land after the Superbowl bet. Gerald was so determined to get Sad-ham because of this that his domestic policymaking went to hell because his mind was so entrenched in revenge that he could not see straight enough to run his own government and lead his own country.

In small windowless rooms in CIB headquarters, once stationed in Langley, Virginia moved to Puget Sound, Washington, and moved back to Octagon City, Virginia, the behind the scenes plotting, the war games being played out to determine outcomes of many scenarios and possible conflicts, the deepest level of deception found light on a cosmic level. Harry Houdini, working directly with one of the most brutally decisive militant thinkers on earth, Betty Johnson, constructed a long-standing hypothesis that would eventually pit the two earthly superpowers, the United States and its allies against China and all of its allies, in a standoff. This was a game played out by Betty and Harry in secret meetings, usually in one of coastal Maryland's quaint villages, at cafés and other romantic places, in which Betty was disguised as Kra and Harry was unrecognizable by most living human beings. The game consisted of mathematical probabilities using scales of economics, politics, history and multi-dimensional travel. It was this game that proved the most maniacal, as Betty's quest lasted much longer than anyone might imagine. In fact, it lasted so long that her disguise, even until just a few acts prior to this one, was unrecognized by the ghostwriting staff, despite the earlier guidance from Helen Keller. After their discovery, the staff examined their own abilities to think with clarity until depression and thoughts of suicide descended upon them, which is theoretically impossible since the ghostwriters are already dead. However, the fact that suicide occurred to them demonstrates with wistful overtones the seriousness of their mindsets.

Harry Houdini was no stranger to the Johnson family. He had helped Gerald escape many difficult moments, and he would probably, working closely with Betty, Gerald and BS, also help Winchester escape many difficult moments. Harry had help in his labors. He was not schooled in military strategy, only in self-reliance, which can go either way. One direction is a disposition of awkwardness in social settings by way of making one feel isolated and self-defeating. However, Harry learned from a master of deception, someone he met in galactic prison long before he met Betty. The man in question paraded around in his time like a warrior and a crusader, but he was a criminal, a thief, a murdering thug. He carried the name of Christ and used it as a weapon, and while he would not be the first to do this nor the last, nor would Christ be the only divine icon's name to be used slanderously, used to kill for, used to control with, his dual standard was obvious on so many levels that Harry's greatest techniques of escape were, in principle, learned from this man's existence. Harry's ability to be placed in the most difficult positions a man could find himself imprisoned in only to be able to solve the mystery of how to escape was overshadowed by something much deeper in his soul. Harry posed the following query: If played out properly, could humankind bring itself to the brink of destruction only to escape? Harry's game is a deadly one, and not many would choose to play it if given the option; but Harry, never a man who did things because others would not, chose to do everything he could to bring humanity to the brink of disaster as a game so that he might witness the potentiality of human nature's survivalist resolve.

One man was working intimately with Harry Houdini, one man who was confided in and even given access to all of Houdini's secrets in exchange for strategic thinking on a broader scale. Despite Harry Houdini's illusionary tactical enterprise, there was one man he looked up to for larger answers, and these answers would play very dark roles in the coming moments for humanity.

Imagine a chain of influence, starting with those who were soul-deep in the great darkness of the Middle Ages, these people's ideas influencing those who lived and ruled during the inquisition, and both influenced the tactical awareness of those who ran things in the century of wars, the 20th century. All of these ideas have survived through changes of perception relating to time and physics and into the present, where all of life's information exists at one's fingertips, all of its lightness and darkness, its joys and humors, its knowledge and wisdom—all stirred up as if in a giant black cauldron over a consistent flame and steaming. All that knowledge making its way into the mind of one person, a woman, who is in many ways a sorceress and who has direct access to and influence over the mind of the President of the United States, the former President of the United States and chief intelligence strategist and covert planning officer. This single mind has potential power that is frightening at a level no one could withstand should they discover it. Betty Johnson sits behind the scenes of every meeting, every maneuver, every strategy, carefully planning the future direction of mankind, darkness in her soul and pithiness in her words and absolute certainty in each step along the way. Betty deals only in absolutes, only in end results. She may appear to be a fragile, nurturing, somewhat worn elder, but the strength in her bones and in her darkened heart is beyond human imagination. Those surrounding her daily do not see her influence on them, her manipulation of time and life's resources for her own end-game, which will end with only one winner and many losers.

After Harry's final lesson, the crusader is able to begin his explorations once again. Robert de Craon finally escaped galactic prison after years of guidance from Harry. Galactic prison is something virtually impossible to escape from, like escaping from Hell, and in many ways, galactic prison and Hell are the same place. In no way does Robert de Craon deserve the same reputation as history's great monsters, but for reasons only known by the playwright (and his mentor), the criminal Robert de Craon, second Grand Master of the Knights Templar, crusader extraordinaire, was imprisoned in galactic prison for centuries. His release was never to come, but his persistent training with Harry over the better part of the last eighty years would provide enough practical exercise to understand the nature of imprisonment and how to escape it. As Harry always told him: to escape is simply to imagine yourself not imprisoned and then to go backward, step by step, until you reach your current state of imprisonment and executing one's escape based upon the principles discovered in the backward traverse. De Craon tried for years to grasp this concept metaphysically, but it was not until he learned of his direct influence over the most powerful men on earth that he decided, once and for all, that he would find that route to freedom in order to play a role in the final scene. Robert de Craon's ego was tremendous, as is the ego of anyone consumed with power.

Aleister Crowley, once deemed a mutant sorcerer by some of the elder Magi appearing from time to time behind Wall's wall, is too dangerous and too sinister to be allowed access to the club. He does, however, have roaming capabilities that afford him the access he needs to communicate with those in the know. Aleister Crowley befriended Zim some years ago. While Zim's state of consciousness is never quite understood, especially because of the secretive manner that shrouds his being, Crowley predicted years before Zim's birth that a man would have access to Hell and to the living world simultaneously, that one man would cross over, that one man would be born with the metaphysical talent, notwithstanding ability or skill level achieved, to exist in two dimensions. Crowley, to his credit, recognized that with this power comes great responsibility. Crowley had been waiting for Zim's presence in Galactic prison soon after Zim's birth. Crowley knew that Zim was the one, the chosen one, and while there are many others considered Zim's equal on earth, or even his superior regarding predator-like actions against the human spirit, none have the wherewithal to exist simultaneously in multiple dimensions like Zim. In galactic prison, Crowley and De Craon were aware of Zim's skill set influencing him, and subsequently, they were influencing Betty masked as Kra back on earth, for she stayed close to the real monsters because they provided an abstract point of view that no other being could. Crowley and Houdini were not very friendly in prison, and while Houdini found the way to escape completely, Crowley did not mind occasional prison life. He was above it, below it, side by side with it at times, so much so that he laughed at the notion of Hell or any other prison as a system to isolate and cause one to suffer. Since Crowley did not believe in the rules, he was not subject to all of their manifestations. Crowley is aware, even now, of the influence he has on President Johnson through Zim and Betty, but his larger purpose is yet undefined and may remain so.

Some might consider Zim to be schizophrenic, a logical and perhaps even accurate conclusion in its scientific roots, but this label does not tell the whole story. Zimmydom, on earth, is considered evil, but in galactic prison, Zim is considered only a "little bitch" by some of the monsters there. Mentioning the names of these historical monsters only gives them notoriety, something the playwright does not want. It must be understood that one's actions and the ramifications of said actions are solely responsible for the elementary understanding of how to measure degrees of suffering. Consequently, Zim's formulation of existence lacks certain elements that most decent human beings have by nature, and hence, he rarely suffers. What he does not lack is determination. It seems that anyone seriously involved in any endeavor has unrelenting determination, whether their agenda is light in nature or dark as a black hole, whether it is to construct or destroy. Aesthetically speaking, recreating the substantive arguments as to where humanity is going or not going can simply be a matter of measuring our collective determination. What does this mean here, now in Act 22? Is there a catch to this? Is there some deeper ideology or method or formulation that is being left out? Does the playwright wish that only the deeper elements in this moment be revealed, while what exists on the surface careens around destroying everything in sight? Why has humanity been drawn to a notion that these are the end days, that the notions of heaven and hell, good and bad, light and darkness have not actually been superseded and modified? Perhaps, a conclusion is coming to the play of humanity, and perhaps the stage props are erect and the lighting system has been tested and the sound system has been adjusted for this final scene. The actors and actresses are in the dressing room, preparing their lines and their voices for final scene in which all is revealed, all is understood and all can be maintained in a single breath.

Robert de Craon finds Betty sitting at small café in Bethesda, Maryland waiting for Harry, who notified her that he has some critical information to share and this is the time to share it. Robert's meeting with Betty, or the fake Kra, as it were, satisfies his wish to hammer out his plans and to make sure that she is on the same page as Harry and himself. Robert de Craon is chasing the secret information with Betty's help. This secret information was always at Betty's fingertips, as her husband dictates much of its movement. However, Gerald and Betty, despite occasionally sharing the same bed, do not share the same agenda. Betty's desire to become one of history's great crusaders has been difficult to maintain considering her political standing. By becoming Kra, maintaining relations with a schizophrenic serial killer and pedophile, Zim, she can carry out her romantic fantasy. Who better to understand a romantic fantasy than an escape artist, and who better to help execute a romantic fantasy than a crusader? Hence her relations with Harry strengthened over time, and her desire to have Robert de Craon as a bedfellow is imminent.

Robert de Craon has been desperate to get the 1st run copies of the play so he can capitalize on the information. He knows that there is a race to control the information and then to use it to misinform. The disinformation campaign is nothing new; he has seen it for centuries. He also knows that Winchester has a connection with ZZ and that ZZ has access to the play. Robert knows that, if he can get in bed with Betty, he will surely reach Winchester and possibly get to ZZ. As a payoff, he has agreed to cut Betty in on the deal once he capitalizes on all the information, for who better to understand levels of riches and wealth than someone who began chasing it almost a millennium ago and has kept tabs on the nature of wealth ever since. Imagine the strangeness for Betty of having sexual relations with her own son, or don't if it makes you squeamish, but any understanding of the relationship she has with her son is very deep and complex and perhaps dates back to classical antiquity at the least. However, for purposes of clarity, this will be left as is. Betty was never comfortable with being on stage, and so, being in costume allowed her to live out her fantasies.

"It's all in the teaching methods," de Craon used to say from prison. "Teach your children how to bo obedient, then disobedient. It is really good training for life." Wild Will Shakespeare scowls in response to the quote.

Harry knows that Robert de Craon and Hughes de Pains are in galactic prison for the grounds they laid, and since he helped design the prison's newest security system, he assumed that no one would escape. However, he did not know that Hughes de Pains was recently pardoned because of a lack of proof of his crimes. De Pain's legal team, headed by Thomas Aquinas, got him acquitted on all counts of grand theft. De Pains knows of de Craon's desire to reenact the crusades in today's world, for, as he put it, "the riches are so many, and so vast, and so accessible, I need to feed the beast within, and it is so easy to convince people you are doing the right thing, as long as you get on television and say that Jesus is behind you." But Hughes de Pains does not share this agenda, and he does have direct access to ZZ.

"Hughes, I want you to keep on eye on Robert de Craon. He has escaped prison and he is dangerous, and considering everything that is happening, I need some help with this one."

"Sure ZZ, but how am I to monitor his actions. I mean Crowley is on his side, and Harry has become quite sinister as of late."

"Yes, but you have us on your side, so worry less about who is watching you and do everything you can to keep tabs on him."

This is no small task. Elusive magicians and escape artists are very difficult to monitor. Former crusaders are easier to follow, as their actions are less complicated to maintain from a rational perspective. Hughes finds out that Gerald and Robert de Craon share a castle in Languedoc, France in the summer, and in the winter, Hu Jintao wines and dines Robert as his most honored guest. Betty plays both sides of the fence, a true capitalist like her mentor, Robert de Craon. She stays closely in touch with the crusaders while keeping her finger on the pulse of the intelligence community at large, the community that dictates what actions governments take. Betty's desire to pass on this legacy from mother to son is, in all likelihood, not going to happen, and so she searches desperately for someone to pass the torch to. Unlike her husband, Betty does not curtail her actions because of political or economic pressures, and unlike her son Winchester, Betty did not lose years of her life worrying about soiling herself. Betty has a strong inkling that the torch cannot be passed to her granddaughter, Winchester's daughter, either, as she seems to be fostering some kind of relationship with someone close to the family, with whom is unknown, as she maintains complete privacy, but day by day, Jennifer seems to walk with a lighter step, a bounce, a twinkle sparkles in her eyes, and she speaks of life, not death as previously. She now speaks of the future, not the darkness of days past, and she smiles instead of frowning. Her military history fascination seems to have given way to fascinations with the earth, alternative energy sources, and maternity. Betty finds the link to the future quite a surprise.

Meanwhile, Broken Stream is building an argument to present to Congress supporting his desire to take Sad-ham down once and for all. Lying was never a problem for BS, and all he needs to do is show Congress that Sad-ham poses an imminent threat to the US or to those on soil that the United States occupies or oversees in the Middle East. Gerald has been insisting on this ever since the election went his son's way in 2000. After Origami toppled the symbols of capitalism in New York and a wing of the Octagon in September of 2001, Broken and Gerald have been plotting to finally take out Husselini. There was a small delay as public pressure pushed Winchester to declare war on the Talibanian devils of Afghanistan in response to Origami's attack. So, President Johnson ordered the troops into Afghanistan needed to overrun the militant faction running the country and replace it with a leader who would instill democracy and stability to the country. Then he sends special forces units "trudging around the tundra, mile after mile"—Frank Zappa gives a hearty laugh at the inference—"from cave to cave to smoke the devil from his hole." Then, the games can begin, the game of revenge and especially the game to finally hand over that swath of land; but this time, as Gerald has indicated to BS on numerous occasions, "I don't just want that slice of good ol' oil rich pie. I want the whole damned well!"

Since the end of World War II, a uniform intelligence system was modified to allow all major English-speaking nations to fluidly communicate with one another. After numerous secret meetings linking the chief intelligence officers of all English-speaking nations, it had been collectively decided that a new approach was necessary if any progress were to be made in penetrating the small terror cells spread out, and going undetected, across the globe. From thin air, BS emerged with a new doctrine from which the world would later come to understand as a prime number: The number 1. This was not a urine-based analysis of DNA structure, but the allowance for any possibility of threat, even if it is only 1% of a threat, to be acted upon, swiftly and decisively. This new edict would prove to change everything. It changed how the leaders of English speaking nations would eventually distance themselves ideologically from the rest of the planet, as the leaders of other nations were not present at these meetings, and they could not possibly fathom the breadth and strength of such a posture given to them hearsay. However, all in attendance were persuaded to call upon their non-English speaking allies for complete military and intelligence-gathering support. Whether or not this will work as a formulation for reorganizing the world's strategic powers is yet to be seen. What is clear is that BS's edict is now a matter of principle and this principle would reach into the lives of many unsuspecting innocent people across the world, into their bank accounts, into their buying habits, their credit card receipts, their telephone calls and emails, and even into their homes; and while this was nothing new in the spy game, what was new was that each nation was now spying on its own people.

As with any complex set of rules governing multiple bodies interacting on every possible level of existence that seem to matter as human beings, there comes great responsibility. For years, America was viewed as one of the only true and honest power brokers in the Middle East. Gerald was careful in the way he handled relations, for his ties to the Saudi King and his family were intricate and delicate. Despite the countless billions that traded hands in business, the Saudis still donated much of their resources to an ever-expanding Muslim organization base that promulgates victory over the West, including biting the very hand that feeds that nation, for without the American, Japanese, European and rising Chinese gluttony for oil, the Saudis would be completely irrelevant. Of course, not all Islamic peoples want death to the Western ideologies of Capitalism, Democracy and Fast Food Culture, many countless Muslims will go to MacDiddy's to order some greasy french fries from time to time and attend movie theaters and laugh at the comedy of Benny Hill. But these people crave theocracy for they cherish such order. Moreover, to belong to a theocratic order is to belong to something meaningful as well as organized, as long as one plays by the rules, and rules in Islamic culture are very strict. But fundamentalism is not necessarily associated with violence, although a leap it is not to connect the two for fundamentalism in any regard can lead to extreme behavior, and while this is obvious, it has never been more important than understanding the role of the Saudis in the world. In fact, the Saudis play a critical role as the balancer in the entire Middle East, as they are relevant in every possible way to every aspect of power in the area.

The Saudi power brokers have come to meet with Gerald's disassociated son, the current President of the United States, and most of his inner-circle present at Winchester's Gold House West, his Texas home. "President Johnson, we would like to approach peace in an entirely different way. We want to redraw the map of the Middle East like it was before the 1967 war," states Crown Prince Smullah.

"1967? War? What war? Hey, I was getting laced at Yalow in '67. I don't know what the fuck you're talking about."

The Saudi Prince winced and looked around as President Johnson's inner circle simultaneously closes their eyes and prays silently that the Prince will laugh.

"Okay, President Johnson. I can see where this is going." We will be in touch.

"Wait, wait, wait. We've got some good Texas grub here. Let's eat, talk about baseball, talk about some terrorists, and maybe we can agree on something."

The Saudi Prince agrees, thinking that perhaps President Johnson's madness had another side to it, a side that is irrational; and since irrationality is so unpredictable, it is possible that, in a time of intense uncertainty about who is on whose side any more, uncertainty might serve as a stabilizer. The only constant available is money, in this case money transacted for the buying and selling of oil. President Johnson knows that America still uses a lot of gasoline, more than anyone else in the world, and therefore, the Saudis will still do business with Americans, and this is enough to keep relations chugging along in spite of his stupidity.

Gerald calls a meeting in the Pyrenees so that Ka Zin can meet with Robert de Craon. Gerald has ideas about modern economics that he would like to confirm with Ka, and Robert has human experience beyond anything Gerald can even understand. Ka and Robert hit it off immediately and begin sharing stories about accumulating wealth in odd ways. Gerald is almost out of his league intellectually, and this frightens him. Ka feels Gerald's awkwardness, tones down his economic dissertations, and gets Gerald more involved in strategies. Robert is careful not to shed too much light on his ultimate goal, to control the lock and key to all of the earth's wealth and resources. Ka and Gerald would not respond favorably, and Robert knows this. Robert's presence is enough to keep Gerald and Ka in awe without waking them up to the reality of why a man who has been dead for a little more than 850 years is dining with them in Toulouse. Robert understands that the world has changed, but his determination has not, and he is a learned man. While he is certainly not up to speed on modern economics and the intricacies contained in an interdependent world economy, he is savvy enough to see that Ka is one of the best. He understands that, as long as he stays close to Ka, he stays close to the source of knowledge regarding wealth and how to accumulate it in the modern twisting, turning gyre that is macroeconomics.

Robert de Craon is very aware of the rising tide of material-starved citizens from the People's Republic of China that is bringing that nation out of its isolationist shell and deep into the lives of everyone on earth. Rin Chin Chin is somewhat of a Chinese cultural aficionado, and Robert has asked Betty to set up a meeting for him with Rin. While Rin is as clever a chin can be, he would probably not be able to dance toe to toe with Robert, an experienced pirate. Robert has learned that Rin is very close to Winchester, almost to the point of willingness to sacrifice himself for the greater good of his father, but he also senses that Rin has become quite perplexed with the decision making and maneuvering in the Gold House offices. So, while Rin's allegiances are clearly with his father, Robert knows that the chin's intellectual curiosity may lead him to places unexpected, and Robert knows from history that, if a man or a body part has his back in a corner, or if it is a back that is in a corner, and the options are quickly laid out as to possible routes to escape this corner, most will react instead of think things through regardless of their intellect or lack thereof. So, his goal is to get Rin alone so he can put some pressure on him, but his methodology is not quite worked out and so he waits before approaching the jarred chin.

"Gerald, I think the timing is right to follow through with our plan. The public is very occupied with suffering from their trauma following 9/11, and they are very supportive of smoking the towel-headed devil from his cave. The weapons of mass destruction strategy is perfectly timed. Also, I have freed up enough human resources in Hellburden to rebuild Iraq after we invade. I mean we can make a KILLING here."

"Listen Rickey, you better be right. I don't have any more patience. I want that son of a bitch Sad-ham blowed up once and for all."

"Do you mean blown up, sir?"

"Did I say anything when your mother was blowing you in your junior high school parking lot?"

"No, sir. Forget it, sir."

The invasion of Iraq by the United States and its allies hangs on the intelligence community's findings regarding weapons of mass destruction, or rather, whether or not they existed, they were found. The final step was to convince Congress that war is the only solution. This was clearly the easiest step, as the Congressional oversight committee dealing with war apparatus and strategy was already on GWB's team, for they only needed the word, an official gathering, and a vote to give the green light, all systems go, fire up the engines boys—we're going in.

Orchestrating an invasion in modern times is not easy, however. All the pieces must be in place. It is no longer sufficient to have the military might, the strategists, the financial support, and the vote to go to war. The public policy must be sound. It is fundamental to have support of the people, for any public image gaff can mean the end of an administration. Rangerover worked night and day with Jimmy Zorro, the President of Pseudalopex, to stage the ultimate spin. Zorro is known as "The Good Doctor" by Broken and Gerald for his ability to spin a story. Any time Winchester has botched up a speech, Zorro's personal touch produces the final product, and some of Hollywood's best known movie critics have credited his work with "Two Middle Fingers Up" and have called him "The Best Damned Spin Doctor on TV." But Pseudalopex has a competitor on the other side of the fence. Al Sneezera Network out of Doha, Qatar uses similar spin tactics to show what they want to show. They operate as a "free" press establishment in very closed societies, an experiment of Western-like freedom-dabbling, but they cook their ingredients using different spices, fats and liquids, for they do not want a roast Thanksgiving Turkey emerging from their oven with all the fixin's like mashed potatoes, chestnut stuffing, and cranberry sauce. They want some hearty falafel, some tasty hummus, and perhaps some sweet stuffed cabbage. Food preparation is as important as spinning a good story, and PNN and Al Sneezera are two of the best cooks on earth. The Spin Chefs, a new reality television show, originally set to debut on American network television, was scrapped due to concerns of allowing an Arabic-speaking media network to get primetime viewing access. Now the show is set to debut in Australia in 2008, pitting the world's best media spinners in a contest using all the same film footage, interviews and landscapes, in order to mold their story in front of a panel of celebrity judges. The two finalists will compete in a cooking run-off, where they will be matched with internationally acclaimed celebrity chefs to spin and cook simultaneously. Apparently, Michael Hackson, the great American pop star icon turned pedophile, turned down a $50 million contract to be the host despite his Bruneian attorneys advising him to take the deal.

The fictitious staging of Iraqi people celebrating the invasion by the United States and the overthrow of a hiding, cowering-for-his-life Sad-ham on network television was comical at best. Some two hundred and thirty paid Iraqi theater actors sang and danced in the streets, but with all the cameras amongst them, it appeared as though thousands and thousands were celebrating like it was the end of days as special forces and ground soldiers systematically raided peoples homes, shooting unarmed civilians and blowing up important military and economic installations and effectively rendering the Iraqi people foodless, waterless, securityless, and many of them shelterless.

This invasion of Iraq was merely the sheath of skin covering the body's guts, the innards. Iraq was merely a bargaining chip in a poker game that Gerald and BS were carefully plotting. Gerald's strategy is not a new one, though this particular move may be miscalculated. Yes, it is well known that keeping a region destabilized for one's own political strength and economic development is usually a valid strategy, and of course, war causes destruction that requires money to accomplish and then more money is required for reconstruction. And yes, the shortest route between tax money and Gerald's and BS's bank accounts is through war. However, it is unclear how far Gerald and BS have taken this strategy. Time will show that destabilizing in one sense means stabilizing somewhere else, and that somewhere and the people inhabiting that somewhere may not be exactly what Gerald and BS are counting on.

Act 23.

Untitled

Not coincidentally, the number 23 has been mentioned frequently enough to warrant leaving this chapter out. Ptolemy is saying that, if any further information is revealed regarding this matter, he will stop sending messages and cease assisting the ghostwriters with mathematical related questions.

Act 24.

Catch 22 + Pi (minus 1.14159265358979323884626): The Time Has Arrived To Plan The Final Stand

If humanity has learned anything, it is that one cannot take anything on faith alone, or on facts alone for that matter, because as we all know, faith and facts are subjective; and most things that are prejudiced are discomforting, whether one is conscious of the source of that discomfort or not. There has to be something else that allows human beings to see clearly without the hazy mist that covers the eyes of most. Some call it instinct while some call it a third eye. Some call it second sight while others call it divine intervention. Some call it a predisposition for which we are hard-wired, DNA coded memories of the future, while others determine that we are being given signals from some alien universe directly to the radio transmission receivers in our brains. Some call it intelligence gathering while others call it a blatant disregard for personal freedoms, but what is it really? Disinformation enthusiasts tend to unite, for misgivings are usually clearer to see than real connections to things. It is easier to think about death than to think about life, but it is more complicated to desist searching for what death actually means to us as individuals, as a species, as a giant organism that can be construed as consciousness, or our planet, mother earth. Why is that? Why do humans continue searching, at least those with curiosity? Logicians think that they understand everything because in their world everything is rational and reasonable, and perhaps so, for why should it not be? Can the right and left hemispheres unite to create perfect balance, a balance of analysis and imagination, of visual, auditory and analytic methods of learning and understanding, or are they forever doomed, as in the lore of the ancient past, to be divided, creating havoc for lovers of both peace and war.

The ability to fall in love with someone, something, ourselves, an invisible ideal, a moving landscape is as critical as our ability to procreate in order to continue the human folly over and over and over until something, somewhere actually makes sense. It is as though, as we continue forward in time, the more something makes sense to us. The more it makes sense, the more we lose touch with it. Love, like war, must be flexible and ever changing, a consistent morphing assimilation to the unknown. Otherwise, it dies in its tracks. But love must be a rock, unmovable, for at times, love is all humanity has to hold on to because the patterns have become so bleak and filled with so much potential doom. We lose our path and regain it. Our hearts beat out of great excitement, and then we rush to shield them. We fear giving too much, and yet, we seek out the most we can at all times. For some, the process of searching is like deciphering a hidden code in something obvious: whether or not it even exists from design, it exists because humanity needs it to exist. For others, it is a matter of purposefully confusing each other as to the nature of something that is clearly lying before us, perhaps always looking for alternate reasons why something should be or should not be. Each person follows different roads, but, everyone is on, as one might say, the same road. How can this be? How can this not be?

This is where the confusion sets in, and where Winchester Buckley Johnson realized he was completely lost forever. He knew he would never quite understand the big words or be able to speak in complex sentences using multiple tenses to arrange a certain notion of spherical time within a singular thought, nor could he decipher this sentence, but that did not stop him from realizing his complete shortfall. And maybe this was a notable strength. He knows he cannot read well so he does not pretend as if he can. Predisposed to a certain functioning way of being, then giving way to a sense of evolving, then returning to the predisposition as if evolution never quite happened. Is this a way for any rational person to behave? Is this a way for a man with a chin in a jar for a son is to look at the world with all the confidence one can muster, that the jar he holds dear to his heart, the one containing the only genius in the family, is not real? Sometime after he stopped drinking daily and the incessant partying and the lost time, he had found his higher calling. He was going to be a man of importance and nothing would get in his way. He did not mind that people scoffed at him wherever he walked, frowned, farted, burped, slurred, attacked, cried, whined, or whimpered. He simply did not care. He is one of the fortunate souls to be disconnected, to follow his, and only his, agenda; and despite his weaknesses, his agenda once included proving to himself and to his father, proving that he could succeed. But now his agenda is more accurately portrayed as, "I don't give a shit anymore what my dad and mom think of me. So what if I am an idiot. I am the damned President of the United States, the most powerful man on earth." This is instrumental in understanding the bigger picture portrayed by the broad, wide-reaching strokes from the quill, the picture of today's human landscape: technology, warfare, disease, poverty, ocean currents, melting ice, quantum physics, dreams, desperation, sport, achievement, inner spaces, outer space, deep sea apparatus, the rape of earth's resources, the rape of our neighbors, a morphing humanscape of taking without giving back anything except destruction. This is relevant, for as the Great Winchester Buckley Johnson, President of the United

States, has his weaknesses, he also carries in him a special strength.

The greatest gift a man can have is hypocrisy. It enables him to detach from his own conscience. Imagine a man who does not owe anything to anyone despite the fact that he borrows everything from everyone, a man who does not need to give back to the people who voted him into office, for his higher calling put him there, not Carlos Rangerover, not the disenfranchised, let alone the voters in the voting booths. Imagine a man who does not need to give back to the earth what it gives to him, a man who can move forward faster than time itself. To breathe or not to breathe? For Winchester Buckley Johnson, the question simply does not matter, for as long as he can prove to himself that he is doing better than he did yesterday, he does not need to do anything more. He does not care about the consequences of his actions or his inaction for, to his knowledge, most people like him—his advisers tell him so. Consequently, he continues doing what it is that he is doing: taking orders and disassociating himself further from the results of his actions.

What would happen in the days, months and years following this time would be later understood as "the moment of reckoning for humanity." It was not so clear to those who were headfirst into whatever subject they chose to assimilate, or to those who did not pay much attention to interests that did not immediately concern them, but for those who kept tabs on the course of things, and there were many, all the points in the converging roads were now ahead, within sight. All of the transparency or lack thereof, all of the clues or hidden meanings, the whole range of exponential functions now yielded the same result, clarifying many questions about what we are as a species, what role we play on this earth, and how, if ever, we would be able to survive as a race. And time was the mostly dysfunctional tool of this enterprise, for man's time, the one dictated solely by gravity, solar positioning and productivity, was a liar, a trickster. There is so much more to the universe than our dedication to the slavery of time, and yet, as in all things, we prescribe ourselves something we can understand, collectively. Perhaps, as Victor Hugo once pointed out to Mahatma Gandhi during a game of Backgammon, "Maybe this is why man needs war to understand ourselves, for the inner-conflict is so deep, that if we had peace with one another, we would need to fight 'something.' We are clearly destroying the planet already, consciously and unconsciously. This 'something' would have to come from somewhere else, and perhaps this is why our Gods fight each other. We need *something* to be in conflict, right?"

Gandhi's response was so confident yet without predisposition to a particular fundamental theocratic or philosophical position regarding the query. "If man needs to fight something, then if it were only so easy as if each man fought himself, our Gods would not have to fight and we would still serve them, and therefore, we might understand the nature of peace, but I do not necessarily agree that man *needs* to fight something, for this decries the clear existence of the nature of balance and of Maya, that invisible veil separating the conscious world from the next world, invisible even to us here in Wall, unless we look hard enough, but it is there and it certainly exists as part of the whole. So, why fight anything? We are already part of everything."

"Bullshit!" Cries out Hegel. "Try wearing a pair of pants inside out during a German Parliamentary meeting! That will answer all of your stupid questions! You think that history and Gods and self-awareness and suffering and veils and unity and this and that and pee and poo mean anything without the opposite?" He walks away, disgusted, ranting to himself about the stupidity of Hugo and Gandhi's profundities.

"Hugo, Gandhi and Hegel's points of view are all relevant, and this is important: no one is right and no one is wrong in speaking of the nature of conflict. There are many ways to understand conflict and how conflict affects each individual as well as each mass or representative peoples. What is important is that, because of man's increased awareness of language and symbols, physics, math, chemistry and other fundamental disciplines of learning, laboring in the theoretical quest to understand the elemental nature of how to measure things, we have arrived at a crossroads of knowledge, one that, like in critical intervals for the past eleven thousand years, survival of the species is our greatest and only desire. Behind the quibbling and power mongering, beneath the sedatives and opiates of the masses that allow us to sleep without dreaming, cutting through the lines that separate us by socio-economic or religious standards, or by levels of faith to our particular beliefs, or our dedications to upholding the clear guidelines set forth for man to obey, or our imaginations, the new battle we face is the race to survive. Interpret this as you may, but this is where we are in time." That would be the last edict given by the playwright. His doctrine has been to guide the ghostwriters. Not discounting their prolific dedication to their respected crafts, their skill sets, the seeds that gave birth to their prominence, the ghostwriters are still blocked by nature. It is the nature of man to not fully absorb all that he or she have been given to use, but the development is simply not advanced enough. Blame could easily be placed on the playwright and on ZZ, for it is they who guide mankind through all of the mediums they choose to use. But it is mankind who is at fault, for his stubborn adherence to a position that bears witness to our true faults and inherent self-destruction has finally tipped the scales of balance.

Akira Kurosawa directs a small group of former United States Presidents and early American intellectuals gathered by a small bright blue lake surrounded by exquisite blueberry bushes behind Wall's great wall to reenact the signing of the Declaration of Independence in a transitory dream state. Those gathered around him are excited, for Kurosawa was already a legend behind the Wall before he arrived. This is the first incident where politicians, military strategists, philosophers and artists from the period following colonization to the end of the American Civil War gather, linking together many of the important characters from a linearly understood timeline. There seems to be a kind of collective ideal that still exists in their minds as to what the United States represents in the world, both in terms of interpersonal relationships and in terms of symbolizing the ideal breadth of modern political and economic life, and a master filmmaker catching this on film is very exciting for them. The debate is fierce and filled with fiery tongues and razor sharp proclamations. Kurosawa is a one-man army, and since he needs only to imagine lighting and angles to be a certain way and it becomes that way, he is able to truly capture the scene as his singular imagination sees it. The gathering came about as a result of a very pressing situation in the eastern Mediterranean during the summer of 2006, a serious conflict in the hallowed border grounds of Israel and Lebanon. Does the melting pot, as it is called, truly exist? Or do people remain segregated out of fear, or do people just not like each other if they share the same space but not the same belief system or the same God or the same language? The American intellectuals gathered because they are trying to determine if people can actually coexist peacefully, especially if they have long brutal histories of hating one another; and moreover, what of the people who cannot use as much of their brains as these illustrious thinkers do? These others outnumber all of history's great thinkers almost 10 million to one. Given these odds, is it even possible that the earthly situation could have been different than the direction taken?

George Washington, American President, is the first to speak by the lake. He is removing the small stem from a blueberry he just ate and he flicks it to the ground as though he is flicking a cigarette butt. "I vote for a vote. Does anyone want to just vote?"

"What does voting have to do with this?" chimes in Ben Franklin.

"Voting means everything. Did we decide to revolt against the British Crown by one man's edict? No. Was the Declaration of Independence forged by one mind? No. Did only one man construct a new set of proclamations for hundreds of millions to obey as their societal laws? No."

"Will my anus get probed if we vote?" adds Doc Whitman to bursts of laughter from the others.

"My point is this: Can't we decide to help if we want? ZZ has insinuated that we can cross over if we want. Now is a time to help. Of course, we need discretion, but we can cross over to help if it is absolutely needed. The time is getting short, and I would love to see more future humans gathering in our special club—we will not see that or each other, I fear, if we do not intervene."

Emily Dickinson adds, "I vote to move the club out of Wall. I think it would be far more exciting in New York, London, Paris or Tokyo. I would even vote that we move it back to Marseilles where it was for years before we set up shop in the Badlands." Immanuel Kant cries out in joy at the suggestion, and the Americans look around to see who is spying, but to no avail as he is well hidden sitting high in a tree nearby discussing Newton's flawed connection between Johannes Kepler's laws of motion and the idea of gravity and comparing the ritualistic practices of ancient Micronesians to T.S. Eliot's grand work, *Four Quartets,* with Galileo, Niels Bohr and Dot Parker.

Former American Presidents Thomas Jefferson and John Adams (the elder) approach ZZ, who is learning to use lasers to clean her fingernails. Einstein showed her how to make a laser from a tree trunk. This still baffles the other scientists, especially the early chemists.

"ZZ, we have been talking and..."

"Yes Thomas, I know. You want to interfere with humanity's course in order to save humanity."

"ZZ, we just think it is the right time. We can teach the people of today." John Adams is appealing to her better nature.

"That's what books are for," replies ZZ quite candidly.

"No one pays attention to what they are reading anymore. The absorption is gone. The human brain is too undeveloped to retain the mountains of information being launched at them everyday. How can they be expected to make good decisions? Their brains are full of pizza commercials and crime shows. Their brains are busy pondering how to save themselves from being kidnapped or shot because of tightening of the drug trade or because they have a nice car and the kid watching TV in the favela, the slum, the ghetto, doesn't even have food. Moreover, governmental leaders teach their citizens that it is acceptable to be uninformed and unintelligent, and of course, social violence and rape are permitted in parts of the world, and if it is permitted in any part of the world, it is permitted everywhere." Thomas Jefferson has done his best rationalizing to encourage ZZ to listen more to the result of their discussions by the blueberry lake.

"I appreciate the wisdom, Thomas. Really, I do. However, the time is not right to interfere. I do not have permission to let everyone interfere."

"What about those who already do? Why did you let them?"

"I did not let them. They do it on their own, without my consent."

This last part got some of the others to thinking. The rules, as they understood them, were more flexible than previously assumed. Apparently, there is free rein to interact with the living. Perhaps the ideas of quantum mechanics could be brought to action after the body is dead after all, for matter is matter and space is space, and anyone can willfully manipulate the fabric of space if they want. They simply have to believe that they can for the power is in the mind, and the mind is a highly complex idea that is both physical and non-physical. Einstein had been trying to explain this to most of the non-scientists, who understood this theory wholeheartedly, but they seemed to be too preoccupied with other things to care enough to do something about it. Jefferson and Adams informed Ralph Waldo Emerson of their new supposition as he joined them in a discussion while walking back toward the lake where the others were now surfing, which suddenly had three-meter waves and a nice curl before the break about 50 meters from the shore. The best surfer was Diogenes, who had joined the American intellectuals, and despite his cynicism regarding man and his curtailed search for honesty, he proved to be a great rider of big waves. The rules still meant something. This was unchartered territory. The afterlife club was so exclusive that breaking its rules was not on anyone's mind. There was an underlying fear to breaking the club rules anyway. The members were not fearful of breaking the rules while alive, because breaking rules was how they got into this club. However, the consciousness behind Wall's wall dictated clearly that they not break ZZ's rules, for that would be gratuitously silly and unnecessary. At least at this point in time the notion appeared to be impractical.

It was on Christmas Day in 2006 that Broken Stream disappeared from sight. There was much speculation by the press corps as to where he went and why, but no one had the answers. The uncertainty led to rumors of his death as he did have a weak heart, but also to his defection from America. Some speculated that he had joined a radical Muslim group because of his enormous economic interests in the Middle East. Gerald, who was BS's closest confidant, had no idea where he went. Betty was too busy plotting something bigger to care. Winchester and Rin sat discussing the possibilities by a windowsill in the Gold House West in Texas shortly after ushering in the New Year.

"Dad, I think I know where BS is."

"What do you mean, my good son, my friendly chin, Rin?"

"You haven't heard? BS disappeared on Christmas Day and no one has seen him since."

"Oh, he's probably shooting some deer or some bulls, or maybe he is shooting his wife."

"Dad, you're still funny after all this time."

"Who's being funny? You don't think he would shoot a deer?"

"Forget it, Dad. I think I know where he is though. Do you want to know what my thoughts are."

"Sure Chinny Chin Chin."

Rin pauses because he is not entirely certain if he should be the one to inform Winchester what really happened with BS. This is big news, the kind of news that would change most people's lives. Rin is one of those life forms people can confide in. Perhaps it is the nature of one to openly trust a genius body part living in a jar, or perhaps it is his emotionally clairvoyant personality, or perhaps because he is in a jar and can't really get out that he does not intimidate people despite his overtly dominating brilliance. So, the fact that Rin is aware of what really happened is not a stretch of the imagination, and since Rin is loyal to his father, despite the transparent idiocy of his father, he will tell him anything. At least at this point in time he will tell him anything.

"Dad, I have to tell you that BS and Jennifer have left together for Bali."

"What?"

"Yes Dad, I am sorry to say that BS and Jennifer have been having a torrid love affair and that Jennifer is pregnant and her pregnancy did not show because of her anorexia. They went to Bali to have their child in peace."

"I KNEW IT! THAT BASTARD! Everyone is sleeping with my wife! EVERYONE!"

"No, Dad. Stop. I said Jennifer, your daughter, not Johnnie, your wife."

"You say potayto. I say potahto."

"Dad, listen, please, let's do that breathing exercise that mom's yoga instructor once taught you. Okay, ready. Take a deep breath, and now, go ahead and say it."

"My name is Winchester. I am a good man. I am alive and I feel good. I like to read my Ho-Lee Bi-Bill because it makes me happy. I love my son Rin and my daughter Jennifer. Jennifer? Oh, I can't believe this! She and BS are having a baby? This is so bad, so bad. I am not ready to be a grandfather!"

"Dad, I think you should concern yourself with more than just worrying about being a grandfather, although that is a good place to start. Your 25 year-old daughter has been having sex with a 65 year-old man, who is your Vice President, who shares assets with your father and with the Emirs of the Middle East."

"Oh damn, damn, damn. What can I do? Give me a drink! Oh, that won't help. Call my dealer—I need some coke!!! Oh forget that too. This is hopeless. I don't want to show my face in Washington anymore. Can we just stay here at the ranch? We can play games, laugh and eat lots of hot dogs and barbecued beef sandwiches."

"Dad, I am sorry, but I think now is the time for you to take charge. If your daughter is having your political partner's baby, I think it is best that we just tell the world that you knew about this and have stood by this from the beginning."

Within seconds Rin is picked up by Winchester's eunuchs and placed in a cloth sack and carried away. Gerald is standing in the doorway staring unemotionally at Winchester. "I could not allow BS to gain any more power. This was the only way. His only weakness was your daughter. He loves her. I noticed it from the beginning. You and your stupid wife couldn't raise her properly. She was a mess, and BS just stepped in and provided support for her. It's really your fault. But I had to do something as BS was gaining far too much power for his own good."

"You mean?"

"Yes son, I set it up. I gave them roofies and he impregnated her in your bed."

"Wow, that's a relief. For a second I thought you were going to say that he slept with Johnnie too!"

"Stop thinking with your shrunken dick. This is serious. We have to get him removed from office now."

"Sure Dad, whatever. As long as he isn't boinking my wife, I don't care what he does."

A large group of secret service eunuchs escort BS and Jennifer back from Bali to Washington where they are debriefed and stripped of their citizenship and sent to Vietnam, where they are accepted as honorary citizens. Rin is placed in a military prison in the naval station in Guantanamo Bay, Cuba awaiting arraignment because he knows too much. Winchester is pleased that Johnnie has not been sleeping around, and although his daughter is now a Vietnamese citizen, he knows that she still loves him, even from a distance. BS will not lie down so easily, however, and he sets up a meeting with Gerald and Ka Zin Flow to discuss how he can still maintain his position in the ranks so as not to destroy their strategy of taking over the world. They agree to meet in Singapore, where Gerald plans to buy up some apartment buildings and Ka Zin has a lecture in the University of Singapore's business school.

"Look, I don't know what happened. I love her like a daughter, not like my lover," starts BS.

"Look, don't BS me BS. I am not my son," interjects Gerald.

"Let him speak, Gerald. Maybe he is willing to offer something." Adds Ka Zin, "He might be willing to offer something very, very valuable to be let back in the circle."

"Don't count your chickens Ka. I have a mind to blow a hole in your head right here and now." BS opens his suit jacket to the side where a double action Chinese QSZ-92 semi-automatic pistol lays snuggly in its leather holster.

"Calm down, BS. I am just saying that it would behoove you to think about rejoining with some moderation in mind instead of just taking everything you want just because you want it and you want to be a bully just like the bullies that bullied you when you were a child." Ka is staring BS squarely in the eyes and knows well they had him emotionally pinned against a wall.

"Okay, listen, we have all known each other a long time. We all have skeletons in our closets and we can work this out. I think the Chin kid is a real problem, however," states Gerald. "He just knows too much."

"But your son loves him so much that it would destroy him if something ever happened to the kid." BS throws this in under the assumption he is apparently back on the team again. "I don't want my son Benjamin to be raised a fucking gook though. I want him to have a life in the good ole US of A."

"We'll think about that. Let's just take care of the chin once and for all. I say we gas him. Just fill up that stupid jar with Sarin and he's done," states Gerald.

"Maybe that's not so easy. He doesn't have any lungs and it might not affect him," adds BS, whose knowledge of chemical weapons was just achieved in recent CIB debriefings.

"Why don't we just send him to China as a gift to the Chinese government? This can take care of two issues. One is getting rid of him, and being out of the Gold House, he will immediately lose touch with what is going on, what plans are moving forward and which plans were tossed. And two is showing the Chinese that we are respectful of them so that they do not see what we are really up to, what our true plans are." Ka dictates the plan with conciseness.

"I don't think they are that stupid, but I agree that dumping the chin on the Chinese is a brilliant idea. We'll tell Winchester that his son longs to visit China and we are sending him there as an envoy. He will not know what that means, but he will be pleased that his son is traveling because he knows how much the chin kid likes to travel." BS is remanding his old position of power back from his brilliant strategic posturing.

"So it is done. Let's eat," says Gerald as they feed each other some grilled sweet and spicy Thai chicken satay in a semi-homoerotic gesture symbolizing a passage to greatness.

Rin waits patiently and quietly in his jar, which is inside of a cage that is inside of a small windowless cell in the military prison. He knows very well that the current situation is not good, and he knows better than to have spoken what he knew, but his loyalty to his father is unquestionable and so he had to tell him the truth. He fears the worst now, certain that he will be executed and then someone will say his death was an accident, maybe a transportation disaster or something like that. He thinks that the time is near so he requests some newspapers because he loves to read so much. The guards and the officer in charge of the prison do not see harm in this, and so they bring him a New York Thymes newspaper to peruse. He reads news that his father has stood steadfastly against stem cell research. "How can a man stand against stem cell research when he has a body part in a jar for a son?" he wonders. This makes him very sad, and then he begins to feel alienated, insecure. His paranoia really takes over and he prays in the night for a cure to his newfound fear, but it never comes. He wishes that he never read what he did for he would have been much happier without this knowledge. He knows his father is not very clever, but he was not aware that he is against the very nature of how his son exists. The betrayal goes very deep and his thoughts turn violently against his father. ZZ comes to Rin in the night to speak with him about the dangers of switching allegiances, of treason. Rin expresses his desire to remain part of his father's life, but he says maybe it is time for him to move on, to grow a little. But ZZ knows differently. She knows that Rin thinks that his death is at hand, but she also knows what Gerald, Ka Zin and BS have planned for him, and so she alerts him to be very careful in how he approaches these next few days.

Rin is visited by Winchester the following day. Winchester has great news for him and he wanted to share this news himself. "My great son, you have been chosen to be the point guard on the Chinese national basketball team."

"Dad, I am so happy to see you. There is something I want to say to you, but I am not so sure I should say anything right now for fear that I might break our relationship completely apart if I open my chin and speak."

"Rin, what are you talking about? You are going to China! I have set it up myself. You will be the official convoy of the government there in BeeChing."

"Dad, do you mean you want me to be the envoy in Beijing?"

"Yes! That is what I said! You get to travel and meet new people and you can speak in Chinese with the all those yellow chinks."

"Wow, Dad. That is quite an honor. Does your father approve of this?"

"Approve? He told me himself. He said I should be very proud of you and this is the best thing for everyone."

"Just one question, Dad: if you are the President and I am your son, why am I being imprisoned by my own grandfather if now I am going to be the main envoy of the United States to China?"

"Dad told me it is the same reason that I wear a diaper—
it is for everyone's protection."

Immediately Rin feels disassociated from everyone except
his not-so-bright father. He thinks that maybe opposites
really do attract, not only electrochemically but also
intellectually and spiritually as well, in that his father's
gullible mobility is perfectly matched with Rin's rock-like
immobility and all the while their intelligence could not
be further apart. Rin knows that he may never see his
father again after this moment, and he is satisfied with
that, because even though he is being sent somewhere
against his will, that place just may be the perfect place
for him. So he has decided to go with the flow, as his
father once told him Jener used to do, but right now, he is
uncertain of most things as he and his father are about to
be split apart and this really bothers him.

Gerald is in Riyadh giving a speech before the Arab
League's assembly of leaders. He is proposing that the
session be closed to the media for the delicate subject
matter might be misinterpreted if reported to the world's
mass populace. Since a very popular friend of the Arab
League, Ka Zin Flow, is flanking Gerald to his left and
the Emir of Saudi Arabia is to his right, the Arab League
agrees to this notion of privacy. Although the speech
itself, the actual words in it, was difficult to monitor, even
for the ghostwriters, the content was well known ahead of
time. Gerald argued that China was plotting to take over
the world economically, then militarily. He made a
motion to drop the warfare between the West and the
Arab nations to focus on dismantling the growing power
that is China. He argued that, if China ever developed
alternative energy technology in the near future, they
would no longer depend on the Arab nations for energy.
He also argued that, since the US was to soon invade
Venezuela, the Chinese would still need, very much need
in the short term, the oil and natural gas excavated from
the Arabian Peninsula. After some deliberation, the Arab

League concurred, but only if the US gave up Israel to the Palestinians, who in turn would have to agree to not obliterate Israelis and Jews generally. Although they said they could not speak for Iran, they could guarantee this would be a new edict from that country, and they agreed, after a motion from Ka Zin, to publicly state their new allegiance with Israel. It was also agreed that the United States would vacate Iraq since all Arab peoples would follow the edicts set forth by the Arab league, and hence, there would be no more bloodshed on the streets of Baghdad and Basra. Gerald said that he could get this done with the Israelis, though it would take some serious negotiating, and he would be happy if the United States was able to leave Iraq, which would be success for his son's ego if they could leave Iraq in a state of peace after all the Iraqi War protests by American citizens. This move would all but assure victory for Winchester in the folklore of Presidents, for he was able to liberate, successfully, a poor country from a murdering tyrant, which was, as he had been declaring every chance he got, a victory for freedom and democracy everywhere. So after a brief handshaking session, the new international policy was set and clear. The Arabs would join the West in taking on China, and while stage props were quickly removed and new stage props were set up in their place, the act to be delivered would be the greatest act ever to be staged by the playwright.

Meanwhile, high above the Arctic Circle, a C-17 Globemaster III transport plane carries Rin Chin Chin in his cage toward Beijing. Rin is given a window seat at his request, and he stares down toward the melting polar ice caps that are breaking off in great chunks and falling into the Arctic Ocean below. He is busy preparing his mind to speak both Mandarin and Cantonese, at least the more widely used subdialects of each dialect. He does his best to put his fears behind him, his loyalties, his family, his love of being part of the United States. He is excited in a way, for he feels something good can come out of this, perhaps a new life. He thinks that maybe he will find so much beauty in the lives and history of the Chinese, that he will determine this was to be his destiny all along; and he is happy with that, comfortable with that. He imagines a mental picture, as best he can, of his arrival. He sees the parades through Tiananmen Square, the tanks, the soldiers, the flags, and he imagines that his life is of importance. He never had this feeling in the Gold House or the Gold House West. He always considered himself somewhat of an oddball, well, he *is* a chin in a jar, and he knows that to be accepted, he had to roll with it, pay attention but not rock the boat, for as soon as he spoke up against his better instincts, he was whisked away within minutes, imprisoned and then deported like so many other intelligent beings who could not stand to witness lies any longer without speaking out against them. So, he has decided to make the best of his new life, his new friends, and maybe even his new family.

When the air transport lands, he sees an entourage of limousines with American flags waiting on the tarmac. This is not quite what he expected. Gerald waits at the bottom of the ramp with the Paramount Leader of China, Stu Rinkow, the Communist Party General Secretary, the President of the People's Republic of China, and the Chairman of the Central Military Commission. What the world does not know is that, in a very clever shell game, Gerald and Ka Zin did everything economically and politically they could think of to get Rinkow into office, for Chang Showmin was getting in the way of Gerald, BS and Ka Zin's plans. If they could push Rinkow into office, they would got his allegiance moving forward, and as long as Rinkow assumed that the Arab League was the biggest threat to the United States, then he would align himself with the United States against those who have power over China, the Arabs. What Gerald, BS and Ka Zin did not count on, and for these three to overlook this element was quite understandable considering their single-mindedness, was that Rinkow is Chinese to his marrow.

He will make allegiances but only if they serve China, for he is not a man of fear, only a man of a very deep cultural loyalty. What Gerald traded Rinkow, with Ka Zin's support, were United States Treasury notes numbering in the hundreds of billions. And by the time that Rin Chin Chin was being delivered to the Chinese, China could all but sink the American economy with one, complete and unaided swoop of the quill. While the Saudis bought up American real estate and the Chinese held all the United States' treasury notes, the land between Hawaii and St Thomas, between Alaska and Florida, between Maine and California and Michigan and Texas, was a virtual battle map for the Arabs and the Chinese. And who better to represent the United States of America on such a critical battlefield than Winchester Buckley Johnson, the Great Winchester, arguably the finest President to traverse the hallways of the Gold House, the White House or the old Presidential Palace, the most well-known gut-wrenching American intellect since, well, Walt Whitman.

"WHAT? How can you compare that imbecile to me?"

"Sorry, Walt, but you have been showing off too much," states a slightly annoyed Rumi.

"Fine, I quit. I am going to hang out somewhere else, maybe, I don't know, Fire Island or Provincetown, maybe South Beach." With that Doc Whitman disappears forever from the club. He is angry and he feels betrayed, but his overwhelming overacting throughout has annoyed the ghostwriters enough to finally do something about it.

The Arab liberation of Israel began on cue, but first, blowing up Iran would set the stage for the newfound peace between the Arab League and the Israelis, a necessary step preceding the liberation. Throughout the Arab nations, real estate gurus and investment bankers set up special Israeli neighborhoods with all the best the world has to offer: culturally, socially, technologically.

Israelis, completely unhappy with the agreement but forced into it, can visit their former land but only with special visas issued by the US and Saudi Arabia conjunctively. Gerald sold all of his shares in the movie studios to Israel's Prime Minister Eckmud Flobert, who then sold them to the Saudi Royal family. who then sold them to the Emir of Bahrain, who then traded the shares to an 11 year-old contract software hacker trillionaire for the island of Tahiti, the young hacker who bought most of French Polynesia from France as his own personal playground, and he purchased this stock for an added amount of cash roughly equivalent to 40% of Bahrain's GDP for the next 30 years. So while the Emir of Bahrain now owns Tahiti, an 11 year-old Nevada middle school genius owns all the Hollywood Studios. Pressure from entertainment lobbyists and the American federal government caused the United Nations Security Council into making certain concessions, and they voted to make the entertainment industry a global security asset and movies made in Hollywood were declared the only form of legal entertainment worldwide. Following a final edict from Winchester in front of the UN General Assembly, the other representatives from the G9 and the rest of the world's UN representation, all of whom had lost their respective wives and husbands to the entertainment industry, agreed. Television and broadcasting equipment, like televisions, computers, satellite dishes, etc. have been replaced by small Macrohard LCDs called eye visors, which are worn on each person's head like a cap and the LCD flips up and down like a sun visor over the left eye to watch up to the minute news and entertainment. The eye-visor's process software programs are based purely on thought and can transmit data to a recipient of choice using small nuclear powered microwave devices on the cap's small infrared receptors/transmitters. The implants were failing frequently, however, and the eye visors gave the impression that the people had a choice in the matter. Since Macrohard had purchased the shares of all publicly traded technology and service-oriented companies during the worldwide recession of 2007 and 2008, the distribution of the LCDs to every person on earth was flawlessly executed, whether they could afford one or not, and it was known immediately if they could, since all of their personal data, including family history, DNA, susceptibility to potential diseases, likes and dislikes, spending habits, total assets and all other relevant life and lifestyle tidbits, factoids, factors and predispositions were on tiny, mobile clandestine servers owned by Silverman Big Sacks, the investment bank turned hedge fund turned traditional bank turned Securities apparatus. Thankfully for humanity, or not, Bill Grape of Macrohard and Floyd Bankfiend of Silverman hate each other and will battle it out for complete economic control of the world until the end, or until one of them loses, or until someone else takes their place.

The invasion of the joint Arab-American forces into Iran was quite a sight to behold on the eye visor. Ground troops, air attacks, and special forces jihadists coordinated a perfect and swift strike against the Iranian government, which was just days away from testing its first nuclear device. And while they still had nuclear devices procured from the black market, the attack was too swift to use them on anyone except their own people, and so they decided not to go through with it. The biochemical destruction of Tehran sent fear deep into the minds of governments worldwide, especially of the Chinese, for Stu Rinkow is aware that Gerald, BS and Ka Zin are plotting something against him. At least, he has been told by Rin that something does not smell good, and although this odor is not coming from his father, it is nevertheless a familial stench. Stu Rinkow immediately recognized Rin Chin Chin as a being with a mind that is clear and extremely insightful. Rin and Stu have spent many a night together, alone in the Forbidden City's courtyard, playing chess and speaking candidly about politics, economics, and human relationships; and while

Rin is also quite a theoretical scientist in his own right, theory never becomes a part of any conversation. Rin Chin Chin's knowledge and relentless pursuit of Chinese history becomes obsessive. In the coming months, he makes startling mystical connections between the legendary Emperor Qin, the first Emperor of Unified China, and himself, and he really begins to struggle. Although he now considers himself Chinese in many ways, his deeper allegiance is to his father, and although not to his ex-country, to his family. In an unplanned speech before the Chinese Communist Party, he reveals secret American plans, and at that moment, the overwhelming notion that ran through the minds of all in attendance was that he may have a connection to, or possibly even be a reincarnation of, Emperor Qin, or as he himself pronounces the name in Mandarin-American, Emperor Chin.

"I remember overhearing a conversation between Secretary of Defense Ramrod and President Johnson's father, my grandfather, Gerald, in the Rectangular Office in the Gold House about the future takeover of China and that all "peace-keeping" missions and maneuvers are simply strategies to join the world together against China. I am not saying that they will do this, but we must learn from our ancestors, especially the Great Emperor Chin, that if we are to fight the oppressors, we must first mobilize our armies and allies into cohesive, structured units of completely trained and prepared warriors."

The assembly of the Chinese leaders gasps in awe at their new spiritual and military leader, and while the Communists propagate an atheist belief system, they submit to the immediate fact that this chin in a jar, the son of the President of the United States, is in fact the reincarnation of Emperor Chin, the first emperor of a unified China. As though he were watching himself in a movie, Rin becomes aware that something is just not right. Is it possible that he fell prey to a maneuver that he has yet to discern? His struggle deepens, for while Rin's genius is unmistakable, his paranoia begins to grow beyond his jar. His paranoia is now dictating every move he makes.

Act 25.

The Final Stand
The End? Or the Beginning?

"Dad?"

"Rin, is that you?"

"Hi, Dad."

"How is my boy? How's your trip to Russia going."

"I am in China, Dad."

"China? What in the fuck are you doing with those chinks? Lookout for those gook towelheads—they're nasty little devils who live in caves and wear long beards and they hate America."

"Dad, you never fail to entertain."

"Hey Rin, I heard that you might make the Chinese National baseball team. Is that right?"

"Listen Dad, let's talk seriously. I have some very alarming news. I heard the rumbling voices throughout the spaces between the walls of the Forbidden City, which I have been informed by a close confidant doubles as a galactic prison for the departed. I know this sounds crazy, but I have every reason to believe this is the truth based on all things that have happened, and based on the fact that my existence is predicated on the understanding that anything is possible. The lingering voices are also saying that Jennifer has been kidnapped by North Korean Special Forces while vacationing in Laos."

"What is she doing with a louse? I thought she was in the Gold House's Vietnam room studying her acting classes."

"Dad, she was deported almost a year ago to the country of Vietnam, not the Vietnam room in the Gold House."

"She is with the gooks? Oh, this is awful, just awful. What do I do?"

"Dad, this is insane. Is Mom there?"

"No, I haven't seen her in months. I hear that she is making a movie with Nickel Marshstall. They really hit it off in the Gold House's Pink Room during a reception for the Lost Animals of the Desert fundraiser. They have been sharing an apartment ever since in Beverly Hills."

"Well listen, you have to find Jennifer. She has been detained by that psycho Ken John-Sik, the schizophrenic North Korean leader with the comical semi-pompadour hairdo, and I fear that she is going to be executed. Didn't you hear about this? Didn't they ask for anything in return? Was there no ransom demand, no demands of any kind, like lifting sanctions, nothing?"

"Maybe, I haven't being paying much attention. The baseball playoffs are on Pseudalopex this month—this is great TV."

"You may want to check with intelligence, Dad. I am being listened to on this call, but I wanted to warn you as it is your daughter, my sister, who has been kidnapped."

"Sure Chinny Chin Chin. I will do everything I can to make sure that she finishes her studies. I know how much you guys like to speak other languages together."

"Bye, Dad."

"Goodbye, son."

Jump cut to somewhere in Hollywood and a voice on the other end of the line. "Johnnie?"

"Rin?"

"I was told you were in Beverly Hills. It was so difficult finding you. Getting through the Hollywood maze is like trying to translate Babylonian-Assyrian signs into Danish street slang."

"How are you? I am so sorry I couldn't do more about your deportation, but when your grandfather and Broken Stream make a decision, well, that is it. There is absolutely nothing I can say that would change anything."

"Mom, it's alright. I have grown quite a bit since we last spoke and I now accept certain realities. But listen, this is much more important. Jennifer has been kidnapped by North Koreans. I told Dad, but he thought she had been in the Gold House for the past year—he has no idea what is going on."

"Does he ever?"

"Well, I don't know. Sometimes I wonder if he is plagued by complete and utter idiocy or if there is pure genius hidden in the shadows of his behavior."

"Trust me, my good son, there is *no* genius hiding behind that wall of stupidity."

"Why have you stayed with him all those years if this is how you feel?"

"Because I, on the other hand, am *not* plagued by stupidity."

"Gotcha, Mom."

"It was so nice speaking with you. I hope you are having a nice time in China."

"Mom, I have become very close to Stu Rinkow. He has taken a fancy to me, and there are rumblings that I may be voted into a top level position in the Communist Part of China."

"Wow, that's great son! Congratulations!"

"Mom, this will be terrible for Dad, terrible for all of you. Think about it."

"Don't worry so much. What is the worst thing that can happen?"

Winchester gets word from newly appointed CIB Deputy Director Pat Ramrod that Jennifer and her son have been kidnapped and taken hostage by Ken John Sik. He organizes a highly modified team of American Navy Seals, British Royal Marine Commandos, and ex-Russian Spetsnaz Special Forces, who now run hand-to-hand combat training classes in the greater Los Angeles basin's finest athletic centers, to invade North Korea clandestinely to retrieve Jennifer from the grips of a madman. Winchester holds a press conference just prior to the departure of Air Force Winchester from Washington.

"We have reason to believe that my daughter, the First Daughter of the United States, Jennifer, has been kidnapped by Ken John Sik Chink Fuck Asshole while vacationing in Madagascar, or maybe Australia—I am unsure right now. This is not confirmed. I mean, I think it has happened but I am really not sure since I am not there, but if we do decide that this is what happened, based on our vast network of intelligence, we will invade that smug little son of a bitch's know-nothing of a country, find her, and chop his fucking balls off."

His message is edited for mass consumption and the worldwide television audience hears the following: "We have reason to believe that my daughter has been kidnapped by Ken John Sik while vacationing (followed by a long pause while his lips moved fluidly) based on our vast network of intelligence, and we will find her."

The pauses in the satellite transmission during Winchester's deep inner plight gave it the right texture and tone of gut wrenching sadness and emotional instability, demonstrating to the people of the world that even a man in his position can suffer, and instantly, globally, people began holding candlelight vigils for the departed First Daughter of the United States. Johnnie's plea to join Winchester in the search was granted by Gerald, BS and Ramrod because, well, they could truly give a damn if she died today, tomorrow, or just disappeared altogether. She served no use to them anymore as Betty has worn out her use to them.

Following the team into North Korea by boat was PNN's leading war journalist, Jimfaldo Primavera, who delivered a stunning play-by-play of the Special Forces maneuvers live for a global audience. Johnnie and Winchester joined Jimfaldo on the journalist boat, which kept a safe distance of a hundred meters or so from the Special Forces' boat, and Winchester had demanded that American flags be displayed on the journalists' boat so as to "avoid any trouble with hostile gooks."

"Here we can see just ahead the prison where the First Daughter of America, Jennifer Johnson, is being held captive by the ruthless North Korean dictator." Primavera stares into the camera lens, twirling his bicycle moustache so the ends curl slightly upward. "I think that our boys in the boat just ahead of us will make their move soon. I have been told that they might jump from the boat with their diving gear and then emerge on the shoreline in full North Korean military outfits to trick the enemy into letting them through in plain sight." He pauses and points to the Special Ops team now jumping from the side of the boat. "See, the timing is just right, and with some luck from the sun going behind the clouds," he points to the sky, revealing some cloud covering moving in from the west, "we can be sure that they accomplish their mission under cover of partial darkness during this, the hour of dusk, the hour of reckoning." Just as he completes speaking the word reckoning, a sniper bullet comes from the Special Ops boat, fired by the commander in charge, blowing a four-inch hole in the back of Jimfaldo Primavera's head.

"Can't stand that asshole," muttered the commander as the Special Ops boat sped away, leaving the journalists' boat stranded on the river and in plain view.

Rin Chin Chin watches his father, mother and a cameraman on the Forbidden City Network News (FCNN). They are drifting along the river with American flags waving proudly on display from the rear of the boat, floating by Pyongyang's riverbed prison fortress where Ken John Sik has Jennifer and her son safely restrained. As the team approaches the prison camp from the water's edge, which is marked by large American flag signs with giant red X's drawn over them, a team of Chinese Special Forces agents swoops in unexpectedly from the sky, breaks Jennifer free, and after a brutal series of gunfights, knife fights and hand to hand combat, the Chinese team, due mainly to the element of surprise, kills the International Special Forces team and takes Winchester, Johnnie, Jennifer and her son hostage. The

PNN cameraman immediately pledges his allegiance to the Chinese by tearing the American flag in half to show his desire to defect without being imprisoned. The hostages are quickly airlifted out and flown to Beijing as prisoners of war. An enraged Kim John Sik declares war on both China and the United States during a live-feed from a heavy metal music festival he is emceeing in Gothenburg Sweden, except no one in China or in the United States has access to the satellite transmission as matters of national security prohibit it.

Meanwhile, back in Washington, unbeknownst to the American people, Gerald and BS have all but dismantled the CIB. As the stage was being set to rescue the First Daughter, Gerald used the rescue operation as a highly skilled decoy to pressure Congress to approve the CIB's integration with the Executive Office. Broken Stream argued before a Congressional Oversight Committee on Bad Governmental Ideas (COC-BGI) that the integration would alleviate mistakes of much magnitude in the future, and his compelling argument was instantly voted as a statute, word for word. While the Committee voted, the entire intelligence gathering power structure was already being moved to the Executive Office, and most CIB field agents were killed or relocated to civilian jobs in one giant house cleaning.

The former CIB wings of the Decagon are now empty, and finally, the Octagon's nomenclature is accurate, as although there are now two empty wings in the Decagon, the volume is missing, so it can be imagined that the clandestine wings where the CIB once stood are not only clandestine but they are also empty, finally leaving the Octagon appropriately as the Decagon minus two sides. The Executive Intelligence Office (EIO) has emerged as the new all-in-one governmental office of absolute power and intelligence, the only remaining relevant federal governmental functionary. Congress simply became a tool of the EIO, who would periodically make demands like a dog's bark only to be thrown small fragments of a bone from time to time. While the Republican Party lost control of Congress in both the House of Representatives and the Senate to the Democratic Party in 2006, too many laws had already been passed that all but eliminated Congressional powers to counter what the President wished or did not wish. The Judicial Branch, which lost all credibility once Winchester began declaring laws like he did as President of the Nation-State of Texas, simply maintains order for the Executive Office already anyway, so now, its role as a highly modified maintenance organization for the EIO's law making prowess was fundamentally secured. Quickly, many of the EIO's officers in the know are dismissed or executed, a train of the most informed governmental and intelligence officials chugging breathlessly down the tracks to destruction, to the station at the end of the line deep in the desert where they are dumped off the moving rail amidst the wolves and vultures waiting to pounce on the weak then destroy the carcasses. At the top are only Gerald, Broken Stream, Carlos Rangerover and Candy Couscous. Pat Ramrod, whose stunt double had been publicly executed for treason against the administration, was placed secretly back in a top EIO position by Gerald. New untrained subordinates, like highly patriotic uneducated children who are mostly illiterate, are hired to perform menial duties in the EIO offices and bonded warehouse spaces, as complete power emanates from the new leadership group.

Betty, as Kra, had been given access to the Forbidden City. She befriended Stu Rinkow in her singular quest for vast power, which led her to the proverbial pocket of every remaining major leader in the world. She was astute enough to avoid Rin, who was busy learning more than 6000 years of Chinese history, including lesser known tales and myths passed on only from family to family. Rin knows Kra, but he is unaware that Kra is Betty, as Winchester's denial about his mother's role in his life never led him to leaking anything about the masked crusader to his son. She learns of the kidnapping of her son, daughter-in-law, granddaughter and great-grandson but decides to maintain her cover. She is tormented, the kind of suffering one naturally feels when a close relative or friend or lover is in danger, but she maintains her cover for the greater good, or for the greater greed, for it is unclear which is more relevant in this instance.

Betty and Robert de Craon have been devising a new type of crusade for years now, and de Craon, like Betty, shares beds with many people, and all of them lend an invisible hand in helping him achieve a crusader's ultimate goal. De Craon takes this very seriously and will stop at nothing to achieve what he wants. The *new* crusade measures time against wealth, the time it takes to achieve complete domination through economic might, and with the help of Ka Zin Flow and other leading Nobel Prize winning economists, they created a new formula to achieve this goal utilizing such functions as gold futures, currency futures, likelihood of terrorist activities, emerging capital market growth potential, quantum physics and astrophysics, spatial theories and consumer reliability based on global recessions or inflation. As a team, Robert, Betty and Ka Zin Flow are certain that they are well on the road to world domination, as does Gerald and Broken Stream with the help of Ka Zin Flow, as does Stu Rinkow and his leading military and economic thinkers with the help of Ka Zin Flow. What no one is aware of, besides Ka Zin Flow, is that Ka Zin Flow is on everyone's team, and this ensures him victory in terms of world domination no matter what political games are played, no matter what economic positions are modified, or so he thinks. As he will soon learn, playing all sides of the zigzagging fences of politics and survival is not very clever in the long run.

Rin asks Presiding Chairman Rinkow if, instead of real prison, they could be detained in his new Shanghai high-rise flat, and Presiding Chairman Rinkow, being a man of tolerance and compassion, agrees to this. So, high above the streets in one of Pudong's most modern architectural wonders, one of the many hundred skyscrapers that top 60+ stories, nestled right along a well-groomed East China Sea thoroughfare where human energy combines with nature in an overwrought polluted landscape teaming with unimaginable levels of excitement, especially for Winchester, as he stares down from the 90th floor of the Johnson' family's detainment center in an enormous 4000 square foot luxury condominium given to Rin by Stu Rinkow in celebration of the emergence of China's great reincarnated Emperor Chin, the Johnson clan is held comfortably captive. Rin still has a very emotional connection to his father and to Jennifer. He never quite connected to his mother in the same way, as he represented something of a vile nature to her. Although he is her adopted son, Rin grew to display the kind of behavior and intellect that consistently reminded her of what a buffoon she married, for this small being, this creature who was merely a small part of a body, an almost insignificant part relative to other organs and body parts and vestiges, showed more promise as a thinking, feeling soul than her husband ever did. While her reaction was unconscious, nevertheless a disconnecting mechanism within her switched to the on position, the same mechanism that exists within Winchester, though his is relative to everything in his life. Johnnie often thought, why couldn't we adopt an ear, or a heart, or even a finger, why a chin? That day confused her often, as one might imagine it should.

Back in Wall, everyone is gathered in a reconstructed ancient Greek amphitheater built into a hillside, one that is acoustically perfect in nature, where one by one, each approach a podium on the stage to contribute their two-cents regarding what course of action could be or should be taken considering the highly tense and potentially devastating immediate future of humanity, a similar tension as to when the young Serbian commando, Gavrilo Princip assassinated the Archduke Franz Ferdinand and his wife in 1914 sparking what would later become known as World War I, or when US Congress passed the President Winchester Buckley Johnson's Dropping out of School for a Year Day holiday. Some of the most innovative thinkers and deeply humanitarian soul searchers stepped forward and gave their vote to intervene, for this was a time when the entire planet's survival, including all that exists on it, seen and unseen, is at stake. Most vote to send one or two representatives to explain with complete candor what is actually at stake, while some vote to just have certain world leaders who are disturbing the balance of mankind assassinated. But, all in all, the vote was overwhelmingly in favor of intervention.

Jener enlists a small group of religious historians, scientific thinkers, and mystics to confront ZZ, who will then, hopefully, confront her mentor, the same mentor as the playwright consults. This strategy goes nowhere, as her mentor wants nothing more to do with the path that the human race has taken, the path to self-destruction. He claims that he gave the playwright and ZZ ample opportunities to change things, that, in many ways, the direction was up to them as well as their students and subordinates. Jener decides to take it to a different level as he implores ZZ to hold a meeting with Jesus. In a very short meeting, one that neither the playwright nor ZZ nor Jener, who was allowed in only under a veil of secrecy, it is Jesus who stands firmly on the issue of intervention He will only intervene if it is entirely right for him to do so, and even so, he said, the solution is beyond him, for humanity has been given every chance to live well and peacefully and learn about themselves and each other, to maintain a complete understanding of balance and unity and synergy its mother earth over thousands upon thousands of generations. While all is not lost, he maintains that the path has become overwhelmingly destructive, and with this admittance, the fear struck so deeply inside of the playwright and inside of ZZ that their entire existence, as individuals and collectively, were questioned. When ZZ thought about making one more plea to Jesus, he read her mind and responded, "How many times can God forgive humanity? The answer is an infinite number, but forgiveness is not the solution. Humanity simply does *not learn* from its mistakes."

A parade is held in Tiananmen Square to usher in the new age of China, the one that brings balance back, that unifies the people and their beliefs, the restoration of a higher ideal and a model to live life by, as the reincarnated Emperor Chin is announced to the world via satellite. PNN was picking up the feed but was *urged* not to send the signal to the 300 million+ Americans' eye-visors, for the sudden political downfall of the Republican Party was imminent since the President of the United States had been captured by China and the son of the President of the United States is now the inaugural leader of China. Back in Washington, Carlos Rangerover is busy enlisting a whole new set of people to follow Zimmydom. The demise of the current regime was imminent, and Carlos would certainly not be the one to take the fall. Carlos was one of the many leaders in the EIO who bounced about among Universities, and he, like so many others who surrounded him at this highest level of bureaucracy and governing, never finished school. Amazingly, in his studies, he failed American history yet he somehow became one of the most important political leaders of the federal government of the United States, and while this is not all that impressive, the fact that he is a wizard in underwater basket weaving is.

The Chinese people came to accept this appointment wholeheartedly because their belief in destiny overshadows their fear of conspiracy. Although other high level members of China's Communist Party remained skeptical, Stu Rinkow made the call, and the new leader of China was introduced to the world. As China's new leader, Rin Chin Chin decided to fortify his command by political dictum, releasing the Johnson family from custody to maintain relations with the West in an uneasy but safe accord. Immediately, just hours after his proclamation, Chinese military commanders commandeered the army and marched on Shanghai to stop the extradition of their enemy's leader. A coup d'etat was being staged in China just as quickly as the new leader was given power by the people, and this coup of a coup heightened tensions across the globe, everywhere except in the United States. The EIO's stealth security blanket blocked the news from all public media domains with complete and fortified censorship. All air traffic was subsequently blocked in and out of the country, and no further border crossings were allowed between the United States and their neighbors Canada and Mexico. All emails and telephone calls were intercepted and filtered for content. Only a small group of teenage computer hackers were able to gather the news from hidden mirrored sites of some Australian news sources, and while they had enough sense to find the information without detection, they did not have the social savvy or the political astuteness to share it with anyone. Hence, the news out of China was unknown to almost 100% of the American population. Americans, in essence, became prisoners in their obese, comfortable, and powerless system.

In a state of pure paranoia, the usually mindful and confident Rin decides that one last-ditch effort to find peaceful measures is worth the burden, for the days to come and perhaps the years to come are at stake. This kind of pressure is new for Rin and he does his best to make logical deductions while being highly charged with energy and inventiveness. He convinces Stu Rinkow to take him to Shanghai, to where his family is detained so he can speak with them about what the options are. Former leader Rinkow convinces the Chinese military that this is the right thing to do, and no one will get away anyway, so Rin is allowed to reunite with his family in his new lavish suite high above Pudong. The Chinese General who staged the coup, General Sanders Lee, the Chinese fast food fried chicken restaurant CEO and military strategist, was already in negotiations to sell the Johnson family to the new military dictator of East Timor who, simultaneous with China's coup, overthrew the office of former Nobel Peace Prize winner, Jimmy Manny Raymond Horticulture, the Prime Minister of East Timor.

"Dad?" Rin bellows as Stu Rinkow carries him into the suite.

"My boy!" Winchester sprints across the living room, trips over the modern low-lying glass coffee table, does a somersault, then stands erect as though nothing had come in his way. He is wearing only his rubber ducky boxer shorts and smoking a Cuban cigar. He cuddles Rin's jar in a true moment of emotional sincerity. Jennifer introduces Rin to her son, Benjamin, and Rin wishes his sister and nephew only the best things in life. Johnnie is in the bathroom soaking in a giant pocket missile-shaped Jacuzzi bathtub talking on her cell phone to her Beverly Hills roommate about upcoming film projects, oblivious to the fact that her son has arrived.

"Listen, Dad. I think I can get us out of here. We will have to move quickly, but my friend Mr. Rinkow can get us to safety. China has been taken over by the military."

"Who would have thunk it. These little yellow bastards can be downright brutal. Look down though—looks like thousands and thousands of yellow ants running around on the streets."

"Yeah Dad, well, anyway, I think it will be best for us to get going now before they change their minds."

"Sure. I just want to get some fried chicken on the way out. There's a joint in the lobby that delivers the best fried chicken this side of Kentucky!"

"Dad, there's no time! We'll eat once we are safely out."

"Damn these chinks! A President's gotta eat!"

The Johnson family thinks that they are being extradited back to the United States with the help of some paid Indonesian mercenaries. However, in mid-flight, Rin realizes that this is a trap, but, alas, it is far too late. They are taken to Dili, the militarized East Timor capital, for trial.

Despite the fact that the word Islam derives from the word for peace, and that most of the world's billion and a half Muslims are very nice people, the relative few that have taken extreme action use Islam as their basis to destroy, just as some Crusaders have historically used the name Christ to destroy, just as some crazy Sri Lankans use the name Buddha to destroy (this fact is still being checked, as it is virtually unthinkable to imagine a Buddhist using the name Buddha for an excuse to kill). After a very short and mostly unemotional trial, filled mainly with militant extremist rhetoric like "Death to Americans," "The Great Satan has met Allah and Allah kicked his ass," "Kill the Zionist-loving Americans," and "I likey the Mecca it brings mc happiness so Fuck the Americans," the Johnsons are sentenced to death in the Ring of Fire, a ceremonial volcano built on the island of Bali by the Saudi King. Like when they were alive on earth, Frank Zappa once again asks Johnny Cash if he will perform with him, specifically, a Bee-Bop rendition of Mr. Cash's *Ring of Fire* that Zappa had re-orchestrated for Wall's elite on the Greek Amphitheater stage, and once again, Johnny declines. However, Elvis did join Frank, Miles Davis and John Coltrane on stage for a hyper acid jazz version of Blue Suede Shoes, which really sent the German philosophers into a frenzy.

The ceremonial execution of the Johnsons was to be broadcast live on the Internet, and anyone could watch for a fee of $1000 US dollars, and if one was fortunate enough to view the event in person, a meager entrance fee of $50,000 USD could satisfy the most insatiable of death lovers. Although American cable companies begged PNN to send the signal through for huge fees, the EIO said no. A crowd of more than 10,000 paid the fee to view the event live. A giant carpet made of pure crushed rubies led the witnesses to this event into the viewing area. Included in the crowd were Hollywood movie stars, Bollywood movies stars, well-known politicians and business leaders from all nations, all cultures. A "rimside seat," right along the volcano's eastern rim, cost an extra $1 million and this exclusive club of 500 came to watch the American President and his family get sacrificed in the volcano as the setting sun provided a stunning backdrop. The event was co-sponsored by Origami bin Louis and Broken Stream's company, Hellburden, the contractor supplying the stadium seating around the volcano's rim and the supplier of machinery used to build the man-made volcano. The Johnsons are placed in a large net lowered down to the rim of the volcano's mouth by Hellburden steel cables and crane. Winchester, for the first time in countless years, is doing his best to be a husband and father.

"Johnnie, Jennifer, Rin, I am so sorry for all the pain I have caused you over the years. I am not very smart. I know that. My father hurt me a lot when I was young, and my mother..." He pauses and changes his mind. "Well, and my brother probably deserved to be President more than me, but I want to say that I am so proud of my family. It means a lot to be a Johnson, and you have made me very happy in this moment."

Jennifer responded first and quickly. "Dad, I love you, and my son would have loved you, and I am proud of you."

Johnnie went next. "Winchester, I noticed you haven't soiled yourself. Maybe you are cured after all."

"Wow, she's right! I am not wearing the diaper or anything. Oh wait, no, that's not it. I just used the bathroom on the airplane about 3 hours ago and I haven't eaten in 2 days, so I am empty. Sorry."

"Dad, the fact that you are proud is all I need to know. I have worried that you and your family would never really accept me, a chin inside of a jar, especially because of your stand against stem cell research, but you have proven to be a valiant man after all, and I want you to know how much I respect you."

The Johnson family huddles together and they pray quietly to themselves. Winchester's prayers are a little louder than the others, and the microphones catch his muffled prayer and the viewing audience gets to hear first-hand some of Winchester's more intimate thoughts broadcast live: "Oh Lord, I am so scared to die. I love all the chinks and gooks and Jews and Palestinians and the Russians, and even my mother, who I had sex with. Please forgive me for my physical ailments and my balls of steel. And please fuck the Democratic Party, those fag-loving, candy-ass, left wing intellectual unpatriotic jerk-offs."

As Winchester prayed aloud, Gerald and Broken Stream emerge from the clouds with forty Apache helicopters to save the First Family at the brink of death while a potent rendition of soaring human voices stream downward from Carl Orff's finale in his *"Carmina Burana, Fortuna Imperatrix Mundi."* As the Johnsons are rescued from the brimstone and raging fires, Gerald notices Hellburden signs everywhere because Broken Stream's company is one of the co-sponsors of the execution, and in a moment of clarity and rage, he throws Broken Stream into the boiling lava of the recently constructed volcano. As Broken Stream's body hits the molten lava, it appears as though the stream of fire, the one that exists inside the volcano but comes through the earth's upper crust all the way from proverbial hell, was split in two and in the center of this broken stream, Ricky Chester enters a domain most fitting for him and his namesake. Jennifer screams in agony, throws her young son Benjamin into the air, and throws herself into the flames, following her dearest love to their collective death. Johnnie, who is screaming, crying and kicking, is held back by Marines sympathizing with the self-sacrificial action performed resolutely by Jennifer, and in their minds, they are unsure if this act was patriotic, for love of a man, or just plain psychotic. Winchester catches Benjamin and stares into his tightly shut eyes, for despite the heat from the boiling lava below them and the noise of the helicopters Orff's opera and gunfire from the stadium guards, the young man lies soundly asleep, as though this were just a bad dream.

Sun Tzu quickly leaves Wall and enters Beijing through a portal in the Forbidden City. He calls upon China's General Sanders Lee in the Government House to quickly mobilize support from all of China's allies, Russia, Cuba, Venezuela, the African continent and Latin America as Pat Ramrod is mobilizing friends in Canada, Mexico, Western Europe, the Middle East, Australia, Japan, South Korea, Vietnam, and India. Very quickly, the nations of the earth divide against one another, and in a matter of days, there are only two sides, and all on each side are vehemently aligned against those on the other side, in all respects: politically, economically, ideologically, religiously and spiritually. Strangely, it is as if the earth had two souls, and while the two souls intermingled for centuries, everything was clearly divided in a single breath. Many began calling this moment the "Dividing Sneeze," The moment that the earth sneezed and its heart rate stopped and started again instantly, but now, split in two.

Simultaneous to the great dividing of the people of the earth is the drying up of the earth's supply of crude oil. Who needs it anymore? Alternative energy is rampant now in the West, and American and Japanese scientists are creating new innovations almost daily, especially in the fields of biochemistry, astrophysics and geochemical research. As most tax dollars have been diverted toward education and science because oil was simply no more, and therefore tax dollars could be evenly distributed among the people, almost like dividends paid out by a large corporation, and defense spending has quintupled as Gerald and Ramrod beef up the American military might to levels unthinkable during times of détente. Similar to World War II, the massive industrial military conglomerate, the EIO, almost wholly drives the American economy, as unemployment is virtually zero, as building new weapons technology supersedes all else. Even the once homeless eat three solid fast food meals a day, as radioactive cleanup duty has an average tour of three months, and all medical benefits for those ending their EIO radioactive cleanup tour are somehow "lost" just after death. They are led to their graves very quickly, albeit with bellies full of hamburgers, french fries, pepperoni pizzas and chocolate milk shakes. The East suffers from petroleum shortages, however, and within weeks, civil wars break out across those lands, and despite strong technological innovations, the people cannot find the energy supply needed to survive in real time.

By Ka Zin Flow's recommendation, the EIO becomes a privately owned company and its subdivisions are whatever is left of the federal government—its market value instantly exceeds $6 trillion dollars. State governments splinter and exist only as tax collectors for Gerald and Winchester's new Commerce Party, the fundamental ruling political party, which is basically the board of directors of the EIO Corporation. The West begins to celebrate, as it appears that victory is in sight.

PNN broadcasts the demise from satellite feeds. As they broadcast desolation from civil wars throughout the East, small late-night raves break out in Wall in order to cut loose some of the extra fearful energy held tightly inside by the members of the elite club. Macrohard purchased every company of every industry: technology, biotechnology, pharmaceuticals, service industries, including Stoogle, the last bastion of Internet commerce and unorthodox corporate culture. However, Macrohard was unable to swallow anything in the financial services sector.

After 2006 and 2007, the skyrocketing number of mergers in the corporate landscape gave rise to supreme financial power for those managing the mergers and sweeping acquisitions, takeovers and brutal assaults on financial independence. In an unfailing procurement sweep of the financial corporate landscape, Silverman Big Sacks used their new position to first buy the world's largest bank, CitiAmerica Bank Group, then used their purchasing power to swallow every bank and financial institution in the world, and all of their holdings including the World Bank, the IMF and all the gold reserves in the West. Silverman, the EIO, and Macrohard are the Western World's last three companies, and they control *everything* in the Western lands. The world's stock markets, commodities markets, and bond markets are dissolved and Silverman Big Sacks controls all money, and they invariably control the flow of all commerce outside of that which China and its allies, the Eastern lands, conduct. Silverman attempts to garner a position as the tax collectors for the EIO, but Macrohard assertively takes that role as they hold the key to regulating it—software. Trade has completely halted between the East and West, and the East has begun to suffer more greatly on all fronts despite their enormous human capital. Macrohard battles Silverman endlessly, until they arrive at a stalemate because Silverman relies on Macrohard to exist and Macrohard relies on Silverman to control piracy.

China's Government bought up everything in its wake among its allies, and its attempt to sink the American economy by liquidating all of the US Treasury notes that it held completely flopped on its face as Silverman's CEO Floyd Bankfiend countered the measure by devising a new currency that left the old United States Treasury notes, in essence, useless, as new treasury notes were now shares in Silverman Big Sacks Corporation, and, appropriately, are now called Balls. The new US Balls instantly became the benchmark global currency.

Despite the growing power balance between the East and the West, the two hemispheres suffer numerous terrorist attacks. Small rebel groups splinter from both sides and begin terrorizing their own people. While this is not surprising, the problem began to grow geometrically, for while small rebel groups in the past were mostly a nuisance for the powers that existed then, they now represented a much more important role, that of defenders of freedom against the tyranny of the all powerful corporation-governing bodies. Iran had sold off its nuclear backpacks to rebel groups all over China, India, Australia, Japan, the United Arab Emirates, Slovakia, Kazakhstan, Ireland, Canada, Brazil and the United States making billions of US Balls and Chinese Yuan. The Iranians were attempting to reestablish their semi-destroyed status and reenter the fray of world domination, on one side or the other, for at this point it simply did not matter to them what side they joined as long as they were part of a dynasty.

Former British Prime Minister Tommy Scared and former US President Bill Clifton joined pop-rock star Bonio in making a plea to the people of the world via satellite, with the help of world-renowned hacker the Pulsar, who now works with Silverman to battle his hated enemies Macrohard and the EIO, who fired him when he was working with Homeland Security because he was a dangerous looking African American man. He hacked into both PNN's and FCNN's mainframes to broadcast the video. The plea was perhaps the last effort before PNN's and FCNN's anti-hacker software kicked in automatically as security layers devised were so complex in their server mainframes that no one, not even the greatest hackers on the planet, could penetrate them once the software was engaged.

"We are sending this message to the people of the world. Our planet will not last more than 5 years at this rate. The Americans and the Chinese are building nuclear weapons at an astonishing pace, and while the stockpile was gigantic prior to this effort, enough to blow up the earth 40 times over, it is now 50 times its original size. This has to be stopped. No one will win. Everyone will lose. Diseases and climate shifts are already taking countless lives each day as medicinal treatments for diseases simply don't work anymore and turbulent weather patterns are becoming impossible to predict due to global warming and desalinization of the ocean's currents. Despite our efforts, global poverty has been replaced by global killer strains of malaria and HIV, and now, fighting it all appears to be hopeless as drugs are so expensive that no one can afford them without mortgaging their assets, and most people don't have any assets." Bonio pauses as Bill Clifton whispers in his ear. "Turning a blind eye to this madness is no longer excusable. You must stand against this. People of the world, there are so many more of you than those in power and you simply need to rise up and not stand for this anymore."

The feed was cut simultaneously by both PNN and FCNN, but most who heard the message forgot about it in a matter of minutes, as anti-hacker videos that were ready to go at any moment were engaged showing the American and Chinese governments feeding the poor people of the world, building free housing, and distributing symbols and paraphernalia of patriotism throughout their respective hemispheres.

Ex-EIO geochemists and astrophysicists discover the methodology to construct recyclable oxygen by positioning receptors to suck the dark matter headed toward black holes into containment systems that have the power to alter molecules on a subatomic level in order to create energy and viable survival tools. Recreating simulated black holes in deep subterranean tanks was enormously dangerous, for at any moment, the simulation could break out of its boundaries and swallow the earth up like a python swallows an alligator, slowly but surely. However dangerous, those conducting the experiment were so confident of their abilities that they had to, at least, "try it." A self-propulsion system is generated using the same containment device, and this was the key to future travel. The discovery of how to use dark matter to move, and survive the process, was the inaugural moment of true scientific renaissance, albeit that not a single soul outside the immediate group of scientists had a clue that this groundbreaking discovery occurred, except those in Wall—and the scientists in Wall shared laughs and tears for all of their hard work has finally paid off by providing something meaningful for the ultimate survival of humanity. A shape-shifting paradigm that was passed on across the ages, based on principles which they discovered and then taught, was finally rearing its tedious head from the sand to catch its moment in the shaded sun.

A prominent group of scientists, doctors, artists, philosophers, psychologists and two attorneys, just in case there is any trouble among them, have finalized the permanent space station residency possibility after years of squabbling and power mongering. A shuttle launch to carry a statistically sound, mathematically formulated group of permanent residents to the international space station, which survived the political divisions, was set for early 2009 because scientific progress was forced, once again, entirely underground as Winchester Buckley Johnson's Dropping Out of School For a Year Day was denounced and replaced by a new holiday. Winchester Buckley Johnson's Universal Appointment of State Government Officials Day kicked off the complete dismantling of elections in 2008.

Since most Americans stopped going to school, in spite of the fact that the year of dropping out had come and gone, to work for the EIO's defense sector, join the military, or watch their eye-visors 24 hours a day, Winchester's sole purpose is to sit in his office and appoint people he likes to any position in the company he deems fit, just like he always has in his former positions. His old Yalow University cheerleading buddies seem to get first nod at high-level management positions in the EIO. All Asian Americans, African Americans (except African American Candy Couscous because she had Michael Hackson surgery in early 2008, changing the pigmentation of her skin to make her appear white as a Nordic sun), Arab Americans, Jewish Americans, Polynesians, Micronesians, Inuits, and, well, anyone else who, simply stated, did not have the same skin tone as Winchester were instantly removed from any high level in the corporation. Winchester now surrounds himself with as many people that looked like him as possible. The only exception is Rin, who abandoned his post in China's new illustrious leadership to be back with his father and mother and nephew in Washington.

"Dad?"

"Yes, Rin?"

"May I speak candidly? I don't care if I am detained again. In fact, I don't care if your father wants to feed me to the new Sarin Chamber in the Supreme Courthouse, or if he wants to devise anything else that might threaten my existence, for I am nor scared anymore."

"There's a Supreme Courthouse? Cool!"

"Dad, I have tolerated many things, one of them being your blindness to horrible things."

"Hey Rin, don't be mean. I am not blind to horrible things. I just choose to ignore them if they don't involve me."

"My father, that is one of my points. They do involve you. All of your actions have reactions. Every time you move something from one place to another, it causes another entirely new set of actions that follow. Don't you understand what I am saying? I know you are not as stupid as everyone thinks you are."

"Listen Rin, I have seen many things. I have traveled to the Kong, and I have been to Shanghai, to Bali, to Egypt, to Wall, to Los Angeles, and one night, my brother and I jumped the fence into Mexico and had a 'real' burrito and I can tell you that what you are saying does not make sense to me. I am sorry, but you are wrong."

Rin pauses. He is ready to give up, but then he decides upon a different approach.

"Dad, I understand that Mom is sleeping with Nickel Marshstall."

In a breakthrough moment, Winchester elatedly proclaims "WOW! That whore! Think I can get in on a three-some?"

"Forget it, Dad."

Rin sits contemplating his existence in the windowsill. He notices a man approach from the old cannon that still sits across the street in the park facing the Gold House's front entrance, the one closest to the streets. He is wearing a bright orange backpack and he is screaming in Javanese.

Marine snipers pick him off from the roof of the Gold House turret, where an entire army's worth of weapons are organized and pointed deliberately at every inch of space surrounding the Gold House. A group of Indian tourists are busy taking pictures of the man sprawled out dead on the sidewalk as a small Goan girl opens the backpack, revealing a ticking bomb with a digital LCD that reads 00:07:12. She screams. Everyone screams. The guards atop the Gold House begin firing at everyone in sight, not knowing why the screams took place, killing dozens of curious tourists. A homeless man waves his arms, pointing to the backpack, and instantly the interior of the Gold House is lowered deep into the earth, 500 meters deep, as the echoes of an explosion are barely audible resonating above the chamber.

Thankfully for humanity, the bomb was just a little pipe bomb and killed no one. It only did a little damage to the sidewalk, but it did a lot of damage to Pat Ramrod's recently reinstated career. His inability to keep the Gold House's perimeter secure was the focus of everyone from Congressional Oversight Committees to daytime talk show hosts to an elderly couple making dinner conversation in suburban Phoenix.

"That no-good Ramrod might as well just stick a Chinese cannon up our healthy clean American assholes and fire away."

"That's what my biology teacher told us today, Grandpa."

That was the end of Ramrod. He was relocated to a military base in South Africa.

PNN picked up the story quickly. The top news headline read, "Chinese Spy Terrorizes the Gold House." The story that was published in 11 different media formats simultaneously declared, "Within America's well-guarded borders, dozens of his Chinese secret agents posed as Indian tourists and were executed by EIO snipers as a large-scale terrorist-effort to blow up the Gold House was successfully repelled." The EIO decided to stay with the brilliant spin and declared war on China.

"These fucking chinks think that they can come into my house and blow up my things." President Johnson gave an address by direct feed from his office to 3.3 billion eye-visor wearing citizens of the Western Lands. Macrohard fitted infants with special filtering devices in their eye-visors, using subliminal messages buried in candy commercials and visions of small penguins playing cards with sea lions. It was determined that starting them young, to "get them on the right track" was essential for continuing Western domination. "This war is just getting started. We'll fuck these little yellow fucks up so hard that they're going to wish that they were still living in caves."

Corporate spies within Silverman Big Sacks and Macrohard immediately alerted the Chinese Government. They had been paid a huge sum of money by the Chinese to pass on any word of dangerous threats by the Americans and their allies at once, and, of course, vice versa of American spies inside the Communist Party Corporation for the Advancement of China. China began to mobilize its forces for either a solid defense or perhaps a first strike, which path to take was debated heatedly in the Beijing's Government House.

Sun Tzu decides to meet with General Douglas MacArthur to discuss potentially running interference, for while both Sun Tzu and MacArthur would normally jockey to win at any cost, they do not want earthly destruction either.

"Heads I win, tails you lose."

"Sun, I am not playing that silly game right now."

"Right, right, serious business, I know, this game we are playing."

"Who says that this is a game? I don't want to lose. I love winning. I should have bombed China back in 1950. But, I didn't. I thought we could all just get along."

"Well, time's up," states Sun.

"Time's up? That's your final word?" rebuts Macarthur.

"Yes, either we destroy everything, or we convince our leaders to meet and work this out."

"I would love to bomb the hell out of Shanghai, but I think that diplomacy is the best option."

"Where?"

"Where else?"

The scene breaks to two women face to face. Their lips are so close they can hear each other's saliva swishing around in their mouths.

"Oh Betty, Betty you are so sexy, so sexy!"

"Oh ZZ, I have been hoping for this for so long. I have dreamed of making love to you. This is perhaps the greatest moment of my short life."

Betty is wearing a Kra mask and ZZ is wearing Winchester's clone's mask, which is the same as a Winchester mask would be but without the goofy smile. They are lying in a small garden, naked, atop a Bangkok high-rise with Thai beach beds scattered about. The afternoon sun shines off some nearby buildings, which are reflecting the light furiously toward them, casting a bright spotlight effect on the trees and flowers in the garden. They are caressing each other's skin. ZZ doesn't mind the wrinkles so much, and Betty is ecstatic, for she never would have thought that a 6000 year-old woman would have silky smooth skin with a tone like a white pearl.

"Betty, I have to tell you that I have been sexually inactive for lifetimes. Forgive me if I seem a bit rusty."

"Don't worry, ZZ. If you give me a looksy at the play before it is published, I will do anything for you, I mean anything."

"That's what this is about! A bribe! Forget it." ZZ furiously places her robe back over her figure. She was about to be duped by one of mankind's leading romantic crusaders.

"No ZZ, wait, wait. I love you."

"Yes, just like you love your son."

"If you let me, I can make that a reality."

ZZ vanishes like mist into the morning fog covering a mountain lake in an African spring. Betty sits motionless, staring at the reflection of light coming off the building facing her. Her cell phone rings. It is Robert de Craon. He is calling her to join him São Paulo, but it has to be before the 15th of March. Will Shakespeare simultaneously high-fives Jane Austin, who proposed using this specific date, and Joan of Arc for her dogged work helping him interpret "Midsummer Night's Dream" into Swahili for the ancient African chieftains who frequent Wall every new moon. She informs him that she can get there in two days. They agree to meet at the fashionable Jardins Hotel Emiliano. He will be perusing the book and magazine collection in the lobby next to the bar. Betty catches a flight from Bangkok to São Paulo and is dreaming of what it could have been like to get a peek at the play, but not all is lost, for she and Robert have a plan, and according to Robert, the plan is solid as can be.

The island of St. Barthélemy is completely surrounded by military forces as battleships sit in a large circle. While there is no looming fear of an Eastern bloc battleship strike so close to Western lands because Western battleships hover close to Eastern lands globally, there is a tinge of serious tension.

The Garden of Eden Flock Hotel is a venerable gathering ground for the world's political elite, and to the astonishment of those leaders who have had no contact with the dead, for history's elite. The Be In the Flock restaurant is completely filled with the contemporary as well as long deceased leaders of the earth. Sun Tzu and General MacArthur flank the long table set up along the water's edge. Gerald and Zhu Zen face each other in the center of the table and the others who are present, General Sanders Lee, former American President Bill Clifton, Stu Rinkow, Russia's President Valmir Plukin, India's Prime Minister Narinder Stingh, Brazil's President Fula, former British Prime Minister Tony Scared, Bill Grape from Macrohard, Floyd Bankfiend from Silverman Big Sacks, and rock star Bonio, who happened to be on the island already, are busy eating breast of quail sautéed in lime chutney accompanied by a terrine of fois gras and a seared crab and spring vegetable mousse cake. Federico Fellini and his production team are circling the group while they eat as Fellini is shouting at Sun Tzu, who refuses to stop looking into the camera during filming, a giant 'no-no' in serious filmmaking. The atmosphere is rather festive despite the looming battleships and the world's state of balance being at stake. While the topic of discussion is clear, the negotiations are rather unorthodox.

"Look, everyone here loves Balls. Why don't we just dismantle the East's need for money as well and replace all commerce with dividends using my Balls as the new gold standard." Floyd Bankfiend speaks first.

Narinder Stingh has a quail bone coming out of his mouth. He removes it and drops it onto his plate, and he is staring at Bankfiend. "My friend, your Balls aren't the answer to everything. We have some serious problems and everyone here will attest to this."

"The problem is that none of you, besides Bonio, understand what is really at stake here. You have all done your best to jockey for position in some way. Some of you want to be rulers of the earth, some just rulers of your people, and some of you don't care about ethics or peace or freedom or balance, or anything besides your precious stream of power." Gerald speaks candidly as the group sits quietly listening. "I have watched my son, who is not present here because he missed his flight on Air Force Winchester, go from failed energy company executive to bumbling manager of a baseball team to Governor of Texas to President of the United States, and he can't even read. So, I implore you all to think clearly. There is something wrong with this picture, and I do not want the inevitable to happen. And don't fuck with me. Just ask my old pal Broken Stream what happens when someone fucks with me." Most are shocked, for in this moment, it seems incredible that Gerald can find a moment of human rationale and modestly exposed compassion, as he was one of the world's greatest engines of destruction.

"Gerald you are missing the point." General Lee pauses and looks around. This was clearly not planned, but he suddenly appears to have a survivalist insight, for as danger was clearly imminent, he was attempting to bypass the danger using logic and his pride is glowing from this. "We are here to join together in a festive gathering of powerful men. We are here to celebrate the division of the world among us." The group nods in unison. "So don't worry so much. Sit back and watch the dolphins play in the sea while we eat our fine meal." As he spoke, his eyes glow with a luminescence never seen before in a man's eyes.

Back behind Wall's wall, the members of the club are watching Fellini's film in the amphitheater, and they now have hope, for peace is a very serious possibility. A round of cheers erupts from the stone stadium seating along with laughter, tears, hugging, and giggling, as though every one of the human elite is transported back to their childhood, the moments that were innocent, happy. Aristotle is searching for Beethoven, wanting to share a moment of bliss with his second favorite composer. He cannot find him.

Suddenly Beethoven appears on the beach next to the Garden of Eden Flock Hotel with a choir of thousands. There is a solitary man on the beach to witness this miracle, an astute, but unworn looking fellow. He is stretched out on a padded beach chair. The sun's ultraviolet rays beam down onto his pale skin and the blood coursing through his veins is ignited to a flame-like temperature. His profession is of a critiquing nature, and hence, this is the perfect situation for a man of his skills to behold. Ludwig Von Beethoven raises his hands, and the choir begins singing the memorable harmony during the finale of his "Ninth Symphony." The notes are carried higher and higher, the volume growing and growing, the emotion taking over the scene with penetrable power. The voices of the thousands standing on the beach and in the water surrounding the hotel are singing *The Ode to Joy* with fervor. Tears begin flowing in the restaurant as the emotion is overwhelming. Fellini is enraged that a German composer is overtaking his scene. He storms out, disgusted, his damaged ego and his film crew in tow. Robert de Craon sits in a café in Marigot, St Martin, not far from St. Barths with a young angry Egyptian man who is giving him instructions. For de Craon, this is the greatest and perhaps the last move of his illustrious career as a crusader. If he can destroy the world's elite, he can claim their treasures. Jener arrives in Marigot with a small group of elite to intervene, to stop the man from carrying out his mission. Unfortunately, the moment was missed by seconds, as shortly thereafter, from a small catamaran leaving the port in Marigot, a small mushroom cloud appears, billowing into the bright sapphire sky. This angry Egyptian rebel who swore to bring the earth back to the time when the lands of the Pharaoh were the center of all relevant human life was coerced by Robert and Betty during a fateful meeting in São Paulo to destroy the gathering of leaders and take over the earth. This was to be their one and only chance. There were literally millions who would now destroy themselves to destroy the powers that be, for the powers that gathered in the Garden of Eden Flock Hotel have stopped at nothing to get where they are, leaving a trail of carnage in their wake. Mass destruction is romantic for Betty, and she always felt that if fucking her way to the top failed to reach her desired objectives, then she would kill those that are on top of the mountain. Being alone on the summit is what she craved, not to share the space with anyone, living or dead. It is a feeling more than anything. It is not based on any set of known parameters. She has had no critical incidents in her life to shape her motivations, but when she was a young girl she did once beat a morning dove to death with a doll. Perhaps the signs were clear early on and that no one paid much attention to her. Her own family did not know the extent of her actions. It is not completely unclear why Winchester turned out the way he did.

That fact that peace was a ferry ride away did not matter for the young Egyptian. He believed in his heart that the world had already gone to hell. He has no rounded or profound sense of history, only of the mockery he feels the world has placed on his beliefs. Martyrdom is, in his estimation, the only reasonable solution. His plan was to catch the high-speed ferry to St. Barths to blow up the

Garden of Eden Flock. However, he could not catch the high-speed ferry to St. Barths in time, as his plane from France was late and his backpack nuclear bomb that was safely concealed in his checked-in luggage was already on a timer. So he was forced to highjack an engineless catamaran, and the winds happened to be rather calm that day. Hence, just above an ancient coral reef, with thousands of parrotfish, angelfish, damselfish, bigeye toro, triggerfish, blacktip and reef sharks, dolphins, octopi, and a couple of divers meandering about, life ends in a flash.

The teary eyed living and dead elite stop eating and look across the Caribbean Sea to the first noticeable sign that the end is not only a real possibility, but alas, a firm probability.

It is not clear if this was what the playwright had originally intended, but it is becoming clear that there is to be a winner, all of humanity, or a loser, all of humanity, and a few that were able to escape if, in fact, there is a loser. The historians, the artists, the theologians, the philosophers, the politicians, the military strategists and the scientists were all jockeying for positions behind Wall's wall, behind the Forbidden City's walls, and out in the conscious world. A few human beings were using their powers to make life better, well, at least they were attempting to make life better, and for them, there is applause. (Applaud now please.) Who will win? Will the winner hold a particular ideology? Will the winner simply be a solution for life's problems? Will having a loser mean the end? Is death something transcendental, or something like an end of all ends? Will anyone be left to care? Will conscious life exist beyond earth for humans?

Johnnie is in heaven already, back in Beverly Hills, precisely the way she has always dreamed. Johnnie likes it when Nickel tells her how well she organizes the mess that is her Hollywood lifestyle. Their Beverly Hills apartment overlooks the Beverly Hills Hotel where the stars lounge by the pool with fruity frozen drinks, apple martinis, and lots of silicone implants, plastic surgery, and Botox treatments. They are completely unaware of anything except planning the next feature film as a mushroom cloud forms softly, gently, like a pillow on the winds overhead.

Winchester Buckley Johnson is rocking on his favorite old wooden rocking chair on his porch at his beach house in Maine. He is reading, well, actually, he is looking at the pictures in his Dr. Seuss books with his grandson Benjamin sleeping on his lap. He is babbling softly to himself about his religious beliefs, the Ho-Lee Bi-Bill, dreams, power, chinks, niggers, towel-headed Iraqi insurgents, Jews, Palestinians and fags and about how he is tired of not being recognized for how smart he really is. Rin Chin Chin sits quietly by his side at the edge of the porch gazing at the sea. The moment is captured like a photograph in time, and it hangs there motionless, for what seems like an eternity.

In each and every nation that has a bustling economy, numerous militant factions split from the pack as racial indignation and economic envy further segregate the people from each other. Those who once proclaimed holy wars, secular wars, and economic wars on enemies outside their borders are now solely opposed to their own leaders, as blame has come full circle, back to the roots of the problem. The world's elected leaders, whether the elections were fair or not, the ones who took control by force with military might, espionage or bribery, or those who were the next in their royal bloodlines, are all sentenced to face the consequences of their actions, which were never inert despite the little thought they gave them.

Shortly after the nuclear explosion just off the coast of St. Martin, PNN and FCNN are taken over by American, Canadian, Arabic, Chinese, North Korean and Indonesian mercenaries, and acting on their own volition, yet somehow working together intricately, the death-starved militants around the world operate in unison as though a dark consciousness drew them together. With help from former disgruntled fired Macrohard software engineers, all transmissions and satellite feeds turn to static. Rogue nuclear missiles procured in the black market, which is really controlled by Silverman's Board of Directors, and from North Korea, what is left of Iran, and former Russian Republics, having dumped them for quick billions of Balls, are set off simultaneously. Origami bin Louis, who was virtually invisible since September 11, 2001, had been living in a submarine that was remade as a casino deep beneath the Andaman Sea, occasionally coming up for fuel, some nude sun bathing, and coconut retrieval from the scattered smaller Thai and Indonesian islands, initiates a reign of fury that sweeps the globe as small backpack nuclear and chemical weapons blow up the world's major cities one by one. In a state of complete panic, Candy Couscous, alone in the EIO office, presses the button for launch against China as Winchester's voice rings fervently in her head: "Those fucking chinks, those fucking chinks, those fucking chinks." As the US launches all of their readied missiles, China's second in command, General Tako Belle, in response, launches China's entire nuclear arsenal. Twelve ICBM's go awry, six from each nation's supply, and hit the poles, simultaneously blowing up the glaciers and sending ice and a mix of fresh and salt water funneling into the air. Within hours, the destruction of the missiles lay waste to organic life on just about every acre of land mass as twenty-two tidal waves join the destructive party to completely demolish the earth's land surface.

Just as the nuclear end-all commenced, the launching pad in Cape Canaveral was already filled with reporters and jealous, less-respected scientists and tourists looking to see the Space Shuttle carry the fifty humans to live permanently in outer space. Twenty five men and twenty-five women, all whom have been pre-tested for signs of cancerous tissue, schizophrenia, Alzheimer's disease, or any major ailment that could quickly end their procreative abilities board the shuttle, ready for lift off. At the last minute, Betty, dressed as a technician, sneaks on the shuttle, but as always, she wears the mask that she loves the most, Kra, and thus it is unclear one way or another what this means to the equality and balance of the group.

*

The angle cuts from slightly above capturing the entire room in full wide-angle view. The playwright, adorned in a soft white linen-like robe, finishes reading through the final edits. He quickly and rather excitedly types a telegraph message to Will Shakespeare, the now assumed head of the ghostwriting team, that the manuscript is finished and it will get the okay to be published soon. He smiles as he gathers up his finished masterpiece that was scattered across the floor. He places metal paper clips over the organized pile of documents and sets the manuscript down on the small black marble table, looks upward toward the ceiling, and smiles. Isbil Satar, the infamous Broadway and West End theater critic, adorned in the snappiest suit, enters through a narrow doorway in the rear of the room, his skin appearing red as though burnt by the sun. Emerging behind the playwright quietly, he grabs hold of the playwright's forehead with his thin, wiry arm, and cuts his throat from ear to ear, leaving him to die. As the playwright grabs hold of his neck and the blood streams down his white robe and body, Satar fills his mind with well known religious symbols, a cross, a star, a crescent moon and numerous, inexplicable in simplified terms, other shapes and symbols, perhaps those from millennia past, perhaps dating from before the time of the conception of King Hammurabi's Code. Then, one by one, he extinguishes these symbols in a ceremonial bonfire, each one exploding gently into the winds carrying the flames into the sky in his mind.

The crow feather quill hits the floor like a bull's eye in the center of the small pool of blood like an ancient tribal spear penetrating a blazing red sun in the center of the solar system.

Mozart stands on the launching strip with an orchestra of twenty-three thousand performing his "Fortieth Symphony," a sendoff for the space shuttle carrying its permanent space residents, and just in time, toward a recently completed intergalactic space station. Rodin sculpts the shuttle speeding away, and somehow, miraculously, he is giving the shuttle itself a soul, as if life poured out from its inorganic hull. Michelangelo puts the final touches on the flame coming out from the main thruster as it carries the last humans toward the stars, out of sight, back to the birth of dust from whence life came as an epic imaginary guitar solo resonates across the Universe.

Steven Polederos grew up in West Warwick, Rhode Island. He matriculated to and graduated from Wesleyan University in 1992 with a degree in Government. While living in Boston, he traded commodities and as an entrepreneur, he started and grew two international distribution companies.

He has written numerous short stories, meditations and poems. The Big Rip Off (of Significant Proportions) is his first published novel.

He currently resides in Coconut Grove, Florida where he works in Aerospace.

LaVergne, TN USA
22 January 2010
170878LV00001B/34/P